THE REINDEER PEOPLE

Megan Lindholm is the author of over nine successful fantasy novels, and has been shortlisted for both the Hugo and Nebula Awards. Under the name Robin Hobb, she is the author of five critically acclaimed fantasy trilogies: *The Farseer Trilogy, The Liveship Traders Trilogy, The Tawny Man Trilogy, The Soldier Son Trilogy* and *The Rain Wild Chronicles*. She lives and works in Tacoma, Washington, and has been a professional writer for over 30 years.

MEGAN LINDHOLM

The Reindeer People

HARPER
Voyager

HarperVoyager
An imprint of HarperCollins*Publishers*
77–85 Fulham Palace Road,
Hammersmith, London W6 8JB

www.voyagerbooks.com

This paperback edition 2011
1

A catalogue record for this book is
available from the British Library

ISBN 978 0 00 742544 0

Set in Sabon by Palimpsest Book Production Limited,
Falkirk, Stirlingshire

Kerlew: The Smoke

'Go deep,' he told the boy. 'Follow the little brown mouse when she takes her seeds and hides from the winter. Go to where the water bubbles up in a spring, and dive into its secret source. Follow the roots of the grandfather spruce down deep into the soil and beyond. This I tell you, for while every shaman must find his own entrance, these are ones that are known to have worked for some. Not all, but some. They are worth trying.'

Kerlew swallowed and tried to keep his drifting eyes on the old man's face. But Carp added another pinch of herbs to the lamp flame, renewing the wavering curtain of smoke between them. 'What do I seek?' Kerlew asked with difficulty.

Carp's tone was patient. 'I have told you. You seek for a magic, and a brother. Find a path into the spirit world and it will lead you to a deep room. The walls are of stone, and water drips down them. Roots hang from the ceiling. You must go through this room and out, into the spirit world. Do not speak to anyone in the stone room, not even if he calls you brother and offers you many fine gifts. For if you

1

speak, you must remain there, and he will be free to take your place. Thus are many shamans trapped. I myself have seen them as I passed on my way to the spirit world. Don't speak to them!'

'I'm afraid,' the boy said suddenly.

The old man only shook his head, softening the gesture with a smile. 'You will go past those ones, and out into the spirit world. I cannot tell you what to expect, because for each shaman it is different. But when you meet your spirit guardian, you will know him. He may choose to test you. He may show you his teeth, or trample you beneath his hooves. He may rend you with his claws, or seize you in his talons and carry you up into the sky. Whatever he does, show no fear. Be bold, and set your palm between his eyes. Then he will be your brother, and he must give you a song or a magic to bring back with you. But if you cry out or flee or strive to hurt him, he will not be your brother. He will kill your spirit, and your body will waste away after you.'

Kerlew clenched his fists to keep his hands from trembling.

Carp saw, and for an instant the sternness of the instructor left his face. He looked down on his apprentice fondly. 'It will be all right,' the old man said kindly. 'Go ahead, now. Don't be afraid.' He touched the boy's cheek with his weathered old hand, dragged his fingertips across Kerlew's lined brow to soothe away the worry wrinkles. 'You will be a great shaman, and all will point and tell tales about Carp's apprentice.'

The boy gave a brief nod and tried to swallow the anxiety that started in his stomach but kept trying to squeeze up his throat. Old Carp smiled at him reassuringly, his pride and belief lighting his seamed old face. His teeth were yellow, separated by black and empty gaps. Kerlew thought his eyes must have been brown once. Now they were skimmed with gray film that reminded him of the green slime that clouded the surface of summer ponds. Kerlew knew that if one stirred the slime with a stick, the depths and wonders of the pond beneath it were revealed. Sometimes when he stared at Carp's clouded eyes, he thought he glimpsed the depths and wonders beyond the gray that misted them. Gray as the smoke that drifted and wandered through the tent. When he breathed it in, it was like breathing cobwebs. It clung to the inside of his nose and lined his throat with dryness.

Carp's withered lips were moving, and Kerlew focused on them with difficulty. He was supposed to be listening, he remembered belatedly. The smoke was supposed to make this easier. Instead it was making it harder.

'Just breathe deeply and listen to the drum. Let the drum guide you. Listen now.'

The drum. Kerlew shifted his eyes to Carp's hands. A little drum with a yellow-leather drumhead was gripped between the old man's knees. In one of Carp's hands was a tiny hammer, made from a bear's molar mounted on a stem of birch. Kerlew watched the molar lift and fall, lift and fall, lift and fall. Each time it struck the taut leather it made a sound. Listen to it. He was supposed to listen to it. The old shaman's fingers were the same color as leather that had been used a lot and hung up inside a smoky tent. Like this smoky tent. His eyes drifted away from the drum and fingers, rose to follow the gray smoke as it swirled silently through the tent.

Carp was still talking to him. His words drifted through the tent with the smoke. 'Listen to the drum and let go

3

of this world. Breathe in in this world, breathe out in the spirit world. Let go and go down, into the spirit world to seek out your spirit beast. Go down, follow a mouse, follow a beetle, go down into the spirit world, followatrickleofwatergodowndeepintotheearth . . .'

The words mingled with the smoke and swirled through the tent and up. Up and around, past the patch sewn on the tent wall, past his leggings hung to dry on one of the tent supports, past the old shaman's head. Kerlew lay still on his pallet of hides and watched them. His tongue was gummed to the roof of his mouth and he could not let out his breath. He could take in air, and he felt his chest swell tighter with every breath. But he couldn't let the air out. For a slow moment he noticed this and it troubled him. Then his attention was caught once more by the swirling smoke. He watched it glide, so gray and soft and free. He let out a long sigh and followed the smoke.

Once he had fallen into a river, and before his mother could snatch him out, he had been washed downstream on the buffeting flood. This was like that time, except the smoke was warm and soft and there were no great stones to batter him. It carried him up and around, toward the peak of the tent and the smoke hole. He brushed past the old shaman's bent head, heard a few lingering notes from the skin drum. For that instant he remembered that he was supposed to be going down, into the earth to seek the depths of the spirit world. Then he swirled past Carp and was carried aloft on the smoke. The old shaman's instructions no longer seemed important. He floated up and out of the smoke hole.

The night was black, studded with stars. Winter was but a breath away, yet Kerlew did not feel the cold. He hunted across the sky, the smoke soft beneath him, his every stride

4

a stag's leap. Then, as he felt the smoke grow thinner and fade, he began to step from star to star just as one could step from stone to stone in a stream crossing, or from hummock to hummock in a bog. Gone was his usual clumsiness and halting stride. Here he walked as a hunter and a man. The night wind touched his hair.

Higher and higher into the sky he climbed, until far ahead of him he saw the pale hides of the moon's caribou. Far above the stars behind the moon, the herd was scattered out across the black sky. Kerlew stood on the highest stars and lusted after them. Their coats shone like lake ice and their antlers swept white and gleaming over their backs. Their heads were down and they grazed across the night sky. He knew that the smoke of their breath formed the clouds, and the clash of their antlers presaged thunder and lightning. Their power and majesty made his heart ache. He knew that if he touched one between the eyes and claimed it as his spirit brother, he would be a powerful shaman indeed.

But between him and the herd the stars were few and widely scattered. He stood teetering atop two stars, yearning after the sky caribou, and wondering what he should do. Briefly he recalled that Carp had told him to go down into the earth, not up into the sky. With a sinking heart, he knew he had disobeyed his master; he would fail in his hunt. He would return from this journey, no shaman, but only the healer's strange boy. At the thought, sickness washed through his belly and throat and tears nearly blinded him. He forced a shuddering breath into his lungs. Unless, perhaps, he could claim one of these creatures as his spirit brother . . . He centered his courage in his belly and prepared to jump to the next star.

But from behind him came the sound of panting, and he

felt hot breath on the backs of his legs. Turning, he beheld Wolf racing up the stars toward him. Wolf's coat was gray streaked with black, and his lolling tongue was red while his eyes glowed green. His great paws splayed wide with every stride he took, and Kerlew noticed every black nail. Then his eyes met Wolf's, and in that moment he knew his brother.

He set his feet well and lifted his hand. Palm out he waited for Wolf, and when he was but a few stars away, Kerlew cried out, 'I claim you as my spirit brother.'

Wolf didn't pause but laughed savagely as only the wolves can. 'Fool!' he howled. 'You cannot claim me here!' With a sudden leap he sprang high over Kerlew's head, beyond the reach of his outstretched hand. To the next star and to the next he sprang. The great white herd of sky caribou suddenly marked his coming. They threw up their antlered heads and bellowed to one another in fear. As one creature, the whole herd leaped into flight, bounding away across the night sky with Wolf panting behind them.

All this Kerlew saw in a teetering instant. The winds of Wolf's passage swept his balance away. His arms flapped vainly as he tried to keep his precarious perch, and then he was falling, tumbling down between the stars that snagged and caught at him like brambles. The bright light of the moon faded into a mellow darkness as he fell, and to his ears came the far sound of Wolf's hunting cry. Kerlew knew he called to his brothers, and he snatched at the words as they whispered past his ears.

'If you would be Wolf's brother, learn to follow the herds!'

ONE

The birthing had been long, though not as difficult as Tillu had feared. Elna's thick hair was sweat-soaked to her skull; in the heaviest of her labors, she had thrown aside furs and skins, panting with the heat of her struggle. But soon after the child emerged, she was shivering with cold and asking that her pallet be moved closer to the fire. The young mother slept now, her fat babe nestled in the crook of her arm, soft furs tucked closely around them both. Elna had been so proud when she saw her baby, her cry of joy louder than her cries of effort had been. He was the first child for Elna, and a large one. Tillu had feared that in her inexperience the laboring woman would push too hard and tear herself. But all had gone well.

She spread one more covering of soft fox furs over mother and child and bent to gather the bloody scraps of hide the newborn had been cleansed with. Tillu straightened slowly, wishing she could just lie down and sleep. Her back ached from her hours of kneeling and crouching by Elna, and her head ached from the tension of midwifing. The need for a

7

successful birthing had been like a knife at her spine. The other women were gone now, but during the birth, they had crowded inside the tent. Tillu had felt their eyes on her like clinging burrs. Had they believed she would do Elna some ill? She supposed so. She sighed again and rubbed at her weary eyes. A fine healthy boy, she reminded herself, resolved not to let her thoughts drag her down again. She was past that, now. She was going to be accepted again.

Outside the skin tent, Rak sat by a blazing fire, eating boiled meat the other women had prepared for him. On the opposite side of the fire, Benu's hunters shared his vigil. All were dressed for hunting; all looked toward the new father. He gripped his best bone-headed spear, its butt grounded against the frozen earth. His deep voice obscured the crackling of the fire, carrying his proud complaints through the leather walls of the tent. 'No doubt that useless woman of mine has birthed a puny, whimpering babe no bigger than a squirrel. Such is my luck. She is too young and foolish to bear a child.'

'Foolish man!' chided one of the passing women daringly. Her voice carried clearly through the cold night, meant to be overheard by all. 'Your firstborn is so large a child, doubtless your wife will have all she can do to pack him about and tend him, let alone see to your needs!' The laughter of the other women of Benu's band swept the night.

'He will fill her arms and bend her back,' crowed another.

'To sew a shirt for such a babe will be the work of a day and a night, while you, poor man, will go naked in the wind, and spend every moment hunting meat enough to fill him!'

'Bold ones!' chided one of the men. 'Dare you speak to a man so? Get back to your own fire!'

But the shouts of laughter that greeted her daring compliment belied the rebuking words. Such tribute made the young father flush even darker with pride. Meanwhile the rejoicing women were cooking delicacies for him, fresh tender tongues and fat ribs simmering in their own rich broth. The tempting odors penetrated the tent, making Tillu aware of her own hunger. She did not need to peer out to know what went on. The young man basked in the honor due one whose wife had just increased the strength of the hunting band. The men of Benu's folk paid their silent respects with the items they dropped unmentioned at the young father's feet. Sinews for bowstrings and bone arrowheads; fit gifts for a firstborn son. Had it been a daughter, it would have been the women who would have casually 'lost' bone needles and hide scrapers beside the mother's pallet. Such gifts were never mentioned by giver or receiver but were quietly set aside and cherished until the child was of an age to use them. Any birth was a cause for celebration, but tonight the small band of hunters rejoiced as if this were the first babe ever born. After their losses this summer, they needed the comfort of new life, even a babe born this close to the fangs of winter.

She glanced about the tidied tent and poked at the wick of the stone lamp to shrink its flame. Her duties were done here. Tillu scratched away a flake of dried blood on her wrist, thinking. The other women of Benu's folk had already borne away the afterbirth, to set it out on an altar of five stacked stones. Tomorrow, Carp would study the signs of the animals that had visited it during the night, and then would announce the child's guardian spirit. Tomorrow would be Carp's day, to shake his rattles of leather and bone and speak in strange voices. Tomorrow Carp would be very busy, receiving the honor due him as a shaman. All the folk would be caught up in celebrating the birth of a new hunter. Tonight would be a good night to leave.

The decision surprised her. She tried to reconsider it as she lifted the tent flap and peered out into the night. The world balanced on the knife edge between autumn and winter. Only a fool would leave the safety of a tribe at this time of year. The tiny tent village around her was as much civilization as this part of the world knew. Beyond the temporary bounds of this hastily pitched camp was the forest. She knew the forest was not eternal; a lifetime away, to the south and east she thought, was a land of farmers and cultivated fields, of riders of horses and reapers of grain. It was the land of her childhood. But this was the reality of her adulthood: this northern forest, and the small bands of semi-civilized people who inhabited it. From group to group she had wandered; this was the farthest north she had ever been, and Benu's folk the poorest of any she had lived with. Of bones and stones, hides and meat were their lives wrought. She pulled her wolf hood up and forward to shelter her face from the early winds of winter as she left the humid warmth of the skin tent.

The blazing light of the fire against the stark blackness of the night blinded her. The men had built it high, fueling it with branches both green and dry, and sometimes splashing precious oil on it to make the flames roar wildly. The dancing flames cast strange shadows that made the surrounding trees seem to writhe in the unexpected warmth. Close to the fire, the men feasted on the boiled ribs and juicy tongues, their faces shining with heat and grease and joy at the new hunter's birth. Tillu walked past them silently, her soft boots crunching frozen moss and grass underfoot. None of the men deigned to notice her passage. It was unworthy of hunters to pay attention to a woman and a midwife.

For a moment the night held her closer. It was a clear

night of black skies and the stars were as thick as yellow pollen on a quiet pond. The camp had been made in a small vale between two hills, a place protected from most of winter's wind. The forest in this area was an open one, of paper birch and alder and willows that merged with brushy thickets and then bog grasses. Years ago this area had been burned over. Fire-blackened stumps and scarred giants of trees were reminders of that time, but most of the live trees were no bigger than she could span with her two hands. It was fine hunting for small game and browsing deer, and Benu's folk had summered well in the winding river valley. But the sparse leaves that now clung to the branches were gold on the birch, dirty yellow on the willow and red on the alder. The edges of the coarse grasses and fallen leaves that carpeted the ground were outlined tonight with shining silver frost. It was time for Benu's folk to seek out the older forest of spruce and pine that offered more shelter from winter's blasts. There they would cope and struggle through until spring. So Tillu knew from their talk. She had once thought she would go with them. Now she shivered and pulled her arms inside the loose sleeves of her coat to hug her body.

At a proper distance from the birth tent and the men, the women clustered together about their own, smaller fire, discussing every detail of the birth, and arguing as to whether the child was as large as Ardee's firstborn had been, or even larger. They were eating dried egg yolks, passing a sack made of deer intestine, each squeezing up a mouthful of the sticky, rich yolk and biting it off before passing it to her neighbor. Their hoods were pushed back in the heat of their fire. Their sleek black-haired heads showed glints of blue as they nodded to one another, and they muffled their giggling behind small browned hands so as not to annoy their menfolk. The joy of this small band of humans at now being eighteen instead of seventeen folk was a warm and tangible glow in the night.

Tillu could have gone to join the women at the fire. On this night, at least, she would have been welcome to share their yolk-sack and to chatter with them of babies and births she had presided over. She would be but the Healer and Midwife, just another woman at the fire. No one would mention the events of the summer. No one would speak of her son, Kerlew.

Tillu turned away from the small fire and the congenial women. She was too tired, she told herself. That was all. And her decision, sudden as it had been, was still strong. She was going tonight, and that would take some preparation. Besides, she was hungry for more than the rich stickiness of egg yolk. Her midwife gift would be in her own tent, borne there by the women as soon as the child's cord had been safely bitten. The father would know nothing of it. Among Benu's folk, birthing and midwives were the province of the women, and for a man to stoop to being interested in such things would be strange indeed. And dangerous, for spirits had been known to become offended at those who did not keep to their proper roles. The child was still especially vulnerable until Carp announced his guardian spirit tomorrow. Thus the huge fire that burned before the birth tent, and the father's brave vigil through the night. The spirits could be jealous and vengeful to those who flaunted their will.

Like Tillu.

She pushed the thought away. She had not been brought up to believe in such spirits as populated every cranny of these hunters' world. She would not be cowed by them now. Had she lived so long among wandering hunters as to share

12

their childish fears? Then it was time to move on. Somewhere there were other folk who would welcome a healer and midwife, people who knew more than skin tents and tools of bone. She squared her narrow shoulders against the night fears she would not admit and hurried through the darkness and clustering trees to the isolation of her small tent.

Yellow lamp light escaped from the ventilation flap and seams to welcome her. She would have to scold Kerlew for letting the lamp burn so brightly and use so much oil. But if he had been talking to Carp, as he did too often now, he would tell her that the tending of a lamp was woman's business, and not for him to worry about. She sighed a tiny sigh. It was not that Kerlew was harder to live with these days; it was just that she had been accustomed to his old differences and difficulties. These new ones were heavier to bear.

She lifted the tent flap, grateful for the light and heat that flowed out to greet her. It was good to be in her own tent again. She became aware anew of the tension that energized her whenever she had to move among Benu's folk. Uneasiness, she tried to tell herself. Not fear. But only when she was alone with her son did she feel safe from their accusing eyes. Only when she could actually see Kerlew did she stop worrying about him, lest some small but deadly accident befall him. She threw back her hood as she entered the shelter, ready to relax. The sight that greeted her stiffened her weary muscles.

The dished stone of the lamp was heaped with lumps of melting tallow. The twisted moss wick that drew up the melting fat smoked and flared dangerously high. The gift of food left for her by the other women had been reduced to scattered fragments beside the blazing lamp. The old shaman was licking gravy from the side of his hand as she entered.

He gave her a gap-toothed grin. His face was like wrinkled leather dried after a rainstorm. The smell of his magic clung to him like the stench of carrion to a bear's hide. When he stood staring at her as he did now, bandy legs spread wide and head nodding, her aversion to him was like a physical thrust. She wanted to strike him, to drive him from her territory. She suspected he sensed it. Sensed it and enjoyed it. So she ground her teeth but forced herself to keep the custom of Benu's folk. Carp was the shaman. No one could begrudge him anything. And no woman denied any man a share of the food in her tent lest she insult her own husband by implying he was too poor a provider to feed a guest. The fact that Tillu had no husband made no difference at all. Guests were always to be honored with food, to be pressed to eat and enjoy, while the host always bemoaned the fact that what he could offer was so unworthy. Then the honored guest would protest that the food was of the finest quality, much better than anything his own poor household could provide. And the next night, the guest would be the host, and the roles would be exchanged. Unless the guest were the shaman. Then the host knew that the spirits were pleased by his fine treatment of their friend, and would bless the household. Was not that honor enough? So Tillu chewed and swallowed her outrage. For the last time, she promised herself.

'This one is honored that you would be so kind as to share the small and stale provisions of my tent,' Tillu greeted him formally.

Carp belched politely and rubbed his belly to show the extent of his satiation. 'Your home has been generous to me.' His eyes followed Tillu as she bent and pulled her reindeer coat off over her head. She sat on her pallet to draw off her knee boots of fox fur soled with winter-taken

14

deer hide. She pulled out the felt padding made by drying and pounding the tough supple stalks of sedge grass and put it by the lamp to dry. She stood barefoot on the cold packed-earth floor. The shaman stared. She was so different from the short stocky women of Benu's folk. She was small, as short as they, but to look at her was to see her as a smaller, fine-boned specimen of a larger people. From elbow to wrist and knee to ankle, her long bones were proportionately longer than those of the women Carp knew. The difference made her unattractively thinner in his eyes. Her hair was finer, more brown than black, as were her eyes. The color of her skin was subtly warmer, as was her temperament. But Carp was willing to overlook these flaws, for she was strong and healthy, and almost young. Besides, women were scarce among Benu's folk, and mostly taken. She would do.

Tillu avoided his gaze but could feel his thoughts. When she had first joined Benu's folk, he had been more subtle. But Tillu had resolutely ignored his courting gifts and the unsubtle hints from Benu's wives. She had no desire to be the shaman's woman. No man had owned her since Kerlew's father had left her, heavy with the child. She had not missed belonging to a man. Yet, among Benu's folk, a woman without a man to rule her was but half a being. Women had their fathers, their husbands, then their sons to order their lives and protect them. At first the other women had pitied Tillu, alone in the world. But as time passed, she had become an uneasiness among folk. Could the spirits be pleased with such a creature as she? By their traditions, Carp could not force her, though she knew that if she stayed much longer with this group, the social pressure could become unbearable. Then, if Carp did take her against her will, no one would intervene, but would say that the shaman knew the desires of her spirit guardian better than she did herself.

At the thought, Tillu clenched her teeth. It would never come to that; she was leaving this night. She could afford to be civil, for one last time. She drew a silent breath. 'And my son?' she asked courteously. 'Has he shown you the respects of our home?'

Carp rubbed grease from his chin. 'The man of this tent has been most gracious to me.' He inclined his head respectfully toward the pallet at the back of the crowded tent where Kerlew reclined. The shaman's dark old eyes, flawed by gray clouds, voiced a silent challenge. Tillu took a step nearer her son.

Kerlew lay on his side, staring up at the shadows on the slanting wall of the tent. He wore only his breechclout of yellowed leather. His coarse black hair was unbound and cascaded about his face and shoulders. His gaze was empty, wandering. For an instant, she could almost see him as strangers did, as a boy rather than as her son. His face always attracted stares. His hazel eyes were very deeply set on either side of the narrow bridge of his nose. The closeness of his eyes to one another made his passing glance seem a peering and his stare an unbearable intrusion. More than one adult had cuffed him for that seeming rudeness. His lips were full and his prognathous jaw emphasized this. Small ears were flattened tightly to his large head, nearly hidden by his hair. His narrow hands waved gracelessly in the air, and he stared, entranced, at their shadows as they flowed and danced on the hide wall. At rest, his fingers curled in toward his wrists, and the thumb stayed in close to the fingers. It gave his hands a blunt and helpless look. But now they flapped at the ends of his arms, and their shadows mimicked them. As he dreamed, his mouth moved silently, speaking, and then laughed gutturally at some pretended reply. Anyone else would have assumed that he was feverish and wandering, or in a shamanic trance.

Tillu knew better. This was Kerlew, her strange one, in but one of his own peculiar self-amusements. A child not only homely but almost repellent in his strangeness. That which would not interest a sucking babe held him fascinated for hours. While other children built leaf boats to sail on a stream, Kerlew would stare, entranced, at the sunlight glancing off the whirlpool. Silent and dreaming, he would come home from such a day to be caught by the dancing of the lamp flame or the movement of his own shadow on the wall. He could forget to eat in his fascination with the globules of oil floating in his soup, or stand soaking in the rain watching the circles of the drops that fell on the puddles. Silent, staring, unresponsive to a gentle voice or his mother's call. But Tillu knew he could be cuffed or shaken out of it and told to bring water, or fetch fuel, or take broth to one who was ailing. Last summer he had all but given up such foolishness, for she wouldn't let him indulge in it. She had filled his days with simple chores, giving him no time for mindless staring, and telling him it was infant's play not fit for a boy of nine summers. She had forced him to learn, repeating aloud to him lessons other children learned without words. 'Kerlew. It is not polite to stand that close to someone. Move aside. Kerlew. Lower your eyes before a stranger. Kerlew. Do not touch another's food.' The endless repetitions of rules which children of two summers already knew instinctively, but which Kerlew had never noticed. Slowly, slowly, he had begun to learn and abide by it. But that was before Carp had taken him over. Before the plague of the bear. Tillu sighed at the memory and, as she took in a fresh breath, caught a peculiar odor in the air of the tent.

'What have you given my son?' she demanded in a low voice. She stepped forward to touch Kerlew, to check for the fever some of the wandering herbs could induce, but before she could lay a hand on him her wrist was gripped and Carp jerked her back.

'Do women ask of shaman's doings? A fine thing indeed! Shall I take up a needle and sew mittens for you while you venture out to bring down meat with a bow?'

'He is my son!' Tillu cried in anger.

'No! He is my apprentice! And he must be trained, and initiated by rites that are not for women to know of. Your time to be his mother is over. I am the one who guides him now. Ask no questions, Tillu, lest the spirits be angered.' He gripped her, eyes and wrist, and for a long moment she believed. Meeting the gaze of those clouded, gray-on-brown eyes that should not see but did, she felt her soul flutter within her, threatening to leave her body and take her wits with it. She felt the coldness of Kerlew gone from her, the pain of watching helplessly as he changed into someone she feared and loathed. She could smell the fetid breath of the magic, a dark and slinking thing that Carp could call out of Kerlew himself, a thing that would steal her son away from her more permanently than death itself. Then the anger in her hardened to resolve, and cunning. She freed her wrist with a quick twist and turned aside from the shaman and her son.

With pretended docility, she moved to the pots the women had left for her, helping herself to some bits of boiled meat still swimming in lukewarm water and oil. She kept her eyes averted before the old man, thinking quickly as she chewed slowly, and then licked the dripping juices from her fingers.

18

'A hunter was born this night in the tent of Rak,' she announced casually. 'All the men feast about his fire on tongue and ribs. A fine healthy boy, as large as Elna could pass.'

'That is a good sign,' Carp announced officiously. 'The spirits once more turn their faces toward us. My gifts to them and my hours of dancing have changed their hearts.'

'So were many saying about the fire,' Tillu agreed smoothly. 'Some were saying that Rak would surely gift you well for the health of his firstborn.'

Carp immediately took up his coat and dragged it on. 'Then they will be calling for me soon, to chant for a new hunter. Such a burden for an old man such as myself. Rak will press me to eat much meat to celebrate a new hunter, and to chant late under the stars, lest spirits come to steal his son before he has a guardian of his own.' He pulled his hood forward to shelter his wrinkled face. 'Then I shall have to arise early tomorrow, to read the will of the beasts to determine the boy's guardian, and to mark him as a hunter with the first blood spilled tomorrow, and to offer the feast of the first kill to the spirits. Uh-yah. An old man must do without his sleep to secure the hunters of tomorrow.'

'And your apprentice? Will you not stay to guide him out of his trance?' Tillu pretended unconcern as she spilled a vessel of blood into the remains of the warm oil and water and stirred them into a thick soup. She hung the pot near the lamp to warm it further.

'There is no need. He does not need the Smoke of the Traveler. I but burned some as an offering. The boy is gifted, for the spirits are ever with him, talking in his ears as loudly as chattering women. He will be a powerful shaman, and all will know him as my apprentice.' There was undisguised

19

pride in the old man's voice as he pulled his skin boots up over his bony knees and knotted the thongs around them. 'My thanks for the hospitality of this house.'

'My thanks for honoring our cold and humble tent, and seeing fit to share in these poor foods.' And her heartfelt thanks that he was finally leaving.

'Uh-yah,' Carp grunted. He stood a long moment, holding the tent flap up and looking at her. 'Woman.' Tillu flinched at that tone, like a dog nudged in a sore spot. 'Tomorrow you will move my tent. Down here, next to yours. After the ceremonies. I will show you where I want it.'

She managed to keep her eyes and voice steady. 'Why?'

'Does a woman question a man when he says he will do a thing? Then a woman has lived too long alone, and has forgotten how the world is ordered.' He let the tent flap fall. Tillu listened to the crunch of his retreating footfalls. She swallowed her sickness, her mind racing. Soon he would be at the fire, and the men would press him to eat boiled meat with them and drink the rich broth to celebrate the new hunter. There would be chanting far into the night. Carp would be very busy.

She poked at the wick in the oil lamp so that the flame burned lower. The light in the small tent faded, and the soft murmur of Kerlew's voice ceased. His hands curled and fell to the skins beside him. He would be close to sleep now, full of his own idle stories. Well, let him. The work of this move would be Tillu's, for the boy was still more hindrance than help with these things. Tillu stirred her blood soup, then took the vessel from its hanging string and drank slowly of the warmth. It gave her strength, and her courage grew.

She began to tidy her tent, eating what Carp had left of the delicacies the women had brought for her, wiping each

20

pot as she finished with it and setting them aside. She set them on their sides on the earth floor of the tent, for they would not stand alone. Their pointed bottoms were designed to be nestled between the hearth stones in a fire. Their sides were rough where pebbles had been accidentally mixed with the clay that formed them. She set them down carefully, taking care not to crack any. She would take nothing that was not hers. She finished eating what there was and wiped her face and hands on a piece of skin. Putting her hands on her hips, she surveyed the task before her.

She wished that she had more to worry about. A little skin case held her sewing needles, awl, and sinew. Another larger bag held her healing herbs and the other supplies she used in treating the various ailments of the folk. A skillfully pegged-together wooden box, remnant of a stay with another people, held her extra reserves of herbs and roots and seeds. Besides that, there were her two cooking vessels made of baked clay and several baskets for gathering. Their sleeping pallets were no more than skins on top of piles of brush gathered each time the folk decided to stop and make a village for a few days. She had two stone lamps and a sack of oil. She thought regretfully of the dried slabs of fish, the pokes of berries in oil, the scored and smoked twists of meat she would have to leave behind. Some she could take, but not a winter's supply. She could only drag so much. Her wits would have to feed them.

Luckily their winter clothing was new, sewn for them by Reena before the disaster. It would last them most of the winter. She would worry about replacing it when that time came. The tent itself was no more than stretched and scraped winter hides sewn together. The poles that supported it would become the poles of the travois she would drag it on. It was a heavy load for one, but such was the fate of a woman with no man and a son with the mind of a babe.

No! That wasn't true! She fiercely rebuked herself for the thought. Kerlew was a good boy, a capable boy, and could grow to be a good man, if only Carp would leave him alone. His 'training and initiation' only made the boy grow more childish each day. She hated watching him revert to the strange, introverted behavior of his earliest childhood. Carp had undone the work of months. Once Kerlew had helped her gather her healing herbs, had done simple tasks of fetching and tidying. But all that had been changed by the bear.

Tillu mourned the event as she gathered her possessions and bundled them, grieving as if it had been her own son lost. It had been a tragedy, but only that, until the old shaman had cast his shadow over it.

Kerlew was terrified of bears. Tillu had seen to that, and refused to regret it. Mother and son were too often on their own, traveling alone, for her to think of a bear as prey. Her rule for the boy had been simple, the only kind of rule he could remember and keep. 'If you see or hear a bear, you leave any meat or berries you have, and come quickly to me.' It had always worked well for them, when they were traveling as two alone. But last spring they had joined with Benu's folk. The other children had speedily learned of Kerlew's differences, but nothing had given them as much joy as his fear of bears. It was sport for them to rattle the bushes like a bear, snarling and snorting, so that Kerlew would flee and leave them whatever fish or berries he had painstakingly gathered. Back at the tents afterward, they would gleefully tell how he had run, and how they had enjoyed their ill-gotten gains.

All of Benu's folk, big and small, had found it humorous.

Tillu had tried to believe it did not matter. Why let it rankle, when Kerlew himself would uncertainly grin as they told of it? Trying to tell him that he did not have to flee from the bear sounds made by children younger than himself only confused him. His old rule was too deeply ingrained in his soul. The children growled and Kerlew fled, to be teased later. Reena's two youngsters had taken the most joy in it. Scarcely a day passed that Kerlew did not come racing home, empty-handed, after an afternoon of foraging. Tillu had hoped they would weary of their sport. Instead they carried it one step further.

It had been close to the end of the summer. Mornings dawned clear and cold, and it took the sun longer to warm the chilled earth. The long days grew short again. Soon the brief season of warmth would be gone and winter would seal the earth beneath her white mantle. The plant life of the land was in a frenzy of bearing. In the shadowed woods grew the lingonberries, dangling red under great leaves already gone scarlet. Blueberries on twiggy bushes ripened on the sunny hillsides, and in boggy places the ground was carpeted with red mossberries growing on their tiny, round-leaved plants. Under the clear blue skies, the children collected baskets of them, to mash and cook into pudding with suet, or store away in leather pokes filled with oil. Small hands and faces were stained purple and red at afternoon's end.

Kerlew excelled at the montonous work, crawling diligently over the ground, absorbed in his gathering long after the other children had abandoned their half-filled baskets to play. Reena's small boys had made no effort at all to fill their vessels, for they had plans that would let them play all day and still return to the village with a trove of berries. They giggled but refused to confide it to the other children.

23

Kerlew had been picking alone, the other children long gone, when he heard the first of the growls. That much Tillu had been able to piece out from his hysterical account. Then he had seen Reena's boys stagger from the bush, screaming and choking, red flowing down their faces and hands. 'The bear has crushed us and clawed us, we die, we die!' With a terrified howl, Kerlew had fled, racing back to the tents, where he screeched out the news of the slaughtered children. In moments the armed hunters and frantic women converged on the berry-covered slope, to find all the children clustered about Kerlew's near-empty basket, filling their mouths with the sweet berries as they shrieked with laughter. The red stains had been only the crushed juice of berries smeared on their hands and faces. After the first commotion, all saw the fine jest that Reena's boys had played. There was much laughter that night around the cooking fires.

But in Tillu's tent, a shaking Kerlew refused to believe that all was well, that it had been but a jest. 'The bear got them. The bear got them!' he tearfully insisted. His breathing would not slow, and Tillu heard the long thundering in his thin chest. His eyes darted about the tent, and he winced fearfully from the shadows he himself made. She put him to bed and urged errimi tea into him, which he drank in gulping gasps. His face was white, his lips red as he panted. And as she knelt beside him that night, silently hating all children but her own, he had sunk finally into a stillness deeper than sleep.

It frightened her and she tried to rouse him, with no success. Abruptly his body began to jerk in sudden, painful spasms like a fish on a riverbank. His face contorted; he opened his eyelids on white eyeballs that stared blindly about. His breath shrieked in and out of his body, and yellow foam gathered at the corners of his mouth. In all her years as a healer, Tillu had never seen the like. She was trying to still his frenzied jerkings with the weight of her own body when she sensed the others behind her.

Carp had pulled her roughly away from her son, his face tense with excitement. 'He sees, he sees!' the old man had exulted, and, as if in answer to these words, Kerlew had begun to speak. The voice was not his. He sighed and moaned the words. Tillu's Kerlew spoke as a child still, in a voice that piped like a shore bird. The voice that came from his heaving chest and snapping mouth now was the deep voice of a grown man. 'Ah, they bleed, they bleed!' he gasped. 'The bear has found their blood! It spills from their mouths, see it drench their shirts. They will die now. They will die!' The last words came out as a roar as Kerlew sat up on his pallet. His eyes rolled suddenly and were their startling hazel again, their foreign, empty hazel, as awful as their whites had been. He bit his tongue, and the froth that dripped from his lips was suddenly pink.

The children had shrieked and tumbled from the tent, with their frightened mothers close behind. Even the stalwart hunters had muttered uneasily and found reason to leave. But Carp had been exultant, and had sat by the now quiescent boy, holding his thin hand until the day dawned again. The next day he had claimed the weak and baffled boy as his apprentice.

Kerlew had no recollection of his seizure, but rejoiced in the sudden exclusive attention of a man held in such great respect by the rest of the folk. In the old man he had found not only a willing audience for tales of his fragmented dreams, but one who attached great importance to them. He had begun to mimic Carp's gait and inflection, even his overbearing manner that made every request a veiled demand. He absorbed avidly all of Carp's teachings about the shaman's world, learning it as easily as other boys learned to make a spear head or draw a bow. After her first resentment, Tillu had grudgingly told herself that it might be a positive change in the boy's life.

Then the children had begun to sicken. Reena's boys were first, becoming weak and irritable, as their bodies spattered out all nourishment. Their bellies swelled, their skin stretched tight over the bones of their ribs and faces. They cried tearlessly, writhing in pain on their pallet. Tillu made root tonics for them, put poultices on their aching bellies, boiled pine needles for tea, to no avail. On the fifth day, they vomited great scarlet gouts of blood that drenched their shirts and bedding. They died.

The other youngsters of Benu's folk sickened rapidly. Tillu was powerless, and Carp chanted and made sweet smokes to no avail. Before ten days had passed, of nine children there were four, and they but pitiful, staggering shadows of themselves. Kerlew alone of the children remained untouched by it. He no longer cringed and crept about in fear of the older boys' beatings. Without the other children, he romped fearlessly on the hillsides, gabbling his stories to himself and laughing his strange, broken laugh. Carp watched him and nodded knowingly. Kerlew alone ran and shouted and played unmolested among the tents. Until the day Reena came shrieking to her tent flap, to fling bones and stones at him. 'Leave us alone, brat!' she had screamed at him. 'Cannot you stop rejoicing in what you have done to us? Have not you punished us enough?' She had voiced the fear the others wouldn't speak; her husband beat her for her boldness, fearful of what she might bring down on them.

Kerlew had been touched by the spirits; he was theirs.

Carp had helped Tillu to move her tent, setting it up outside the village. Carp had forbidden the others to drive Kerlew and his mother away, saying that the spirits who had chosen Kerlew to be his apprentice would turn against the people that sent him away. Did they want to feel that wrath?

And thus had they lived these last two months, apart and yet united with the people who still ached from her son's curse. Until tonight, when in her birth pangs Elna had called for Tillu, and Tillu had come. Tillu sensed a healing in this night, as well as a birthing. If she wished, if she were willing to pay the price, she would be a member of Benu's folk. There would be other women to talk to, the work of a healer to do, the security of having a place within a people. All she had to do was abandon Kerlew to the old Shaman's grip. She could give the boy to Carp, and stop worrying about him. She would become the shaman's woman, under his protection. Carp never went without food and clothing. The best could be hers.

She shuddered. She knew she could never bear the touch of the shaman's hands upon her. No matter how she stiffened her courage to endure it, she knew she would writhe and struggle against him. Better to be mounted by an animal than by one such as him. Better to flee these people, to be cold and hungry. Those things she could more easily stand. But the boy?

She looked down into the sleeping face stained with his father's wildness. She could travel more rapidly without him. Carp could give the boy an easy life. He would not have to be forced to grow and change and learn. As the shaman's apprentice, he would not be cuffed for staring, nor mocked for his awkwardness. Benu's tribe would grow to prize his

27

strangeness, to feel pride in their new shaman. It might be for the best.

Alone, her needs were simple. Since he had been born, he had made her life harder. She had gone from being a girl to being his mother. And he had never been an easy child. Even as a tiny babe, he had cried and struggled uncomfortably in her arms when she tried to cuddle him. No one would blame her. Not even Kerlew? She smiled ruefully. A season from now, he would probably be unable to remember her. What mother could love a child like that? Who would choose to be bound to such a burden? Her fingers reached, to push back a lock of his rough hair.

'Come,' she told him as his amber eyes fluttered open. 'It is time for us to travel again.'

'I have already been far this night,' he murmured drowsily.

'I doubt it not,' she agreed. 'But tonight we shall go farther still.'

TWO

She made her own trail, threading between trees just far enough apart to permit passage of the travois she dragged. Behind her, her long trail meandered through the forest, swerving and winding among the trunks but always bearing north. Benu's folk had been bound southward. She knew it was foolish to move north at this time of year, but Carp would not expect her to be foolish. Even if he guessed that she had gone north, Carp could not follow them, not unless he was stubborn enough to leave Benu's folk and travel alone. Perhaps, she thought as she plodded on, perhaps he could convince a few of Benu's hunters to track her, for a day or so. But they would be unwilling to trail her for longer than that, for they were anxious to get themselves south, to their own winter grounds. And despite Carp's power over them, they would be reluctant to go after his strange apprentice. No. Carp would be the only one with any reason to wish them back. She moved her fingers inside her mitten. Six days since she had left, and two falls of snow. If he had been following her, he would have caught her by now.

Safely out of Carp's reach, she told herself. She waited to feel some lightening of her heart but only felt her burden dragging at her shoulders. Out of Carp's reach, and into unknown areas and dangers. The straps of the travois cut into her flesh until she wondered if it was sweat or blood that damped her shoulders and back. Heavier than the drag of her tent and possessions was the weight of the task she had taken on. To do all, for herself and her son, in an unfamiliar territory devoid of human life. And to somehow change Kerlew, she reminded herself. To make him less strange, less difficult for other folk to understand. To drive Carp's strange notions out of his head and replace them with the skills he would need to live. To cleanse him of the magic Carp had started growing in him, just as she would cleanse a wound of an infection. Her determination set her teeth. She would do it. And until it was done, they would live alone and apart from other folk. No more Kerlew being hurt. No more hurting of others.

Her mind traveled back through the catalog of folk they had lived among. Before Benu's hunters, there had been a river tribe. Tillu had liked them, enjoyed their cleanliness and the songs they sang as they tended their nets. She and her skills had been welcome among them, until Kerlew had come seeking her one evening, walking boldly into the women's hut where no male ever ventured, into the midst of a womanhood ceremony. When Tillu protected Kerlew from the flung stones, they had both been driven from the river tribe with little more than the clothes on their backs. She flinched at the memory, and the others that crowded up behind it. Kerlew eating the jerky a hunter had set out as a spirit offering, Kerlew following a hunter of Oslor's folk and springing every trap he had set, Kerlew noting aloud that

Trantor's son looked more like Edor than Trantor, to the great dismay of Trantor's wife. Kerlew, Kerlew, always in the wrong place at the wrong time, with the wrong words in his mouth.

'Kerlew?' she called questioningly, realizing it was some time since she had last heard his voice. There was no answer. She halted, stilling the scrape of the travois's poles over the frozen ground and thin layer of snow. Awkwardly she turned in her harness, looking back past her left shoulder. 'Kerlew?'

'I walk where no one else has ever walked before.'

She snapped her head about, found him just slightly behind her and to her right. 'I thought for a moment I had lost you,' she told him. She began walking again.

Some moments passed. Then, 'Not me.' The boy chuckled.

'Not you what?' she asked absently.

'Not me you lost. Carp and Benu's folk. We should find them soon?'

'Maybe.' She walked on a little faster. The first night they camped she had tried to make him understand why they had to leave Carp and Benu's hunters behind. But as he realized she meant that they were running away from Carp, he had become agitated. The more she explained, the more upset he had become, swiftly reaching a point where he was not hearing anything she said. 'Carp, Carp!' he had wailed, rocking back and forth as he crouched on the frozen ground beside the small fire. 'Carp! Carp!' Until she had feared that if there were any of Benu's hunters tracking them, the sound would attract them.

'Hush, hush,' she had comforted him, choosing any words that would quiet him. 'Tomorrow, then, we'll go back. Just be quiet now, Kerlew, and tomorrow we'll go back to find them.' And then, cruelly, because he wailed still, 'Hush! Or

31

a bear will hear you!' That had silenced him, leaving him shaking with his pale eyes wide. 'We will go back tomorrow,' she had assured him, repeating the words until he slept. But when morning came, she had continued on her trek away from the hunters' camp, Kerlew none the wiser. A few times each day now he asked when they would find Carp, and she gave him nebulous answers. Soon enough he would forget. She knew her son that well; nothing stayed in his memory for long.

'I walk where no man has ever walked before!'

She glanced over at him. His smile was too wide, too wet. Sometimes she longed to slap it from his face, make pain chase away the vacuous, idiot smile and the foolish words. But she did not. She knew only too well the consuming self-disgust that would follow such an act. 'You chose to keep him with you,' she reminded herself. 'You could have left him to Carp. You know you cannot beat sense into him.' To Kerlew she said, 'That's silly. Just because you cannot see a trail does not mean that no man has ever walked there before.'

'On this snow!' Kerlew explained, smiling at the thought: 'On this snow, no one has ever walked before, for the tracks would be here. This snow fell new last night, and the first tracks on it are mine. I walk where no one has walked before.'

'Mmm.' Tillu kept walking. There were times when the boy almost made sense, when she believed that, to him, his observations and statements followed some mysterious logic of his own. Carp's shamanic instruction of the boy had made him more vocal; there was that she could say for it. Unfortunately, what Kerlew vocalized was the mystical gabble he had picked up from the old man.

She glanced across at her son. If only he would stand straighter, not drag his feet when he walked. If only his eyes would not wander and stare through things, he would not be such an awkward-looking boy. Not handsome, perhaps, but no worse than some she had seen take wives and build homes. Perhaps she could change the way he moved and spoke. Alone and apart from all others, perhaps he would turn once more to her, listen to her again. She would teach him, and this time it would be different. This time he would learn and grow. He would walk at her side through the forest and learn, not only her herbs of healing, but a hunter's skills. He would learn silence, and swiftness, and skill with a bow. As he grew, he would stand tall and move as a man should move. And one day she and Kerlew would be hunting, and they would come across strange hunters. Kerlew would be standing straight, having just brought down a fine deer, and the hunter folk would smile at the sight of the tall young hunter, and there would be a young woman who would look at him just a little longer than was quite proper, and she would be the –

'I'm hungry.'

The complaint broke the dream. Tillu sighed, both at her own foolishness and at Kerlew's request. She had taken what supplies she could, but already they dwindled. The boy ate so much, so fast. She glanced again at him. Skinny. Perhaps she should give him the worm tea again.

'I'm hungry,' he repeated into her silence.

'Soon.' One more hill, she promised herself, and then, if the valley beyond it were a likely one, she'd stop for the night. This time she'd set up their tent and stay a few days. Carp's seamed face came suddenly to her mind. Well, perhaps not just yet. Sleeping in skins was not so bad, it was not all that cold yet. Tomorrow she would push on for a day or so more, or perhaps three. She shivered. If Carp did come after them, with Benu's hunters, her fate would be sealed. The shaman's woman, prey to his withered hands and lined face, servant to his commands. To be touched by one such as that . . . She walked faster. She would not. That was all. She would not.

They crested a hill, and as they descended its other side, they passed abruptly into a forest. Here, for whatever reasons, the ancient forest fire had stopped. They stepped from a region of cottonwood, birch, and alders into the older pine forest. They went from trees that permitted light and snow to pass and settle on the forest floor to mossy-trunked giants that sealed out most of the light and snow. They moved through greenness, the air silent, almost opaque in the dimness. The poles of the travois hitched and bumped uncertainly over the deeper, softer moss and uneven blotches of snow. This part of the forest was older, more silent, generating a soft green gloom that seemed to well up from the dense moss and deep drifts of brown needles that peered from the scattered mosaic of snow that had penetrated the canopy of the forest.

There was a sense of peace to these huge trees. Their trunks rose straight and branchless for many man-heights before extending their needled limbs to block the sky. The underbrush was very sparse. Here, Tillu thought, I could set up my tent and the trees would keep most of the snow and wind away from us. I can see well in every direction; I would know if Carp came to seek us long before he was in reach of us.

'. . . and she lay down on the deep moss to rest, but in the night it grew swiftly and covered her over, sealing her eyes and filling her mouth, and a tree, small and green, grew up from where her belly had been.'

Tillu shivered at the words and scowled at Kerlew. 'What are you saying?'

'A vision Carp showed me. Of a place like this, and how there came to be one small tree growing in the midst of many great ones. Like that one,' he added, pointing to a young spruce, its needles pale green in the wash of the forest light.

It did grow from a hummock in the forest's green floor. Tillu shook off the chill that came over her and set her shoulders more firmly to the chafing leather straps. 'We have to go on. There's no water here, and it would be hard for me to come up on game without it seeing me first. And there are too many trees to allow me a straight shot at anything.' Suddenly the deep forest seemed a very poor place to set a tent.

'We will go on.' Kerlew nodded agreeably.

The tongue of the old forest was not wide. They were out of it as suddenly as they had entered it, the snow once more crunching under Tillu's feet. The mellow green darkness of the great trees was left behind. The light of the young forest seemed too bright, the edges of the trees' pale trunks too sharp to look at. She struggled up a new hill, the travois bumping against trees as it jerked along behind her. Kerlew walked behind her, taking advantage of the broken trail.

At the top of the hill she paused, taking in great lungfuls of the chill air. The sky, so bright only moments ago, was dimming now. Night would come early and swiftly. She glanced at the low-riding sun, trying to estimate how much farther they could safely travel today. The fire should be kindled before the darkness was complete. 'Kerlew. Start picking up branches for tonight's fire,' she called over her shoulder. He muttered a reply.

'What?'

'Woman's task to gather the wood. Not a fit task for a shaman,' he reminded her calmly.

Tillu straightened suddenly in her harness. An anger like pain jolted through her. She twisted to look back at her son. Kerlew stared up at her, his eyes suddenly going wide. He shrank from her fury. 'You are not a shaman!' She spat out the words. She glared at him, her fury strangling her. No more words would come. 'Pick up firewood!' she snarled at last, turning away from him. The straps cut into her shoulders savagely as she jerked against her burden to get it moving again. She could hear him muttering sullenly behind her, but she also heard the snap of a dry lower branch broken from a tree. He would obey. She thought of Benu's son, who would have run ahead with his bow in hopes of a rabbit or grouse. He had been no older than Kerlew. An alert boy he had been, his eyes large and bright, his hands already clever at carving. He had died of the bear plague. All the women had mourned his death. But Kerlew had lived. They had hated him for living.

The tears that stung her eyes were cold on her cheeks. She wanted suddenly to throw off her harness, to turn to Kerlew and hug him and tell him she was glad he had lived, that she loved him, would always love him, no matter what. But she could not. She had to get to the top of the hill, she told herself, and the boy would only have leaped away from her, struggled against her embrace. He did not need her tears and hugs. He needed her strength. She panted as she drew the travois over the crest of the hill. Standing still to breathe, she heard his muttering.

'. . . and I will be treated better there, when I walk among the reindeer-folk. Yes, I will lead them all, and Tillu will be only a woman who must tend to the men.'

The valley ahead of her was a deep one, full of darkness and reaching trees. Tillu began the long descent.

THREE

Heckram stood alone on top of the pingo and looked back the way they had come. Winter had already claimed the tundra. Diffused moonlight seeped through the overcast and reflected off the snowy plains, giving a false aura of dawn to the scene. But dawn was many hours away, and wiser men than he were sleeping.

Cold emanated up from the frozen heart of the giant frost heave he stood upon. The dark earth covering it was carpeted with lichen and vegetation; they in turn were frosted by last night's sprinkle of snow. The cold of the pingo's heart tried to numb Heckram's feet through his thin boots as the chill night leaned down on him.

The peak of the frost heave, a crest near sixty times the height of a man, lifted Heckram and made it seem that the tundra was a flat land, pale and featureless as the surface of a frozen lake. Distance and the uniform whiteness of the early snow cloaked its rolling swells and masked its long flat river valleys. The scouring of ancient glaciers had ground this part of the world into submission long ago. Ice had shaped it and mastered it and retained its dominance here. Freezes and thaws cracked its rocky bones and tortured its flesh into distinctive patterns, stripes and checks of earth separated by lines of ground frost. Even the long hours of daylight in the summer barely penetrated it. The skin of the tundra might thaw and bloom, but its heart was an icy secret.

A shallow blanket of powdery windswept snow covered all but the tallest grasses and brush of the tundra. There were no trees to stand tall and give a sense of distance to the vastness. The black line where the horizon met the night could have been but a step away, or mythically far. Clouds blanketed the sky this night; no stars betrayed the jest.

But Heckram had climbed the pingo to regain perspective, not lose it. He blinked his weary eyes and turned south, toward the foothills and forested mountains that were their winter goal. Ahead of them, perhaps two or three days as the herd traveled, they would find browse for the reindeer and fuel for winter fires. There, too, were the sod huts that offered as permanent a shelter as the nomadic herdfolk would ever know. In the winter camp, the older people and smallest children would shelter out the worst of the cold, while the herdfolk guarded against wolverines and wolves as their reindeer foraged on the snowy hillsides. For some, the camp ahead meant rest, and a time spent by the fires inside the kator. Some would slaughter their extra beasts and make blood sausage and boil marrow bones. The women would bow their heads over their ribbon looms, and some men would tell their children stories and make shadow plays with their rough hands against the walls of the sod huts. Some would take their excess wealth of animals and hides south to trade, while their relatives watched over their animals and families.

But not Heckram. While other men enjoyed the peace of the fireside, he would be raiding the wild herds, hoping to carry off the calves that had summered beside their mothers. His winter meat would be tough wild sarva or lean rabbit. While other women amused themselves with pretty-work, his mother would protect their animals from predators. What it all came down to, he reflected, were the beasts, tame and wild. If a man had enough reindeer marked with his mark, he lived well and easy. He had meat and hides to spare, and the time to hunt wolves and foxes for the lush winter furs the traders so valued. He had leisure to follow streams, looking for lumps of yellow amber washed loose by the spring floods. He had time to travel south through the hills, to walk proud among the southern traders and bring home the goods and stories of the south. He had time for the things that made life more than another day of survival. If a man had enough reindeer. Heckram did not.

The knowledge roiled bitterly through him. He lifted his eyes as if to see over the blocking hills and beyond them. Beyond them were more hills, and between them ran the trails that a good harke and a pulkor could travel easily. A man could load his pulkor with winter furs and lumps of amber from the spring-rushing streams and follow those trails. And if he did, he would come to the camps of the southern traders. They would make a man welcome with tongue-stinging wines from still farther south. A man could trade furs and amber for good bronze tools, or woven cloth of soft wool dyed to flower colors, or ornaments of gleaming gold, or flint worked as bronze, ground and polished with spiraling decorations. There men were tall and pale of eye and hair, as Heckram's father and maternal grandfather had been.

And beyond the trading camps? There were tales. Beyond, men lived in tall houses with many rooms, an entire village in one shelter, and turned up the soil with wooden plows. They rode beasts with but a single toe on each foot, and brewed potent drinks from the seeds of grasses. The water of their lakes leaped and splashed by itself, and it was always summer. So he had heard. From his own father, so long ago. So he had seen, once, on a long-ago journey. Before the Plague Summer.

'It's useless to think on such things,' Ristin would say, her head bent over her work, a small frown dividing her brows. 'Stories and memories are fine for old folks and children. But you are neither, Heckram, and there are other things you should attend.' His mother's bright black eyes would send him a peering reminder that was also a rebuke.

Useless. But there were times when he felt hungry for them with a hunger worse than the starvations he had known. Times when the dreams of far places and better days were all that could sustain him. It was a hunger that ate at him, that set him apart from the herdfolk and made him a foreigner among his own people.

'I want more than this,' he heard himself say. The words didn't impress the night, and he himself heard their foolishness. He closed his eyes, letting his mind wander back. When he had been small, his father had led their string of harkar. His mother had followed, leading her own string of reindeer oxen, and Heckram had ridden, clinging proudly to the pack saddle on the back of the most docile one. His clothing and the harness of their animals had been bright with ribbons of dyed sinew and grasses woven by Ristin's clever fingers. He had worn woven shirts made with wool from the south, and his father's knives had been of ground flint and gleaming

41

bronze, not bone and horn. His mother had worn amber beads, and even a bronze armband. There had been extra animals and soft furs to trade south for luxuries, and plenty of rich reindeer cheese and blood sausages to share. Their tent had been a bright warm place in the winter evenings. His mother had helped him nock his own mark into the ears of his first calves, and he had tended them proudly. They had laughed often, in his childhood. Who would not dream after days like that?

But few of the others ever did. Or if they did, they seldom spoke of it, for on the heels of those memories came the other ones. The memories of the Plague Summer. Heckram shook his head, trying to dislodge those other memories that settled and burrowed into him as relentlessly as warble flies.

The preceding winter had been mild. He had played in the snow beneath the eaves of the forest, and watched his calves grow large and strong on the easy grazing. Spring had come early, to green the forest before the herdfolk had even begun their annual migration to the summer grounds. They had followed the wild herd coming down out of the forest-sheltered foothills into the wide tundra. The early warmth softened the tundra's frozen face, thawing a shallow layer of the perpetually frozen soil beneath the hooves of the herd. The freed moisture and the brief warmth were all the vegetation of the tundra asked. Greens, purples, and golds with a scattering of blue, the hasty flowers of the tundra had leafed out and bloomed, so that the herd passed over a sweet carpet of lichens and mosses interspersed with the tiny bright flowers of the subarctic's stunted flora. Then warm weather had descended upon the herd when it was still on the flats of the tundra, far from the upthrust of the Cataclysm with its cooling ice packs. The warble flies, the midges, and the mosquitoes had swarmed. They were far from the sanctuary of the glaciers. In the evenings the people had burned wet moss on their hearths to drive the insects away, but there had been no place for the animals to shelter from the stinging pests. The warble flies had driven many beasts to madness. The reindeer had galloped and fought the air as they were stung, pawing vainly at their nostrils when they inhaled the tiny, hateful creatures. The herdfolk had pushed on desperately, straining toward the Cataclysm and its blessed, cooling glaciers. Bewildered calves died in the unseasonable warmth. Full-grown animals galloped in maddened circles trying to escape their stinging tormentors until they fell of exhaustion. Yet the majority of the herd had reached the Cataclysm and moved up its steep sides, to relief in the winds off its permanent ice fields. The trials of the herdfolk should have been over. But of those reindeer that did survive to reach the Cataclysm's height, where the stinging flies would not follow, many died anyway, coughing and choking and gasping in the sweet air of autumn.

He tried to rein his mind away from the memories, but like an unruly harke new-harnessed to a pulkor, bitterness dragged his thoughts once again through the misery of that time. The family's string of twenty harkar was reduced to four. Heckram had walked back from the summer pasturage that season, his small feet dragging behind his burdened mother. There was no trading trip south, no shower of bright gifts on his father's return. His family no longer possessed enough breeding reindeer to slaughter several for winter meat. Instead, his father had fed them on lean rabbit and squirrel and tough wild reindeer, and spent every spare moment stalking the much diminished wild herd to steal calves to bring home. Until the day he had not come back from the hunt. Heckram and his mother had searched the empty hills in vain. No one could say what had become of him. And that had marked the beginning of Heckram's manhood, come before its time.

He had been tall for his age, his southern blood showing early. His mother's father had been a tall, pale southerner, and his father's father, it was said, had hair the color of a summer fox. 'He's more southern than herdfolk,' he had heard the old Capiam say once. And so he sometimes thought of himself still, with unease and wondering.

At twelve, he had stood as tall as most of the men of the herdfolk. It had not made things easier for him. Folk expected a boy with the stature of a man to have the skills and control of one. His clumsiness shamed him often, his inexperience and impetuosity even more frequently. He often felt the lack of a father's teaching and protection.

The quickness and high spirits of his early years grew into silence and caution. He felt no kinship with the short, stocky boys of the herdfolk. Not even with Joboam, whose ancestry shared some southern blood. Joboam, fully as tall and awkward as Heckram, had a father who matched his height and was pleased with his son's growth. Growing with the plenty of his mother's and father's reindeer, Joboam's size seemed a credit to their wealth. His tunics were never too short; he was never solemn and anxious. By comparison, Heckram was gaunt as a wolf in hard times, and in his eyes was always the hunger of the wolf. He was a brooding youth, staggering under the burden of his manhood, the intensity of his dilemmas burning in his eyes. The herdfolk compared him with casual, confident Joboam, and in the comparisons he suffered. Failing too often, being less than competent at a man's skills, made him wary. To keep from losing, he would not compete. Even now, grown and competent, he hunted alone and did not boast of his kills. He was most comfortable when he moved unnoticed, whether he was stalking an animal or moving about the tent village. His solitude and his silences worried his mother.

Tonight her worrying had taken on a new barb. He shook his head grimly, his mouth set. 'Twenty-four years old, and what do you have?' she had rebuked him as she mended a mitten by the fire. 'Where is your wife, your children, my grandchildren? Do you think you can wait forever? Other men your age have three, four children at their hearth. Not yet, you say, and another year slips by. Do you think you have forever? Elsa is patient, perhaps too patient with you. But a woman cannot wait forever. No honorable man would ask it of her. She is a pretty girl, a good herdwoman, all a man could ask. She is strong and clever, a good hunter, too. Do you think no one else sees her worth? You will wait too long, and another will not ask her to wait. And then you will be too old to catch the fancy of the younger girls. You will be alone.' She shook the mitten at him.

So he had risen, to drag on his heavy tunic. As he had pushed open the door flap, she had demanded, 'Where are you going? To Elsa?'

'No. To practice being alone,' he had retorted, and left. To climb the pingo and think.

Now he regretted his snappishness. It wasn't like him and would only upset her more. But too many of her words had been nearly true. He had wanted to answer her, but the habit of silence had grown strong. Talking was an effort, especially the painful talk of explanation. She didn't want to hear his truth. She wanted his agreement; she was so sure it would make him happy. He knew it wouldn't, but couldn't tell her why.

His thoughts turned reluctantly to small, dark Elsa. She was all his mother said she was. And more, for in their childhood, they had shared friendship. He knew her. There was gentleness in her, hidden behind her self-sufficient toughness. And a warm ardor she had shared with him more than once, when they were children no longer but not yet grown. And yet . . . He did not want her to wife. He didn't want anyone to wife. Not yet. He wished his mother had not been so openly hopeful of a match. Already folk had asked him if he and Elsa would join by the Cataclysm next summer. And Elsa herself blushed whenever he tried to speak to her. When he approached her, her friends drew aside that he might be alone with her. And then he wouldn't be able to speak at all, for the bright hope in her eyes. He wanted to tell her not to wait, to look elsewhere for a mate. But how did one tell a friend that he didn't want her for a wife, no matter what his mother had noised about? Soon, he'd have to. Soon. His heart went out to her with fondness and sympathy. He hoped she wouldn't hate him.

Without conscious thought, he reached inside his shirt and drew out a length of sinew with tiny flaps of skin strung on it. This was the tally of his calves this year, the soft bits of ear cut from each miesse to mark it with his own private mark. It was pitiful. Five tiny flaps, and three of the calves were male, good only to neuter into the load-bearing harke, reindeer oxen, or to slaughter for winter meat. He would leave but one a sarva to service his vaja. His animals multiplied so slowly. Each vaja could bear but one calf a year, and there was no guarantee that it would survive the winter. The mysterious coughing sickness still claimed animals every summer. The diminished wild herds had forced the wolves and wolverines into new cunning and boldness as they preyed on the herdfolk's domestic animals. Heckram felt a twinge of despair as he wondered how he would protect his beasts from the marauding carnivores, and still find time to steal calves from the wild herd.

His mother's reindeer had done little better. Her tally string had but eight flaps, and five of the calves had been male. How could she urge him to take Elsa to wife? How did she think they would manage? Heckram reached up a mittened hand to rub at his face, to force the tightened jaw hinge to relax. He eased his heart by looking out over the herd and tents of his people.

The kator had been pitched in a village for the night. All had smelt the snow in the air, and sensed the storm to come. Better to set up the tents now, in the lee of the pingo, and be in shelter when the blast hit, instead of trying to struggle on toward the forest and be caught in the sweep of snow across the plain. Glows and streaks of light escaped from the simple hide tents, and he smelled the smoky fires of dried lichen and dung that warmed them tonight. It was a homey smell. The hobbled strings of harkar scraped away the shallow layer of snow to graze on the lush lichen of the tundra, awaiting the morrow when they would once more be loaded with the possessions of their owners and led on, toward the sheltering forest.

The herd, too, sensed the approaching storm, and had drawn themselves into a moving huddle of beasts. Their gray and brown backs were like a rippling sea in the moonlight as they shifted and stirred. The exhalations of their warm moist breath created a mist that drifted and rose from the herd in a cloud. The cold air carried the softly distinctive sound of their clicking hooves as toe bones flexed against stretched tendons. Their light-tipped tails flicked in an ever-changing pattern. Most of the great sarva had lost their antlers in their fierce autumn battles over the vaja. Gone were the great bulging withers of the bulls, their fatness battled away. In contrast, the neutered harker still carried their proud crowns, and their fur rippled sleekly over their muscles and fat. One would have thought them the monarchs of the herd. Even the vaja still bore their smaller, sharper antlers. The females would carry their antlers longer than the males, and would use them to full advantage for much of the winter, to make sure they and their young ones were not driven away from the best feeding. Heckram could imagine the soft grunts and mutterings of the settling herd, and the warm smell of the living beasts in the cold night. Wealth uncounted grazed there, his own paltry fortune among it.

'Heckram!' A thin panting voice sounded in the night behind him. His eyes sought and found the struggling figure that had ventured up the pingo to find him.

'I'm here,' he called back softly to Lasse. The boy made his careful way across the broken crest of the frost heave. Heckram found himself studying the boy as coldly as he would study one of his yearling calves. His short legs were already acquiring the typical bow of the herdfolk. When he finished growing, his head might reach as high as the point of Heckram's shoulder. But he would never fill out to be a sturdy, thick-shouldered herder like his father and mother had been. His body had known too much privation, too soon. Had he been a calf, Heckram would not have considered him worth gelding into a harke, let alone using as a stud. With a snort of self-mockery, he shook such images from his mind, and once more saw Lasse as Lasse. As reluctant as he was to have his solitude broken, at least it was Lasse who had come to do it. The boy seemed to sense his mood, for he was silent as he approached. Lasse was nearly ten years younger than he but Heckram never treated him as a boy. Lasse, like Heckram, had become a man before his time. If anything, Lasse and his grandmother lived in circumstances even more straitened than Heckram's. But Lasse never complained. Perhaps because he had never known that life could be any different.

'See them?' Heckram asked softly, and Lasse nodded. Both sets of dark eyes were fastened on the distant smear that was the wild herd. Vast it was, and yet still but a splinter of the thousands that moved from tundra to forest to tundra in their annual migration. And before the plague, the herd had been even larger. He knew Lasse found that image hard to comprehend. But Heckram remembered. In his boyhood, the wild herd had flowed before them like a river making its own bed. Brown and heaving it had surged across the tundra, leaving a swath of grazed earth in its wake. It always ranged ahead of the domesticated herd, but followed the same migration path. It was closer to the forested foothills but it had settled for the night.

'How many shall we take this winter?' Lasse asked boldly, as if it depended only on skill and determination, and not luck.

'Ah, perhaps a hundred,' Heckram blithely estimated. 'Eighty vaja for me, and twenty sarva for you.'

They both laughed short, quiet laughs at the bitter jest. 'As many as we can, my friend, and it will never be enough,' Heckram amended.

Lasse grunted in soft agreement.

'I've been thinking,' Heckram began.

'Not much else one could do up here,' the boy commented.

'About our hunting,' Heckram went on firmly. 'What if we were to shoot the vaja as she grazes, and then try to lasso the calf? The calf would tend to stay by its mother, not understanding what had happened to her. And it would give us meat this winter.'

They were both silent, thinking. A live animal weighed about three hundred pounds. A good portion of that would be guts, but that was not wasted. Heart and liver, bowels for the dogs, intestines and blood for sausages, bones and sinews for tools. Still.

'Tough meat,' Lasse qualified. 'And a calf with no antlers is not as easy to lasso. And it has less of a chance of surviving the winter without its mother's protection.'

'True,' Heckram agreed. 'But in a case where we couldn't get close enough for a good throw, it might at least be a chance for meat and a new animal.'

'But the calf would be too young to bear that spring and would not fare well without its dam. If we take the vaja, even if the calf doesn't follow, we have an animal that will bear again in the spring. Whereas we may shoot the vaja, and find we have made all that effort for a male calf.'

'Better than no calf at all,' Heckram rumbled.

'Or only an antler to show for it,' Lasse suggested wryly, and they both laughed companionably. It had been last winter. Lasse had stalked a vaja and her calf. He had thrown his lasso well and true, and the bone runner had slid smoothly as the loop of woven sinew had settled around the vaja's antler. But it had been late in the year, and with a sudden jerk the vaja and her calf had been free and fleeing through the woods, leaving Lasse with but an antler caught in the loop of his lasso. He had taken it back to the village and worked it into a needle case for his grandmother. The incident had become a joke among the herdfolk. But Heckram had admired the boy's pragmatism and went out of his way to befriend him.

'It's foolish to try and decide it now,' Heckram conceded. 'Better to wait until the vaja and her calf are before us, and then see which is more likely to work.'

'Snow,' observed Lasse.

It had begun to fall, tiny crystalized flakes that sparkled in the moonlight. In the dry cold, the flakes were like icy dust. It did not cling, nor dampen them as it settled on their shoulders and hats. A gust of wind stirred it, and the icy bits stung Heckram's face. He turned aside from it. 'Time to go back to the sita,' he suggested, tossing his head at the tent village.

'Sitor.' Lasse suggested the plural with an edge of mockery in his voice. Puzzled, Heckram looked at the tents again.

He saw what the boy meant. In a sense there were two villages below, not one. The division was subtle, but obvious once he looked for it. Closest to the base of the pingo, in the most sheltered area, was the tent of Capiam, the herdlord. Beyond it were the tents of the elders and his favored advisers. Beyond them, the tents of those wealthy with reindeer: perhaps a score of them. In a migratory caravan, such as the herdfolk were now, it was customary for each household to have two or more rajds. Each rajd was a string of neutered reindeer, usually about seven. Those tents nearest the pingo boasted three or more strings each, and some of them as many as five.

Then there was another village, pitched beyond the rajds of the first one. The tents of this village were clustered more closely together. More light gleamed from the seams of the worn tents, and fewer animals were picketed between them.

His mother's tent was there, with the rajd of seven harkar they shared. Lasse's tent was beside it, and Elsa's not far from that. The poorer folk of the herd had drawn together in their own separate village, just as the wealthy had set themselves apart from them. It was a cold thing to feel, and but one more sign of a trend that Heckram despised.

'Did Joboam apologize?' he suddenly asked the boy.

Lasse gave a disdainful grunt and turned to spit into the snow.

'Did he?' Heckram pressed.

'No. Not that I'd have stood about to listen to it if he did. I've no use for anything he says.'

'He should be made to apologize, publicly.' Heckram's deep voice was soft, his words hard as polished flint. 'If Capiam were all that a herdlord is supposed to be, he'd have seen to that. And made him pay, too, for the insult.'

'Let him call me what he likes.' Lasse stooped to crack a stone from its icy bed and shy it down the frozen crust of the pingo. 'Those who know me know I'm not a thief. And who cares what the others think?'

'I do. And you should. It's not just you, it's your family he's insulted. Isn't your grandmother upset?'

Lasse sighed and turned away from Heckram. 'Let's get back down to the sita before the wind really comes up.'

Heckram reached out to put a hand on Lasse's shoulder. It made the demand of friendship as it shook the boy's stiffened shoulders. 'What is it?'

The boy's voice came thickly. 'She heard that Joboam had accused me of stealing milk from reindeer that were not mine. A stupid accusation! Is a vaja going to stand still while a stranger milks it? Only a fool could believe that. And my grandmother is no fool, even if she thought that I would steal.

52

But she is proud, in the old way, and she was angry. So she chose to show her pride and anger in the old way, to shame him with a gift. She sent three cheeses to his tent. "He will see these," she said, "and he will know what I think. I think that if Joboam is so poor a man that he worries about the milk of a reindeer, then we should give him cheeses to ease him through his hard times. When folk see the cheeses from my molds, they will know we have shamed him." She still lives in the old days.'

Heckram winced for his friend. The cheeses alone were a gift the family could ill afford. But, worse than that, Lasse's grandmother did not understand how deep the changes in the herdfolk went. The cheeses she had sent as an insult to one who accused her grandson would be seen as an effort to pay back a theft. She had as much as admitted Lasse's guilt to the rest of the herdfolk. The older people would know the meaning of her gesture. But it was the younger ones that Lasse had to contend with every day. In her pride and anger, she had shamed him deeply.

'It is as you say,' Heckram said with false heartiness. 'Those who know you know the truth. And those who remember the old ways will understand that your grandmother knows you are not a thief. Who cares for the rest of them?'

For a long moment Lasse was silent, and a wind laden with ice crystals rushed between them. 'There's a good fire in my tent,' he said at last. 'How about a game of tablo? You owe me a chance to beat you.'

Heckram managed a grin. 'This time, I'll be the Wolf,' he offered. He put a mittened hand on the youth's shoulder and they started down the pingo.

FOUR

The sun had not risen. Nor would it, for the next twenty days or so. Yet there was not absolute blackness, but a diffused grayness of moon and stars and white snow shining. It was a shadowless light that filtered through the outstretched branches of the trees and rested coldly on the snowy ground. Tillu moved through the dimness, a shadowy figure that left crumbling footprints in the powdery snow. The cold had turned the snow to dust and crystals. At least it no longer clung to her boots and leggings, to melt and sog her clothing against her. Now there was only the absolute of water turned to dust, of cold so intense it made the hairs inside her nose prickle and her eyelashes stick together momentarily whenever she blinked her eyes.

She was carrying a dead hare. She gripped it by its hind legs, letting its skinny body swing. Ordinarily, she would have tied her kill to her belt with the thongs at her hip, to have her hands free to shoot if she saw other game. But her fingers had been too numb to manage the laces, so she carried the dead animal in one mittened hand. She had drawn her other hand and arm out of her sleeve and into her coat. Her arm hugged her chest, her hand in her armpit for whatever warmth it might find there. If she saw game, she wouldn't be able to shoot, but it didn't worry her. She was too cold to worry, and too tired to believe she'd see any game within the range of her crude bow.

The dead hare slipped from her fingers. She heard it hit the snow and she stopped, to look down at it dumbly. She had to move her whole head to see it, for she had tied the drawstring of her hood so tightly that the opening was just enough for her to see straight in front of her. She breathed shallowly through the long fur that edged her hood, feeling the frost form and melt with every breath. After a long pause, she pushed her warmed arm back down her sleeve and out into her mitten. Then she wriggled and tugged until the other arm with its numbed hand was inside the tunic with her body. Stooping, she picked up the hare and trudged on again.

On days like these, she regretted leaving Benu's folk. Among them, she had not had to hunt for her meat. Her skills as a healer had fed them both and kept warm clothing on their backs. Now she was alone again, dependent entirely on herself. She had never been a skilled hunter. She had grown up among farming folk.

As she walked, her thoughts wandered back to the village beside the wide river. She remembered cutting the ripe grain with a flint-toothed scythe. The heat of those days had glazed everyone's body with sweat. But in today's cold, the heat of those days seemed but a child's dream. So was it all, no more than a child's dream. She stumbled over a buried snag and dragged her mind back to the present. She wondered if they would survive the winter. The boy grew so thin, and she herself grew so stupid with the cold and the ever-present twinges of hunger.

She crested the last hill and looked down into the little glen where her worn tent was pitched. Nearly home and safe, she told herself. Useless to think of those lost days in that far-off place. As useless to think of Benu's folk, a hundred hills and valleys from here. She started down the long hill, nearly stumbling in her weariness. Her lips were dry and she longed to lick them, but knew they would only crack in the cold. Nearly home. Halfway down the hill, she halted and stared. Something was wrong. Her heart slowed its beating.

No smoke rose from the tent's smoke flap. Frost was heavy on the flap, showing that no residual heat clung there. The pieces of broken branches she had left by the tent for firewood were undisturbed. The still gray tent reminded her of scraped hides swinging in the wind. Dead and empty.

She ran. Her numbed feet felt the shock as they hit the frozen ground and plowed on through the loose snow. 'Kerlew!' she called, but her voice was dry and cracked as a dead leaf. It floated weightlessly away from her. A wolverine, guessed a part of her. A wolverine was afraid of nothing. It would not hesitate to enter a human's tent and attack a ten-year-old boy. Or perhaps he had gone outside the tent to relieve himself and wandered off. He never paid attention to tying his hood tightly, or putting on extra leggings. In this cold it wouldn't take long. The cold could do it, even if he didn't run into the wolves she had heard this morning. Hadn't she herself assured him that they were on the other side of the ridge, and no threat to them? Would wolves kill a child? They'd kill a calf that wandered from the herd. What about a calvish boy, all long awkward legs and flapping helpless hands?

It took her forever to reach the tent and burst inside. Her lungs and mouth hurt from the frozen air she dragged in with every breath. No matter. Where was the boy? 'Kerlew?' she asked breathlessly. The ashes were gray on the hearth stones. Nothing moved. Her life thudded to a slow halt in her breast, fell endlessly into the cold pit of her belly. The only sign of the boy was the bundle of hides on his pallet. Thoughts of bears and wolverines, of wolves, and of bands of wandering hunters sometimes more brutish than any animal rushed through her mind. And she had left Kerlew alone to face such things. Her throat closed. The dead hare slipped unnoticed from her hand.

'Kerlew!' she cried again, the sound ripping the stillness of the tent. She slipped her bow from her shoulder and gripped it. Tracks. Perhaps he had left some tracks. But as she lifted the tent flap, a tiny clucking came to her ears. She turned her head sharply, saw the pile of furs on his pallet stir. Stepping forward, she jerked the furs back, to reveal Kerlew on his side, talking softly to a smooth stone in his hand. Relief was overwhelmed and lost in the sudden rage she felt.

'What are you doing? Why is the fire out?' she demanded angrily.

'I forgot to put wood on,' he replied, not stirring. He stroked the rock in his hand, not even looking up at her. 'But it doesn't matter. I got under all the hides and stayed warm.'

Tillu stared down at him, feeling the cold eating through her clothing, feeling the hunger that would have to wait to be satisfied, but, most of all, feeling the despair that her son awakened in her. Would he always be this way, waiting for her to come home and care for him, heedless and helpless in the world around him? She didn't move, she didn't speak, she only looked on him, wondering what was missing in the boy, what she had failed to teach him, what it was that kept him from belonging to this world. She tried so desperately to make him right. But nothing changed him. He couldn't even see his own wrongness. All her waiting, all her efforts at teaching him were useless. Lost in the swirling hopelessness, she stared at her only child.

'Aren't you going to start the fire?' Kerlew demanded petulantly. He tugged at the covers she had pulled away. 'It's getting colder and I'm hungry. Is that all you killed today?'

The old rage, the rage she had thought left behind with his baby years, rose in her. The unfairness of this burden chafed and burned her soul. She towered over him, her anger giving her strength. With one hand she seized his shirt front, dragged him from the blankets to his feet. She all but threw him at the cold hearth stones. He staggered sideways, caught his balance awkwardly, and then suddenly crouched down, cowering before her.

'No!' The word ripped her throat. 'No! I am not going to fix the fire! You are! You, the fool that let it go out! Even the youngest babe of Benu's folk knows that the fire must be always tended. Without the fire we cannot live! But you, old enough to hunt, if you were not so stupid, you let the fire go out while you huddle like a baby and fondle some stupid rock. Give me that thing!'

She wrenched the reddish stone, polished by Kerlew's touch, from his frantic grip and flung it through the tent door. Kerlew's face went white. The stone vanished into the snow and Kerlew cried out. He dove after it, but she caught him by the back of his shirt and dragged him back, to dump him roughly on the cold earth by the hearth. She was shaking with rage and despair. This was her son, her boy who would soon be a man? This crouching creature that wept with anger because she had thrown a stone from the tent? It was unbearable.

'I want my rock!' he screamed furiously. He tried to rise from his place by the hearth, but she shoved him back. She snatched down the leather bag that held the dry tinder high above the earth floor. She flung it at him. The boy cried out as the bag slapped him and fell to the floor. She followed it with the fire-bow. She had no flint and strike-stone.

'Make the fire!' she commanded in a voice that shook the tent. 'Now!'

'I can't. I don't know how. I want my rock!' He scrabbled away, but she seized him by the scruff of his shirt and dragged him back. Tears streaked his face.

'You try. Now. You've seen me do it a thousand times. Now you try. Now!'

'I can't! I can't! I want my rock! It was my rock, not yours.' There was fear in his voice as well as defiance, and any other time it would have melted Tillu's anger. But she was too cold, too hungry, and too tired of being the entire support of his world. She knelt behind him and seized his thin wrists, forced his hands to the tools. His hands were limp. He would not pick them up.

'Pick them up! Right now, Kerlew! You pick them up and you try! Do you think I will always be here for you, to come home and make the fires and cook the food? What if I had gotten lost today? What if a bear had killed me, or I had fallen and broken a leg? Would you sit in this tent and cry, "I can't!" until you froze or starved? Would you? Would you sit and stroke a rock until you died? Would you? What if I hadn't come back today?'

The boy craned his neck to look over his shoulder at her. His mouth hung open and his closely set eyes goggled at her in terror. 'Not come back? You not come back? Kerlew alone?' His fear had reverted him to babyishness. His mouth hung askew, his bottom lip trembling wetly as he stared at her in mindless fear. Tillu was ruthless.

'That's right. Tillu not come back. Now you try. Try!'

The boy took up the implements awkwardly, waved them about helplessly, and then tried to fit them together. She held her anger as he made three faltering tries, then slapped his hands aside. 'Fool! Like this. Your top hand here, like this. Your other hand here, on the bow. Try!'

He shrank from her touch, but she seized him roughly and put his hands in place. He moved the bow awkwardly, his hand bent in toward his wrist as he sawed back and forth. The stick, trapped in the loop of the bow string, moved unevenly, dancing out of its nest, spending the heat of its friction as it skittered over the face of the wood. Tillu reached past him to set it firmly in place.

'Try!' she rebuked him again. There was no encouragement in her voice, only command.

'Ma-a,' he began pleading, but she jerked herself away from him, stalked to the door of the tent.

'Call me when you have fire.'

Despair was on his face, his breath coming in short sobs, but she lifted the tent flap and went out into the darkness.

The cold of a subarctic winter night snapped against her flushed cheeks. It made her realize she was sweating, that her anger had put heat back in her body. She trembled still with the force of her fury. Why did he always do these things? Why?

Then, as her anger died in the cold blackness of the night,

shame came to warm her cheeks. She could hear the steady rasp of the fire drill from the tent behind her, and Kerlew's voice as he sobbed and ranted to himself. The world loomed large and empty around her, but there was nowhere she could flee to escape that small mumbling voice and the angry confusion in his eyes. Tillu's angers seldom left Kerlew repentant for his misdeeds. Instead, he would offer her his childish sullenness, and the wincing fear of her touch that cut her soul.

She had pitched her tent in a clearing in a small vale. At the edges of the clearing the forested hillsides rose. Pines were darker in the darkness, their swoops of branches laden with snow. Sometimes she felt a deep peace welling from the trees and snowy hills, felt cupped and sheltered in the palm of the forest. She heard the soft whicker of an owl's wings as it drove into the clearing, the thin cry of the seized prey as it rose. The sound scraped her raw nerves and she shuddered. Tonight she sensed only the deep and eternal struggling of life to master its harsh environment. The most blind of newborn mice was better fit to survive than her son. Why could not she admit the futility of trying to make him learn? Kinder by far to let him go on as he was, until he met his eventual end. What good did she do him by forcing him to learn, by throwing him into the struggle and insisting he try?

He was as he was. Beating him would not cure it, as well she should know by now. Neither her tears nor her pleading had any effect. He was as he was. The most she could do for him was to let him take what small pleasures he could find in this world, and to bury him when he had finally blundered his way out of it. But what she was doing to him tonight was no better than beating him. Hadn't he had enough punishment in his life? Had not other children and sneering adults given him enough misery to last him until the end of his days? Her heart swung in its orbit, and she felt her anger rise against those who mocked his differences, who pointed out his lacks. Who were they to judge? Who were they to say that what made him different also made him wrong and weak? Her anger burned hot at the women who shook their heads over him and turned away, at the men who looked at him with distaste and cuffed him aside. And she herself? She was no better.

She thought of his red stone and shame stung her. Futilely she turned to where it had landed. Whatever dent it had made in the snow cover when it landed was hidden from her in the dark. She stood indecisively by the area for a long time. She longed to get down on her knees and paw through the snow for the rock, as if this useless endeavor would somehow prove her love for Kerlew.

Tears stung the corners of her eyes and she brushed at them with the back of her mittened hand. Tomorrow, she promised herself. Tomorrow, when the day was lightest, she'd come out here and find it for him. And now she had better go back inside the tent and make the fire and cook some food.

The surging storm of anger and frustration had passed, leaving her feeling only empty and tired. Vaguely she wished she had hugged him more when he was a baby, cuddled him more. But the thought brought back the memory of his small body rigid in her arms, his infant face red as he fought her embrace. She remembered the painful thudding as he banged his over-large head against her bony adolescent chest, over and over again, battering her with it as she carried him so that by nightfall both his face and her breasts were black-and-blue. When she had put him down, he screamed. When she picked him up, he went rigid. But perhaps she could have tried harder. Maybe if her mother or aunt had been there, someone could have told her what she was doing wrong.

But they hadn't. She wondered if they had even survived. The raiders had carried her far from her home on the river. When her swelling pregnancy made her an unattractive bed partner, they had abandoned her, with less thought than they had given to abandoning a lamed horse. She had never even known which of them had fathered the boy. When she thought of them now, she could not even remember them as individuals. Their coarse black hair and sallow faces blended into one nightmare of a smelly, heavy male pinning her down and hurting her. Trapping her against the rocky earth, all hot breath in her face and heavy weight on her torso and laughter all around as she struggled. She jerked her mind from the memory, shuddering.

She was shaking, she realized suddenly, shaking with the deep tremors that were the body's last effort against cold. She had stood still too long, and the night had sucked her warmth away. She had to have fire and warmth now, if she were to live. And she had to live, if Kerlew were to live. She turned to the tent wearily. She would take the bow and make the fire. She would take up once more the weight of their survival. Then from the tent she heard his shrill voice cut the night and the cold, his triumph ringing brighter than the stars.

'Fire! Tillu, Tillu, it burns, it burns for me!'

FIVE

Cold air moving against her face. As cold as it would be outside, not inside, the tent. Tillu released her grip on sleep and stirred slightly beneath the hides that covered her. Had the fire gone out? She dragged her eyes open and peered out from her huddle of skins. No, the fire was still aglow, though it would need more fuel soon. The draft came from the open tent flap, where Kerlew stood in his long nightshirt, staring out into the darkness. 'The wood is right by your left foot,' Tillu pointed out. 'You don't need to chill the whole tent to find it.'

'Not looking for wood,' Kerlew mumbled. Cold air flowed in past him, misting slightly as it met the warmer air inside the tent. Kerlew stood motionless in the swirling fog as it eddied past him.

'Well, put some on the fire anyway,' Tillu instructed him grouchily. She pulled the hides up to her chin again. Kerlew still stood in the doorway, staring out into the snowbound darkness.

'I heard Carp.' He swayed slightly, as if he were still asleep. 'Calling me.'

A chill ran over Tillu and the hair on the back of her neck hackled. Stupid! she chided herself for her reaction. But there was something in the boy's slow words and unseeing gaze that spooked her. In the dim light from the dying fire, he turned his face to her. His eyes were black holes beneath the straggle of his hair, no trace of sleep in them. His intentness reminded her of a great wolf sitting, ears pricked, as his prey moved into his range. Not for the first time, she said, 'Carp isn't coming, Kerlew. You dreamed it.'

'I know.' The boy spoke in his hesitant way, as if each word had to be found before it could be uttered. He strung his words on the threads of his thoughts, visibly manufacturing his sentences. 'But it was one of the real dreams, like he taught me. I saw Carp, walking through the snow of the forest.' Wonder transformed the boy's face. 'He looked up at me and smiled so I could see where his teeth are gone. He was leaning on the staff we carved together. And I knew he was coming for me. He said, "You are mine, Kerlew. And I will come for you, because the spirits will it. Be patient, but do not forget." Then it started snowing and it fell between us until everything was white and I couldn't see him anymore. But I thought I heard him calling me, so I woke up and got out of bed to see.'

'Kerlew.' Tillu kept rigid control of her voice. 'Carp is not coming for you. He doesn't know where we are. And we have come a very long way since we left Benu's people. They don't come this far west. We are out of their territory now. I don't think we will ever see Carp again.'

Kerlew stood silent, his brow crinkled, nodding slowly. Then he let the tent flap fall, shutting out the night and the greater darkness it sheltered. The tent became a small, safe place again, and Tillu could look at Kerlew and see her child.

65

His bare legs stuck out from under his soft leather night-shirt. His thick black hair was tousled, some dangling before his strange eyes. For an instant she saw all his vulnerability and loneliness, and her conscience smote her. In all her travels, Carp was the only adult male who had ever shown anything near tolerance for her son. To some, Kerlew was an object of ridicule; to others, disgust. He had always been taunted by other children, ever since he was old enough to betray his differences with speech. Women either pitied him and treated him as a babe, or pitied Tillu and treated him as a misfortune. In running away from Benu's folk, she had taken him from the only person who had ever befriended him.

'Then why did he say he was coming?'

Tillu tried to keep her patience before the slow words of the dogged questions. 'Because you only dreamed it. He didn't really say it.'

He stood nodding by the fire, his mouth slightly agape, his tongue wetting his lower lip. Then his lips moved as he carefully repeated her words to himself. 'Ah,' he said, nodding at the flames. 'A dream.'

Tillu sighed in relief and began to settle back into her nest of hides.

'Do you think Carp will come tomorrow, then?' Kerlew's hopeful question jerked her back.

Tillu sighed. 'No. Carp won't come tomorrow, either. You never hear a word I say, do you? Bring in some wood for the fire.'

He stooped to obey her, dragging in sticks of wood frosted with last night's snowfall. They sizzled as he dumped them clumsily onto the red coals.

'Not too many at once,' Tilly cautioned him. 'You'll put it out.'

'Then I'd have to start it again,' Kerlew observed, an edge of resentment showing in his slow-spaced words.

'That's right,' she agreed firmly.

They both fell silent, feeling the silent tension hanging between them. Part of her said it had been necessary, that the boy had to learn, however he could be taught. Part of her felt only sickened and sad. How well he remembered anger and hurt. He might forget what she had said to him moments ago, but his memory of last month's confrontation was still fresh. It was how his mind worked. As if he could sense the things that pained her and chose to keep those things for himself.

She looked at him now, saw his eyes steal up to the tent support where the meat hung. She smiled at him slowly, remembering his face shining with the triumph of fire. That she would keep for herself. He stared back at her, then smiled uncertainly.

'It's nearly time to get up, I think. Shall I bring snow?' he offered hopefully. Then Tillu knew what had really awakened him. He was hungry.

She pushed wearily at her blankets. She knew she should make him go back to sleep and wait to eat until the true morning. But she felt guilty and, she realized, hungry herself. She was not providing well for them. She knew the forest offered ample food, even in the hardest winter, for the skilled hunter. But she was not skilled.

In the time since they had left Benu's folk, she had been feeding them on rabbits and ptarmigan and the like. At first, there had been the dried meat and oil to supplement what she caught, and the late vegetation of autumn. But snow had locked the plants away now, save for bark teas and the like, and they were reduced to whatever meat she could bring home.

Yesterday it had been two hares, neither of them large. She had stewed them up, reserving the hindquarters of one for breakfast. The little creatures had already lost their autumn fat. The lean, stringy meat had been more tantalizing than satisfying. She craved fat, and no amount of stringy hare could satisfy that craving.

She gave in to Kerlew with a curt nod. He snatched up the pot and ran to pack it with snow, not even bothering with his boots. Tillu pushed her sleeping fur back and dressed hastily in the chill of the tent. She added more fuel to the fire and set the pot of snow close by it to melt. The semi-frozen hindquarters of the rabbit were hanging from one of the tent supports. She took them down, shaking her head at how small they were, and cut the meat into tiny bits that would cook quickly. Bones and all went into the pot. She poked at the fire to bare the coals and set the pot among them, screwing it into place to brace it. Kerlew had dressed quickly. Now he picked up the bone knife she had used to cut up the meat and licked the traces of blood from it. Tillu chided him: 'Don't cut your tongue.'

'I'm careful,' he told her and ran his fingers over the piece of wood she had cut the meat on, licking them eagerly. His hunger and the crudeness of their surroundings struck her suddenly. Shame vied with anger, but weariness won over both of them. If she didn't start doing better, they weren't going to last out the winter. She stirred the pot of stew thoughtfully. Everything they had was on the verge of wearing out. The bone knife needed to be replaced, mittens needed sewing, the small scraped hides of her kills needed to be worked into useful leather. But there was only one of her and most of her time was taken up with hunting. The solution would have been simple with any other child: Put the boy to work. But experience had taught her that teaching Kerlew a new skill took more time than doing it herself.

Still. He had relit the fire. And he had been responsible for gathering the wood since then, without being reminded. Maybe the harshness of the fire lesson was what he had needed. Maybe it was time to expect – no, demand more of him.

He had come to hunker beside her, watching like a camp-robber bird as she stirred the stew. The water was beginning to warm, and she could smell the meat cooking. She added a handful of dried ground lichen to thicken it. Kerlew's nose twitched and he sighed in anticipation as he crouched beside her. Sitting down flat on the cold earth floor of the tent, he leaned against her, taking comfort in her closeness and warmth as if he were a much younger child. Tillu reached to rumple his hair. He flinched, then looked up at her questioningly.

'Kerlew. We can do better than this, but only if we both try harder. I need you to learn to do more things, make more things for us.'

His wide eyes looked up at her in alarm. 'I brought the firewood yesterday.'

'I know. I know. You've been very good about remembering to do the things I asked you to do. But you're big now, and it's time you started to do even more things. I could show you how to stretch the rabbit hides, and you could learn how to fix your own mittens, and –'

His lip jutted out rebelliously. 'No. That's women's work. Carp said so. I'm not supposed to do those things.'

Tillu clenched her teeth, biting back her anger. Carp. Always Carp. How far would she have to travel to escape that man? She began again carefully. 'Different groups of people have different ways. We are on our own now, so we can make up our own ways. We can do any kind of work we want. And there are many kinds of work we are going to have to do if we are going to survive on our own. We can't trade healing for meat and garments anymore. So I am going to have to sew our clothing for us, and hunt our food. Even though I never used to do those things. And you will have to do things you didn't do before, either.'

Tillu paused to look at him. His brow was wrinkled, but his look of stubbornness had diminished slightly. He had pushed his lips out as he thought. It was a lesson that her years with Kerlew had taught her. Other children might be told firmly, or be persuaded with the threat of punishment. Kerlew would go unmoved by such tactics. As slow-witted as he seemed, he would not do a thing until he had firmly in mind the reasons why he must do it. Once persuaded, however, he would not be swayed from what he perceived as necessary. Such as the need to flee from bears, and to keep the fire burning.

'So why can't I hunt, then?' he asked suddenly.

'You don't know how. I thought you would want to learn simple things first, like carving and making tools for us, while I hunted.'

'Other boys my age hunt. Graado was always off hunting, before he died.'

'I know. Graado was a very good hunter. But it had taken him a long time to learn. Now isn't a good time for you to be learning to hunt, because if you accidentally miss, we won't have anything to eat that night. But it is a good time for you to learn to make bowls and knives and other useful things. Do you see what I'm saying?'

'Yes.' Grudgingly. 'I'd rather learn to hunt.'

'You'll learn to do both this winter,' Tillu promised, surprised to find she meant it. Now, living alone with the boy, she could teach him some skills, both useful and social. Perhaps the next time they joined a group of people, his differences would not be so apparent.

'It would be easier for you if we just found another group of people for you to heal.' Kerlew spoke with insight Tillu had not known he possessed. She looked at him sharply.

'What makes you say that?' she demanded.

He shrugged stubbornly.

'Well, it might be easier, but there's no one around here for me to heal, Kerlew. So we'll have to do for ourselves.'

He looked at her without speaking, not denying her words, but withholding his agreement. She sighed. He had made up his mind that there was another way to solve their problems. And he'd cling to his own solution for as long as he could.

'Is it done now?'

She gave the meat soup another stir and nodded. He jumped up to fetch the carved wooden bowls, and to watch ravenously as she poured out their shares. They drank it in a companionable silence, Tillu thinking and Kerlew completely absorbed in eating.

It was finished too soon. Tillu rose to gather her supplies for the day. Taking up a soft leather pouch, she tied its sturdy belt around her waist. Into this went the bone knife, a long hank of braided sinew, and the smaller pouch that carried her healer's supplies. Ever since her days on the riverbank when her great-aunt had first instructed her in the skills of a healer, she had carried such a pouch. In it were a few powdered herbs in bone vials and a roll of soft leather for bandages. Over all, she dragged on her heavy outer coat. It had been cured with the hollow-shafted hairs on it and, when new, they had trapped the heat and held it close. But reindeer hair was brittle, breaking off easily, and in places the coat was now rubbed nearly bare. As she often did, she wondered if the weight of the leather was worth the warmth. But she knew that if a storm came up, or if she were caught out overnight, she would be glad of it. The garment was a long-sleeved tunic that could be belted at the waist.

As she tugged up her mittens, she told Kerlew, 'Today you should tend the fire and gather firewood, as much as you can. Pile up a lot so that you won't have to go after wood tomorrow or the next day. And watch for pieces that might make a good bowl or spoon. Tonight, when I get back, we will try some carving.'

'Can't I go hunting with you today, so I can start to learn?'

Was he back to that idea again? 'Tomorrow, maybe. When we have a good supply of wood, so we can bank the fire for the day. Remember, you have to gather lots of wood today if you want to hunt with me tomorrow.' She took up her bow and paused. 'Watch, too, for a piece of wood to make a bow for yourself. You'll need one if you're going to hunt.'

'Shall I chant to the spirits to bring you good hunting?' Kerlew offered cautiously. She could tell that he expected her usual snort of refusal at his offer. But what could it hurt?

'While you gather the firewood,' she agreed and ducked out the tent flap. She heard his thin voice rise behind her in the strange monosyllabic song Carp had taught him. Tillu had never been able to decide if the song was in the words of some strange language, or was merely monotonous noises to lure Carp's spirits closer. She thought briefly of the beautiful carved goddess of her river-village childhood. The raiders had dragged the image down and burned it as fuel to roast the fat piglets that Tillu had once tended. She had not trembled before any spirit-being since then.

Graceful white birches edged the clearing around her tent, while tall dark pines made the hills around it green. A clump of twisting willow grew at one end of the glen; Tillu suspected a summer spring hidden beneath the snow. The glen itself seemed an open, airy place in contrast to the hills around it. Sunlight struck the hide walls of the tent during the day and helped warm it, while the pine forests on the surrounding hillsides sheltered it from storms and provided firewood and game. It was a good place to shelter out the winter.

Tillu spent her days hunting in the surrounding hills. She was beginning to know them now, and to think of exploring the neighboring valleys. It was still dark as she entered the silent pine forest. The cold of night had put a good crust on the snow. Tillu walked on top of it, heading steadily west, instead of having to plow through it. She picked her way carefully, following old game trails and avoiding the snow-laden swags of the pines. She didn't expect to find game close to the tent. She and Kerlew had been camped there nearly two months now. Their noise and smoke would have spooked away most small game. So she strode along, seeking to put distance between herself and the tent before the brief hours of light dawned.

The hours of light were few, but the day was long for her. She hunted first under a starry sky disturbed by the pale ribbons of the aurora borealis. She did not turn her gaze up to that spectacle, but peered into the shadows of the forest as she strode silently along. The stew had warmed her stomach but not filled it, and hunger soon chewed at her concentration.

The gray light of 'morning' found her moving silently,

arrow ready, through an open forest of pine. The great trunks soared up around her. Brush was sparse, making it easier for her to walk, and to watch for the small game that was her target. She hated the constant tension of keeping an arrow ready to fly, but knew that any game she spotted would be aware of her. A movement such as drawing out an arrow and setting it to the bow would send them fleeing.

She watched, not for rabbit or squirrel or ptarmigan, but for movement and shape. The flash of an eye or the flick of an ear in a clump of brush, the white curve that might be the haunch of a rabbit beneath a tree. She loosed once and missed, both bird and arrow vanishing silently into the snowy forest.

Her first kill came close to noon, and had nothing to do with her shooting skill. She had emerged from the forest into a small clearing. A blackened stump and a few fallen trunks protruded from the snow, showing where lightning had started a fire that had not spread. The open meadow was thick with brush. Tillu stood silently on the edge of the clearing, only her eyes moving. Dawn or gray evening would find this clearing alive with small game, she suspected. But she had discovered it at the wrong time of day. It was empty.

Or was it? A tiny clump of snow fell from one of the bushes, jarred loose by movement when the air was still. Tillu shifted her eyes to study the bush, while keeping her head still as if staring in a different direction. The hare was crouching motionless beneath the bush, thinking his white coat would conceal him. She clenched her teeth. The branches of the protective bush were just thick enough that they would probably deflect her arrow and let the hare escape. She could spook him into the open and try for a running shot. But she knew her limits. There had to be another way to take him.

As long as he thought he was undiscovered, he would stay frozen there. Tillu began to walk slowly forward, looking everywhere except at the animal. She kept her head high, as if she stared across the clearing, and walked casually. But her eyes were turned down on the crouching animal, and her path carried her within a body's length of his hiding place.

The snow crunched lightly under her tread. The bright sun off the open meadow threw light up into her eyes, dazzling her after the soft shadows of the forest. She wanted to rub her eyes, but dared not move her hands. Closer. She was passing him now, and still he was motionless, his ears drawn flat to his back. She did not spring. She fell on him, letting her body crash down on both bush and animal, pinning the wildly struggling animal to the snowy earth in a tangle of snapped brush.

She gripped at him frantically with both hands, caught a leg, felt him kick free, clutched his body, felt him wriggle from her grip, then closed her hands on his neck. She had him. With a swing and a snap she broke his neck, the tiny pop sounding loud in her ears. She hefted the warm, limp body. He was larger than the other two had been. He'd make a good meal. She pierced the thin skin between the two long bones of his hind legs and strung a fine line of braided sinew through them, knotting the ends. It made a long loop that went over one of her shoulders, so that he dangled upside down by her hip. The weight of her kill felt good. Now, if she could only get one or two more . . .

But luck deserted her. She crossed the meadow and moved on, into somber woods where the branches that met overhead defeated the brightness of the short day. Nothing stirred. When the waning light of afternoon forced her footsteps back toward the tent, the stiffening hare was still her only kill.

She crossed over her morning's trail and worked the hillside above it hopefully. Most animals that browsed or grazed on hillsides kept their attention fixed downhill. Often they paid little attention to the hunter who stalked them from higher ground. But the light was going bad, and she wondered if a chancy shot would be worth the risk of losing one of her precious arrows. She gained the crest of a small hill and looked down into the next valley. She hadn't hunted this area yet. She wondered if she should take the time to explore it now, or head home with her kill and save this for tomorrow.

She froze for an instant, peering into the shadowy forest below her. She heard several tiny clicks, then the soft sound of snow being moved. A clack, as of wood against wood. She could not see, and then, as her eyes adjusted to the gloom and distance, she did see. Trunks and branches of trees interrupted her view, but the hump of an animal moved briefly in the snow and was still. It stirred again, and, as it did, Tillu slipped behind the cover of another tree. The creature was large, with a brown coat. But stare as she might at the shadowed shape, she could not resolve it into the outline of any beast she knew.

Then the female reindeer lifted her antlered head from the hollow she had pawed into the snowdrift. She peered about alertly for danger as the calf at her side butted up against her for warmth. Tillu grinned silently to herself: two animals, not one, and the adult with its head invisible. That was what had baffled her. She gripped her bow tightly and wondered.

She had four arrows left. But she did not deceive herself about their quality. Their tips were no more than fire-hardened wood. She had made her bow herself, and knew all its faults too well. The force that was sufficient to stun a bird or pierce a rabbit's thin hide would probably do no more than bruise the animal below. But the lure of that much meat wrapped in a useful hide sent her slipping from one tree's shelter to the next, getting ever closer as she worked her slow way down the hillside.

The mother pawed snow away to bare for her calf the tender lichen beneath. While the calf fed, she lifted her antlered head and stared about, watching for wolves and wolverines and the occasional lynx. When she was sure all was well, she dipped her own head into the hole. It was during those moments, while the mother's watchful eyes were below snow level, that Tillu advanced.

Tillu halted while she was still out of range. Her heart was high with hopes, her head whirling with plans. If she didn't spook the animal now, perhaps she would still be in this area tomorrow. Even if she weren't, sighting this reindeer meant there would be others in the nearby valleys and hills. Their winter hides would be thick now, good for boots and coats and bedhides. Their long sinews made fine thread, their bones and antlers good tools. To say nothing of rich slabs of red meat frosted with layers of fat, or the steaming liver and succulent marrow bones from the new kill. Tillu let her hunger rise as she thought swiftly. What would it take? A spear? And Kerlew to spook the animals to where she waited? It was possible. The mother lowered her head again, and Tillu peered out from the cover of the tree.

And froze anew.

She was not the only hunter here. Even as she watched, two shapes were converging on the deer, rising from the snow to creep forward. They were a mismatched pair, and she watched them curiously. One was a man, tall and wide-shouldered, dressed in tunic and leggings of reindeer hide. His dark hair was touched with bronze when the light hit it. It was cut straight, jaw-length, and swung forward by his face as he scuttled soundlessly on his hands and knees. A bow was slung on his back and his eyes were fixed on his prey.

The other was a youth, or a very small man. He was short, not only in height, but in every measurement. His short, thick legs were slightly bowed. He did not move as smoothly as the older man, but twitched along like a nervous weasel. His hair was black and dense, lying flat on his head and framing his wide face. His cheekbones were high, his nose broad, his lips finely drawn. Tillu studied him as he studied the deer. An odd thrill of recognition ran down her spine. He was not so different from the raiders who had snatched her away from all she had known. He had a coiled rope of some kind in his hands. He was in the front, and seemed intent on getting as close as possible, while the other seemed content with getting within close bow-range. The men exchanged glances, and the older man nodded to the youth. One rolled into place behind a tree, to unsling his bow and draw out an arrow, while the other slithered forward, rope in hand. When the feeding reindeer lifted her head, the youth froze, belly and face flat to the snow. The animal widened her nostrils, snuffling audibly in the cold evening air. But the air was still beneath the black-barked pine. No wind carried their scent to the mother. She began to lower her head again.

Tillu never knew what turned her eyes. There was no sound, so perhaps it was a tiny bit of movement at the edge of her vision. Whatever it was, she lifted her eyes from the scene below and looked down the hill to her left.

Years ago, one of the forest giants had fallen. Its great trunk lay prone, half submerged in snow. Its bare reaching branches rose from its trunk like a screen. When it had gone down, its great roots had torn up a huge mass of soil with them. Parts of the tree were still alive, nourished by the half of the roots that were buried still, while some of the roots clawed blindly at the air, the mass of earth that had surrounded them slowly eroding away from the clump still clinging to them. It was a tangled, brushy place, perfect cover for any small animal seeking shelter. Or for the bowman who stepped out suddenly from its cover.

Tillu saw no more of him than the shape of his hat, the outstretched hand that gripped the bow, and the long black curve of the bow itself. She sensed the tension in the bowstring she could not see. A smile cracked her cold face; he wasn't going to wait for his fellow hunters to get closer. He was going to take the deer now, and, from the steadiness of his hand, she'd wager his shot would be true.

The reindeer lowered her head, and Tillu fixed her eyes on the scene. She wondered if they would carry it off whole. She decided to wait. She was not too proud to take whatever they might leave.

The bow sang just as the youth reared up to swing the rope over his head. Tillu cried aloud in horror, a warning that was too late. Swifter than sight, the black arrow ripped the air, snatching itself in and out of the boy's upraised upper arm, to go wobbling off, its flight spoiled by this unexpected obstacle. It buried itself in snow.

Reindeer and calf bounded away, crashing awkwardly through the snow that would not support them. Tillu clung to the tree trunk that had hidden her, feeling giddy. The tall man who had signaled the boy sprang out from his hiding place to dash to his side. The boy wallowed in the snow, his bright blood staining it. Of the other bowman, Tillu saw no sign.

She would be wisest to flee. She was a woman alone, and she knew nothing of the men below her. Perhaps the wound was but a scrape; perhaps they didn't need her skills. If she went down there, she could be putting herself in their power, men she knew nothing of. Foolishness. They could kill her or drag her away, and Kerlew would never know what had become of her. She stepped deeper into the cover of her tree, watching.

The big man pulled the youth's tunic off over his head, more swift than gentle. He seemed smaller without his coat, younger than Tillu had first estimated. The boy wore a shift of some woven work beneath it. Tillu was startled. How long had it been since she had seen folk who wore woven cloth? The shirt was the color of ripe grain, save for the one sleeve that was brilliant red and dripping. The youth gripped his arm, his gasps of pain audible even to Tillu. He sank suddenly to his knees, his companion following him down. Shock and pain were overpowering him. The big man supported his body, speaking hoarsely to the boy who wasn't listening. His ignorance was obvious. Bleeding like that had to be stopped right away, or the boy would not live. Tillu began a stumbling run down the hillside.

Heckram knelt in the snow, Lasse half in his lap. He could hear nothing but the thunder of his own heart and rasp of breathing, and Lasse's thin cries as he squirmed and clutched at his arm. It was a nightmare. Soon he would awake, sweating in his bedskins. He tried once more to see the damage to Lasse's arm, but the boy only gripped his own arm the tighter, his eyes squeezed shut against the pain. Heckram had seen the black flash of the arrow that had ripped from nowhere to slide through Lasse's arm. He held Lasse tighter.

'Calm down. Please, Lasse, calm down. Lasse! Let me see your arm. We have to stop the blood.'

Lasse gave a sudden whimper and went limp in his grip. The boy's head rolled back, and for an instant Heckram's soul froze. Then he saw the wildly jumping pulse in the boy's neck. He was alive still, just unconscious. Perhaps for the best. He pulled at the stubbornly yielding weave of Lasse's wool shirt, trying to expose the wound. He had nothing to bandage it with, nothing, and the talvsit was a day's hike from here. He could carry the boy that far, but if this wound didn't stop bleeding, he would soon be carrying a corpse. Lasse had no flesh to spare, and his face was now near white as the snow he lay in. The arrow had pierced the heavy leather of Lasse's tunic, opened a deep gash in his arm, and ripped out the other side of the sleeve. The wound was a gaping, ragged thing. Heckram thought he caught a gleam of white bone deep inside it and felt dizzy.

Someone dropped into the snow on the opposite side of Lasse. The stranger was dressed in an oddly cut coat and leggings, hood pulled forward as if against a snowstorm. A bow was slung on his back. Sudden fury rose in Heckram, and when the bowman reached for Lasse, he pushed him roughly back. 'Did you come down to see what meat you had taken?' he demanded angrily. The man was even slighter than he looked, for Heckram's push sent him sprawling in the snow. He sat up, spitting snow, his hood fallen back to his shoulders. The small man yelled something angrily at Heckram and in that instant was revealed as a woman, not a man at all. She tore her bow from her back and flung it down into the snow, followed by a stiff hare on a string.

81

Lifting the skirt of her tunic, her hands worked at something at her waist. Heckram could only stare at her. Was she going to disrobe here in the snow? Why?

Then she was dragging out a pouch of soft leather and opening it. Taking out a roll of very fine, thin bird skin, she shook it in his face. She knelt again in the snow on the other side of Lasse's body. Her black eyes flashed at him as if challenging him to push her away again. He didn't. But he kept his grip on Lasse, holding the youth close, trying to put his own warmth into the boy's body.

Her skill was apparent as she eased the torn fabric back from the gaping wound. She was talking fast, in what sounded like a strange parody of his own language. She said words he could almost understand, then shook her head angrily at him. In sudden silence, she firmly gripped Lasse's arm above the wound, nodded violently at her own hands, then released Lasse's arm and grabbed one of Heckram's hands. She set it where hers had been and told him something commandingly. He stared at her in puzzlement, then gripped the boy's arm as she had. She nodded her violent agreement, and turned aside from Lasse to scoop up a double handful of clean snow.

The boy jerked slightly as she applied it directly to the wound. Heckram kept his grip. The snow reddened in her hands, but the bleeding slowed. She bent her head over his arm, studying the wound, then applied more snow. This second treatment seemed to satisfy her, for after examining the wound a second time, she spoke softly in reassurance.

'It's not that bad?' he asked and she seemed to understand, for she nodded, but again patted his hand and told him, 'Grip!' The word was strangely accented, but he understood. She rummaged again in the leather bag and brought out a container made of a deer's hollow leg bone. She pulled a wooden stopper from it and shook a grayish-brown powder into her hand. 'Willow bark.' She spoke very slowly and clearly. She trickled a pinch from her fingers into the open wound. The bleeding almost stopped. Gently pinching the wound closed, she wrapped the soft skin bandage over the wound. He watched the practiced way she slipped a finger under the binding to be sure it wasn't too tight. Lasse began to stir, and she spoke to him as she worked. The boy's eyes were huge in a face gone sallow.

'Who is she? What happened? How bad is my arm?' The rising urgency in Lasse's voice reached the woman, who knotted the bandage gently and patted his shoulder. She motioned to Heckram to loosen his grip. Lasse hissed in pain as he removed his hands. The woman spoke again, more slowly this time, and Heckram understood enough to tell Lasse, 'You're to rest and not try to move your arm for a while. And eat or drink something.'

'Of course,' Lasse agreed calmly. 'Before or after I pass out again?'

'I don't blame you.' Heckram pulled his eyes from the reddened patch of snow. His face was so pale. He kept his hand companionably on the youth's shoulder, but suspected that if he moved it Lasse would topple over.

The woman was already gathering her things. 'You! Healer!' Heckram called to her. She looked around at the familiar word. 'Are your people close by? Is there any kind of a shelter close by? A kator? Talvsit?' At first he thought she couldn't understand what he was asking, but then he caught the wariness in her eyes. 'It's the least you can do after you shot him! All we ask is shelter for a night. Look at him! I can't drag him home this way. If he doesn't bleed to death on the way, the cold would get him. After all, you're the one who shot him!'

He gestured angrily at her bow. She seemed to finally catch the idea, for she shook the bow at him and flooded him with words. He caught 'hunter' and 'accident' and watched her gesture vehemently at a fallen snag uphill of them.

With a wave of his hand, he accepted her story. 'Seems to have been an accident, though she doesn't seem too apologetic. I suppose she feels we're the ones who carelessly got between her and her prey. Lasse, if I can get her to take us to her shelter for the night, is that all right with you?'

'You mean because she shot me? It was an accident, Heckram. And she could have just run away and left me to bleed in the snow. No. There's no sense in holding a grudge, my friend. Besides, I don't think I have the strength if I wanted to. Has it gotten colder?'

'Yes. Night's coming on,' Heckram lied easily. He picked up the boy's coat to shake the loose snow from it. He couldn't pull it on over his head, so Heckram wrapped it around his shoulders. Lasse rose slowly.

'I could carry you,' Heckram offered softly. Lasse shot him an offended look that rapidly became abashed. He gave him a grin that was part grimace. 'Not yet, anyway,' Lasse told him, but he put his good hand on Heckram's shoulder, and with it a part of his weight. 'I wish we had brought a pack-harke. I'd ride him like a child.'

Heckram looked at the woman. She had retrieved her bow and hare. Hesitation was still evident in her eyes, but Heckram stared at her coldly. She owed them shelter for the night, and she knew it. For Lasse's sake, he wasn't going to let her out of it. At last she nodded curtly.

'Tent,' she said, and, with a beckoning gesture, she started off slowly through the snow.

SIX

Tillu's mind seethed with plans. She set a pace through the snow that kept her well in front of the two hunters. As soon as they sighted her tent, she raced ahead. The glow of the fire showed through the worn seams and the ventilation flap of the tent. She pushed hastily inside, scarcely noticing the wealth of firewood Kerlew had stacked by the entrance. Inside the tent, she dropped her bow and hare on the floor and looked about frantically. How to give the impression that men shared her tent and were expected to return soon? Quickly she snatched half the hides from her pallet and heaped them on the floor to make them look like a third bed. No, that wasn't right. She should have spread them out to make it look like two persons slept in her bed. She snatched them up again.

'There is blood on your hands. But the blood on mine will be darker.'

Kerlew's words jerked her attention to him. He hadn't moved since she came in, but remained sprawled on his pallet, staring into the fire. His arms dangled over the edges of the rough bed, his hands resting palm up on the floor. His eyes were unblinking and unfocused, his voice deep and dreaming.

'Kerlew! Wake up and help me!' she snapped irritably.

The boy took a deep breath and rolled over. He looked up at her. 'You were gone so long. Was the hunting good?' His voice was his normal halting speech and she breathed a sigh of relief.

'Help me get ready. Two men are coming. One of them is hurt. Don't talk to them, for they can understand some of what we say, and you might say the wrong things. I want them to think that someone else lives with us, a man who may come back –'

'I found my rock.' Kerlew grinned uncertainly as he interrupted her, holding up the polished red stone for her inspection. She glared at him.

'A lot of good that will do us! Get busy!'

Kerlew was still gawking in confusion as the man pushed the tent flap open. The youth staggered in before him, dropping instantly to his knees before the fire. He swayed in place, and the big man steadied him as he glanced about. He scuffed his foot against the scraped earth floor of the tent and asked something.

'Birch?' Kerlew guessed, his tongue slow but his face eager. Tillu frowned, but the big man nodded. The boy shrugged his lack of comprehension, and the big man hissed in exasperation. Tillu spread out a hide on the floor beside the youth and eased him down onto it. The big man made a gesture for waiting and disappeared from the tent. The youth closed his eyes. Tillu watched him breathing. He was too pale. He had bled more than such a wound should, and he seemed more exhausted than should a boy of his years. She narrowed her eyes, looking at him shrewdly. He was not as robust as the man he hunted with. She would guess that he had not been eating well recently, perhaps not for a long time. And she surmised from his growth that he had never been a sturdy child. But, for all that, he was healthy enough. He'd live to hunt again.

She knelt and checked the bandage on his arm. He opened his eyes to watch her, but tolerated her touch. The bandage was damp, but the blood had not soaked through it. Better to leave it alone than to open the wound trying to change it. Food and warmth and rest were what he needed now. She scowled at the stiffened hare that would have to feed four instead of two. Nothing to be done about it except to do it. She took the pot outside to pack it with snow, leaving Kerlew to stare curiously at the injured stranger.

The big man made a strange profile in the dark as he returned. She held the tent flap open for him. He unslung a huge bundle of birch twigs from his shoulder and pushed them in before him. Tillu followed, setting the pot of snow by the fire to melt, then watching him curiously. As he began to spread the birch twigs in a layer over the earth floor, she wondered if this were some healing ritual of his people. She had been taught the uses of the birch tree: Oil from its bark soothed skin disorders, and syrup from the tender roots pleasantly eased a cough. One could steep its tiny cones for tea to ease a mother's body after a difficult childbirth, or toast the same cones over coals, that the fumes might clear a stuffy head. She watched carefully to see how he would use such a quantity of twigs on a bleeding wound. But then he boldly took another hide from her bed and spread it over the twigs. Careful as a mother, he helped the injured boy move on to this softer resting place. Then he straightened

87

and looked around her small tent curiously. She could not tell what he was thinking.

Abruptly he placed a hand on his own chest and announced, 'Heckram.' A gesture toward the youth. 'Lasse.'

'Tillu,' she replied and, pointing to her son, added, 'Kerlew.'

'Tillu,' he muttered and, turning, left the tent again.

'What happened to him?' Kerlew demanded, pointing at Lasse as she knelt to open up the hare.

'Some fool shot him instead of a reindeer,' she told him tersely.

'The big man?' he asked with interest.

'No. Someone else, someone who ran away instead of staying to help as he should have. So I had to help them instead.'

'Why?'

'Because they needed help. Isn't that a good enough reason?'

'I guess,' he subsided. He watched her with interest. 'Is that all you killed today?'

'Yes. And we're going to have to share it.'

'Sharing makes less,' he observed without rancor, returning to staring at Lasse. The youth opened his eyes and at first looked confused. Then he smiled weakly at Kerlew and made a vague effort to sit up. 'Better lie still,' Kerlew advised him. 'Or you'll be bleeding all over. Bleed too much and you die.'

'Kerlew!' Tillu chided him, for the youth had understood enough of his words to look stricken. 'Be quiet, as I told you. The less you speak, the less chance of making a fool of yourself. Besides, you say things I don't want said. So, be quiet.'

Kerlew went into a sulk, poking angrily at the fire and

nearly upsetting the pot of warming water. Tillu turned back to Lasse. She spoke slowly and carefully. 'Don't try to move right now. I'm fixing something to eat. Your friend will be back soon. Your arm. Does it hurt much? Much pain?'

'Yes, pain. Sick.' He made a vague gesture with his good hand at his head and stomach. Tillu understood. The shock of the wound, the long cold hike, and the unrelenting pain of the jagged gash made him feel weak and ill. She wasn't surprised. She moved to her healer's pouch and began to sort through it. 'Heckram?' he asked anxiously as he watched her.

'Yes. He'll be back very soon.'

As if in answer to her words, the flap was pushed open once more. Heckram and more birch twigs came in. He spoke reassuringly to Lasse, and the youth visibly relaxed. He spoke to Tillu over his shoulder as he spread the second bundle of twigs over the floor and blithely covered them with hides from her bed. The gist of his words seemed to be that this was warmer and better than the bare earth floor. Tillu nodded curtly and went on with her work. Anything that occupied him without bothering her was fine.

She poured a small measure of the snow water into a cup. From her healing supplies she took several small packets made of gut and an assortment of bone vials. Inside each were herbs or ground roots or bark. She opened several, frowning at those that had not kept as fresh as she might have wished. She chose carefully from among them, taking a pinch of willow bark and crumbling it finely into the water, adding a thumbnail-size piece of sorrel root and letting it steep. She added a small portion of dried anemone flower. It was a potent sedative, one that would cause collapse in a patient if too much were taken. In the boy's weakened

89

condition, she would use too little rather than too much. After a few moments of steeping, she dipped her little finger into the mixture and touched it to her tongue. Heckram unnerved her by squatting down on his heels by her fire and watching her with friendly interest. He nodded in turn to Kerlew, who sulkily turned aside from him. The big man did not seem offended, but rose and moved casually around the tent, pausing to rearrange some of the hides on the birch twigs. He spoke softly to Lasse as he crouched by the boy and then returned, sighing softly as he seated himself on a layer of birch twigs and hides near the fire. Tillu rose as he sat, to take the cup of amber liquid to Lasse.

'For pain,' she said, searching his face for understanding. He looked to Heckram, who nodded to him slowly. The boy drank. Tillu took back the empty cup, ignoring the wry face Lasse made at the unfamiliar taste. She knew his pain would ebb now. And he would probably just have time to eat before sleep descended. The willow bark should keep fever away as well. She nodded in satisfaction and crouched again by her fire to carefully rinse the dregs from the cup with more of the snow water. Heckram watched her intently, apparently curious about the herbs and roots she so carefully repacked. She paused a moment, thinking. Then, hoping her face didn't show how reluctantly she parted with her precious store, she mixed more of the herbs and root in the now dry cup. With mortar and pestle of calf's bone she ground them to a powder and rolled the mixture carefully in a tiny square of skin. 'For tomorrow,' she told Heckram as she offered it. 'Only if pain.'

He studied her face, then asked, 'Pain again, new day?'

She nodded, hoping he understood. She busied herself once more with the hare, hoping he would return to his friend. But he continued to crouch amiably at her side, looking from her to Kerlew with friendly curiosity. Cocking his head, he asked something in a casual tone.

Tillu shrugged at him.

'He asked if we live alone,' Kerlew interpreted helpfully.

She glared at him as Heckram nodded, clearly understanding the boy's rewording of his question. 'Don't you remember that I asked you to be quiet?' she hissed at him, speaking as rapidly as she could. To Heckram she made a vague gesture that could have signified anything and said, 'Soon. Very soon.'

The man looked slightly puzzled, but nodded and smiled in return. Then he transferred his attention from her to the obviously rebuked boy. 'Come,' he said, speaking slowly and plainly. 'You help me.' His gesture could not have been misunderstood even if Kerlew hadn't known his words. He glanced at Tillu for permission. She nodded, her lips tightly pressed. Kerlew rose to move around the fire and squat at Heckram's side.

The man rose, to open his loosely belted tunic and take out a packet from inside it. Then he pulled off his heavy tunic of reindeer hide, revealing a woven shirt beneath. 'What fur is this?' Kerlew asked in amazement, instantly reaching to touch the fabric. The man smiled at his curiosity and suffered the boy to pluck at the sleeve of his shirt. After a moment he motioned at the package and took a knife from the sheath at his hip. Tillu watched from the corner of her eye. The sheath itself was woven, from sinew or something. The knife was flint, ground, not flaked, to a fine edge. Beside it, her bone knife looked like a child's crude toy. As the man unwrapped the package, a smell at once familiar and foreign filled the tent. Kerlew wrinkled his nose at it, but Tillu could not keep herself from turning to stare. Cheese.

A half round of yellow cheese filled the man's hand, marked with a woven pattern on its rind. He set it down atop its wrappings and began to cut it into portions with his knife. Lasse called something to him and Heckram rose to remove a similar package from the youth's pouch. This one contained a piece of river fish with its smoky smell. Tillu understood that they were sharing their hunting rations and nodded to indicate her thanks. At the same time, her mind was racing. A folk that knew weaving, and the making of cheese, that used ground flint tools as casually as Benu's folk used bone. These were no stray hunters from some wandering tribe. Surely cheese meant a settled village somewhere, and woven goods meant livestock kept, crops grown, and village life such as she had once known. And where polished flint tools were known, there was usually bronze as well. She pushed down a vague hope and dropped the last piece of hare into the pot.

Heckram was offering a piece of the cheese to Kerlew. The boy took it, sniffed it suspiciously, and glanced at Tillu in confusion. 'Cheese,' she told him, but had to revert to the language of her childhood to find a word for the food. 'You eat it. Try it, it's good.'

The hungry boy needed no further encouragement, but crammed most of the chunk into his mouth, then made a wry face at the unfamiliar taste. Heckram burst into a roar of laughter that Lasse weakly echoed. Tillu felt her face flush, her nerves prickling as they laughed at her son. She kept her head bent over the fire so they would not see the flash of anger in her eyes. Always it was this way; adult men either made sport of the boy, or dismissed him in disgust. It did not help her spirits when she looked up to see Kerlew smiling vaguely at their laughter. He had swallowed some of the

92

cheese in his mouth, but still looked like a squirrel with its cheeks pouched.

'Eat nicely,' she hissed at him. 'What must they think of us?'

He gulped to clear his mouth. 'It tastes funny,' he tried to explain.

'Then don't eat any more,' she snapped, letting her anger find a target.

'But I think I like it,' he hedged, unwilling to surrender anything that resembled food.

Tillu felt tension pull tight in her. The two strangers had noticed the exchange between her and her son. They were trying to ignore it politely, talking casually to one another as if they did not sense the unease. Tillu stirred doggedly at the stewing hare, feeling the familiar ache of the emotions Kerlew roused in her. She had to protect him, but wished there were no need. She loved him as he was, but wished he were not that way. She wanted others to accept him, to see the value in the boy as he was, and yet wished his differences were not so apparent. Everything she felt for Kerlew was a contradiction. Her mind snapped back to the old midwife putting the tiny baby into her arms. She had shaken her head, patting a soft skin around the babe, her mouth pursed. Tillu had still been amazed by the reality of this new being when the old midwife spoke. 'Love him while you can, but don't lose your heart to him. He has the look of the ones that don't live long.'

That had been the first time she had felt the now familiar anger at the unfairness. All were so quick to judge the child. She had left the wandering tribe and their midwife as soon as she was strong enough to travel. The people had watched them go, and in their eyes she saw their belief that her tiny mewling babe would be dead soon. But he had not died, she thought fiercely. He had lived and he was hers, and she would fight for him, every day of his life. The sooner these men were gone, the better. She needed to be alone with Kerlew, she told herself fervently, to teach him slowly what other children learned rapidly, to give him manners and skills so he could merge unnoticed with other folk. She would not follow them back to their village. And as soon as she had that thought, she was surprised at the poignancy of the regret she felt. Were woven cloth and cheese, the idea of a village and a settled life, such a powerful lure to her? She pushed the thought away.

A hand plucked at her sleeve, but she rudely pulled away from him. She didn't want to touch Kerlew just now, lest in her frustration she strike him. But it was Heckram's voice that spoke, saying, 'Fish,' 'for you,' 'eat,' and other words she could not understand. His tone was the excessively polite one of the guest who had given offense. Tillu's embarrassment deepened. She thanked him without looking at him or at the food he placed carefully beside her. Instead, she gave the stew a final stir and rose to go to the door flap and lift it. She peered anxiously out, as if awaiting someone's return. The coolness soothed her flaming cheeks, and the necessary deception gave her a measure of control again.

'What's wrong, Tillu?' Kerlew asked anxiously. He felt his disgrace without understanding why.

'Nothing,' she replied evenly. 'I just thought I heard him coming.'

'Carp?' asked the boy excitedly, rushing to the door. He poked his head out under her arm and stared wildly into the darkness.

'Mmm,' she said, neither agreeing nor disagreeing. At least

Kerlew was convincing in his appearance of waiting for someone. She hoped they would think her man delayed somehow on his hunt. She turned from the door to find the strangers watching her expectantly. She shrugged. Lasse lay on his side, holding a bit of fish in his good hand. His color was still not as good as it should be. She went to kneel beside him. She inspected the bandage once again, then felt the hand below it. It was a little cool, but the stricture of the bandage was necessary to hold the flesh together. 'Make a fist,' she told him, then demonstrated. Lasse winced, but was able to obey her. She nodded her approval, but his eyes were cast down before her. His youth suddenly struck home to her. He was, at most, five years older than Kerlew, and obviously unaccustomed to a woman's touch. He was shy. Yet she knelt by him a moment longer, savoring the fantasy that Kerlew would grow this well, would hunt like this youth did, and bear himself with a man's dignity. 'He's a good boy,' she said, more to herself than anyone, but looked up to find Heckram nodding with a vaguely paternal air.

'Brothers?' she asked aloud, to break a suddenly heavy silence.

'Friends,' Heckram explained gravely. 'Hunt together.'

She nodded her understanding. But for the accent, the languages seemed to share many common words. She was unprepared for his question.

'Little brother?' He nodded toward Kerlew. 'Father comes? Mother comes?'

Tillu snorted. 'Son,' she explained, then wondered if it wouldn't have been smarter to let him think them siblings. What difference could it make anyway? But now the big man was anxious to talk. Words and questions spilled from him.

'You come from . . . far? South?' He added other words she did not recognize. The intensity of his interest gleamed in his eyes. It made her uneasy. Why did he want to know so much about them? She picked up snatches of his meanings, but tried not to let it show. Had her man gone to trade to the south, or was he hunting? Where were the rest of her people? She let the questions flow past her, smiling apologetically as she shrugged, and then covering her thoughts by bringing out bowls to divide up the stew. Kerlew had his in his cup, and Tillu had hers in the cooking pot, to make enough dishes. She saw the big man's forehead wrinkle in puzzlement at this, but decided to let him think what he would. He made another slow appraisal of her tent and its contents. Tillu covered her nervousness by eating.

The fish had been smoked into a hard slab and tasted of salt and summer fires. It had been so long since she had tasted cheese that she was not sure if the flavor had changed, or just her memory of it. She ran a fingertip lightly over the rind, feeling the woven impression where the curd had been packed into the mold. After the weeks of lean hare, it seemed unbelievably rich, and the stew tasted heartier in its company. She looked up suddenly from her empty dish to realize she had ignored everyone else while she ate. But Kerlew and Lasse seemed likewise occupied with their food, with only Heckram's eyes wandering about the tent as he chewed.

Their eyes met and she dared not glance away in what might be a submissive gesture among his folk. They looked at one another, while she struggled frantically to think of something to say, anything to fill this silence. But it was he who spoke.

'. . . hard . . . winter . . . wild . . . herd . . . but . . . hides . . . payment . . . heal Lasse . . .'

96

She listened carefully, trying to string the words she knew into some kind of sense, but finally had to shrug at him. He gave his hands a small toss to indicate the dilemma, and then said quite clearly, 'Wait. Understand soon.'

She nodded and rose to gather the various vessels and clean them. By the time she had finished, Lasse was sprawled in sleep. She knelt by him to check him. No fever, the bandage seemed comfortable, the hand below it warm. She looked up to find Heckram's eyes upon her. 'Thin,' she said, spanning the boy's wrist with the circle of her fingers.

'Thin seasons,' he agreed solemnly. He covered Lasse with one of the bedhides and then his own coat.

'Kerlew,' Tillu rebuked the dreaming boy, jerking his attention from the fire. 'Don't sit and watch it burn out. Put some fuel on it.'

The boy moved slowly at her bidding, bringing in frosty wood that he heaped carelessly on the coals. 'Are we going to carve tonight?' he asked her.

She had forgotten her lecture of the morning and was not inclined to do any kind of work just now. The unexpected strains of the day had tired her, and her full stomach was making her sleepy. Evenings for most hunting folk were a busy time of day, for making household items, for conversation and stories. She realized that she had let them become idle times of silence and staring, sometimes because she lacked materials to work with, but more often because she was simply too tired. Heckram was glancing about as if wondering what to do with himself. Although it was dark outside, it was still early for sleep. So Tillu nodded stiffly to Kerlew, who seemed suddenly energized.

The boy darted to his pallet and returned to her with a great armload of sticks and chunks of wood. He rattled them down in a pile at her feet and sat expectantly. She smiled wearily at the boy. 'I tell you to find one or two pieces, you bring me a forest.'

He smiled proudly back at her as she began to sort through the sticks. She felt Heckram's eyes on her, and her reluctance toward the project grew. Her skills for this were rusty; she didn't enjoy the idea of someone being amused at her awkwardness. Even more daunting was the prospect of someone watching the painfully slow way that Kerlew learned. But to do this was better than to sit idly through the long evening, avoiding the stranger's uneasy glances.

Many of the sticks were plainly unfit for use, dry and brittle ones, ones so small they would be carved to nothing before anything could be made of them, some so full of knots they would defy any shaping. These she set aside, until of Kerlew's bundle there were five pieces of wood left. She chose one at random and put it into his hands. He looked up in surprise, and she had to smile at his expression.

'You thought I would do it while you watched, didn't you? No, there has been too much of that. Now Kerlew starts to do things while I watch. There is the knife, you have the wood. Wait a moment.' She rose to rummage through her possessions and returned with bone scrapers. They were for hides, but they would have to serve. She put them out in a row by the boy. He sat holding the wood and knife in his lap, not moving. Heckram was watching them both silently, his face mildly puzzled, but friendly. She refused to be ruffled by his scrutiny. Sitting down beside Kerlew, she said, 'First, you strip the bark from the piece.' He met her gaze, unhappy in his uncertainty. His anxiety wrinkled his face, pushing his lip out like a shelf. 'Go on,' she encouraged him, and he took up knife and wood.

She watched the boy attentively, flinching each time the knife skipped over the bark by his fingers. He hit a stubborn knot and tried to hand the work back to her. 'No. Keep trying,' she told him gently. He pursed his lips, his eyes going darkly bitter, and went on picking at the stubborn bark. It would not yield to his awkwardness, and she saw his chin start to tremble. The boy knew failure all too well; even the threat of it could cripple his efforts. She forced herself to sit still and watch him struggle, believing he must learn his own way. Kerlew's breath began to catch. He curled himself around his work, as if to hide it from her, but doggedly continued to dig at the unyielding knot.

Then a large shadow moved between them. Heckram did not look at her, but crouched behind the boy, and when he spoke there was only interest in his voice.

'What do you make?' The meaning was plain even if the words were not.

'Probably nothing,' Kerlew replied sulkily. He was already braced for the expected blow.

The man reached out a slow hand. Kerlew flinched slightly as the hand settled on his wrist, and Tillu readied herself to intervene. Some men thought Kerlew pretended his difficulties and tried to make him learn by cruelty. If this Heckram . . .

The boy hastily tried to surrender, pushing the knife and wood into the man's hands, but Heckram only pushed them back, then rearranged them in the boy's hands. He shifted the boy's small hands on the wood, and then his own large hand engulfed Kerlew's small one on the handle of the knife. He guided it as the edge of the knife went under the stubborn knot. 'See?' he asked Kerlew, and, as the boy nodded nervously, he added his strength and the bit of bark went flying across the tent, to bounce off the hide wall. The man laughed easily, and after a moment Kerlew joined him. The piece of wood shone white and smooth in Kerlew's hands. 'What you make now?' Heckram asked easily.

'A spoon,' Kerlew decided.

Heckram tapped the wood gently, asking permission to take it for a moment. The boy released it, and the man took it, turning it this way and that as he perused it thoughtfully. Taking up the knife, he marked the wood with shallow cuts. 'Here cut,' he instructed softly. 'Here cut. Here,' he made a scraping motion of the knife near the knot. 'Make strong. Hard, strong.'

Tillu rose, feeling suddenly excluded. Kerlew didn't even notice her departure. His head was bent over the wood as he carved with more energy than skill. She stepped outside the tent into the crisp cold of the night. The night was clear, the cold settling over the world like a blanket. She gathered an armful of Kerlew's wood and took it back into the tent.

It could have been someone else's tent, with the one youth flung wide in careless sleep, and the other crouching by the man, carving diligently as the adult worked more sedately at a piece of his own. Heckram said something to Kerlew as he tossed a handful of parings into the fire, and the boy grinned, though Tillu was sure he didn't understand the words. She set down the firewood and felt suddenly at a loss for what to do with herself. The two muttered to each other as they carved, ignoring the language barrier. After a moment's hesitation, she took up Lasse's coat, covering him with another hide. She rummaged through her sewing things and then examined the ragged rents the arrow had made. She threaded her needle with a length of sinew and looked up to find Heckram's eyes on her.

'Thank you.' The courtesy was clear and honest.

'Thank you,' she replied evenly, nodding at the intent boy. Heckram touched his own chest. 'Heckram . . . no father. Hard learn man's work. Understand.'

Tillu nodded and then felt her face burn as she realized she had betrayed herself. He knew no man was coming back this night. He was smiling at her easily, but she didn't return his smile. She sat as frozen as the hare had earlier, but felt her exposure keenly. For a long moment he watched her, and the smile faded from his face. He made a motion of his hand that seemed to indicate it was no concern of his and went back to supervising Kerlew.

By the time she had finished mending the sleeve with tiny, tight stitches that would keep out wind and weather, Kerlew's eyelids were drooping over his work. He was obviously sleepy, but loath to surrender Heckram's attention and guidance. It was part of his nature to accept people at face value. If Heckram had cuffed him and pushed him away, Kerlew would have seen it, not as an offense, but simply as part of the man. That the older man accepted him and took time with him he assumed just as easily. He held up his rough spoon for inspection as he rubbed at his eyes. Heckram set down his own more finished product and took the boy's. Turning it, he muttered approvingly at some parts, and pointed to others that needed more smoothing. But when Kerlew would have immediately gone back to work on it, Heckram made a show of yawning. He sheathed his own knife, and the boy was quick to follow his example.

'Sleep,' Heckram said simply. He glanced about, including Tillu questioningly. She stiffened with wariness, but held up the mended garment. He crossed to take it from her. He nodded slowly over her work as he ran his fingers over the place where the sleeve had been torn. She was suddenly conscious of his tallness, the depth of his chest as he stood over her, blocking the fire's light and warmth. She shrank before him. But, 'Thank you,' he said again and then stepped away, to spread the coat once more over Lasse. Without a glance at Tillu, he lay down not far from his companion. Kerlew was suddenly at his side, offering a sleeping hide from his own bed. The man gave him a grin and a friendly poke of thanks, and settled for sleep.

Tillu rose to bring in wood to bank the fire. Kerlew followed her out into the cold to relieve himself, then brought in an extra armload of fuel.

'I like them,' the boy said suddenly. 'Let's go live with their people. You can be the healer and I can be the shaman.'

'Shush!' Tillu glanced warily at the unstirring men. 'Go to sleep now. We'll talk about that later.'

She arranged the wood with care, thinking of Kerlew's words. Could it be he missed being part of a people as much as she did? A foolish idea. What had folk ever meant to him besides beating and taunts and mockery? Except for Carp. And this man, tonight. But the way a man behaved around a child when he was alone with him and the way he treated him in public were two different things. She remembered a man, several years ago, a man who had seemed to like her. He had courted her with meat and gifts, and then, one night as Kerlew slept, he had offered, with the kindest of smiles, to take the child out and leave him 'where the wolves would find him quickly, so that you and I could have children of our own. The gods never intended one such as he to live this long.' Tillu and Kerlew had left that folk before the sun rose the next day. She and Kerlew had both liked that man, too. She shook her head, felt the sting of fool's tears.

She banked the fire so it would burn long and then retreated to her own pallet. But she could not relax with strangers in her tent, and she lay for a long time, staring at the slow fire and dreaming. She glanced at the sleeping Heckram and found herself speculating. If she had not seen them hunting together, she would never have guessed that he and the boy were of the same people. The boy had a short, broad build. His thick black hair and yellowed skin reminded her of Kerlew's parentage. But Heckram, while he showed signs of kinship in his high cheekbones and dark eyes, also reminded her of the men of her own people. Blood and people had mixed somewhere. She lay still, smelling their unfamiliar odors. There was the smell of blood, sharp and disturbing, from the boy's injury. But beneath that there were the subtler odors of hides tanned by a different method, of the cheese and fish, and of the man himself. Inexplicably, he smelled of reindeer. Not the dead odor of meat and hides, but the subtle wild scent that she picked up when she stalked such game. He smelled of living reindeer as her own father had once smelled of his sheep. It was a puzzle. She meant to stay awake and ponder it, but didn't.

SEVEN

Lasse put out a hand and steadied himself for a moment against Heckram.

'I'm out of breath,' he explained.

'Me, too,' Heckram agreed, standing still while the boy panted. 'But there's not far to go now.'

The last hill had been a steep one, but now they stood on the final ridge. The barking of the dogs bounced echoes through the hills, and the wood smoke of the talvsit was a distinct tang in the air. The forested slope below them hid the winter camp with its huts of sod and bark, but they were nearly home.

'And just as well, too,' Heckram muttered to himself. Lasse had not asked for any help, but he walked awkwardly, his injured arm held close to his chest. Usually the boy plowed eagerly through the snow ahead of Heckram. Today he had followed in his wake, taking advantage of the trail he broke, and Heckram had consciously slowed his pace. Now relief lightened Heckram's mood. The brief light of the day was already fading. He was glad they had made it home before dark.

'Just as well . . . what?' panted the boy.

'Just as well everyone will be busy at their chores when we come in. Bad enough to come back empty-handed. Worse to come back saying, "Here's the only meat that was shot, and it's not worth eating."'

Lasse snorted his contempt for the weak joke, and they began to make their way down the hill. They soon intersected one of the many trails that led into the winter encampment, and the going was easier. On the trail the snow was packed, and there were no overhanging branches to duck. They passed a few harkar browsing on the outskirts of the camp. Their ears swiveled toward the men curiously but the deer didn't pause as they nipped the tenderest tips of the naked branches. The rest of the domestic reindeer would be either with the herd grazing up on the hillsides or harnessed to pulkor, journeying south with the traders who sought wool and bronze tools and other supplies.

Elsa was drawing water from the spring as they passed. She straightened with her dripping buckets and called out as she caught sight of them. 'You're back! What kept you? Too much luck, I hope.' Her voice was warm with welcome and relief.

Heckram felt the familiar tightness in his chest, that sense of a duty shirked. It made him brusque. 'Too much luck of the wrong kind. Any news here?'

She shook her head, walking ahead of them as she talked. 'Not much. Wolves got one of Jeffor's vaja last night, so most of the sita has been out hunting today.'

'And not you?' Lasse asked. 'Then they won't get much.'

The girl smiled at his compliment. 'Not this time. My mother is not feeling well, so I stayed behind to bring in the water and do the heavier chores. Father went with the hunters.'

'Well, the man who taught you to shoot so well can surely shoot as well himself,' Lasse observed.

Heckram was silent on the subject. He knew that Kuoljok's eyes were starting to fail him. The same thought must have crossed Elsa's mind, for her face saddened for an instant. But she recovered well, easing her heavy buckets to the ground outside her tent, then straightening with a sigh. Then, as she noticed Lasse's odd posture: 'What's happened to you?' she demanded.

'A mishap,' Heckram said and suddenly did not want to say much about it. 'A strange hunter. She must have been taking aim at the same vaja that Lasse and I were stalking. Lasse stood up with his rope at the same instant that she let fly. The arrow took him through the arm. But he'll be all right. She had some skills as a healer. That's why we were out overnight.'

Elsa nodded and spoke to Lasse. 'Your grandmother was worried, but refused to make a fuss over it. She just said that doubtless you'd had better hunting than you expected and were having a hard time getting it home.'

'I wish,' Lasse snorted.

'This strange hunter? Is there another talvsit close by, then? I've bone needles and antler work I'd like to trade. I tried to send some south with the traders, but they said they'd already packed as big a load as their sleds would carry. Still, another village might –'

Heckram shook his head, but Lasse elaborated. 'No. No talvsit at all. Just a woman and her son living in a skin tent alone. And not even much of a tent at that.'

'Outcasts, perhaps?' Elsa asked, her curiosity piqued.

Heckram shrugged. 'I doubt it. They've a foreign look about them, a strange way of cutting their clothes, and their speech is different. One can barely understand them.'

'Still,' Elsa persisted in wondering. 'How do folk come to be alone like that? There must be some evil in their past . . . like a plague that destroyed the rest of them, or becoming separated during a river crossing,' she hastened to explain at Heckram's puzzled look.

'The boy has the look of something like that. Did you see how he watched us leave this morning, Heckram? More like a black crow in a tree than a child. Like he knew too much of life to be a child, but wasn't concerned by any of it. He watched us go, but I would swear he didn't see us. It seemed a very strange look for a little boy,' Lasse added, shaking his head.

Elsa's eyes brightened with curiosity.

Heckram shrugged uneasily. 'You're imagining things, Lasse. Let's get you home to Stina. She's been worried about you all this time, and my mother as well. As if we were children out playing late.'

'Not too far off the mark, if you ask me,' Elsa commented lightly, then waved a farewell as she ducked into the domed sod hut with her buckets of water.

The winter camp was quiet as they wended their way between sod and bark shelters to Stina's hut. They passed the meat racks and storage huts of their neighbors. Here were the atti, platforms on four tall legs where frozen sides of reindeer meat were resting. They passed njalla, tall racks set high on a single smooth, slippery pole, the best way to guard food against voracious wolverines. A row of reindeer sledges, turned upside down to keep out the snow, looked much like a row of upended boats, with their keels, sterns, ribs, and bulwarks. There were the covered akja for hauling loads, and the half-covered pulkor for driving. Lasse drew energy from the familiar sights of home. But Heckram found he dreaded seeing Stina.

Every winter the herdfolk returned to the talvsit for a few months of rest. The sod and bark huts were patched, or new ones built by younger couples. Fresh birch twigs were cut and spread on the earth floor and covered with a layer of hides. Down from the storage racks came the sledges and winter skis that had rested there all through the summer while the folk were on the wide tundra, and up on the racks went the summer gear that would not be needed until the spring migration began. Their lives made an elliptical orbit between this winter talvsit and their summer camp at the base of the Cataclysm.

Heckram loved the site of their talvsit. He had visited other ones, when he was but a child on the back of one of his father's harkar, but thought none of them were so well placed as his own. Here were deep fresh springs that never failed, steaming in winter as the cold water gushed out of the ground and made contact with the colder air. The forested hills offered plenty of fuel for the fires and ample birches with their tender twigs for flooring and their knurled bark for the carving of utensils. The snow fell deep on the hillsides, but beneath it were tender lichens of the pine fells, no inedible soggy green moss. The herd wandered, but never far from the camp. The watchful herdfolk guarded their beasts as they pawed deep holes in the snow and shoved their hairy muzzles down to feast on the revealed lichen.

The old woman's winter shelter was on the outskirts of the sita, where she and her husband had built it when their life together was new. Heckram lifted the door flap of Stina's hut and motioned Lasse in. He paused outside to stamp the clinging snow from his boots, then gritted his teeth and ducked in to face Lasse's grandmother.

It took a moment for his eyes to adjust from the sun-bright

snow to the fire-lit dimness of the cosy hut. Flames burned cleanly on the stone hearth, the arran, near the center of the hut. Stina knelt nearby, tethered to the center pole of the hut by her belt weaving. She did not deign to notice their entrance, and both stood, feeling awkward.

She was dressed in worn but brightly colored woven garments decorated with the bright ribbon weaving of her own hands. Her deep black eyes flashed at them once from their deep nests of wrinkles. Then she looked away as if they were of no consequence to her. Her thinning black hair was pulled back from her face in a severely neat roll, and her busy hands never paused in their manipulation of the bright fibers she joined. Neat shanks of dyed fibers and grass rested near her, waiting their turn to be worked into the bright pattern. Everywhere was the work of those same tireless hands, in the cheeses and blood sausages that hung from the rafters, in the cheese molds and salt flask woven from grass fibers, and the traveling baskets with their intricately simple patterns. The water buckets stood brimming with fresh water from the spring. Here a roll of shoe grass hung from a rafter, ready to insulate the laced boots her hands stitched. The carved shoe-grass comb near it had been worked by Lasse's father and was older than the boy. The hut smelled of the birch twigs and clean hides, of the fire's heat and the cheeses. It was a homey, welcoming smell, and Lasse sighed as he sank gratefully by the fire.

Stina knotted a bit of the fibers and slowly unfastened the work from her waist. 'So. You've found your way home, have you? Never mind that someone might have been worrying about you, out hunting two days when you said you'd be back in one.'

The two men looked at each other, and Heckram

shrugged at Lasse and whispered, 'You tell her. She's your grandmother.'

But Stina's ears were as keen as ever, and she went on mercilessly, 'Never mind that someone's old grandmother has to fetch her own water, and check her grandson's harke as well as her own. Never mind that she cooked food enough for two last night, and kept it warm far into the night for someone who wasn't coming. Never mind that she must spend an hour looking for the milking scoop that someone had hung up out of sight and reach, and then struggle to milk a vaja that hasn't been trained to stand properly still. Never mind –'

'I got shot.' Lasse's words dropped on the lecture like a load of tree snow on an unsuspecting hunter. 'Heckram, help me get my coat off.'

But before Heckram could move, Stina was there, tugging gently at the sleeve as the tone of her lecture changed abruptly. 'It's just as your mother was saying last night, Heckram, when the poor woman stopped in to see if Lasse had taken supplies for more than one day. "Off they go to hunt, with never a care as to whether we'll see them again! Off chasing the wild vaja, when they'd both be better off at home, tending to what they already have, yes, and perhaps looking to a future that is not so far away." Oh, but what does a man care when he worries his mother and gives her a night without rest? Nothing.'

Her tongue stopped for a moment as a tousled Lasse emerged from his coat. She handed the garment to Heckram for him to hang up and knelt by her grandson as if he were a child. 'Well. You may be a bad shot, Heckram, but at least you made a neat job of bandaging it. Here I expected blood and a mess, with a piece of leather strapped over it. But this

110

is as nice a job as I've seen since Kila the midwife went south with the traders and married there, never to come back to those who needed her, never even thinking of her old uncle left alone. But look at your shirt, boy! Now where am I going to get the wool to mend that, and this your father's own shirt, made for him by your mother's little hands. You've bled all over it! She traded the hides of her own reindeer for that wool, she who could scarcely afford to, and worked into the night by the firelight to weave –'

'Heckram didn't shoot me,' Lasse cut in mercilessly. 'It was a stranger, hunting alone and on her own. And she's the one who bandaged me.'

'Well!' Stina rocked back on her heels, to regard him with wounded anger. 'And never a word of this do you tell to your own grandmother! I suppose the whole sita is buzzing with this tale, and I shall have to hear of my grandson's adventure from that gossip Bror. Well, what am I to expect? What am I, just a worthless old woman, fit only to weave and cook and mend and clean and milk and . . .' She added sting to her words as with seeming meekness she turned to the fire, to move a simmering pot from its edge. Turning her back on them, she shuffled with exaggerated care to the wooden trunk to take out bowls and spoons.

'You are the first to hear of it,' Heckram declared hastily. 'But for a word or two to Elsa, just enough to be polite. She knows she'll have to get the gist of the tale from you, while Lasse eats and sleeps. No, thank you.' He shook his head to the proffered bowl. 'Now I must leave, so that Lasse can tell you all of it. I've a mother of my own to return to, and no doubt chores to catch up on.'

'Listen to him! As if Ristin would let her home go to wrack and ruin because her son is gone for a night. It isn't so long, young man, since she was bringing in wolf pelts, and you but a brat in the wood komse hanging from her pack saddle, yes, and bawling so that she had to stuff sweet marrow in your greedy little mouth to keep you quiet. But no, now he's a man, and the only one who has ever hunted or worked, I suppose. Well, Lasse, are you going to tell me of this strange woman who shoots my grandson and then mends him? Or must I wait to hear the tale from Ristin?'

Lasse rolled his eyes at Heckram, but he only grinned as he ducked from the hut. He took a deep lungful of the cold air, grateful that Lasse was in competent hands, and that Stina was not angry with him. Evening had fallen swiftly, and the only light in the sita was that which leaked from the huts. He hurried over the familiar paths between the huts, avoiding sleeping dogs curled before their owners' doors, ducking around the looming storage racks. A figure stepped suddenly from the darkness directly into his path, and Heckram halted abruptly to keep from running into him.

'Sorry,' he murmured as he moved to pass him.

'Of course you are,' drawled the other, and Heckram halted, turning slowly.

'Do you have a problem, Joboam?' he asked with excessive courtesy.

'Only with fools who charge into me in the dark. You're late back from the hunt, I hear. I thought perhaps I'd seen the last of you. But here you are again, no doubt with a fine kill.'

'No doubt,' Heckram said lightly. 'But you're far from your hut this night, Joboam. Looking for something?'

'Perhaps. Capiam likes to know what goes on in all parts of the talvsit. He knows it is easier to stop trouble before it starts.

So, on his behalf, I take an evening stroll, to make sure all is well. Surely you don't object?'

'Why should I? If the dogs run about between the huts by day, why shouldn't Joboam by night?'

'I'm sure Capiam will find your jest very amusing when I report it to him.'

'If he's half the man his father was, he'll find it more than that,' Heckram replied recklessly and pushed past Joboam on the narrow path, not quite touching him. He strode on, his shoulders tightened, wondering if Joboam would jump him from behind. But all remained silent behind him as he walked on.

He pushed his seething anger down, telling himself he really had no reason to be incensed. So Joboam walked among the huts by night, checking to be sure all was well. What was there to be concerned about in that? Only his superior attitude as he deigned to walk among the humbler huts. The man was assuming authority to himself. Capiam, as the leader of the herdfolk, should not have to ask others to be sure the sita was secure at night. Had he not legs of his own to walk among his own people? But no, ever since the older Capiam had died last winter, his son had taken himself seriously, acting more like some barbarian tribe chief than the leader of the sita. His spare time was spent in his own hut with his wife and son. If Capiam had to send someone to patrol between the huts at night, then why not send his boy, Rolke? Let him start learning to act like the son of the herdlord, instead of crouching by his mother's hearth all day. She was as wealthy as Capiam himself. She did little sewing or weaving or hunting anymore. Stina had once wondered aloud what the woman did all day, other than berating their daughter, Kari, for her laziness. Yet she herself looked as heavy as a pregnant vaja, while the girl looked starved as an orphaned miesse. Heckram shook his head in distaste. Capiam seemed proud of his wife's girth, as if she were a harke fattening for a winter feast.

'I'd never share a hearth with a woman like that,' Heckram vowed heartily, and was surprised to hear himself speak. What kind of woman, then, *would* he share a hearth with? That was the next question, and one he'd already banished from home conversations. He detoured to his meat rack with its scanty stores. Climbing up, he took out his knife to carve a generous chunk of meat from one of the haunches there and to lift down a blood sausage as well. He was hungry after the day's effort with no rations to sustain him. So he would eat now, leaving his rack barer than ever, and hope for better luck tomorrow. And what kind of woman, he wondered, would sit at hearth with a man with an empty meat rack? He dashed the thought from his mind with a shake of his head and lifted the door flap of the hut he shared with his mother.

The fire on the arran was nearly out. Ristin knelt by it, feeding it bits of twigs to coax the coals back to flame. For an instant she looked small as a child to Heckram. It was the shadows diminishing her. Not that she was a large person. She had the short, stocky build that most of the herdfolk shared. At times, Heckram felt like a lumbering elk in a herd of reindeer. So had his grandfather been, a big man from the south who came north to trade and never left. Even his hair was pale, Ristin would say, light as the flash of a reindeer's tail. Short and dark herself, she showed no sign of her mixed blood. Only in her son had it come to bloom. She still wore her warm furs, and her bright wool hat covered her hair and cheeks. Her mittens hung from strings at her wrists, baring her hands.

'Just leaving?' he asked, coming in quietly.

Ristin made a startled noise and dropped the piece of wood she held. 'Oh, it's you. Well, I'm glad you're finally back. No, just coming in. I've been hunting today, but without much luck.'

'Oh. For wolves or sons?'

Ristin shrugged lightly. 'A little of both. I was worried about you, and a new pelt would be nice. So I took my bow down and went out. Why, does that surprise you?'

'Not from a woman who was hunting wolves when I was a brat in a komse with a mouthful of marrow to keep me quiet.'

Ristin laughed quietly. 'Sounds as if you've been talking to Stina. She was worried about Lasse. I'm glad to see it was without cause.'

'Not quite.'

'Oh?' Ristin had been shrugging out of her coat, but she paused, peering out the neck hole like an owl from a tree.

'Nothing serious, but it could have been. A strange hunter, hunting alone, aimed at a vaja and got Lasse instead. Not seriously!' he added hastily as Ristin's face went grave. 'But it might have been. Luckily she was skilled as a healer. She bound up his arm, and gave us shelter for the night in her tent. I . . . I said I'd pay for her healing. I'm not sure that she understood me, for she speaks our language poorly. And I know that if Lasse knew of it, he would say it was his debt.'

'But you feel responsible for his injury?' Ristin guessed.

'Somewhat.' Heckram scratched at his ear and the day's growth of stubble on his chin.

'Could you have prevented it?' Ristin pressed.

'No. Probably not. But he is only a boy, in some ways,

115

and Stina trusts me with him. I don't like to have that trust betrayed, even accidentally.' He paused and cleared his throat. 'But that isn't the only reason I want to pay the healer for her work. There was something about her and her son.' He stared into the fire as he shrugged off his outer garments. 'Mother, do you remember the year, several years after the plague, when we lost the two calves at the river crossing, and you decided we couldn't slaughter any of our animals for winter meat?'

Ristin slowly put her coat on its peg, shaking the garment out to air it well. She sank down by the fire to loosen the laces on her boots. Her eyes were distant as she pulled them off and drew out the handfuls of shoe grass that insulated them. She fluffed it out and set it by the fire to dry.

'Do you remember that winter?' Heckram pressed.

She turned to him. 'How would one forget such a time? Your father was gone, we had no fattened autumn reindeer meat, no blood sausage, no marrow bones. Only hare and ptarmigan and fish from the summer catch. The wild reindeer were still decimated from the plague, and what there were of them, the wolves hunted better than I. It was a hard time for us all.'

Heckram shook out his tunic and hung it to air. He turned to her, his face grave. 'Her son eats like I did then. He watches food cook like he's afraid it will leap out of the pot and run away. Their tent is not sewn well, the hides they sleep under are thin. Worse, the knife she has looks like something I might have made back then. I do not think she is the hunter you are, either. Other than winging Lasse, the only meat she had shot was a thin hare.'

'It is not as if we are wealthy ourselves,' Ristin began slowly.

'I know, but –'

'Don't interrupt. But there is much cluttering this place that another might put to better use. I do not know why I keep mittens that are too small for you now. And how many bows can I use at one time . . . though if her bow was good enough to down Lasse, perhaps that is something she does not need.'

Heckram chuckled softly. 'I admit I did not notice the condition of her bow. It was the boy I looked at.' As he spoke, he took down the tablo board and turned it over to show its scarred back. Setting the meat atop it, he began to carve it into slices that would cook quickly. He was hungry tonight, hungrier somehow for having met the boy and the healer. 'They were so strange. I wanted to talk to her, to ask her where they had come from and why. She has a look of far places to her and acts as if she doesn't really know how to provide for herself. I am sure she has tales to tell, and I wanted to hear them. But she didn't want to talk. I think she understood more of my words than she let on. But she was fearful, as if talking to me might leave her open to harm. And the boy . . . He was all eyes, and so quiet, staring all the time.'

'Hunger can do that to a boy.' Ristin paused, remembering. 'And being alone can make a woman that cautious. But Heckram . . .'

'Yes?'

'The worst of those days, for me, was the pity of those around us. We had the village to help us, and some were kind. I cannot count how many times you were fed by Lasse's father at his tent. Some mornings there was meat on our rack that I knew had not been there the night before. I knew it was done out of kindness, but it was –'

'I know. Some I shall take as payment for Lasse. She also had a bag of herbs there, and seemed to know the mixing of them. It has been long since there was a healer among the herdfolk. I am sure there are medicines that would be useful to us and that she might make. I will leave her pride intact.' He had spitted the meat pieces and now set them to cook over the revived flames. The fat sizzled and his stomach rolled yearningly.

Ristin nodded thoughtfully. 'Sometimes it is all one has left to lean on. You might talk to Elsa as well. She had some bone work and ribbon weaving she wanted the traders to take. She might be willing to trade some of it for something to ease her shoulder when the days are cold and wet. It has never been the same since that fall. Perhaps you should even take her along when you go to pay the healer. The girl works so hard, and this chance to trade might be a bit of a rest for her. Is it far to the healer's hut?'

'Not by skis. If we had not been on foot, hoping to drag a vaja home alive, Lasse and I would have been home by noon. And now that I know where it is, I should be able to get there in a short time. I will tell Elsa I am going. If she wants to come along, I'm sure she will.'

'You might treat her with a little courtesy.'

'I do. With as much courtesy as I give to Lasse, or Jakke. Or any of my friends.'

'Heckram . . .'

'Are you hungry? The meat is nearly ready.'

Ristin noticed the tone of his voice with a sigh. 'Yes. But I'll remind you once more that you aren't getting any younger. Nor I.'

'Nor Elsa. I know. But I won't have a hungry child at my

hearth, mother. I won't look for a wife until I am sure I can care for one.'

'If you wait until you're ready, you'll never be wed.'

'Mother.'

Silence fell. Heckram drew the still sizzling meat from the flames, portioning it into the wooden trenchers his mother set beside him. She brought juobmo as well, sour milk preserved in a small keg and flavored with sorrel leaves. With cheese and blood sausage, it made a pleasant meal, although it was a quiet one. The meat was more flavorful than tender. Heckram chewed the fine-grained chunks, watching the fire and thinking. After the dishes had been cleared away, Ristin took up a half-finished basket. She seemed to give much thought to which fibers to choose and then abruptly set it aside. She stared at him until he lifted his eyes to meet hers. She spoke softly.

'Heckram. Your father and I . . . we never intended to have a hungry child at our hearth.'

He shrank at the pain in her voice. 'I know that,' he said gently. 'I did not mean my words as a rebuke to you.'

But she spoke on relentlessly. 'We never expected the plague, and I never thought to lose him while you were just a boy. But for all that, Heckram, even knowing all that was to come, I would do it again. I'd take him as husband again.'

A small silence was planted in the hut and grew. Ristin took up her belt weaving and knelt to fasten it to the center pole. Drawing it out taut, she knelt and took up colored root fibers for the pattern, some stained red from alder bark, some yellow from wild onion. She sorted out a handful.

'When I feel that way about Elsa,' Heckram offered, 'I'll ask her. But only when I feel that way.'

Ristin looked up from her work, holding her son with her

eyes for a long moment. Then she slowly nodded. 'That's fair,' she said softly as her head bent over her work again. 'That's fair to both of you. But let us hope she still feels that way about you when you get around to asking her.'

EIGHT

The ptarmigan were small. She hefted them by their feathered feet, studying the scarlet eyefeathers that had betrayed them. But for that shot of color, she would never have seen them in the willow thicket. But even two of them weren't much more meat than a hare. Well, she would be able to skin them carefully and keep the feathered skins. And their succulent flesh would be a welcome change from all the hares they had eaten lately. She would spit one and cook it over the fire, and stew up the other with herbs and lichen to thicken and flavor the broth. Two dishes might make Kerlew feel as if there were more to eat.

The long shadows of the trees crossed her trail in a bluish network against the snow. Evening was seeping up the hillside, rising about her as if darkness began in the hollows and shadowed places of the land and welled up to meet the night. Already the brightest stars were beginning to show in the deep blue of the sky. The sun itself had but peeped over the horizon today and sidled along the skyline. Soon it would dip out of sight again. She'd best hurry.

Tillu ducked under a branch, careful not to disturb its load of snow. She moved silently, always watching for that flicker of movement that might give her one more target for her bow. She was getting better with it. She grinned to herself; soon she'd have as much skill as one of the children in Benu's band. But the landscape around her was still. The slowly encroaching twilight was darkening the green of the pine boughs into near black, merging the ranked tree trunks to either side of her trail into a curtain of grayish bark and shadowed snow. Perhaps if she had not wasted so much time watching the herd of reindeer and trying to think of a way to kill one. Her mind swung back to that challenge. She had already proved that her crude arrows from her flimsy bow did no more than bounce off the animals' thick hides. All she had accomplished was spooking them. A flung spear would do no better, for she hadn't the skills to make a good one. And even in the deep snow, the reindeer would easily flounder away from her before she could get close enough to use a jabbing spear. But there had to be a way, and she would discover it soon.

She tried not to think of the long nights of winter that still remained. She should remember that the darkest part of the cold time was behind her now, and they were still both alive. She sighed lightly, promising herself that things would get better. Look how Kerlew was changing. In the three days since the strangers had stayed with them, the boy had turned out twelve spoons. True, some were cruder than others, but each one seemed improved. And, in typical Kerlew fashion, now that he was confident of one implement, he was not inclined to try to carve anything else. She would let him enjoy his success for a while, and then persuade him to try something new. The point was, they were surviving, and Kerlew was growing. She wouldn't worry any further than that. Tillu crested the last rise and started down into the sheltered dell that held her home.

The strange tracks cut across her path, the twin lines of them looking almost blue against the snow in the evening shadows. Tillu froze, looking up and down the line of the trail's passage, but seeing nothing. They vanished into the snow-mantled trees, with no sign of what had made them.

She crouched down to study the track, to touch its clean edge with her mittened hand. She had seen nothing like these before. The tracks were long and narrow and continuous, almost as if a man had dragged something long and narrow through the snow. But there were no footprints beside them. Indistinct dents in the snow alongside the long narrow tracks at irregular intervals puzzled her. Nothing about them resembled the footprints of any creature she knew. She strained her ears, but heard nothing. She couldn't even tell if the mysterious tracks were going or coming. But as she continued on her way home, she found her tracks paralleling them. As it became more and more obvious that her tent was either their destination or source, she hurried.

She was panting when she arrived at the clearing. Her eyes followed the strange trail right up to the edge of the beaten snow that surrounded her tent. She approached cautiously, heart thumping and ears straining. Four long, narrow planks of wood with strange leather fixtures rested on the snow outside her tent. The tips of the planks had been warped up at one end. Four staves stood in the snow beside them. Tillu had never seen anything like them. Muffled voices came from within the tent, Kerlew's piping one and the deeper voice of the stranger. Worry squeezed her stomach as she ducked into the tent.

Within, the fire burned merrily, casting its dancing shadows on the skin walls. Kerlew, his finished spoons in a row before him, crouched on his heels, busily explaining to a nodding Heckram exactly how each had been made. Another stranger, not near as tall as Heckram, stood by the entrance, looking down on the boy with a strange expression on her face.

The woman turned to Tillu as she entered, regarding her with wide black eyes above high cheekbones. Her fine lips parted in an uncertain smile. Her hair, shining black, had been coiled around her head under a bright cap of yellow and red knotted wool.

Tillu could only stare, feeling a strange ache of homesickness such as she had not experienced since Kerlew's birth. Over the years she had grown accustomed to seeing folks in clothing of leather or fur, skillfully designed and sewn, functional, sturdy clothing. Such did this woman wear, also. But at the cuffs and hems and throat, on the band of her hat above her eyes, everywhere there was room for it, her garments were decorated with woven bands of brightly colored fiber and wool interspersed with strips of fur. Beads of glowing yellow amber, of white and brown bone and horn, clicked against each other when she moved. The bright ornamentation woke in Tillu a sudden sharp hunger for a settled life, for villages where crops grew and domestic animals grazed, where a man or woman might spend a few moments of the day in doing more than simply surviving. She remembered her parents in the evening, her mother weaving something for the beauty of the blending colors, her father carving and painting useful objects to transform them into art. For a world she had long believed lay so far to the south of her that she would never again see it, her eyes stung.

'Heckram,' the woman said softly, and he turned on his heels, to nod easily to Tillu.

'Good spoons!' he said by way of greeting, and Kerlew turned a pride-flushed face to his mother.

'They came while you were gone, to pay for your healing the arrow-shot man.' Kerlew's explanation limped along in his usual halting way. 'I've been showing him the spoons I made. He likes the goose one best.'

Kerlew waved the ladle at her as he spoke. This was his latest creation, with the long curving handle possessing two knots and a stub at the end that suggested a goose's eyes and bill at the end of its long neck.

'Tillu the healer,' Heckram said. 'Elsa my friend.'

Tillu nodded to the introduction, not moving. She had not expected him to return and pay her. Their village must be closer than she thought. She covered her confusion by unloading the game bag from her waist and hanging her bow and quiver from its hook.

'Lasse is better?' she asked as she turned back.

'Much better.' Heckram's teeth were very white in his wind-bronzed face.

'Good. Good.' Her profession came to the forefront, rescuing them both from awkwardness as she asked, 'New bandage? Swell, bleed, hot?'

'New bandage,' he assured her. 'Wound closed. Arm moves, little pain.'

'Good, good.' She bobbed her head like a courting duck.

'You sound like you're talking to a baby,' Kerlew said in disgust.

Heckram caught the gist of his words, for he laughed as he replied, 'Makes easy to understand.'

'And you, don't be rude. It's better to be quiet and learn manners when you are young,' Tillu suggested firmly.

Kerlew hung his head and retreated. Heckram hid a grin

at the familiar rebuke. Even if he had not been able to decipher most of Tillu's words, he would have known what she
said. It was a rebuke he had often heard himself when a
child. Tillu sensed that he shielded the boy from further
scolding with a change of subject.

'Pay healing,' he said to Tillu. He gestured to a hide that
had been rolled into a pack. Stooping, he unfastened the
knots of sinew and unrolled it, revealing various smaller
bundles within. Their wrappings were cloth of woven fiber,
some dyed in bright colors. He tapped each as he spoke.
'Fish. Cheese. Reindeer.' He paused and looked up at her as
if asking her to make her choice. Perhaps he wanted her to
choose what she would take for the healing. She didn't hesitate. She and Kerlew both had a permanent craving for fat
of any kind.

'Cheese.' She smiled as she copied his inflection, remembering his word for it from the last time he had been here.

'Cheese,' he agreed uncertainly, trying to understand why
she had repeated it. Then he shrugged, rolled up the hide
with its smaller packages, and offered it to her.

'All?' she asked, stunned by the size of the offering.

'For Lasse,' he explained.

'Too much,' she refused quickly.

He shrugged innocently at her words, but she was suddenly
certain that he was pretending not to understand her. 'For
Lasse,' he repeated slowly. 'You healed him. I pay.' He kept
his eyes from hers as he set the bundle down on her pallet.

Tillu hesitated, but Kerlew's eyes were on her with mute
appeal in them. 'Thank you,' she said stiffly, but Heckram
grinned at the boy as if they shared a secret. All stood about
silently for an awkward moment.

Then Elsa spoke. 'I come, trade?'

'Trade?' Tillu asked, puzzled. She had not expected the woman to speak. Was not this Heckram's woman? She glanced toward Heckram to see his reaction. She was accustomed to men handling all such negotiations. But Heckram seemed engrossed in some talk with Kerlew.

'Old hurt.' Elsa was not paying the least attention to her man. Tillu turned back to her words. 'Fall into river, hit rock. Long time ago.' The young woman put a hand to the small of her back, then to her shoulder, miming pain.

'Cold, wet day? Swell?' Tillu asked.

Elsa nodded quickly at each of Tillu's questions. Tillu pointed to her knuckles and wrist. 'Swell, hurt here, also?'

'No.' Again she touched the small of her back, and her shoulder. 'Only shoulder, only back. Fall down, long time ago.'

'Elsa work hard? Lift heavy loads?'

Elsa laughed ruefully. 'Yes. Elsa herdwoman. Hard work, heavy loads.'

Tillu nodded back. 'Tillu see?'

Elsa nodded and bent to draw her heavy skin tunic off over her head. She glanced once at Heckram and the boy, and then turned her back on them to pull off her undershirt of woven wool. Stepping to her side, Tillu ran a careful hand over the shoulder. There was no indication of an injury. She hesitated, then pressed gently and finally probed at the joint. A smooth layer of muscle coated the young woman's back. Lift heavy loads? Tillu didn't doubt it. Her diminutive size was belied by the musculature of her shoulders and back.

'Not hurt now,' she reminded Tillu as the healer manipulated the shoulder. 'Only cold wet days. Then ache, stiff.'

Tillu nodded, satisfied. This was a thing she had seen before, and often. Her mind was working swiftly. She had some herbs that would make a tea for that kind of pain. She had others that would work even better if they were blended with fat into a greasy ointment. But fat was something she didn't have.

She made a sign to them to wait and went to the back of the tent for her medicine box. Elsa pulled her shirt back on as Tillu mixed the herbs and placed them into a pouch of dried intestine. 'Mix a little of these with hot water and let them soak, oh, just until the leaves are soft. Then drink, but only one cup, no more. Too much can be bad.' Tillu suddenly realized that she was making no effort to make herself easily understood. She glanced up, but Elsa was nodding, seeming to understand the directions. 'You have bear grease? Wolf fat? Glutton fat?' she asked her.

Elsa nodded slowly, looking puzzled.

'You bring some. I make medicine to rub on. Better kind, help more. Put where it hurts only. Understand?'

'Next time,' Elsa suggested, and Tillu nodded. Next time. So there would be a next time, with people coming and going. Perhaps that was a good thing. Elsa seemed kind, and Heckram did not cuff Kerlew and push him aside. Perhaps it would work out, this limited contact.

'You take for medicine?' Elsa asked. She was offering a piece of carved horn, incised with figures painted red and black and blue. She didn't look to Heckram for permission before offering the trade. If a woman had behaved so in Benu's group, her man would have beaten her for her forwardness. But Heckram was not paying attention to them. Tillu took the horn slowly and turned it over in her hands.

'Open here. See?' Elsa took it back, to pull off the fitted cap. She spilled three bone needles into her hand. They were new and sharp, made by skilled hands. Tillu nodded in

128

appreciation, and reached to touch one shyly. Elsa smiled. 'I make them, and case. My father, no sons. Teach me to carve instead. Now he says I am better than most men at carving. I makes knives, needles, arrowheads, harness rings. Mine are not just strong. Mine are pretty.'

Elsa recapped the carved needle case and offered it back to her. Tillu took it cautiously, to examine the carved and painted surface. The tiny decorations pleased her more than the new needles inside. After a moment, she remembered her guests.

'You stay, eat?' Tillu offered.

Heckram shook his head as he rose from where he and Kerlew had been conferring. 'Dark nearly here. Hurry back to talvsit. You come talvsit, sometime? People welcome healer, much work for healer. You come, sometime?'

'Sometime, maybe,' Tillu agreed slowly as Kerlew bounced in excitement at the prospect. She followed them to the door of the tent, watching in consternation as they strapped the long flat pieces of wood to their feet and took up their staves.

'Skis,' Heckram explained, smiling at her confusion. 'Go over snow fast, not sink. You, skis?'

Tillu shook her head, eyes wide.

Heckram grinned at her. 'You come talvsit, I teach you. Teach Kerlew, too. Good way to hunt, on skis. Go fast, quiet. You come to talvsit, visit, learn skis. Maybe tell about your people, your lands?'

The request and offer took Tillu by surprise and she found herself flushing in confusion. Heckram smiled down at her and nodded assurance at Kerlew, who was capering with excitement.

Elsa settled her hat firmly on her head and glanced at Heckram with annoyance. 'Time to go,' she suggested, a trace of irritation in her voice.

'I'm glad you came,' Tillu said awkwardly, wondering if she had somehow offended the woman. But Elsa's smile seemed warm as she promised, 'Next time, bear grease.' With a wave of her hand she pushed off, sliding her feet in long steps as she coasted over the top of the snow. Tillu marveled at this strange method of traveling. There was no denying it was swift. Already Elsa had reached the base of the trees and was starting easily up the hill. Tillu expected her to have to struggle to ascend, but Elsa leaned into the walk. It looked so easy.

'You come talvsit, soon,' Heckram suggested as he pushed off to follow the woman. His leg muscles worked and the skis carried him forward effortlessly. Tillu watched him go. With his longer stride he would catch up with Elsa easily. She must have known that, for she showed no sign of waiting for him. Still, it was strange to hear a woman announce it was time to go, and stranger still to see a man follow her. Kerlew peered from the tent flap after them.

'Skis,' Tillu told him, pointing after them. 'Would you like to do that?'

'Someday I will. See my knife?' He held up a bone knife in a sheath of woven fiber. As Tillu reached for it, he pulled it close to him. He drew the blade from the sheath and flourished it dangerously near his own face, not letting her touch it.

'Where did you get that? Did the man forget it?' she asked, hoping Kerlew had not somehow stolen it.

'He didn't forget it. He wanted the goose spoon, so we traded.' Kerlew spun away from her touch, eluding her. 'Now I am a man indeed!'

'A knife does not make a man!' Tillu scoffed. 'Let me see it.'

'Look, but do not touch,' Kerlew told her with tolerant pride. 'Carp told me to never let a woman touch my own tools. A shaman can hide his strength in his tools. I put good luck in the goose spoon for Heckram.'

'Carp!' Tillu snorted, but put her hands down.

He held the blade steady for her inspection. It was a fine piece of work, with the handle wrapped in a leather thong to keep the grip from slipping. Away from the cutting edge, decorative lines had been etched shallowly into the blade and stained black. It was worth far more than a crudely carved spoon and Tillu chewed at her lip, pondering. What made Heckram treat Kerlew so kindly and pay her so generously for the simple healing of Lasse? She could not understand it. It made her uneasy. 'I shall find a way to make it even with them, when next they come,' she promised herself softly.

'She will not come again.' Kerlew spoke in a voice that was next to a whisper, but deeper. He stood suddenly still, staring up the hillside. The point of his new knife touched the base of his throat.

The two skiers had appeared on a bare shoulder of the hillside, limned against the darkening sky. Colors had fled from the earth, taking refuge in the sky on the horizon. Branches and trunks of trees had turned black against the pale snow. The people on the crest of the hill were no more than dark shapes against the violet streak on the horizon.

'She has to come back, to bring the bear grease so I can make the ointment for her shoulder,' Tillu pointed out. 'Move out of the way and let me back in the tent. It's getting cold out here.'

'She will not come back, for he is going to kill her. Even now the blackness swallows her down, and she is gone.'

A chill not from cold racked Tillu's body. Kerlew stood in

the entrance of the tent, the knife held before him like a finger pointing at the far figures at the top of the hill. His eyes were full of the setting sun and the violet light made his face look like a corpse's. Tillu could not keep herself from following his gaze. The woman's form went over the crest of the hill, appearing to sink into blackness. The sunset splashed the surrounding snow with spreading pink and shadowed purples. As Tillu watched, the figure of the man plunged after her. A chill wind rattled branches, dropping plops of snow like irregular footsteps. She started at the sound. When she glanced back to Kerlew, he smiled up at her ingenuously.

'Let's eat all that food tonight!' he suggested happily and vanished into the tent, his treasured knife waving in his clutched fist.

'Wait!' Heckram called. Elsa had cut across the smooth face of the snow on the downside of the hill and was nearly out of sight in a thicket of willow. He gave a final glance at the lonely tent with the woman and boy standing before it, then pushed off to follow her. She was right to hurry, with the sun setting and the light changing, but he suspected she was feeling playful as well. They had always competed as children, on foot, on their skis, or in their pulkors as they raced over the snow in winter, shouting wild encouragement to the bounding harkar that pulled them. As a youth, Heckram had strained to stretch his wolf hides tighter as they dried, so they might appear larger than those of his slender young neighbor. In summer they had compared strings of fish and each measured their new calves against the other's to see whose reindeer prospered most. Elsa was a strong herdfolk woman, competent and independent. But he had enjoyed her challenges more when they were younger.

'Wait,' he called again, and she gave in, sinking her poles at the sides of her skis as she paused.

A sting of evening wind kissed Heckram's cheeks as he caught up with her. The same wind, and effort, had reddened Elsa's cheeks. Some of her thick hair had escaped from her bright cap. She shook her hands free of their mittens and tucked it back in. She had dark, liquid eyes that flashed like those of a proud little vaja. She pulled her fingers from her cap, but her hair snagged on them and spilled out worse than ever. Heckram grinned as she ruthlessly stuffed it back.

'Why not just let it hang out?' he asked as she struggled with it.

'And spend all evening picking the snarls out of it? No, thank you. Why didn't you tell me about the boy?'

'I did. I'm sure I did. I told you the healer had a son.'

'That's not what I mean. Why didn't you tell me how strange he was? Lasse said something about it, but when you said he had imagined it, I believed you. But when we first went in there, before his mother came . . . brrr. It was all I could do to keep from turning around and leaving. The way he looked at us!'

'He's just a boy,' Heckram snorted, feeling more annoyed than her remarks merited. 'Lonely, probably, and a bit hungry all the time.'

Elsa dropped her hands from her hat and began pulling her mittens back on. 'You actually believe that, don't you? I guess you haven't been around children that much. That boy is . . . well, he isn't like other children. Look how he behaved when we first got there.'

'I don't know what you mean.'

Elsa shook her head at him. Taking a firm grip on her poles, she pushed off, Heckram following behind her and slightly to one side. 'When traders from the south come to the talvsit, what do the children do?' The rhythm of her words matched the rhythm of her pumping arms as she chose their trail through the woods.

'They rush out, chattering like magpies, making the dogs bark and pester them with a thousand questions,' Heckram replied grumpily. He felt as if she were lecturing him and he didn't enjoy it.

'That's right. But what did that boy do when strangers came? He didn't even come out of the tent, although he must have heard us talking outside. Not until you shouted to ask if anyone was home. Then he came silently to the tent flap and let us in, and sat down by the fire and invited us to sit, as if we had come all that way just to see him. He didn't run to find his mother, or call for her, or even mention her until you asked where she was. And the way he showed those spoons he had carved, as if they were some kind of treasure. You know that spoon you took wasn't worth the knife you gave him. I wonder that his mother allowed it.'

'I doubt that she even knows of it yet. It was just between Kerlew and me. And it wasn't the spoons he was showing me, so much as that he had learned from what I showed him last time. As to his manners . . . Elsa, they aren't herd-folk. They're bound to have different customs. Perhaps among his people it is unseemly for children to be noisy. And I suppose, living alone as they do, he has learned to behave older than his years.'

'That's not it at all.' Now her voice was mirroring his annoyance. 'That boy is not right. He's . . . well, not a half-wit, but only a step from it. Listen to how he talks!'

'He doesn't speak our language!' Heckram put in irritably.

'Even when he speaks to his mother in their own language, he sounds like he doesn't speak the language! Why are you getting so upset? You act as if I were criticizing Lasse or your mother! He's just the healer's boy.'

'Because I . . . I don't know. Because, maybe, he is a bit different. As I was a bit different, with no father to teach me a man's skills. My mother hunted and herded and fished and wove, and I worked alongside her where I could. But there was always that secret worry for me: What if something happened to her? And always the knowledge that our life was different from those around us, in ways they could never understand.'

Elsa had gradually slowed, as Heckram's words and pace had picked up. She was alongside him now, staring curiously at him. He clenched his jaws tight against any more words, feeling embarrassed that he had said so much. And angry. Angry at the past for the way it had been. He could not go back and change how it had been for himself. The most he could do was change how it was for Kerlew now. He glanced across at Elsa.

'There's no talking to you, is there?' she observed. 'A person can't say a word to you without your taking it personally. Is everyone supposed to tiptoe around your feelings? I'm the one who should be hurt. That knife you so casually traded for a crooked spoon is the one I made for you. Remember? At the last herd sorting, I borrowed one of yours to mark a calf after mine broke. And then I broke yours, too. So I had to make two new knives, and I gave the best one to you. But look at me. Am I carrying on about it as if I am insulted because you traded it away? No. But I make one little comment, and you are mortally offended. Over such a silly thing. And Heckram, you were nothing like that boy, and you know it. As well as I know it. I was around when you were a boy, remember? And you were never as strange as that Kerlew. But if you want to carry on about someone else's child, it's your business. I won't stop you. All I was trying to say is that he's not normal. But you'll find that out for yourself soon enough. I don't know how Lasse can bear to hunt with you. Everything has to be so grim with you!'

He let her talk on, hunching his shoulders to her words. He felt shamed that he had traded away her gift knife without even remembering it. She did have a right to feel insulted. But he would rather that she be insulted than that she scold him like a thoughtless child. He should never have told her he was going to see the healer. But, as the old tale went, in trying to please everyone he had pleased no one. He was sure his mother would soon hear about how unsociable he had been.

He glanced across at the girl. Her cheeks and nose were flushed with more than cold. He supposed he had offended her, and she was only saying he hadn't to save his feelings. But that was even worse. With an effort, he changed the subject and asked, 'How is that calf doing? The orphaned one you were hand-feeding?'

'It died,' she said coldly. 'Nearly a month ago. As I'm sure I mentioned to you at the time.'

'That's right,' he hastily amended. 'So you did. Well. That shows you how well my mind is working lately. I've had so much to think on, I can't seem to keep my thoughts together. Even Lasse scolds me about it. I just –'

Elsa abruptly jammed her poles into the snow, halting herself. With an effort, Heckram checked his own skis and looked back at her. He was astonished. She was crying.

'I'm sorry I forgot about the calf,' he said, feeling ashamed of his thoughtlessness and baffled by her response to it. Had one calf become so important in her life?

'You *are* an idiot. You and that boy make a fine pair. I really do believe you don't know anything of what goes on with the people of the herd. All you think of is the reindeer and hunting, and dragging animals back to cut your mark in their ears. Did you know Joboam has said that he will marry me?'

After a moment, Heckram shut his jaw with a snap. His head reeled with contradictory thoughts. 'He's a very wealthy man,' he observed, addressing his remarks to a nearby pine tree.

'Yes. And he smells like an ungutted carcass and has the manners of a wolverine, and I wouldn't have him near me if he were the son of the herdlord. Which he seems to think he is, even if Capiam has a son of his own who will inherit that position. But he comes around, and comes around, and comes around, following me about like a dog follows a bitch in heat. And he gives my mother and father gifts they cannot refuse for fear of offending him, gifts of things I know they need, but I cannot supply for them. Things I cannot hope to pay back for. He sits by our arran late into the evening, and if I go outside into the night to be alone, he follows me. If I say I am going to visit, he says he will go with me. He will not let me avoid him. Even when I say I will not hunt with him because I prefer to hunt alone, he follows me at a distance. I know he does, even if my father thinks I am silly. He has already told Capiam that I am going to marry him in the spring by the Cataclysm. I heard from Marta that Capiam was pleased and said that there would be a fine celebration, with many gifts for us. I feel like I am being swept down a river current, with nothing to grasp at.'

'Tell him no,' Heckram suggested harshly. He felt he was suffocating, as if he were a salmon with the mesh of the net lifting him from the rushing water. The urgency of his mother's matchmaking was no longer remotely humorous. Why hadn't she spoken honestly to him of Elsa's dilemma? Anger seethed through him. Who was Joboam, that all should fear to offend him?

'I did tell him no. He told me to think again. He laughed and told my father that young girls didn't know what was in their own best interest, but that if I thought on it, I would change my heart. I don't want to offend him, but –'

'Why not offend him?' Heckram demanded. 'Surely he is just a herdman, like any one of us? He has no right to force his attentions on you. Is he of the herdfolk, or is he some forest savage who must steal a wife to find one?'

'But what reason can I give him? What can I say to him?'

'Say "I don't like you. Go away and stop bothering me."' He tried to make the words sound like a jest, but the eyes she turned on him were swimming with tears.

'Heckram . . . times have changed. Don't you see that? Joboam has many reindeer, and his rack is always heavy with furs and meat and hides. My parents bore me late. They are getting old. My mother seems always sick, and my father's eyes . . . I cannot hunt and herd for three. And' – she paused. 'Joboam frightens me. When he says that girls do not know what is in their own best interest, his eyes are . . . dangerous. He does not look at me like a man looks at a woman. He looks at me as I look at a harke who must be broken to packing. I do not ask the harke what it prefers, because that has no bearing on what will be. I do not think Joboam cares what I prefer. I think he believes I will marry him in the spring.'

'Why do you tell me?'

It came out harsher than he meant it to. She turned her face from him and he saw her stiffen. Cursing their mothers and their wagging tongues, he maneuvered his skis to where he could reach and touch her shoulders. She turned to him abruptly and he embraced her awkwardly. Little Elsa. Not even as tall as Lasse. Childhood friend. A good-hearted, sturdy woman, independent and skilled, capable of taking care of herself. But that was no longer enough. Her responsibilities were more than she could shoulder, through no fault of her own. He remembered, vaguely, her two older brothers. They had been close to his own age, and as small as Elsa. They had not survived the Plague Summer. He patted her awkwardly and felt her shoulders shake once in a great sob.

'It's going to be all right,' he told her. Knowing it wouldn't. Instead of one woman taking the responsibilities of a family of three, it would be the two of them taking the responsibilities of two households. His own mother was starting to feel her years. Or three households. He supposed they would have to have a tent of their own, and their own string of harkar. Their own cooking utensils and bedding, their own pulkor and meat rack.

He reined his mind viciously from the list. 'I'll speak to Joboam. I'll tell him we have an understanding. That will put an end to him bothering you.'

'I can't ask you to do that!'

'You don't have to. I'm asking you, aren't I? To join with me,' he pointed out gently.

Relief made her tears break out anew. She put her face against his chest and leaned on him heavily. The top of her head did not even reach his chin. 'You say so little. I had begun to think you did not care, would never speak. My

139

mother kept saying not to worry, that you were like your father. Shy. But I was so afraid. I love you, Heckram. I'll be a good wife to you.'

Hampered by the skis and their heavy winter clothing, he patted her back awkwardly. 'You're a good woman, Elsa,' he said, carefully choosing honest words. 'Joboam doesn't deserve a woman like you.' And she deserves more than carefully truthful compliments, he told himself. He tried to find more he could give her. 'I'll be a good husband to you.' He felt the words bind him as he spoke them, and his heart sank beneath them.

'Will you come to my tent tonight?' she asked softly. It was not an unusual question for a woman of the herdfolk. With or without the assumption of marriage, she was free to invite him. Nor was it the first time she had let him know he would be welcome there. But he felt the question like a wolf feels the thud of the second arrow.

'No,' he said quickly. And then, more gently: 'In our own tent, when I have traded for the hides and you have sewn them. Then we will be together, as is fitting.'

'You never used to mind,' she teased him gently, her face against his chest still. 'Mossy hillside or grassy meadow, it was all one to you. Even in the snow that time. Remember?' She turned bright eyes up to him, challenging him playfully. But she found him staring up at the sky as it darkened over the forested hillsides. His mouth was solemn.

'Heckram?' she asked gently.

'Bror has been wanting me to help him make a new pulkor. I've been telling him that I was too busy hunting. But, perhaps if I agree, he will trade me tent hides for the work.' He glanced down to find her eyes uncertain. 'Don't worry,' he assured her quickly. 'I'll find ways to get the things we will need. You won't lack what you need, Elsa.' In the gathering darkness, he stooped to kiss her carefully. Her arms went quickly around his neck, holding his face close to hers as her kiss became warmer. Her weight dragged at him, and his back bent as under a burden.

Kerlew: The Pouch

So Tillu had gone hunting without him. Good. He didn't care. A shaman didn't need to know how to hunt. A shaman had better things to do with his time. He didn't really care if he never learned how to hunt. She could keep her secrets and he would keep his.

Kerlew sat down carefully by the fire, his pouch beside him. He poked at the fire with a narrow willow wand. The peeled stick gleamed white against his sooty hands. He held the tip of it in the coals, watched it blacken and then suddenly flare alight. He lifted it carefully and held it as he would hold a flower with a long stem. He smiled upon it lovingly. It was short and fat if he held the stick still, long and thin if he moved it. He stopped moving it and there was the short fat flame again. Now he gently waved it, and it was long and thin. After a long time, he remembered that there was more to this game than the flame on the tip of the wand. He stared into the flame, opening his eyes wide to the light as the old shaman had taught him. He blinked involuntarily against the light, and started at what he saw with his eyes closed. He closed them again and stared. Pale wolf eyes inside his eyelids. Wolf looking into him as he looked out. Wolf watching, coming to him? He shivered deliciously and opened his eyes to the flame again. The bright, yellow, dancing flame. He brought it close to his face until he felt the heat of the tiny flame against his lips. He stared deep into the flame. 'Carp?' he whispered questioningly.

In an instant the flame was gone, leaving only a thin streamer of spiraling smoke. Kerlew sighed. 'He's still angry at me.' He threw the stick onto the fire. 'He's still angry at me,' he repeated dismally. 'For going up instead of down.' He stared into the fire for a long time. His stomach felt heavy and his throat felt tight and sore. 'Mother!' he called out. 'Tillu, I think I'm getting sick. Tillu!' Then he remembered she wasn't there. She had gone hunting and left him here alone, and Carp was angry with him.

He sighed again and rubbed at his face. He wished the stranger man, the spoon man, would come again. He liked how big he was, and how he didn't hit. And he smiled at Kerlew. Usually the ones that didn't hit didn't look at him either. He pursed his lips and squinched his eyes, straining to group the ones who didn't hit but did smile at him. There was . . . the spoon man and . . . Carp. He smiled. It was the first time he had put them together in his mind, and it pleased him. The spoon man and Carp. Too bad Tillu didn't like them.

Tillu. The fire. He looked at it in sudden trepidation. As he feared, it was burning low. He scrabbled to his feet and hurried to the woodpile by the door. He brought back an armload and let it crash down onto the coals. The fire sizzled and sparks leaped out onto the bare earth around the hearth. Steam and smoke rose as the new wood began to catch fire.

Smoke. If only he had gone down instead of up with the smoke. If he had gone down, he would have a spirit brother now. And Carp would be with him, and he would be a powerful shaman. If he had gone down instead of up, he wouldn't have to tend the fire. All people would respect him, as they respected Carp. They would bring him tongues and livers, gifts of soft furs and new tools. No one would ever hit him again. And if they did? His yellow eyes narrowed. Then he would curse them, would take their hunting luck, would make their women die in childbirth, would make their meat spoil and their children sicken. Yes! Then they would know Kerlew the shaman, would know his power and treat him well. Even his mother would hurry to build up his fire for him, to bring him the best of her kills. Not that she often brought home good kills. Usually it was rabbit or squirrel, little red-meat animals with thin hides. Kerlew liked meat that was edged with white fat, big pieces of meat he could grip with both hands when he ate. He held up his hands, pretending to grip a big piece of meat, and grinned. When he was shaman, he would eat big pieces of meat and wipe his greasy hands on his hair to make it shine. Carp did that. Carp. Carp was angry.

The thought sobered him and the smile faded from his face. His hands fell into his lap and he stared once more into the flames. Maybe he should try to see Carp in a flame on a willow wand . . . No, he had already tried that. What else?

He reached for his pouch and untied the strip of leather that held the mouth shut. Then he put his nose and mouth against the opening and breathed deeply. He liked the smell of the pouch. It smelled of tanned leather and his mother's herbs. For a while he amused himself by taking a deep breath of the delicious smell and watching the leather sack go flat. When he breathed out, the sack would puff up like a fat little rabbit. It was very funny. He giggled into the sack; it sounded different from when he giggled out loud. It made him laugh even more. Finally, when his stomach hurt from laughing, he took the sack away from his nose and mouth. He reached in carefully.

It was important to touch only one item at a time, and to take them out in the order he touched them. Carp said so. He touched the knife first. It seemed he always touched the knife first. It was biggest. Maybe Knife-spirit was trying to tell him something. He took it slowly out of the bag.

The knife pleased him. It was a very good knife. Much better than the one his mother had, and he knew she wished she could use his knife. And it was the first tool anyone had given him. When he had offered the spoon man the special spoon with the good luck in it, the spoon man had seen what a special thing it was. That was why he had given him such a fine knife.

Kerlew drew the knife from the woven sheath. There were reindeer on the knife. One was running, with its head thrown back so far that its antlers touched its rump. Another, near the handle, grazed with a calf at its side. That one had no antlers. Between the reindeer, there were swirling designs, that reminded Kerlew of the stars he had climbed. This reindeer knife was very important. Not only did it have the spirit of the animals he had seen in his first shamanic journey, it was carved from the bone of that animal. He turned it in his hand, gripped it with a tight fist and flourished it aloft. Such a knife! Holding it was almost like touching Reindeer between the eyes. The Knife had a strong spirit of its own. To show his respect, Kerlew pointed it toward the flames and sang to it softly for a long time. Then he resheathed it and set it beside him.

He reached into the bag again, wondering what would be next. His reaching fingers brushed a smooth, cool surface. The red stone. He pulled it from the bag and considered it. He wondered if it was still angry at him, too. He rubbed it with his hands until it felt warm. The time Tillu had thrown it into the snow, it had been very cold and angry when he found it. Now it did not seem so angry. He held it between his palms and sang to it. It was an important talisman, and he didn't like it to be angry with him. The Blood Stone, Carp called it. Carp had shown him how to find it. It was the first sign of his power. That first day . . . Kerlew's brow wrinkled as he reached for the memory. It was such a long time ago, and everything before that time was like a long dream. Carp had wakened him from the dreaming time.

Yes. Carp had wakened him and made him stand up and walk with him, even though Kerlew's legs had been as bendy as the tips of willow boughs. The sunlight was too bright for his eyes, and he had kept touching his head to make sure it was still there. His neck had grown long and his head bobbed at the end of it. But he had felt very good, very fine indeed. And the important man, the shaman, Carp, had held his wrist and led him along. They had gone behind the tents into the hills. Kerlew had felt cold and light; he had feared the wind would blow him away. He had wondered where they were going.

Then they had come to a trampled place on the hillside. Carp had stopped him by a scatter of squashed berries. 'Here,' the old man had said. 'Look for it here.' Kerlew remembered squatting down on his heels and nearly falling over. He had wondered what the man wanted him to do. The shaman towered over him. 'Find it!' Carp had urged him. The man's eyes were serious, and Kerlew had cringed, fearful he would kick him.

But the expected blow had not come, and after a few moments Kerlew had cautiously run his fingertips over the scattered berries. He still didn't know what the shaman wanted, but sometimes they didn't hit you if you pretended to understand them. He let the berries sift through his fingers, peering up at Carp through his eyelashes to see if this pleased him. Was this what he wanted him to do? But the old man had only watched him.

When there were no more berries to handle, Kerlew had dragged his fingertips over the moss and leaves that coated the ground. He picked them up and looked curiously at them and again peered up at Carp. Did this please him? But the old man's face never changed. He stood over the boy and waited.

Kerlew had begun to feel dizzy and sick, but he dared not complain. Tillu was far away. She had gone to fetch water, he suddenly remembered, and she was gone when Carp had led him away. If Carp decided to kick and strike him, she was not there to make him stop. His lip jutted out and began to tremble. He had seen the bared earth through a shimmer of tears as his stubby nails dragged across it.

He had felt very ill then. The earth got far away, and then closer, and then far again. His fingernail caught on something, bent back painfully. Kerlew exclaimed at the hurt and heard the shaman's gasp of interest. The old man suddenly stooped down beside him, watched avidly as Kerlew's fingers pried the stone from the soil. Kerlew had picked it up, held it close to his face to look at it carefully. A tear had fallen onto its dirty surface, and the small drop let a sudden streak of red show through. 'Aahh!' Carp had sighed.

'Is this it?' Kerlew had asked, offering the stone to the old man. Maybe he would take it and leave him alone, let him crawl back to the tent. Maybe his mother would wrap him in a soft, warm hide and make warm, salty soup for him. He hoped.

But then the old man had leaped at him, had seized him in his wiry old arms and clutched him close. Kerlew's breath left him; he had no air to scream and he feared he would die now. But this man did not shake him or pinch him or throw him to the ground. The shaman only held him and muttered words of praise, then had helped him to rise and walk back to the tent. The shaman himself had taken the bowl of warm, salty broth his mother made and fed it to Kerlew and sat by him until he fell asleep holding the red stone.

Kerlew set the stone down reverently. The Knife and the Blood Stone. The two most important talismans in his pouch. Always they seemed to come forth together. Was the Knife asking for Blood? He shook his head perplexedly and wished Carp were here to advise him. He eased his hand into the pouch again. There was not much left in it, and he was not sure if the other items held power or not. He had picked them up because he felt drawn to them, and put them in his pouch because he could not bear to throw them away. There were few things that belonged exclusively to him. He parted with none of them willingly.

The withered but feathered foot of a ptarmigan. He had found it in a bloody patch of snow, amid the feathers that marked the fox's feast. He liked the way the toes were so tightly clutched, a bird fist, while the feathers were so soft still. He stroked it with a reverent fingertip and murmured to it before he set it with the other talismans.

148

Again into the bag. A wolverine's tooth. Tillu would be angry if she knew he had this. She had told him not to touch the dead wolverine when they found it tangled in some tree roots beside a stream. She said it had drowned. If it had drowned, why wasn't it still in the water, he had asked her. And she had said the water had carried the wolverine downstream and put it there. He had thought, and then asked her again, why wasn't it in the water, then? But she only said the same thing over again. Maybe Water-spirit had done it. Water-spirit might be strong enough to kill a wolverine and throw its body aside. Maybe his mother had been afraid Water-spirit would be angry if he touched her kill. Or maybe Tillu had just not wanted him to have the tooth. But he had crept back that night and gotten it. Alive or dead, Wolverine was a fierce spirit. To have one of his teeth might give Kerlew power over him. He rubbed his thumb along it, and then set it back beside the bird's foot.

The pouch was very light now. He tried to think what might still be in it, but could not. There were just too many things in it. He looked carefully over the many objects he had already taken out. There was the Knife, and the Stone, and the bird's foot, and the tooth, and the bird's foot, and the Stone. More than he could count. And there was still something inside the pouch. Something soft. He pulled out the puff of a rabbit's tail. From a rabbit that Tillu had brought home. He patted it softly against his face, feeling the small scratch of the tailbone still inside the fluff of fur. He sniffed it, smelling the smell of Rabbit, and again ran it lightly over his face. Reluctantly he put it down. He liked it. He hoped it had power.

He put his hand inside the pouch and ran his fingers carefully along the seams. Anything left? Yes!

149

It was wedged into the far corner of the bag. He picked it loose cautiously, wondering what it was. It was only when he brought it out into the light that he remembered.

The owl's nest had been wedged high in an old willow stump, on the far side of the dell. He had climbed up it one day when Tillu was hunting. In it he had found the remains of a nestling. He had known it was an owl's nest by the castings and feathers around it. But the tiny beakless skull had frightened and alarmed him. Men's skulls were not so different from this. He had left it in the nest, afraid to touch it. But whenever he saw the nest, he thought of the tiny, fragile skull. It drew him. And finally he had climbed the stump and taken it for his bag. These sockets had held the eyes. They were empty now, just a tracing of old flesh in them. Here the beak had been; he wondered what had become of it. Or what if it had never had a beak? What if it had never been an owl at all? A strange thrill ran through him and he nearly dropped it. Trembling, he placed it carefully among his other treasures. That this one had power he never doubted. Always it filled him with foreboding.

He gazed at his talismans, let the wonder of them fill him until the hair stood up on the back of his neck and prickled along his arms. There was a message here for him: Carp had told him that just by setting out the contents of his pouch, a shaman could learn many things. Again Kerlew's eyes roamed over his trinkets. The Knife, the Blood Stone, the bird's skull. The feathered claw, the rabbit's tail, the Blood Stone. His mind teetered on the edge of knowing all, understanding all. There was a pattern here. Knife wanted something done, something Bloody. And the bird's claw . . .

As rapidly as the ideas had built, they fell apart. He was cold, staring at the arrangement of articles in front of the

150

dying fire. The fire. Tillu would be very angry if he let the fire go out again. He would have to wait to eat if the fire went out. Hastily he scooped the items back into his pouch and returned it to the hollowed place beneath his pallet.

He brought an armload of wood from the pile by the door and tumbled it onto the embers and coals. It hissed, and steam and smoke rose from it chokingly and swirled up toward the smoke hole in the peak of the tent. Smoke. He wondered if Carp was still angry with him. Suddenly he had an idea. Taking the knife from his pouch, he went outside, to look for a good, thin willow wand to cut and peel. Maybe Carp wasn't angry at him anymore. Maybe this time Carp would speak to him.

NINE

It had started out as a journey to no place, a long walk, the pace set fast enough to make himself breathe through his mouth and make the sweat trickle down the back of his neck. Now he stood on the hill overlooking the little tent and looked down, wondering if he had been hurrying here, or hurrying away from the talvsit.

The question irritated him, and he glared down at the tent as if it were at fault. She should turn it, he thought to himself. Turn it so the entrance didn't face the prevailing wind, and she should stack her firewood in the lee of it so the snow wouldn't drift against it. And she should soften the seams with grease, and lace them tighter. She probably didn't think about things like that. There were so many things that could be done to give them an easier life. Simple, easy things. He didn't understand why it almost angered him to look down at the tent and see the things that needed to be done. The things that wouldn't be done.

He started down the hill, his boots breaking through the snow crust at each step. They probably weren't even at the tent, and if they were, what was his excuse for visiting? 'To tell them,' he muttered to himself. 'To let her know I'm to join with Elsa.' Glad news, he told himself, news a man should share with all. Did not all the talvsit buzz with it already? Did not every face smile at him and nod, full of the knowledge of his joining? Every soul he met asked him of it. When would the feast be, where would they build their hut, was he not glad to be getting such a strong and healthy woman? Was he not happy to leave his lonely days behind? Soon he would never need to hunt alone again, or sleep alone, or sit by himself of an evening. Soon Elsa would always be with him, sharing all the moments of his life. He took a deep breath, sucking in air as if he were drowning.

'Kerlew!' he called as the boy poked his head out of the tent. The boy turned his face toward the man, and the smile that dawned there was all a visitor could wish. 'Come in!' he called, his voice going shrill with excitement. 'Come in and visit me!'

He threw the tent door wide to the man's approach and stood barely out of the way to let Heckram enter. His fingers ran excitedly along Heckram's sleeve, daring to touch and then leaping away, like a shy puppy's sniffing. Heckram grinned down at him and put a hand on his shoulder, squeezed it firmly. The boy stood still under his grip, grinning back.

'This is how men greet one another,' he said suddenly, the words awkwardly turned, but the meaning clear. His thin hand reached up to pat Heckram's shoulder shyly. 'Welcome to my tent!' he said grandly and waved an inviting hand at the small fire.

'I thank you for the shelter,' Heckram replied formally, sensing the significance to the boy. He remembered that formless ache of boyhood, the needing to be seen as a man by other men after being 'Ristin's son' for too long. Doubtless Kerlew was tired of being 'the healer's boy.' He pulled his cap and mittens off, advanced to the small fire, and sat. Kerlew circled the fire and sat down facing him. The boy's grin faded slightly. They sat in a silence that threatened to become awkward. He knew nothing of dealing with people on his own, Heckram realized. No notion of how to talk to someone; his mother handled all that for them. Kerlew's smile was becoming desperate.

Heckram spoke, saying anything to help him. 'I thought I could come visiting today, to see how you and your mother were doing.'

'I do well. I keep the fire burning. Sometimes I make a spoon.' Kerlew paused, groping for more thoughts.

'And Tillu? How is she?' Heckram asked helpfully.

'She is fine. Fine. But Tillu isn't here.' Kerlew stopped abruptly, his face setting in a strange expression.

'Oh?' Heckram prodded gently, wondering what the problem was.

Kerlew looked into the fire, then aside into the shadowed corners of the tent. 'Gone hunting,' he mumbled, 'to get meat for us.'

'Oh,' Heckram repeated.

'I keep the fire going. If I went, too, the fire might go out. Or something bad might happen here.' The boy sounded on the verge of tears.

Understanding suddenly dawned within Heckram. He shifted on his heels, hesitated only a fraction of a moment. 'I wonder who will bring back the better kill,' he said slowly, his voice casual. 'Will it be Tillu, or' – he grinned wickedly, and the boy's eyes went wide as he finished – 'us?'

Kerlew had to take two breaths before he could ask, 'We hunt, you and I?'

Heckram nodded, all hesitation swept aside by the boy's eagerness. He was grateful that habit had put his bow on his back this morning. The boy's eyes clung to it.

'Get your bow, and dress warmly,' he told Kerlew, and wondered at the sudden fading of the light from the boy's face.

'Not a good day to hunt,' Kerlew said suddenly, addressing Heckram's boots. 'We wouldn't get anything. And I have other work to do. The fire. And a spoon.' The boy seemed to be pushing the words out one at a time, as if they were jammed in his throat. Heckram remembered suddenly the awkward way the boy had gripped his mother's knife, how she had brought out hide scrapers for the boy to carve with. His own chest tightened. Poor they might be, but no boy Kerlew's age should suffer that humiliation. No wonder the boy groped so desperately for manhood. Could not his mother see? He tried to think of the right way to say it, without making it worse.

'You could learn with mine,' he offered quietly, 'until we can make you a bow of your own.'

Kerlew stood very still and small. He stared into the fire when he spoke. 'If ever you need my life, I'll give it to you,' he offered in a tiny voice. He lifted his pale eyes to Heckram's face. Heckram nodded, knowing the offer was sincere. It was all Kerlew had to offer him.

'Let's hunt, then,' he said, and Kerlew sprang suddenly to life. The boy snatched up his boots. 'Dress warmly,' Heckram reminded him. 'We'll be gone all day. I'll bank the fire so it doesn't go out.'

'Doesn't matter!' Kerlew told him joyously. 'If it goes out, I can make another. Sometime I'll show you how.'

The sun on the snow was brighter than Heckram remembered

it, the air crisper, the sky more blue. Eagerness and inexperience made the boy clumsy, but Heckram was amazed at his own patience. He found good cover overlooking a game trail, and waiting for a rabbit became more engrossing than all the reindeer stalking he and Lasse had done all winter. The bow was hopelessly too large for Kerlew; Heckram had to draw it back and help Kerlew hold it steady. The boy exclaimed over Heckram's brightly stained and feathered arrows and had to examine every one in the quiver before he could decide which one to nock. Heckram blessed whatever spirit made the game move so well today. Of seven rabbits that came their way, they felled three, and made great fun of retrieving the other arrows that had gone wobbling off into the woods.

They spoke little, lest they scare the game, communicating with nudges and nods that made the boy's awkwardness with words unimportant. When the first rabbit fell, he let Kerlew retrieve it. The boy lifted it by the heavy deer arrow that had speared its entire body. He stared at it as if he had never seen a rabbit before. When he stood up, his shoulders straightened and he stood taller, his body opened in the light. His chin came up, and something kindled in his eyes. 'Tillu will see this soon!' was all he said. He came back to their cover to wait for the next rabbit; the smile did not leave his face again.

The sun was fading before they tired, and they walked back in the dimness, his hand on Kerlew's shoulder while the boy hugged his three rabbits to his chest. They said little as they walked back, both too busy imagining how Tillu would react to this magnificent feast. 'They're heavy rabbits,' Kerlew said once, 'very, very heavy.' Heckram knew better than to offer to carry them for him.

The wind was rising as they crested the last hill, and Tillu's voice rose up to them like the ululation of a she-wolf. 'Kerlew!' Her voice drew the name out and threw it to the wind, her hopelessness riding the dark breath of the night. The pain in it split Heckram's soul; it was the cry of a woman who had lost her everything. 'Coming! We're coming!' he roared into the night, and hurried, pushing her son on before him.

They came out of the darkness and she stared at the large silhouette that walked beside her son. Relief flooded her and she rushed to meet them, throwing her arms around Kerlew with a glad cry. He shrugged her off with an embarrassed exclamation. She did not even notice the rabbits in his arms. 'Where have you been?' she demanded of him, and then of Heckram, 'Where did you find him?' She looked down at her son, at the wide grin on his face despite the worry and fears she had endured. Anger rose in her, that he would wander off on his own, and make Heckram interrupt his hunting to bring the boy back. 'Why did you go off like that?' she scolded. 'Do you think I have nothing to do besides worry about you? Do you think Heckram has nothing better to do than look after you? You know you should not leave the tent when I am gone! What if Heckram had not found you and brought you home?'

Kerlew's triumph melted in humiliation. He stood speechless before her growing anger, his worthless rabbits clutched to his chest. Heckram put his arm around him, squeezed the boy's unresisting shoulder. 'We went hunting,' he told Tillu, amazed at the defiance he heard in his own voice.

'I would think you would have asked before you took my son from my tent,' Tillu snapped back. 'You left no sign,

157

nothing! I have searched and called until my voice was hoarse! You had no right to take him without asking me.'

'Kerlew wanted to go,' Heckram defended himself, the woman's words suddenly understandable to him as never before, though their accent remained strange. 'And he hunted well.'

'He is not old enough to decide such things for himself. Is it your custom to take a woman's child from her tent, and make no word to her about it?'

'Is it your custom for a mother to humiliate her son before his friend, instead of rejoicing over his first kill? The boy did well! It is time he learned to hunt!'

'That is not for you to decide! You don't know Kerlew, he is not like other boys! He is –'

'Gone,' Heckram pointed out to her.

It was true. Kerlew had discarded his rabbits in a pathetic heap at her feet and disappeared into the tent. Tillu stood staring down at them silently for a long moment. Embarrassment flooded her face with warmth. How could she have quarreled with a stranger over her own child, admitted to him that Kerlew needed constant supervision? How dare he pity them and make excuses for her son to her. She glared at the meat he had brought. 'You don't have to hunt for us,' she pointed out coldly. 'I can get the meat we need. And I can take care of my own son. Take your rabbits and go.'

'They aren't mine!' Heckram longed to shake her, and the urge echoed in his voice. 'Kerlew shot them. Every one of them. To please you. To be a man. Why do you treat him so badly? Why doesn't the boy have a bow, why do you keep him like a baby? Don't you want him to grow to be a man?'

Tillu sank down slowly, almost collapsing in the snow. She lay her mittened hand on the soft fur of the dead rabbits. 'He really killed these?' she asked, disbelief still strong in her voice. Heckram nodded silently. 'My son can hunt.' She said the words aloud, but Heckram knew they were not for him. They were spoken to herself, in a voice full of wonder and thankfulness. She looked up at him, her eyes shining wetly. 'His first kill.' She paused. Her face clouded as she realized what she had said and done. 'I was so worried,' she said softly. 'So frightened.' She glanced up at him, her eyes dark. 'I'm sorry.'

He shook his head, refusing the apology. 'Tell Kerlew that. I should tell you I am sorry, for taking him in such a way. I meant no harm.' Now that the quarrel was ending, Heckram felt suddenly abashed at the frankness of his earlier words. Who was he, to interfere between Tillu and her son? 'I should go back to the talvsit. It is late.'

'No!' The vehemence in Tillu's voice surprised him. She gathered up the rabbits, cradling them like babies. 'Please,' she said in a softer voice. 'I've all but ruined it for him. Stay and watch me skin out his kill. Eat with us. Celebrate with him.'

'Any mother would have been worried. I was a fool to take him off that way, leaving no sign for you.' His own behavior suddenly seemed reprehensible. 'I should have asked you first.'

'No. No. I am always telling myself, if only the boy would do something on his own, if only he would decide for himself, then I would know there is hope for him. Then, the first time he does, I scold him and humiliate him. I've spoiled it for him, his hunt and his first kill.'

Hope for him. Heckram could not understand the anguish

159

in her voice. How could she expect the boy to learn, if no one taught him? How could she love him so much, and understand him so little? Aloud, he asked, 'How did your own hunting go?'

She shrugged to his question. 'A couple of ptarmigan.'

'Only two?'

She nodded, perplexed.

'Then all is well, still.' He lifted his voice. 'Kerlew! Come out and help with the rabbits. It is as I told you! We two have hunted much better than Tillu. Your kill is three to her two! Kerlew! Hurry! Or do you think I will carry all these rabbits myself?'

The boy's hesitancy was painful to watch. He came forward cautiously, his shoulders hunched as if he feared them both. It was only when Tillu stepped aside that he dared come close to Heckram. The rabbits lay in the snow where Tillu had placed them. His eyes darted from the rabbits to Heckram and finally to Tillu.

'It's a very good kill,' she said softly.

He only looked at her. She lifted her eyes to Heckram, and then met her son's stare. 'Better than mine. All I brought down was two skinny birds. But you, you have brought home all this meat on your first hunt.' Suddenly she straightened, standing braver in the night. 'See how well my son hunts!' she exclaimed to Heckram. The pride in her voice rang true. 'Soon it will be, not rabbits, but fat deer he brings. The fat will sizzle over the fire, and all will smell its richness.'

A portion of his earlier triumph came back to the boy's face. He lifted the rabbits slowly, hefted them in his arms. 'Come into our tent,' he told Heckram grandly. 'My mother will cook my kill, and we two hunters will eat well tonight.'

Kerlew led the way to the tent and Heckram followed.

He had to stoop to enter, and the light from the lamp struck a bronze sheen in his dark hair. The flap fell behind them, and Tillu stood alone in the dark. Had that been her son, speaking so well, standing almost straight? Had he really killed those rabbits, or had he only shared Heckram's hunt? She shook her head, and the question suddenly seemed to matter less than the question of why Heckram would take her son hunting. And then defend the boy from her own hasty judgment. And salvage the boy's triumph from her thoughtless humiliation of him.

Their voices reached her from within the tent, Kerlew's higher as he replied to something the man had said, and then their voices merging in a shout of laughter. I could walk away into the night, she thought. I would walk away and leave my son with him, and he would do well by the boy. I could not let Carp take my son. But I could give Kerlew to this Heckram and not regret it.

The tent flap lifted again, light spilling out. 'Come inside,' Kerlew called impatiently. 'Share my meat and Heckram's news. He is taking a woman soon, that Elsa. Is he not a lucky man?' He darted back inside without awaiting her reply.

'Is she not a lucky woman?' Tillu asked softly, then frowned over her words. She walked back to the tent she shared with her son.

TEN

'Mother?'

The pain in Heckram's voice jerked Ristin's attention from the tent hide she was piercing for lacing. He shadowed the door of the sod hut, the day bright behind him. She squinted her eyes against the glare, and he stepped in, letting the flap fall behind him. He looked stricken. In that moment she knew what he would look like as a corpse. It frightened her.

She tried not to show it. 'That's a long face for the man whose betrothal gathering is but five nights away.' She patted the hide on her lap. 'I've nearly finished boring the holes. Elsa has the sinew ready for the lacing. If you'd but make the time to cut and trim poles for it, this tent could be finished by nightfall. Or are you having second thoughts?'

As if he had ever had the first thought about this joining. He smiled a sickly smile. 'On the contrary. I've just decided to slaughter my fattest harke for the feast. Care to help me with the butchering?'

She stared at him in consternation, knowing full well that he grudged slaughtering any of his animals, let alone his

162

heaviest reindeer ox. 'But I thought you were going hunting for meat . . .' she began faintly.

'So I was, but something's saved me the trouble. It's Bruk. He'll have to be butchered. I'd like some help.'

Ristin stood abruptly, letting the bone awl and heavy leather hide slip from her lap. Without words she followed him out of the sod house and behind it, into the area where their pulkor harkar were hobbled. The sun was bright against the snow, but the air was cold. Ristin wrapped her arms around herself, wishing that she had paused to pull on her outdoor tunic. The back of winter was broken, and the light stretched longer with every day, but that did not mean that the true thaw of spring had begun. She hastened to match her son's long stride, straining to hear his muttered words.

'I was going to harness Bruk up and drive the pulkor over to the healer's. I wanted to invite her and the boy to the betrothal feast. But when I came out here –'

Heckram gestured.

Ristin's two harkar had wandered up to the edge of the woods and were busily pawing up the snow in their search for lichen. The rest of their animals grazed higher in the hills with the main herd. Those two harness harkar and Bruk were kept close by the hut for convenience. Bruk was a prime animal, weighing twice as much as her tall son, even if the harke's shoulders came but chest high on the man. Bruk's coat was sleek, and his neck and haunches rippled with muscle. He could carry his own weight in a pack load, or pull a loaded sledge all day without faltering. Heckram had broken him to harness two years ago when Bruk was a feisty three-year-old. Now he was as responsive an animal as any herder could wish for, healthy and strong, with a long life of usefulness ahead of him. Ristin could not think of a possession her son valued more.

But the harke was down in the snow, not browsing with the others. He rested now, but his sides heaved as if he had run all night. Then, as Ristin watched, the reindeer heaved itself up on its front legs. Panting and grunting, it struggled to rise. But his hind legs were limp and useless, remaining bent in the snow. He sagged back into the pawed snow around him, his exhaustion evident, and sounded his distress with coughing grunts.

'What's wrong with him?' Ristin demanded, fearing some new disease. She made no move to approach.

'His hock tendons are severed. Something did it in the night.' Heckram was keeping his voice carefully neutral, but Ristin knew the effort it cost him. Bruk represented the work of years, had been Heckram's sturdiest and best harke. Now he was useless for anything but meat. It was a staggering blow to a man considering marriage.

And an inconceivable accident. 'But how?' Ristin demanded, her voice rising with her outrage. 'No wolverine kills that way. A bear mauls. A wolf might hamstring a wild reindeer. But any predator would have killed and fed before it left. And we heard nothing last night.'

'Bruk was used to people. He probably just stood there, expecting the harness.' As Heckram spoke he moved closer to the panicky animal. He placed a gentling hand on his shoulder, and Bruk turned puzzled eyes to his master. 'Steady, fellow,' Heckram comforted him. He moved in closer to Bruk as the wearied animal let his head sink, calming him with his touch and soothing words. Then Heckram sank his knife in, a straight swift blow to the heart. He gave a practiced twist to the blade and left it in the wound. Bruk gave one startled bellow, then slowly foundered into the trampled snow. Little blood escaped from the wound. It was the herdfolk's way of killing a meat animal. The blood would collect in the chest cavity to congeal, then to be scooped out with birch scoops by the butchers and made into blood sausage.

Ristin, hardened as she was to butchering time, flinched as the knife went in. She was silent as a final shudder ran through Bruk's heavy shoulders.

'Who would do such a thing?' she wondered aloud in a choked voice. 'Have you reported it to Capiam? He should come and see this before we butcher, to witness the truth of what we say. Whoever did this must be brought before the herdlord!'

'No.' Heckram spoke softly but firmly. He knelt down in the snow beside the fallen animal. His knife haft stuck up from the dead beast, but he stroked the fur on its side as if it would take comfort from his touch. 'No, I have told only you. Nor shall we. Think about it, mother. Has Capiam sent word of his congratulations on my betrothal? Has he sent a gift of food, or offered one for the feast? Who has? Lasse's grandmother, of course. Rilk, and Reynor, Trode and Lanta, Jakke. Ibb and Bror. All of them folk living as close to the edge as we do. Those who could spare it the least have sent the most. And those who wallow in food, and feed their dogs what our children would be glad for? They have sent nothing, no word, no gift, no sign.

'So shall I give them the satisfaction of watching me run to Capiam, bemoaning the loss of one animal and crying out for justice? No. There would be no justice, only satisfaction for whoever did it. He would know his blow had hurt. So. We shall have a butchering instead. You and I. Our finest harke, to honor Elsa and her family. Bruk will be a bit tough.

He wasn't young, and he was struggling for a long time before I even found him. But there will be plenty of him, and it will speak well of our opinion of Elsa and her family.' He ran his hand again over the shining hair. 'He'll make a nice bedhide for Elsa.'

'Shall I ask Lasse if he will help?' Ristin asked softly.

'Not yet,' Heckram replied. 'Later. After he can no longer tell the hind tendons were cut before the animal died. I want no word of complaint from us or on our behalf. Perhaps someone will be cocky enough to betray himself.'

'You suspect Joboam.' It was a statement, not a query. 'Are you going to tell Elsa?'

'No.'

'You mean later.'

'I mean no. These are supposed to be happy days for her. I won't have our betrothal degraded by worry and fear. Besides, wouldn't it spoil the effect of my slaughtering a harke if she knew I had to?' He gave his mother a wolfish grin. 'Let me keep credit for the act in the eyes of my wife-to-be.'

'Heckram, it's a poor way to start out, with secrets and hidden worries.'

'Don't scold me about it, for I didn't choose it.'

'Hmph.' His mother rose from crouching beside him. 'I'll bring the skinning knives. Doesn't look very fat, does he?'

'Not as fat as he was two months ago. But better than anything else I've got set by. Better than a wild reindeer. Poor Bruk.'

A note in his voice turned Ristin back to him. 'Heckram. If you aren't going to seek justice before Capiam, then you must let it go. There is no other way; not among our people. Such is our tradition.'

'New traditions are starting up everywhere, Ristin. Hamstringing the bridegroom's best harke before his betrothal feast, harassing a woman with your attentions because her family is not as wealthy as yours . . . I may start a few traditions of my own.'

Ristin looked her contempt for the idea. 'Are you a man, or a little boy? So do children speak, threatening one another, rolling and tussling in the dirt as if that would prove who is wrong or right. Are you from some forest tribe, where they kill their own folk, and maim one another in their brawlings? No! We are herdfolk. Men do not kill men! If someone becomes so degraded that we cannot let him live among us, we drive him away, and that is punishment enough. Act like a savage, and you shame me, and your father's memory. And you will be the one driven away from the herdfolk.'

Heckram only stared at the fallen harke, silent but unrepentant of his words. Ristin sensed the depth of his anger and came to stand beside him. She spoke more gently. 'You never told me how Joboam reacted when you told him that Elsa was promised to you.'

'There was nothing to tell. I didn't confront him to shame him, though now I wish I had. I thought it better to treat the matter as if nothing were amiss. For the sake of Elsa's pride, more than his. I waited for a time that seemed fitting. A group of hunters had just returned, Joboam among them. They were standing about, comparing kills for the day. I walked up to them and said, "I have fared better than any of you at the hunt today, for Elsa has set a date for our betrothal feast." Some of them wished me joy. Amma, joker that he is, wondered aloud if I were the hunter or the prey. Some said nothing, but turned away to speak of other matters. Joboam glared at me, then turned aside. There was nothing said.'

'It's like him, to slink about like a heel-biting dog. You've a bad enemy there, Heckram. One who has the ear of the herdlord.'

Heckram grunted. 'Well, if he has the herdlord's ear, let him have Capiam's daughter as well. I've heard she's not happy with the mate she'll take this summer by the Cataclysm. So let her have Joboam instead.'

'You shouldn't listen to such gossip. Kari but pretends reluctance, to be seen as more maidenly. As I recall, there was talk of pairing her with Joboam, several years ago. But nothing came of it.'

'I shouldn't listen to gossip? Listen to you. If you must tell it, at least get it right.' Heckram had drawn his blade of polished flint, the legacy of his father. He began a careful incision at the animal's anus, working carefully up the belly to avoid puncturing the gut sac and spilling bile and waste on the meat inside. 'Joboam wouldn't have her. He made his excuses pretty ones, but that's what it came down to. Pirtsi only took her to get a place at Capiam's side. The girl is feckless as a late-born calf, and fey besides. She's always either weeping or moping. Pretty as she is, who'd want to share a hearth with that?'

'And Pirtsi is such a man as should make any woman's heart leap?' Ristin asked sarcastically. 'When he isn't strutting like a marsh-bird in spring, he's rutting with any woman foolish enough to accept him. It cannot make Kari proud to hear such things of the man she will join this spring.'

'I thought she was but pretending maidenly reluctance?' Heckram asked. His incision inched up Bruk's hairy belly. He pulled the knife free, wiped clinging hair and blood from it against his pant leg, and then eased it back into its groove. 'They'll make a fine pair, no doubt. She can weep when he comes near her, and mope when he does not.'

Ristin rose slowly, her knee joints crackling. 'I'll bring the knives,' she repeated, ignoring his comments. But as she went she called back over her shoulder, 'Unless one knows a person's sorrows, one can't sympathize. But one shouldn't assume that misery is groundless, either.'

The hide pulled up, parting from the meat as the integuments beneath it gave way with a ripping sound. Occasionally the knife licked in, to slice across a stubborn bit. But skinning the animal was more a matter of pulling the hide free than of cutting it off. 'See? You keep the tension steady and slice along under the skin as you need to. That way you get a hide without holes, and no big chunks of meat stuck to it that have to be scraped off later. See? You only use the knife where you have to. When you get to the tail . . . *Kerlew!*'

The boy's head jerked around and he pulled his bloody fingers quickly from the dead calf's mouth. 'What?' he asked his mother, shifting nervously.

'Why aren't you paying attention? You need to learn how to skin an animal, so you can hunt and prepare your own meat. What were you doing, anyway?'

'Nothing,' the boy answered guiltily. 'Here, I'll do it now.'

He drew his own blade, the one Heckram had given him. Rising, he took a firm grip on the loosened flap of hide and tugged it upward. The membranous layer that held the hide to the meat stretched tight. It was transparent stuff, bubbly and clear as froth to look at, but sticky and clinging to bare hands. As the boy pulled harder, some parted with a ripping sound. The inside of the hide was creamy white and slick-looking. The meat was covered with thinly transparent integument, the functional lines of muscle bared to curious eyes. The naked animal was purple and white and deep red.

The hide clung at a stubborn place. Kerlew reached down with his blade and, with a slashing stab, ripped a gaping hole in the hide.

The boy froze, staring at the damage. Tillu expelled a long sigh. 'It's all right,' she forced herself to say. 'You're learning. Next time, make your knife follow the curve of the animal's body. Cut close to the meat, not the skin. Keep trying. But don't pull on the hide at the weak spot now, or it will rip further. Go to a different place and work from there.'

The warm smell of the fresh kill filled the air. Tillu had already rolled the gut sac clear of the body. Watching Kerlew's knifework, she was glad she hadn't allowed him to help with that part. One puncture of the gut sac could impart a rank flavor to the whole animal. Once the hide was off, she would butcher the calf into manageable pieces, and then they could lug it home.

She gritted her teeth as she watched Kerlew skinning. He pierced the precious hide again, but she kept silent. She watched it peeling back from the calf, creamy white where she had worked, marred with slices and gobs of red meat where Kerlew's knife cut through flesh instead of joining tissue. Scraping the hide would be a real task. But the boy had to learn. And he didn't learn as other children did, by watching and absorbing. Kerlew could watch her brew herbal tea a thousand times. Yet the first time she had told him to prepare a tea, he had dropped the leaves into cold water and then put it over a fire, instead of letting the water boil and then putting in the herbs to steep.

He tried. Tillu knew he tried and wished it were enough. But it wasn't. A man could die of cold trying to light a fire, starve to death trying to kill a rabbit. Kerlew had to do better than just try. Only days ago, when he had returned from his hunt with Heckram, she had been filled with hope. Her son, her Kerlew, had hunted and made a successful kill. But like his single triumph with the fire, it was an isolated incident, a single success in a row of failures. His memory was like a torn fishing net, now holding the catch, now letting it slip away. He could fetch the water, bring the wood, build up the fire. But if she told him to fetch wood to build up the fire, and bring water to heat for stew, he would lose track of his tasks. Later she would find the water bucket by the firewood stack. At her angry shout, Kerlew would rise from watching a swirl of leaves in the stream, to innocently ask her when food would be ready. Yet he could recite Carp's tales word for word, or casually ask her what she had meant by something she had said months ago.

Beating him did no good. When they were both much younger, she would strike him for such failures, believing him lazy or simply disobedient. She was girlishly envious of other women's handsome, bright-eyed children. She had wanted desperately for Kerlew to be quick-witted, or agile, or sweetly obedient. She had longed to feel proud of him.

Instead she heard the mockery of other children when the little boy spoke his halting words, and the commiserating words of other women for her misfortune that her only child was a half-wit. She would angrily deny it and set him to some task. He would fail. Shamed and angered, she would strike him. Then he would weep helplessly, baffled by the punishment, for he could not remember having done wrong.

The sight of his small frightened face, running tears, would shame her. And her own soul would rise to smite her when she reached to comfort him and he cringed from the hands that had so recently brought him pain, or else stiffened and struggled against her repentant embrace. Eventually she had stopped slapping him or pushing him down to sprawl in the dirt; it did neither of them any good. Folk only laughed at both of them, or turned aside with embarrassed faces. She had grown out of being a child with a damaged doll. Instead she had begun to accept that he did not learn as other children did. But learn he must, and so a new way must be found.

So now she crouched by the dead calf, her chilled feet going numb in the snow, and watched patiently as he mangled the hide away from the body. The luck that had brought them this calf, alone and bawling for its mother, would not be likely to bring them another. It had been exhausted, staggering through the snow. Tillu surmised that its mother had been killed by a glutton. The clever wolverine would wait until the reindeer had its head deep in the hole it had pawed in the snow, nipping up the buried reindeer moss. The deeper the snow, the easier it was for the glutton to rush in and sink its teeth into the tender throat of the grazing animal. Tillu had come across the traces of several such kills in recent days. She had brought home a trove of red-rimmed bones from such scenes, to stew into broth and crack for the marrow within. This calf, smaller than most she had seen, had probably fled from such a slaughter. Only to stumble into Tillu as she hunted, to be stunned with a broken branch and have its throat cut. She didn't regret it. Whatever gods or spirits reigned over these forested hills, they made no distinction between Kerlew and the orphaned calf. So Tillu had chosen for them which creature would survive the winter. And fetched the boy to help with the skinning and packing.

Kerlew paused in his skinning to scratch busily at his cheek. His fingers left red streaks on his face. He had bloodied the knees of his trousers and the cuffs of his coat.

'I'll take a turn now,' Tillu offered. After a moment's

frowning pause, the boy nodded. He stood up, his face set seriously. It was so conscious an expression of maturity that she had to smile at him. He was a good boy, and she did love him so. There were moments, times when he tried and things were well between them, when her heart swelled with love for him. At those moments the future seemed bright and their troubles behind them. She nodded at him now and said, 'You did very good work, for your first time at skinning.'

'I know,' he replied. He touched the hilt of his knife proudly. 'I can do many things. I can carve spoons and make a fire. I can kill rabbits and skin animals. I am more of a man than you know.'

'Men don't boast,' Tillu observed shortly.

Kerlew merely stroked the hilt of his knife, unabashed by her rebuke. She sighed.

'While I skin,' she suggested, 'you carry home the basket. Be careful with it.' She nodded to a dripping basket that had melted deep in the snow beside them. It was heavy with the liver, tongue, heart, and kidneys of the small calf. 'When you get to the tent,' she went on, 'add wood to the fire, so it won't go out before we get back. Then be sure to come right back here, to help me carry the meat home. Can you remember all that?'

The boy nodded vigorously. 'What do you think, that I'm a baby still?' He frowned suddenly, his close-set eyes worried beneath his knit brows. But he slowly repeated, 'I'll take the meat home, build up the fire again, and come right back.'

'Go, then.' Tillu smiled. 'Hurry, but do not spill the meat.'

She watched him trudge away, the pack basket leaving a dripping red trail behind him. The boy was growing fast and well now. Perhaps this was what he had always needed; a chance to be alone with her, for her to concentrate on teaching him.

173

And a chance to learn a man's skills from a man like Heckram. She shook her head. Kerlew could learn from anyone who took time with him. That was all that proved. Now that Heckram was taking a woman, they would see less of the man. But she didn't care. She could take care of herself and her son, teach him all he needed to know. Kerlew was going to be fine, just fine. She smiled to herself. Her son. Soon he would be the man he claimed to be. He would make his own decisions, take his own actions, live his own life. And then? And then could she live her own life as well? She snorted with derision at the thought. She did well enough on her own. She bent back over the animal, pulling firmly on the hide as she carefully sliced it free.

When the hide was clear, she rolled it up, skin side out, and set it aside. She set about dividing the calf up into manageable parts. It would have been more difficult with a larger animal. But even her poor knife could work through the calf's flesh and muscles. She dislocated the legs at the major joints and cut between the ball and socket to break the animal down into four quarters, along with torso and head.

By the time she was finished with the heaviest work, the sun was skimming the horizon. She was sweating inside her tunic, but knew the foolishness of setting it aside. The sweat would chill on her body, and she would start shivering her way into a deadly chill. Better to sweat and keep moving than risk that. She stared a long moment down the trail, expecting Kerlew. But there was no sign of him yet. Perhaps it hadn't really been as long as it seemed. Perhaps he had stopped to eat something at the tent before coming back. The basket was heavy. He would stop to rest, so it would take him a long time to lug it home. She stooped to cut a fine slice of red meat from the calf. She bit off a piece of it, feeling the fresh blood tingle deliciously on her tongue. She finished it quickly, and another slice more slowly. Where was the boy? Well, she wouldn't waste time waiting for him.

With a sigh she turned to the gut sac. She separated the intestines and stripped the dung from them with her fingers. Cleaned, they had a hundred uses. She sorted out gobs of suet and set them in a pile. A slash of her knife separated the stomach, and she emptied its contents into the snow. It became a container for the tallow bits. She would leave little for the ravens to clean up. She straightened a moment, rubbing at her aching back, and then returned to her task. By the time Kerlew got back, she would be finished.

Later, when the shadows of evening had changed from blue to black on the snow, and she could no longer see the colors of the forest, she wedged most of the meat into the crotch of a nearby tree. She hoped no scavengers would find it before she could return. She rolled one hindquarter into the hide that was now stiff with frost and hefted it slowly to her shoulders. Her back ached from bending over her work, her feet ached with the cold, and the skin of her face stung with night's rising wind. She ignored the ache in her heart and the sting of tears that threatened her eyes. Once more she buried her knowledge that Kerlew would never be all right, would never be a fine and laughing young man proudly bringing home a kill. The snow dragged at her feet as she trudged home under her burden.

ELEVEN

The questing tongues of fire popped the sap pocket under the bark of the pine log and crackled suddenly into reaching flames. Heckram opened his eyes to the new light. It felt earlier than their usual rising time, but Ristin was already up, sitting beside the hearth, a cup of tea in her hands. His eyes met hers, and hers suddenly brightened with moisture before she could turn away from him. He rubbed at his face, self-conscious at having caught her watching him sleep.

'Is something wrong?' he asked, his voice still thick with drowsiness.

'No. No, everything is right. I was just thinking it was the last morning that my son would wake up in my home. Tomorrow I will wake up alone. And every day after that.' Her voice tightened as she spoke, and she didn't look at him.

Heckram rubbed at his face wearily, feeling the new stubble scratchy against his palms. He didn't release the sigh coiled inside his chest. Mastering his own reluctance had been difficult enough. He didn't think he could contend with Ristin's new doubts as well. 'Isn't that what you wanted? It seems to me that I've been told any number of times that I should be in my own home, fathering grandchildren for your entertainment. So I finally take your advice, and wake up to find you weeping at me.'

Ristin gave a short, high laugh and then sobbed. She turned to him, her smile showing between the tears that damped her cheeks. 'I am glad for you. So glad, and so pleased that it is Elsa with you. I don't weep for your joining. Only for the changes it will bring. We old people always weep for the change times: for births, and deaths, for joinings and sunderings. They are the proper times for these tears.'

'Old people!' Heckram scoffed at her. He threw back the coverings and rose from his pallet. 'Tell that to the foxes you brought down yesterday!'

'It's not the things you can do that mark your age. It's the things you find you can't do any longer.'

Heckram looked at her sharply, weighing the regrets in her voice. He tried to see her as a stranger, but could not. Ristin was Ristin. A little thinner perhaps, the lines around her eyes more numerous, the joints and knuckles of her hands more apparent, but still capable Ristin. He refused to indulge her melancholy.

'Are you saying you're too old to help build a talvsit hut for Elsa and me?' he asked innocently. 'I suppose I could ask Lasse's grandmother to fill in for you . . .'

'What do you . . . ? You puppy! Don't make mock of your mother's years. I'm not as old as that yet. Get out of bed now. I've cooked for you this morning; maybe the last time I ever shall – not that I regret that! You get up and eat, and pack in water to wash yourself. The least I can do for Elsa is see that she finds you clean, though why she'd want you at all is more than I can understand. Out of there now,

177

you great lout! You've a sod house to build today, and a woman to claim.'

She took down her tunic from its hook as she spoke and dragged it on. She smiled at him as she left the hut, and Heckram found himself grinning in reply. But after she was gone, he found the smile fading from his face. A heaviness weighed on his heart as he clambered to his feet and went over to the cookfire. Today, in the construction of a sod hut, he would be laying a formal claim on Elsa. They would begin their life together today, even if the joining was not formally recognized until they had announced it before the gathering of all the herdfolk at the Cataclysm. He glanced about the smoke-darkened walls of his mother's hut, suddenly sharing her recognition that he would no longer wake up here, no longer share her fire and food. Changes. She would be living alone, and he would live with Elsa.

Resisting the temptation to burrow back into his bedskins, he stretched and then inspected the cooking pots. A porridge of meat and grain was bubbling thickly at the edge of the hearth. Set away from the embers to steep was a pot of herb tea. He dipped a mug carved from knurled birch into the pot and then sipped noisily at the steaming tea. The hot liquid cut the night thickness from his throat and cleared his head of useless regrets.

He ate quickly and as he dressed he tried to recover his acceptance of the situation. Yesterday he had borrowed his mother's young harke on the excuse it needed further training, and had harnessed it to his pulkor and driven off into the forest. The sledge moved well over the snow, the young animal pulled almost willingly, and his head was free of the chatter of the other herdfolk. He had pondered, his eyes unseeing as he guided the pulkor around and between obstacles. He had thought of Elsa, mostly. His knees did not quake with lust at the thought of her; she did not fill his chest with sighs. He had always felt a satisfaction in their friendship, a comfort in her steadiness. He wondered if it would be enough for her. Or for him. He could think of no other herdwoman he found more attractive. She lacked no skills that a woman should have. She was not dull-witted, nor subservient. She had spirit, spirit he admired. And she had courage; not only the courage to resist Joboam's advances, but also to come to him and speak plainly. And she wanted him. Surely that should count for something. He'd heard of women wedded and bedded reluctantly. She would not come to him grudgingly. She could have had a wealthy man, rich in reindeer and bronze tools, a man who would have decked her in amber and bronze and ivory. She had preferred him.

He realized belatedly that three times he had approached and then turned aside from the path that led to the healer's tent. He wanted to go see Kerlew, wanted to see the boy's face light with excitement, wanted to take him driving in a pulkor. He was sure the boy had never seen one. Nor his mother. But Tillu would not light up as the boy did at the sight of him. Tillu would be like the fox watching her cub play. Watchful, ever watchful of harm to her young. So fierce a little woman she was; how she had scolded him for taking Kerlew that day. And when she realized her error, how her face had softened and filled with her love for her son. Ristin was like that over me, he mused to himself. She's a fine mother to the boy. They can take care of themselves; she's right about that. He turned his mind and his harke away from them.

He returned from his long drive as the sun was setting. He was still not in love, but he was not unappreciative of

179

the woman who was giving herself to him. Nor could he deny the stirrings of desire in the base of his belly when he thought of her. He had set his doubts and reluctance aside, resolving to face his obligations. His dreams of the trading villages to the south and the strange lands beyond them were but fancies for a child. Something he had used to soften the harsh realities when he was too young to do anything else about them. Now he was a man, about to take Elsa to wife. He would have other things to think about.

As he dragged on his boots and laced them, he thought again of his decision not to invite the healer and her son. He would have liked them to come. He would have enjoyed watching Tillu watch the people, enjoyed letting Kerlew eat until he was filled. And perhaps she would have spoken to him of the folk she had traveled among. She looked like no people he had ever met. Her appearance was almost as outlandish as his own. But he did not think Elsa would share his enthusiasm for tales of far places, or enjoy the healer taking the attention of the herdfolk away from her betrothal ceremony. Another time, he mentally promised Kerlew and himself. Another time.

Taking up the buckets, he left the hut and went to the spring. Early as it was, the herdfolk were up and about, the talvsit humming with suppressed energy. Heckram was greeted with smiles and knowing nods on his way to the spring. The morning was clear and, though cold, there was a softness in the air that was the early breath of spring. He went down on one knee to fill the buckets, then started back to the hut. He stopped once by Lasse's hut, to get a fresh grip on the wet handles and to incidentally inspect an area beyond the hut that had been swept clear of snow. Yesterday he and Lasse had paced it off. The youth had helped him sweep the snow from the ground with pine boughs and then scrape away a layer of frozen moss and turf. The circle of bare brown earth waited now, looking empty amid the snowy clearing. Stina would be a good neighbor, they were not far from the spring, and there would be good grazing for a pack harke or two behind the hut. It was a good site for a home.

He lifted the buckets again and set out for Ristin's hut. Bror was standing before his own hut, yawning and stretching in the thin daylight. He grinned when he saw Heckram.

'You've a bit of work before you today, young man.'

'A bit,' Heckram conceded with a smile.

'Just remember not to weary yourself too much, if you take my meaning. Stout walls alone won't warm a new hut properly. What's the water for?'

'Bath. And shave my face. I've never minded my grand-father's height, but did he have to pass on his whiskers as well?'

Bror, like most of the herdfolk, was smooth-faced, save for a few fine black hairs on his upper lip. These he stroked as he nodded again at Heckram. 'If it were me, I wouldn't take a bath this time of year, woman or no. A man can get his death-sickness from wet skin in winter. Wait until spring, when the water runs noisy in the streams. That's the time for bathing. A bit of steam, a little oil on your skin to smooth it; that should be enough for any girl. You don't want to spoil her, do you?' Bror scratched energetically at the back of his neck.

Ibba poked her head from the hut to make a wry face at both men. 'Spoil her, Heckram, spoil her. Or you'll be sitting still, as Bror must now, while your poor wife picks the nits from your scalp. Get in here, you old gossip. Heckram has no time to stand and work his mouth today. He's a hut to build and a woman to claim. Get along, Heckram. And scrub the back of your neck well!'

He grinned his farewells as Ibba seized Bror's hand and tugged the old man, protesting, into his hut. He continued to smile as he made his way up the trail between the huts of the herdfolk to Ristin's hut. The mood was infectious. He was beginning to feel as a man should on the day he built his talvsit hut. Anticipatory and glad. He found he was singing softly, one of the long, almost wordless joiks of his people, timing his words to the squeak-crunch of the packed snow beneath his boots. The deep timbre of his voice made it little more than a pleasant rumble under his breath.

'So merry the bridegroom.'

The hard cold voice was like a dash of water in his face. Heckram had been looking at little more than the snowy path before him. As the too familiar voice broke his thoughts, he set the buckets down to either side of himself and casually rolled his shoulders to loosen the muscles. He glanced briefly at Joboam, who leaned against an upturned pulkor beside the path.

'Have you come to wish me luck in my joining with Elsa, Joboam?' he asked pleasantly.

'Would luck be enough, I wonder? It takes more than luck to keep a woman contented and at home. Remember, between now and the Cataclysm, she is still free to leave you without a word. Many's the woman who has joined a man, to find she didn't want to make the arrangement permanent.'

Joboam rose slowly and gave an elaborate stretch. The powerful muscles in his neck and shoulders cracked as he rolled them. Heckram lifted his chin to keep them eye to eye. Joboam was taller than he was, and broader, his muscular build coated with a layer of hard flesh. In contrast, Heckram

182

appeared almost rangy. He'd often wondered which of them was stronger. As Joboam stepped offensively close to him, he wondered if today they'd find out.

'Elsa has said she'll be contented with me. Unlike some men, I'm inclined to believe women know with whom they'd want to mate.' Heckram's voice was low and pleasant. He let his arms hang loose at his sides, waiting.

'It doesn't surprise me to hear you say that. There have always been men in this sita who have been contented to be ruled by their womenfolk, to live in their mothers' tents until women come to choose them.'

'Better than to live in my own tent and never be chosen at all,' Heckram agreed smoothly.

Joboam's eyes went a little narrower. Heckram felt his own breathing deepen, and then the swelling and tightening of his muscles. A deep patience rose within him. No haste to this game. It would never be said that he'd provoked the herdlord's man. A smile bowed his mouth as he waited for Joboam to make the first move. The moments passed, and Joboam's arms hung limp. A small knowing grew inside Heckram. Joboam would make more words at him, perhaps, but he wouldn't push the quarrel to blows. Joboam was not anxious to find which of them was the stronger. Not yet, anyway. Heckram's smile became a grin.

A small muscle jumped in the bigger man's cheek. 'Why be chosen by one woman when a man can choose any, or all?' he demanded suddenly, his voice too loud and harsh. Bluffing. 'The bitch in the heat of her season doesn't go to the slinking dog that whines for her, but is taken by the strongest male.'

'Joboam!'

Her voice was shrill, and both men jerked to it. Fey Kari,

the herdlord's daughter, perched lightly on a nearby pulkor, looking like some airy bird. Her black hair sleeked smooth to the shape of her skull, pulled so tight that the strain of the braid pulled at her eyes. Her black eyes were raven bright, her lips too red, her teeth too white behind them. The fine bones of her face showed against her skin. 'Joboam!' she cawed again.

'What is it?' he asked grudgingly.

'Capiam requires you. Immediately. Twice he has sent to your hut, but neither time were you there. So he sent me to fetch you. Are you coming?'

'I come.' He spoke heavily. He turned challenging eyes on Heckram, waiting for him to speak. Heckram only grinned at the larger man. Kari hopped from her perch, her loose tunic of white fox swirling around her as she moved. She had lost weight again and the looseness of her clothing on her body contributed to her ethereal appearance. She came over the snow to the men in short quick steps, coming too close to them both, all but touching them as she insinuated herself between them. She tilted her face up to Heckram.

'*I* wish you luck in your joining with Elsa,' Kari emphasized. Heckram wondered uneasily how long she had been listening to them. He tried to remember all he had said, and if any of it could be repeated to make mischief. Surely he would have noticed her perched there. Or had she used the white fox furs of her tunic as well as the snow fox himself did when he stalked his prey? Her eyes probed his deeply. 'I hope she realizes her good fortune. To not only know who she wishes to mate, but to have the joy of claiming him! Hurry on your way, Heckram, to make yourself ready for her, and to raise the walls of her home.'

Joboam had backed off a step or two as Kari spoke to Heckram. Now Kari turned back and clapped her hands sharply as if he were a recalcitrant puppy. 'And you! To Capiam, Joboam. Do not keep the herdlord waiting, after he has sent his own daughter to fetch you. Hurry now! Run!'

Joboam glared at them both, but as Kari barked the last word, he set off down the path at a grudging jog.

'Joboam!' Heckram called after him and, when the man glanced back, he said, 'I don't know much of dogs. But wolves mate for life. Remember it.'

'No one who hunts wolves should forget it,' Kari remarked, and her laughter was brittle as icicles in the cold air. She bit the sound off, sighed abruptly, and turned back to Heckram. 'I shall come to your betrothal tonight,' she announced suddenly and stared at him hard.

'You will be welcome, as will any of the herdfolk who honor us by coming,' he replied gravely.

For a moment longer she stood staring up at him, standing so close that her thrusting breasts nearly touched his ribs. 'You smell of butchering and reindeer. Go bathe yourself,' she advised him suddenly. She turned from him quickly and hurried away with her short, hopping steps, her white furs flapping around her like the wings of a crippled bird.

Heckram watched her as she wound her way between the huts and meat racks, never choosing the well trodden path between the rows of huts, but walking where no one else did. His heart was still beating strongly, the excitement of his near fight with Joboam flooding his veins but finding no outlet. He stooped once more for his buckets and hastened again for Ristin's hut.

In the hut at last, he put the water to heat in pots over the fire, set out a large basin, and then rummaged through his possessions for his father's razor. He poured a bit of warmed water into the basin, then stood looking at the implement in his hand. It was bronze, rare enough in this hut. The razor was almost the only bronze tool he possessed. There was a knife as well, one that had been his father's. A knife almost too precious to use. The traders said that far to the south now all tools were of bronze, and only the poor used flint anymore. But in Heckram's village, flint and bone were still the commonest materials used for tools. True, the flint tools were now polished and ground to resemble their bronze counterparts, but stone they still were, and far more brittle than the new metal. More and more bronze was finding its way north these days. Heckram had seen the new bronze axe that Capiam had traded amber and white fox hides for. It was shaped just like Lasse's axe of polished flint, and its handle curved in the familiar curve of reindeer antler the herdfolk had always used for axe handles. But its head was bronze, and every bit but the actual cutting edge was etched with elaborate patterns. Despite its delicate beauty, it would take punishing use that would destroy Lasse's stone one. Perhaps he should think more of gathering amber lumps and hunting the thick white furs the southern traders valued and less of gathering up reindeer. But then he shook his head, the traditional measure of wealth too strongly ingrained to deny it.

The bronze razor had a bone grip carved with close-grained spirals. He damped his face and the blade, then scraped the edged tool over his skin. He ran his fingertips down his cheek, feeling with satisfaction the smoothness that followed the blade. Then, mindful of the time he had already wasted, he finished his shaving hastily.

He mixed steaming and cool water in the basin to a comfortable temperature, and then stripped hastily. Under his fur garments was his long shirt of woven wool. He could not remember when last he had removed it. Before the chill of fall set in? He dragged it off over his head and stood shivering and naked. He hesitated a moment, then stepped to the chest and opened it. On top of the other contents, as if anticipating him, was a leather poke of aromatic herbs and a square of coarsely woven fiber fabric. He took them.

Placing a handful of the herbs in the center of the fabric square, he folded the fabric into a packet. This he dipped into the steaming water. As the herbs took in the moisture, their fragrance filled the sod hut. He scrubbed his face and neck with the rough packet, feeling his skin open to the warmth of the water. Dampening the packet repeatedly, he worked his way down his body. The water turned dingy, and he emptied it and refilled the basin again. He shivered as the water evaporated from his skin, chilling him further, but doggedly finished his bath. Then another basin of warm water, and this time a handful of the herbs floating loose in it. He knelt to pour more water over his thick mane of dark hair and then plunged his head into the basin of scented water. He scrubbed at his scalp, feeling his hair go to silkiness under his hands. At least he had no nits to worry about, as Bror did. Ristin would not have tolerated vermin in her tent. He suspected Elsa would feel the same way.

His fine hair tangled about his fingers, snagging on the work-roughened surfaces. He pulled his hands free, mumbling a curse, and plunged his head into the water again. He came up for air, and his hair swung forward past his face, streaming water into the basin. His scalp felt clean. He wrung his mat of hair over the basin. Elsa liked his hair. Every time he had spoken to her since their agreement became public, she had taken the opportunity to touch it, to stand twining strands of it around her fingers as she talked to him. His hair was finer than that of the other men of the herd, and when the sun struck it, it shone not blue, but bronze. Heckram found its fineness annoying, for it blew into his eyes and clung to his fingers when he tried to smooth it. He shook it back from his face.

Shivering, he picked up his woolen long-shirt from where he had let it fall. But as he bunched it to pull it on over his head, the full impact of its aroma hit him. He dropped it, snorting. He had been wearing that? No wonder Kari had told him he smelt of butchering. He tossed it into the scented water still in the basin and looked for something else to put on.

In his clothing bundle he found two thin shirts of rabbit leather, fine for the mellow weather of summer, but not winter. But when he found nothing else, he regretfully took one and a clean pair of leggings from his bundle. They would have to serve. He tossed them across the hearth so they landed on his bedskins. Picking up his boots, he followed them, then stood staring down.

The shirt stirred dim memories. Images of his father, always a vague, tall man in his memories, suddenly snapped into focus. Heckram suddenly remembered a tall man, impossibly tall, laughing down at him as loudly as a wind roaring. The man had hazel eyes, and his nose was long and thin compared to the noses of the herdfolk. His big hands spanned Heckram's childish chest as the man lifted him up, touching his head to the rafters of the hut. A man wearing this brown wool shirt. Slowly he picked the shirt up and sniffed it, smelling the herbs his mother packed into the chest to keep the mice out. He wondered when she had placed it on his bed for him. Cautiously, as if afraid of shattering the memories he associated with it, he pulled it on over his head. He dragged on a pair of leather leggings and tied them and then stood, rolling his shoulders and trying to get used to the feel of it.

'It's tight on you. You're bigger than he was, I suppose, though I never realized it until now. Your southern blood must run strong, from both my father and yours. Still, the wool will stretch out to fit you.'

He turned slowly to find Ristin in the door, looking at him. Her smile was bittersweet. 'You've a lot of his looks. And his temperament, too. I suppose Elsa will learn to live with your moods as I learned to live with his.'

Heckram found himself nodding slowly. 'You saved this for me?' he asked.

She nodded in return. 'For this day. As he wore it on the day he claimed me.' She turned aside from him abruptly, no longer able to look at him. 'Comb your hair out, and be on your way. I'll clean this mess up for you, this last time, and wash out your shirt as well. Quickly now. Lasse and the others have been waiting for you long enough.'

She moved purposefully as she spoke, returning the bag of herbs to her trunk and pushing his shirt under the water in the basin to soak. He knew she didn't want to talk to him just now, so he ran a bone comb through his hair, slicking its dampness back from his face, jammed his hat over it, and left her tent quietly.

'A fine time of year to be building a sod hut,' Lasse growled mockingly to the other men as Heckram approached. Heckram greeted the men solemnly, touching hands with some, embracing others, and carefully ignoring the cluster of girls and women who had gathered behind Stina's hut to watch them. He thought he caught a glimpse of Elsa's bright blue cap among them, but refused to turn his head and see.

'So, Heckram, you've decided to build a sod hut today?' Bror asked him loudly.

'I might. I thought it might be a useful place to keep my things.' The men were elaborately casual as they followed him across the clearing and up the hillside. They watched in silence as Heckram brushed the snow away from a patch of ground, then forced a bone turf knife deep into the sod. Carefully he outlined a square in the surface of the revealed turf. Working with tools of wood and bone, he severed the thick mat of roots that held the block of sod in place and lifted it from its cradle. Dirt and bits of humus sifted from it as he lifted it. This first block of sod he carried down the hill in his arms, as if it were a fragile child. Carefully he lowered it to the earth, packing it firmly down where he wanted it. 'And here's the start of the wall,' he said loudly.

It was all they had been waiting to hear. Tools and sledges suddenly appeared. Some, more impatient than others, had already cut their blocks of sod while waiting for Heckram to finish bathing. These were off-loaded from sledges and set end to end with his starting block. A circle of sod blocks began to rise as the men moved and added more blocks of sod. In size and shape, the sod house would resemble a skin tent, but its thick walls offered more resistance to the wind and weather. Stout poles appeared, to frame in a doorway, and then more poles for the roof struts.

The roof itself was of birch branches and bark, set over pine poles and chinked with moss. The men returned from gathering the materials to find that someone had hung a hide on the doorframe. They made no comment on this, or on the thick layer of birch twigs that appeared on the floor while they were gone for their second load of roofing supplies. Lasse waved Heckram back from the roof when he would have climbed up to set the final barks in place around the smoke hole. 'You're too big. You'll cave the whole thing in.' Agile as a squirrel, the boy scrambled up and put the finishing touches on the roof.

Heckram walked carefully around the outside of the hut, looking for cracks to stuff with moss, or places where the turves might be set unevenly. But it was a good, tightly built hut, made to stand many a year of snow and rain. By the time he returned to it next fall, the walls would have taken on a life of their own. Small plants would cling to them, and the moss that chinked them would be green and growing. He nodded in satisfaction, then pushed the doorhide aside and entered. The bare birch twigs crackled under his feet. The other men clustered in the door, peering into the new hut.

'No hearth stones!' Bror observed with loud cheerfulness.

'It will be a cold hut with no arran to heat it and cook upon!' Lasse added, his shout ringing in the cold air.

'That it will,' Heckram agreed. The other men nodded commiseratingly as Heckram came back to stand in the door of the hut, crouching but still filling it. 'But what does a man know of building a hearth?'

'Nothing at all!' Stina cackled. She loved the ceremonies of a joining and was always the first woman to speak aloud. 'But here comes a woman to show you how! I bring you a stone for your hearth!' She hobbled forward as fast as her stiffened legs would allow her, to mockingly present him with a crumbling piece of shale no bigger than her fist. But Heckram accepted it gravely and made a great show of inspecting it.

'It looks like a fine hearth stone to me,' he declared,

inviting a chorus of hoots from the women. 'Yet it is not like the stones my mother used. I will not take your arran stone or you into my hut, woman!'

Stina pulled a face of great disappointment and retired to the ranks of the women. Ibba came forward, to offer him a huge round rock as big as his head. Again he examined it gravely, but decided that it was not the same as the stones in his mother's arran. Woman after woman and stone after stone he inspected and rejected, and the roars of laughter from the gathered herdfolk grew louder as the stones were more and more unfit for a hearth. At last came Tranta, Elsa's friend, to insult him by offering him a handful of pebbles and bark bits for his hearth. Again he refused, asking loudly of the surrounding folk, 'Is there no woman here who can build a hearth fit for a new hut such as this?'

The huddle of women parted and Elsa stepped out. Her warm skin was flushed even rosier than usual, her eyes shining bright. She wore a new cap of red wool and her black hair shone where it peeped from beneath it. Instead of a tunic of caribou hide, she wore a cloak of white fox fur over a woven shirt and a knee-length skirt of woven wool with fringes around the hem. A murmur of approval rose from the folk as she slowly approached the hut. In her two hands she held a fine flat arran stone.

Heckram took it from her gravely, their eyes meeting for a long moment as he received the weight of it. He turned it in his big hands, examining it gravely over and over again, until the crowd began to murmur at the delay. Elsa's dark eyes were wide when he finally looked up from the stone. He tried to keep the mischief out of his eyes.

'This, for a hearth stone?' he asked dubiously, and at the outraged cries of the women, he dropped the jest hastily and added, 'will make the finest arran a man could warm himself at. Your hearth stone I will take into the hut, and you with it.'

He put it gravely back into her hands and stepped back inside the hut to allow her passage. In the center of the hut, under the smoke hole, was an area left free of birch twigs. Here she put the stone. She worked carefully to set it into the earth. All was quiet as she left the hut and then returned with another stone to fit into place beside the first one. Again, and yet again, and then at last she came bearing a burning torch kindled from her mother's hearth. Her mother, Missa, and Ristin came behind her, bearing wood for the new fire. Early evening was falling, and the torch burned very brightly in the twilight. Once more Heckram lifted the doorhide to let her pass through. This time Missa and Ristin followed her, and faces crowded the door as Elsa knelt to build and kindle the first fire on the new hearth stones.

When the flames burned hot and high, she moved to Heckram's side. Together they turned to the folk clustered at the door. 'Why do you stand about outside in the cold night?' Heckram demanded. 'Come in and warm yourself at the fine fire my woman has built on our hearth.'

'Do not stand under the sky. Come into the tight hut my man has built for me and warm yourselves. We are poor folk, newly joined, but we will share with you what we have!'

The silence broke in a hubbub of voices as well-wishers pushed inside. All loudly admired the tight walls and bright flames of the fire. Then, one after another, they found fault with the new home. 'Is there nothing to sit on but birch twigs?' demanded Kuoljok loudly. 'Well, I have here a poor rabbit hide that may keep the twigs from their skin!' So saying the bride's father unrolled a finely cured bear hide before the new hearth.

Megan Lindholm

'Will they offer their guests nothing to eat?' panted Stina. 'Well, I've a small pot of tea I can spare them.' With a grunt of effort, she set a heavy pot of stew, still simmering from her own hearth's heat, onto the stones of the new arran.

'And how will they stir it? With a stick or a finger?' demanded Ibba. She plunged a newly carved bone ladle deep into the savory stew.

'She'll be a lazy wife that has put aside no cheese for the winter,' Lasse predicted woefully and proceeded to hang six large ones from the new rafters.

Heckram and Elsa could but sit on the bear hide before the new hearth, admitting their poverty and incompetence at home building, as their friends and relatives contributed to the new hearth. Tomorrow they would fetch from their old homes their possessions, but tonight their comfort would depend on the generosity of others. Elsa's eyes shone as her fingers stroked the bear rug they sat on. Ristin bore in spits of meat to set over the flames, all the while telling her neighbors how relieved she was to get her lazy son out of her hut. Missa, cutting cheese and ladling up stew for the guests, loudly confided to them that her daughter knew nothing at all of keeping a home warm and well supplied. Laughter greeted every disparaging remark, and the predictions of misfortune and misery grew wilder as every guest took a turn.

'So poor a hunter will feed his wife on shrews and mice!'

'The hair will slip from the hides she tans and her weaving come unwound!'

'His crooked arrows will fly into the trees, and her cheeses be rank and spoiled.'

'Am I too late to offer a stone for the hearth?'

All eyes turned to the hut's door and the late arrival who stood there. Kari was framed there, managing to look at

194

once timorous and arrogant. No others of the herdlord's family had seen fit to attend this joining. The slight had been felt, though not commented on. Now she was unexpected, and no one moved to welcome her. Her cheeks blushed dark red, and her eyes shone. In her hand she held out a lump of amber as big as her fist. Kuoljok gasped audibly. Silence fell like a heavy snow, swirling among the guests as all stared at the proffered wealth. It was an awkward offering, out of keeping with their tradition. The quiet grew longer and the girl's discomfort grew.

Lasse stepped into the awkwardness. 'I never saw a stone like that in my mother's hearth!' he exclaimed. The guests laughed nervously.

'I shall set it by the arran,' Kari exclaimed loudly, her voice cracking in her nervousness. Eyes and silence followed her as she crossed to the hearth and knelt to set the yellow lump before the new couple.

Stina looked at Lasse and cleared her old throat. Her voice cracked as she observed, 'Don't set it there! Elsa will mix it with the kindling and try to burn it for wood!'

The jest was close enough for people anxious to be at ease. The moment of embarrassment passed, and the talk and laughter rose again in the night. Kari looked at Lasse gratefully and he responded by offering her some of the freshly roasted meat.

The talk grew louder; a keg of juobmo and then a keg of beer were opened. Someone brought in sausages from the meat racks. The fuel on the hearth was replenished and the flames leaped high again. Ristin made another trip to the meat racks. The air in the hut grew thick with the odors of people, roasting meat, and beer. Dark eyes shone and wide cheeks flushed as unjoined women flirted outrageously with the young men, and the older couples recalled the warming memories of their own joinings.

Several hides now graced the twig-strewn floor, and sundry tools and implements hung from the rafters. These, the poorer folk of the herd, had been generous. A komse, of wood and leather, was propped unabashedly in the corner, in the calm expectation that Elsa would fill it before the year was out. Cradle of a nomadic folk, it was fitted with straps so the baby could be hung from a pack saddle or hooked on a tree branch. The buzzing voices and sudden shouts of laughter spilled into the night as the herdfolk rejoiced. And Elsa, squirming closer to Heckram, observed softly, 'Late as the night is, you would think they would seek their own hearths!'

'But the night is young still,' he protested and then, as he looked down into her face and saw her warm eagerness, felt a similar impatience stir within him. She knelt beside him on the bear skin. He was suddenly aware of her thigh warm against his. Her mouth parted in a smile as she saw the interest kindled in his eyes. Heedless of the others, he bent suddenly to kiss her. Her mouth was wet under his, and warm, tasting of the southern beer.

He did not see Lasse's grin, but heard it in his voice as he yawned loudly and exclaimed, 'Well, some of us have to hunt tomorrow. And those that do will want to sleep tonight.' He rose slowly.

'Kuoljok said he saw wolf signs on the south ridge,' Ristin observed. 'I think I will hunt there tomorrow.'

Lasse was holding the doorhide aside as Kari slipped out into the night. Ibba and Bror were not far behind.

'It's not such a bad hut, after all,' Kuoljok observed, and Missa nodded, her eyes shining with moisture as she stepped away from her daughter's hearth.

'The fire burns well,' Ristin agreed. She followed them out the door.

Heckram and Elsa sat before their hearth as their guests, with various inconsequential remarks, slipped out into the night. Stina puttered about a moment longer after the others had left, banking the fire and lifting a pot from the hot stones. She stared at the couple a moment longer, opened her lips to speak, and then gave her head a short, hard nod instead. After the doorhide fell behind her, there was silence but for the crackling of the flames on the new hearth.

Elsa, suddenly shy in the stillness, exclaimed, 'I should put more wood on the hearth,' and made as if to rise. Heckram felt the blood thundering suddenly in his veins. The fringe of Elsa's skirt dangled at the tops of her knees like an invitation. He stood, pulling her up with him, and became suddenly aware of her smallness. When she buried her face against his chest, he felt the warmth of her breath through his shirt. He looked down on the clean skin in the part of her shining black hair. She looked up at him for a moment, her eyes clear and liquid as the dark eyes of a little vaja. His heart leaped like a wild sarva in rutting time. He knelt suddenly, pushing his face against her shirt, nuzzling her breasts through the woven fabric as his fingers snagged and fumbled at the lacings. Her hands caught in his fine hair and pulled his mouth against the firmness of her breasts. Her nipples reminded him of raspberries still warm from the noon sun, her thighs sleek and strong as polished ivory to his touch. The warmth from the new hearth flushed their bared skin, and the gift hides were silky beneath them.

It was late that night when she rose to put more fuel on the fire. He watched her from the warmth of the bedskins as she moved, gold against the dying gold of the flames, her hair a black wave down her shoulders, and was almost content. Then she gave a sudden cry of dismay and sprang back from the hearth.

'Did you burn yourself?' he asked quickly.

'No.' She turned worried eyes to him. 'One of our arran stones has cracked.'

Between an older couple, it might have been no more than an omen of a quarrel to come, or a day's bad hunting. But this was a new hearth and their joining was new. There could be no worse portent for a betrothal night than a cracked stone in the newly set arran, and Elsa's eyes reflected her knowledge of that. He knew she was waiting for him to scold her, to say she had chosen the stones poorly or made the first fire too hot. Instead he only lifted the bedskins and beckoned her back to his side.

She came in, uncertain at first, but soon was cuddling against him, stroking the hair on his chest. Later they slept. But when he awoke, he could only recall that he had dreamed of watching laden pulkors leaving for the southern trade villages. The morning was cold, and the fire had died on the cracked hearth.

TWELVE

'But I thought we were going to the herd, to check our animals.'

'It's on the way. And it won't take much time.'

'It's not on the way,' Elsa said, a bit petulantly. 'And I don't see why it should take any time at all. Why do you want to go visiting today?'

Heckram slid his skis forward through the crisp snow for another three strides before replying. 'Just to visit.' His big shoulders moved in a shrug. He was glad he was in the lead and she could not see his face. She would have known he was holding something back. As it was, she suspected.

It was one of those rare days that came sometimes in the midst of winter, a day that reminded one that spring must come sometime, that the life of the forest was sleeping in the dark rich soil under the blanket of cold white snow. The sky was a bottomless blue, the dark green of the pines a stabbing contrast. The white snow held a light of its own, glinting so brightly that Heckram squinted and felt the water rise in his eyes. There was a perfection to the scene that nothing man-made could even imitate. Each dark-needled branch balanced its precise limit of snow. They crossed an open meadow where the tall heads of grasses poked up through the snow, each tassled stalk frosted with white crystals that emphasized the asymmetrical beauty of each individual. The coldness of the day burned against his cheeks, but the warmth of its beauty numbed him to the pain.

'But why? There's nothing we need from the healer. And it isn't really on the way; the herd is more west of here, in those hills.'

He didn't look back to see her pointing pole. He knew. A month with her, and already he knew her too well. He wanted her to be quiet, to look at the day as he was looking at it, to share the seeing of the frost on the tassled grasses, to feel the sunlight and the wind touch her cheeks with warmth and cold.

'I want to visit the boy,' Heckram said, surprising himself with the sudden honesty of his words. 'He's too much alone.'

'He's with his mother,' Elsa pointed out bluntly. 'If she thought he was too much alone, she'd move her tent closer to the talvsit. But I think she keeps him alone on purpose.'

'Perhaps.' Heckram's voice was grim; his shoulders worked more than they needed to as he pushed himself along.

'Well, you know how he is. I don't think he'd get along with the other children. They'd have nothing in common. So, even if they moved right into the talvsit, he'd still be alone. Heckram, I've an idea. Let's go to the herd first, spend the day checking the reindeer. And then, on the way back, if we have time, we'll stop and see them.'

'Their tent is just over this hill and down,' he replied and pushed on, driving himself up the hill with a fury that left Elsa panting in her efforts to keep up.

The snow around the tent was trampled, and there were other ski trails now, evidence that several of the herdfolk had had reason to seek out the healer's skills. Tillu was out before her tent, lacing a calf hide onto a stretching frame. She looked very small as she crouched in the snow. Very alone, as if her tent were the only one in the world. Kerlew was to one side of the tent. He gripped a stave and made an elaborate show of stalking a stump. His movements were stylized, more dance than play. His body swayed lithely as he moved, in a manner far different from his usual awkwardness. Now he crouched and plodded toward the stump as if he fought a great wind, now his body lifted on tiptoe, and he menaced the stump with short jabbing thrusts of the stave. A gust of wind carried some words of his chant to Heckram's ears. It was in no language Heckram had ever heard. He stood still on the crest of the hill, watching.

'See what I mean,' Elsa said suddenly beside him. 'What kind of play is that for a boy of his age? Why isn't he doing something useful to help his mother?' Her small face was set in a look of disgust, and the condemnation in her features made them hard and old. Heckram pulled his eyes away from her.

'He's only a boy,' he observed gently, and he pushed off down the hill. An instant later he heard the sound of her skis cutting the snow as she followed him.

Kerlew saw them first and with a glad cry raced up the hill to meet them, coming straight at Heckram so that he had to turn his skis in an awkward stop that all but spilled him into the snow. Behind him Elsa exclaimed in annoyance and swerved gracefully around them. Her action carried her past him and into the clearing before the tent. Tillu rose awkwardly, greeting her with obvious surprise. And Heckram was left alone with Kerlew.

They grinned at one another, in an understanding that was complete without words. Kerlew gripped the man's wrist with both hands. 'You have come to see the calf skin. I skinned it from the deer myself, taking it carefully, carefully, with the reindeer knife you gave me. Tillu has no knife so fine.'

'Um.' Heckram stored the bit of information. 'Then you hunt well, small man?'

Kerlew shrugged, a man's deprecating gesture to cover swelling pride. 'The calf was small,' he said casually. 'But it will feed my mother until I can kill another. Today I do the hunt dance, to bring me luck in hunting.' The boy paused, then said with elaborate casualness, 'Perhaps tomorrow you would care to hunt with me?'

The hidden plea in his words was a thing Heckram could not deny. 'Perhaps,' Heckram replied, already planning the day. He glanced down at the tent, where Elsa stood, the set of her shoulders suggesting both annoyance and awkwardness. Both she and Tillu were staring up at them. He'd better get down there. 'Here,' he told the boy. 'Behind me. Put your feet behind mine. No, you have to hold on to me, I need the poles. Now, when I move my feet, you move yours. First the left . . . now the right. Ready? Here we go!'

It was but a short run down the hill, but the boy whooped all the way, his grip around Heckram's waist surprisingly strong. Crossing the flat was more difficult, not so much because of the boy's awkward weight on the back of his skis but because of the two faces that awaited him. The smile on Tillu's face was a rare and cautious thing, while the look of warning that Elsa wore was becoming all too familiar to him. She did not approve of this silliness and the time it was taking.

'Jump off,' he told the boy when they halted before the women. Yet Kerlew's arms lingered around his waist an instant longer, tightened for a second in a convulsive hug of thanks before the boy stumbled away from him. His small face was shining with excitement.

'And now you will see my calf skin, and then have tea in my mother's hut,' Kerlew began excitedly.

'I'm afraid we cannot stay that long,' Elsa cut in smoothly. 'We have to visit the herd today, so we have still a ways to go. And we must get there soon enough that we can return before dark.'

The light went out of Kerlew's face like the sun going behind a cloud. Elsa went on, 'I was just telling Tillu that we only meant to say hello on our way. It is a nice calf hide; it is only a shame it was cut in the skinning.'

Heckram tousled Kerlew's hair in a gesture that was almost possessive. 'A few cuts in a hide matter little. A clever woman can always sew them shut.'

Now the look of gratitude on Tillu's face was unmistakable. 'If you would care to stay for just a few moments,' she said, her eyes going swiftly from Heckram's to Elsa's, 'you could have a cup of hot tea to warm you. And I have tallow, from the calf. I could mix the rub for you, Elsa. For your shoulder.'

'I have nothing to trade for it today,' Elsa said, and there was no mistaking the chill of formality in her voice.

'There is no need,' Tillu said awkwardly. 'When you gave me the needles and case, I said I would make it for you. It will take me but a moment . . .' She glanced from Elsa to Heckram, plainly puzzled at Elsa's displeasure. Then her eyes went to Kerlew. He was crouched in the snow by Heckram, his hands tracing the pattern of lines and colors that decorated Heckram's ski pole. Her eyes narrowed and the light went from her face. Dullness seemed to flood it, muting the life in her eyes. 'Of course, if you are in a hurry, you could come for it another time. Whenever it is convenient for you. Kerlew. Kerlew! Run into the tent and find the other hide scraper for me. I think it is in the medicine box.'

The boy moved reluctantly at her bidding. And there it is, Heckram thought to himself as he kept a friendly smile pasted on his face. The vixen senses a threat to her cub, and chases him back to the den. Is this why they live apart? Elsa had been right, he realized. The woman lived alone out here deliberately. Not to deprive Kerlew of company, but to keep him from the danger of other folk. To protect the boy from hard looks and mocking words, and sly blows when no one was looking. Something inside his chest squeezed tight.

'I'd like to take Kerlew with us today,' he said suddenly. The idea had been in his mind since this morning. But now it seemed very important to him that it come to pass. Tillu looked wary, while Elsa gasped as if he had doused her with cold water.

'How can we, Heckram? We're on skis; he could never keep up.'

'He could ride on the back of my skis. Or on my shoulders. He isn't that big, Elsa.' Heckram spoke slowly, deliberately.

'But he would slow us down,' she objected in dismay. 'And already we have lost time, stopping here. Oh, Heckram, we cannot, not today.' Her voice was politely firm.

As was Tillu's. 'You are kind to offer, but the boy has work to do.'

He might have argued with Elsa. Tillu's words left no room for any objections. He looked at her, saw for an instant her watchfulness that would not allow her son to go into any situation where she could not be sure of protecting him. Then her face was politely empty. Her eyes looked away from his.

'I had hoped,' he began, 'to take the boy hunting with me tomorrow.'

'But Heckram –' interrupted Elsa, her upset evident.

'No.' Tillu's voice was smooth. 'Tomorrow I will need him here. You must see how it is, the boy and I alone. I depend on Kerlew for many things; I cannot allow him to go with you.'

'Tillu!'

The cry of anguish was Kerlew's. He had come up quietly behind her. The scraper fell from his hand as he darted forward toward Heckram. She caught him by his tunic back, held him beside her. 'They are in a hurry,' she said firmly. Kerlew wiggled, and her bare knuckles went white with keeping her grip. 'They have to leave now, Kerlew, and you must stay with me. Are not you the man of this tent? Have you not tasks of your own to keep you busy?'

Kerlew darted a glance at Elsa's face, saw her disapproval of the entire scene. He turned his eyes, bright with despair and betrayal, to Heckram. It was a gaze Heckram could not meet. 'Perhaps another time, Kerlew,' he muttered and bent to brush imaginary snow from his leggings.

Kerlew suddenly stopped struggling against Tillu's restraining grip. Very still he stood, and when Heckram dared to look up at his small face, it was closed. As carefully empty as Tillu's own. 'And perhaps not,' he said, his voice cracking on the words. His speech came suddenly faster, the words tumbling and twisted on his awkward tongue. 'It is not as if I have time to spare. To hunt is fine, but a shaman has many other things to attend. There is a world other men see not, the world a shaman moves in. It is there that I am more of a man than you can imagine, yes, and it is there that I protect my mother and bring animals for her to kill. It is there that I go and I call to Carp and he will come, very very soon he will come and I will have no time to go hunting, no, nor to use a bow, so there is no sense in your making one for me, for I would never use it, it would only lie in the corner of the hut –'

'We have to go,' Elsa said, her voice low and uneasy. She planted her ski poles firmly, swung herself suddenly away, and Heckram found himself following her, letting Kerlew's words fall to the snow behind him. 'I'm sorry,' he said, knowing the boy didn't even hear the words. He had to hurry to keep up with Elsa; he could not look back to where Kerlew babbled, his words flung like useless missiles against his own pain. Heckram felt as if something within him had torn, as if he had broken a bond and the torn flesh was sore, very sore.

At the crest of the hill he ventured a glance back. Tillu already knelt by her hide again, busy with the scraper. Kerlew crouched in the snow, his face in his hands. He rocked as he grieved, looking like a much younger child than he was. The boy's pain sank its teeth into Heckram's heart. 'Why doesn't she go to him, hug him?' he demanded fiercely.

Elsa glanced back at him. 'What did you say?'

His anger flared at her. 'Why did you behave that way? Didn't you see how the boy's feelings were hurt?'

Her face went stony. 'All I saw was a young boy with no manners. A boy whose mother should teach him better. No wonder they have to live apart from folk. Who could tolerate a child like that in a village?'

'I could,' Heckram muttered.

Elsa's face suddenly warmed. She moved to his side, put her mittened hand atop his. 'I know you could. Who would have thought that a man like you could be such a fool over a boy?' Her hand traveled up his arm. 'We waited too long, you and I. But do not be impatient now. I have no doubt that by this time next year, there will be a little one in the komse. A boy, perhaps, that will look like you and will grow strong and tall. A boy of your own to teach and play with and hunt with. You will have a son of your own to share these things with, Heckram. A bright, well-mannered child.'

He looked down into her face, saw her own hunger. She would be a good mother, full of dreams for her children. She would bear fat, healthy babies, would protect them jealously when they were small. And when they were older, she would set her children free into their independence, launching them like leaf-boats in a stream. Looking into her face, he could see the rightness of her wanting. There would be children for them, a boy of his own, with none of Kerlew's subtle differences. Their son would be a good hunter, would be healthy and strong, all a father could ask. A boy to make a man proud, with none of Kerlew's awkwardness and difficulties. He and Elsa would have a good family. Their children would thrive. But . . .

'What about Kerlew?'

Elsa frowned, then softened the gesture with a laugh. 'Foolish man. Is your heart so easily touched? He is nothing to us. The boy has a mother to care for him. He will be fine. You must leave them to their own lives, Heckram. If you interfere, you will only make things harder for the boy, make him want things that are beyond him. Let them live their own lives, Heckram. You and I have a life of our own to fill.'

She pulled his hand close, cradled it against her breast. Her smile was full of a tender promise. He found a smile of his own to answer it before he pulled gently free of her. She pushed off on her skis, moving silently down the bright hillside, and he followed. But a question followed him, a question merciless as wolves.

What about Kerlew?

THIRTEEN

He should have stayed with Elsa. He knew that, knew that the others had expected it of him, and would be shocked that he hadn't. But he couldn't. He had to move, to strain himself and his animal as the pulkor raced over the snow. In the pumping of his heart and lungs, in the flash of snow and black trees that passed, he found an edge of comfort. He was doing something, not standing horrified and stricken. He could pretend to have some control over what was happening. He fled his own pain and anger. And fear. Yes, fear, but not for himself. Fear that if this could happen among the herdfolk, then anything could happen. Anything. The outrage that had bubbled inside him since Bruk's mutilation rose to a boil that overflowed and scalded his soul.

Short hours ago, the night had been a comfortable place, folk gathered around the hearth, the men to play at wolf tablo while the women wove and talked. He and Elsa had gone visiting to her parents' hut. The yellow light of Missa's fire touched everyone, warming colors and softening lines. He and Kuoljok had set up the board on top of the traveling chest. The heavy wooden chest had once been incised with a brightly painted design. Now the patina of frequent moves obscured the pattern, and the colors were faded. Yet in the warm light of the fire, it seemed handsomer for its scars.

As did the parents' faces. Kuoljok's hair was thin and black and unruly, standing out in a halo about his seamed face. His black eyes were deeply set, the whites of them stained with brown as if by running dye. His sallow skin was reddened by the weather and made ivory by the firelight. He pondered his next move, hiding a shrewd smile behind a hand all knuckles and tendons. Heckram's mother, Ristin, was there as well. She worked at weaving trim for his wedding shirt, stopping often to compare it with the weaving Missa did. The ceremony at the Cataclysm in summer would be the formal one, requiring elaborate garments. The folk of many herds would gather there, and Capiam's herdfolk would be judged by the richness of the pledged couple's attire as much as by their reindeer. Mothers took pride in the weaving of such things.

Both women sat stiffly erect on the floor of birch twigs and hides. Their ribbon looms tethered them to the center pole of the hut. Weaving materials of grass and fiber and strips of fur, bright dyed lengths of wool yarn and leathers, whispered against one another as their busy old fingers danced them together. Small basins held beads of bone and horn and amber to be worked into the design. The two women spoke and laughed over their work, paying it little mind as the intricate patterns flowed from their fingers. Missa's trim would adorn Elsa's wedding garments of snowy white fur. The furs were lush winter-taken fox. Elsa herself sat with her head bowed over a basin as her fingers squeezed excess color from the fibers she was dyeing. The golden firelight highlighted the scene.

'You'll be too hot,' Heckram pointed out annoyingly as

Kuoljok pondered his next move. 'The wedding will be at the height of the summer. No one wears fox fur then.'

'The beauty will be worth a little discomfort,' Missa assured him placidly. 'And Elsa wants the wedding to be in the evening, when the cool wind blows down from the ice packs.'

Heckram grunted his defeat and turned back to his gaming. The dice were made from the toe-knuckle bones of a reindeer calf, while his marker, the pursued wolf, was a larger knuckle bone stained black. Kuoljok tumbled the dice and then smiled as he moved his own markers closer to the fleeing wolf. Heckram picked up the dice and warmed them in his hand, pondering strategy. The smell of freshly carved new wood mingled with the homey smells of the hut. In one corner of the hut stood the beginnings of a traveling chest, chips and curlings of wood littering the area around it. Heckram had been doing the carving, under the watchful eyes of the old man, but both had decided their work had progressed far enough this night and had abandoned it for the game.

Heckram moved his piece grudgingly. Old Kuoljok snickered, cast the dice, and moved quickly. 'That traveling chest could be finished by tomorrow night, if we worked on it tomorrow,' he suggested.

Heckram shook his head slowly as he polished the dice between his hands. 'Lasse and I are going hunting.'

'Again?' Elsa asked in dismay. 'Can't you ever stay at home for two days in a row?'

He closed his eyes a moment, then opened them again, keeping them on the game board. 'Not if you still plan to slaughter two animals for our joining feast at the Cataclysm. If I can drag in a couple of young sarva now, they could be fattened by the time we reach the Cataclysm.'

'Heckram, you sound as if we were starving. One of your

211

animals, one of mine: that's not going to deplete us. New calves will have been born by then. We'll return with as many animals as we started with.'

'I'd like to return with more,' he said softly.

Elsa snorted. 'There's but the two of us to feed. And we've plenty of animals for that. Why must you always be off hunting more reindeer and furs? We have everything we need.'

The dice in Heckram's hand ground against each other. 'I can remember when my father wore his talley string around his waist, and the ear flaps on it were thick as leaves on a branch. Every year he had furs and amber to trade south, and his tools were bronze, not bone. Every year he traveled south to meet the traders. He always had tales to tell, food to share. Always, we ate well and our tunics were thick.'

'Umm,' Kuoljok agreed softly. 'So we all did, in those days. No one had ever seen the herd so large. The wolves grew fat off the weak ones, but the strong ones were so many that they poured over the land like water. Folk held feasts for no reason, and all the meat racks were heavy. For three, four, maybe five years it was like that. More and more reindeer, every year. When they moved, we felt the thunder of their passage through the earth's bones. It was a time of plenty for all. Then, of course, came the plague. And the herd was smaller than I had ever seen it, and the wolves tore one another in their frenzy to feed off a kill. Heckram, there will always be fat years and lean ones, but I do think neither I nor you will see years as fat as the ones before the plague.'

'The wealth of the herd was the plenty of the folk,' Missa added softly. 'No man can hunt enough to create that level of wealth for himself in these times. Not even the best and most diligent hunter.'

Heckram sat silent, his eyes bowed to the board, and did

not speak. A hard determination inside him grew, threatened to split his chest open in a roar of defiance for their placid acceptance of these times, for their dumb contentment in the predictable rounds of their lives. Didn't they want, didn't they wonder? He knit his brows over the game board. His teeth were clenched and he kept his eyes down. The silence in the room passed as Missa and Ristin conferred over their weaving.

'Are you ever going to cast those dice, or are you going to give up the game now?' Kuoljok asked slyly.

'I'm thinking,' Heckram said, trying to make his voice easy.

'That's it. Take your time. Never be in a hurry to lose,' the old man suggested with a cracked laugh, as Heckram warmed the dice in his hands. Heckram growled, but threw the dice anyway, knowing he had already lost. He moved the wolf conservatively, biding his time. Always biding his time.

'There. That's done.' Elsa rose from her work, shaking her fingers. Heckram let his eyes wander from the board to follow her movements. The firelight touched her hair, illuminating the blue highlights of its deep black. Her hands were stained blue from the dye, and there was an errant streak of blue beside her nose. Yet no herdman would have said the evidence of her diligence made her less fair. Her face was still thoughtful of the work she had just completed. But as she picked up the water bucket to pour water to wash her hands, her eyes caught his. She smiled at him, almost shy to catch him watching her. The genuine fondness in her gaze called up his own slow smile, but he dropped his eyes from her look. He felt his heart must break, not because he loved her, but because he did not. She warmed his bed and cooked his meals, she rubbed his shoulders when he came in cold and weary from the hunt, she stroked his hair as he lay breathing deeply after their mating. But the feeling he had thought would grow in him seemed more absent than ever. He liked the girl. But sometimes he longed to put her hands from him, to shake free of her gentle touch and stride alone into the night. She had so little understanding of the determination that drove him. Always she tried to lure him aside from the things he knew he must do, to make him content to sit out a stormy day by her warm hearth. Sometimes he felt he could not breathe. And sometimes he dreamed of another hearth, and a boy who sat beside it.

He had not been back to the healer's hut since that day. He felt ashamed to go back, as if he had committed a great and cowardly wrong there, one there was no explaining. He thought of Kerlew, crouched and sobbing in the snow, and sighed. He was too busy to go, really. He had a wife now, and a life of his own to tend to.

Elsa was right. He had no right to interfere in the boy's life, to make him hungry for things he could not have. He stared at the board and at the trap he had been maneuvered into.

'The bucket's empty!' Elsa exclaimed in annoyance.

'So fetch more water,' Missa told her daughter calmly, not glancing up from her work.

'I'll go for it,' Heckram volunteered. The sod hut seemed suddenly suffocating, closing him in like a sorting pen closes in a herd of reindeer. Like them, he felt the urge to gallop wildly against the boundaries, seeking some way out. But even as he rose, thinking of cool air and the black sky arching over all, Kuoljok's hand closed on his wrist.

'No you don't, Heckram!' Elsa's father cackled. 'You won't slip away from the game that easily. Stay and lose like a man!'

'Finish your game! I'll be back in just a moment,' Elsa promised them. She did not even bother to slip on her outer tunic for the quick dash down to the spring. Bucket in one hand, she lifted the door flap and vanished into the night outside.

'A word of warning, young man,' Kuoljok counseled him in a loud whisper. 'Never do for a woman what she can do for herself. Or soon there'll be nothing she does for herself!'

Missa gave a derisive hoot. 'Listen to the old man! As if this woman ever asked him to do for her! I do my own work, and half of his as well! Where were you when your vaja and calf nearly drowned in that stream crossing three springs ago? This one was in the water up to her shoulders, trying to hold onto the calf, and hold off the mother that thought I was hurting it! And what does he call from the stream bank? "Looks like you can handle it, Missa. I don't want to ruin the new pants you made for me by getting them wet!" Such a help he is!'

The incident had been herdlore for three springs now, but they all laughed anyway, Kuoljok loudest of all. Heckram alone frowned at the dice that had fallen in the worst possible combination. Slowly he slid his hunted wolf from the apex of one triangle to another. There was no winning this game. The old man had him, and he knew it.

Kuoljok shook the dice fiercely, grinning at Heckram's long look. Heckram looked aside, let his fingers idly trace the fading pattern on the trunk top. Joining Elsa had been like wedding Lasse, he thought to himself glumly. A fine and merry companion, honest, competent, skilled, and caring. What more could he ask for in a wife? he demanded of himself. And had no answer. A surge of anger and panic pulsed through him suddenly at the choiceless direction his life was taking. He found himself reaching, to snatch the wolf marker from the board just as Kuoljok's knuckly hand was about to capture it.

'Hey!' the old man exclaimed in surprise. Heckram forced a frozen grin to his face and dropped the wolf marker into the hand that opened to receive it.

'You've caught me, fair enough,' Heckram conceded. As Kuoljok grinned and scooped the markers and dice into their little leather bag, Heckram rose. He stretched, his fingertips brushing the rafters of the hut.

'Elsa has been gone a while, hasn't she? I thought she was just going to the spring.' He idly touched his fingertips to the long fibers of beaten root that she had hung to dry. They came away blue.

'Don't touch that!' scolded Ristin. 'You'll spoil her work. No doubt Elsa ran into someone and has stopped to talk. Don't fret so much over her. You're joined now! Surely you can be apart for a few moments.'

'It just seemed that she had been gone a long time,' he said lamely.

'So it does,' said Missa sagely. 'Put your mind at rest, then, Heckram. Go and fetch her.' Heckram didn't miss the conspiratorial look that passed between the two mothers. Had not they once been young women finding an excuse to be alone under the crisp winter sky with a handsome young man? 'And the two of you might bring some of the good blood sausage from the meat rack. A bite or two would taste good this evening,' Missa added.

'Mind you don't kiss her, Heckram. You'd be playing right into her hands,' Kuoljok suggested wryly, with a look that said that women were not the only ones who played such games.

Heckram snorted noncommittally and shrugged into his heavy tunic. Since he and Elsa had joined, they treated him more as a child than as a man. He, who was several years past the age when most herdmen wed, was addressed as if he were a moonstruck youth. It was but one more thing that rankled this evening. One more goad he would not respond to.

Pushing the flap aside, he stepped out into the night. The winter camp was quiet. Evening chores were done and folk were snug inside their huts. The village dogs slept close to the doorflaps of their owners' huts, savoring the warmth that leaked out. Heckram stretched in the chill night, drawing in a deep lungful of the cold night air. There was a moon tonight, nearly full. The snow reflected its silvering light, painting a world of blacks and silvers and grays. His knee boots crunched on the packed snow of the path as he passed the crouching huts. Light leaked from some of them, voices flowing out with it to warm the night. One dog stretched and rose to greet him as he passed. A quick pat and a quiet word settled the animal again. He passed his own hut, silent in the darkness.

The spring was at the far end of the village, set in a tangle of willows. No huts were built close to it, for in spring the ground became soggy muck hidden by a waving forest of reeds and grasses. Only the freezes of winter reduced its flow and tamed it. The cold water welled up from the earth, black and chill, in a still pool no wider across than a man's two strides. It flowed away in a stream now covered by ice and a layer of smooth snow. But the herdfolk kept open this one circle of water, where they might fill their buckets.

Elsa knelt by the stream, almost hidden in the shadows of the surrounding willows. Her bucket lay empty at her side, and she stared at the black circle of water. Heckram wondered what could fascinate her so, to sink in the snow, so lightly clad, and stare at the water. 'Elsa?' he called softly, not wishing to startle her. She made a guttural sound. Her head swung slowly to face him.

'Elsa!' he cried, and the cold night swallowed his horrified cry and gaped over him for more. The moonlight was gentle as it touched her, but its shadows could not hide the ruin of her face. Her jaw sagged awry and the darkness that dripped from her open mouth stained the front of her shirt. She lifted a hand to him. White fingerbones flashed an instant in the moonlight; then her hand fell into the white snow beside her. Darkness spread from it.

There was no way to be gentle enough. She cried out wordlessly as he lifted her and her legs flailed him with her pain. Running would have jarred her, but his soul fled ahead of him, racing between the long row of sod huts. He couldn't find a voice to call for help, to raise an alarm. They were unprepared when he kicked the tent flap aside and entered the hut. The heads turned slowly, the faces froze as he knelt before them and offered them the broken body their daughter's soul was trapped in. For a long teetering instant, the world balanced in silence.

Then it came crashing back against him, like a roar of wind down a narrow valley, like the merciless rushing of a spring-thawed river.

'What happened?'

'Put her here! Gently, gently! Oh, her hand!'

'Cold water. Clean bandages. She's shivering, cover her. Elsa, Elsa. Lie still, little one, lie still. You are safe now. Give me some cold water!'

'I left the bucket by the spring,' Heckram said stupidly. He stared at Elsa. If an avalanche had caught her up and swept her through trees, then she might have looked this way. If she had been caught in the sudden roar of a spring flood and bashed against rocks and debris, then he would have expected this. But she had only gone to fetch a bucket of water, from their own village spring at night. He stared at her, unable to grasp the reality.

Something had struck the side of her head. It had torn her jaw loose from its hinges so that she gaped stupidly at nothing. The flesh had torn from the corner of her mouth up into her cheek. The flow of blood stained her cheek red and dripped on her chest. He had an almost uncontrollable urge to reach over and shut her mouth for her, to put her face back together. A horrid little sound came from it with each breath she expelled. A useless, hopeless little cry. One arm hung unnaturally from a shoulder that sagged in its socket. The hand of the other arm seemed scarcely a hand anymore.

'Heckram!' His mother's voice crashed against him; her hands grabbed his face and shook him. 'You can't just stand here. Go wake Lasse and send him for the healer. Then get Capiam. Report this to him. No bear did this. This is man's evil. Hurry!'

He felt himself pushed from the hut back into the dark and bloody night. He stood, blinking stupidly, taking in the image of Kuoljok hastening from the spring with a bucket that slopped water at every step of the old man's shambling trot. 'Elsa, Elsa,' he was panting as he ran, quavering out the helpless cry. The sound galvanized Heckram. He found himself running through the night, fleeing before Kuoljok could speak to him.

His pulkor. His mother's harke, a young, strong animal that was still but half trained. But Britsi was fleet and had stamina. Tonight Heckram was not gentling and coaxing. When the skittish Britsi leaped away from him, he seized him roughly by his lower jaw. Britsi tried to rear up on his hind legs and lash out with his front legs, but Heckram was merciless. He dragged the reindeer down to a stand.

The harness went on quickly, the leather collar slung over his neck and the ends pulled down over his breast and between his forelegs. Behind the forelegs it was fastened to the reins, which then ran back between his hind legs to the pulkor. Britsi danced as Heckram leaped into the pulkor and then the reindeer was off, streaking half terrified through the snowy night. The pulkor careened after him, Heckram shouting encouragement.

The keeled wooden sled slid smoothly behind the animal down the packed-snow trail that ran the length of the village. It was slower going when Britsi took to the deeper, less packed snow outside the village. The darkness of the forest closed in around them as they left the village behind. Heckram tried to keep to the more sheltered parts of the hillsides, avoiding the deepest snow where Britsi would have floundered to a walk.

The night was still but for their passage. He struck the vague trail made by their skis the last time they had visited the healer. An image of Elsa struggling to tuck her thick hair back under her cap. He shook it from his mind. Lasse had been to see Tillu twice since then, once for a flux remedy and once to fetch a tonic for his grandmother. The snow was packed enough to take the reindeer's weight. The pulkor slid smoothly and silently in Britsi's wake.

The forest stretched endlessly around him and ahead of him. It was made of the night and his fear, and his unacknowledged guilt lurked in it, as intangible and penetrating as fog.

At the bottoms of the vales they raced through willows

and alder that reached scraggling hands toward him. The frosted tips of the branches glistened white as fingerbones in the moonlight. Then up the side of the hill, through a stratum of ghostly birches, naked and grieving, and into the dark and forbidding pines with their lowering branches. The path seemed endless and he cursed Britsi and yanked the reins whenever the animal stepped from the path and faltered. Then they started a long descent of a gentle hill, and the feeble firelight that leaked from Tillu's worn tent was like a beacon of hope to him. 'Tillu! Tillu the Healer!' he cried, his voice breaking against the cold black night.

Sleep had begun to close over her like a soft blanket when she heard the anguished roar from outside her tent. She rose hastily, pushing the hair back from her eyes and belting her nightrobe more tightly around herself as she stepped quickly through the door.

The scene that met her eyes was like a tapestry of some strange fable. A reindeer rushed down the hillside toward her while behind it came a man atop a sliding log. She recognized Heckram's voice, and as he came closer she caught the gist of his words. 'Elsa . . . hurt . . . must come.' She darted back into her tent and was pulling on her clothes when he burst through the tent flap, still shouting. His hair was wild, his eyes frantic as he caught at her arm. She seized his hands firmly in both of hers and spoke calmly.

'I have to get my medicine bag and waken Kerlew. Calm down. What's happened?'

He let go of her, but the words tumbled from his lips so rapidly that she could not decipher them through his accent. All traces of his former restraint were gone. His shouting awakened Kerlew, who sat up in his sleeping skins and looked about, bewildered. Tillu stepped past him to take down her bag of medicines. She checked quickly through it to make sure she had supplies of the most common herbs. But when she opened a small box to replenish those she was low on, Heckram stepped past her to slam it shut and tuck the whole box under his arm. He grabbed her by the upper arm, dragging her to the door.

'Has he come to take me hunting?' Kerlew asked hopefully, sleepily.

'No. Someone at the village is hurt. Elsa, I think. I have to go to her.' Tillu pulled her hood up against the cold.

'I'll come, too.' The boy kicked off his blankets and reached for his leggings.

For the first time, Heckram became cognizant of the uproar he was creating. He released Tillu's arm and passed his hand before his eyes. He suddenly fell silent and looked from Tillu to her son in worry. He took a deep breath and tried to speak in a normal voice, but he panted out the words. 'Kerlew, you'll have to stay here. No room in the pulkor. Be a good boy?' he asked hopefully.

'Kerlew, stay here and behave yourself,' Tillu instructed him firmly. 'I won't be gone long. Go back to sleep, and I'll be back before you wake up. You're big enough to stay by yourself. You do it all day.'

'Night's different. What if a bear comes? What if Owl-spirit comes to steal me?' His halting words quavered.

'Don't be silly,' Tillu said firmly. 'Those are just old tales. Just go back to sleep and I'll be back by morning.'

'All right!' Kerlew replied savagely. He shut his jaws with a snap, but couldn't keep his lip from trembling.

'We must hurry. Elsa needs healer very much. Kerlew be brave boy. I'll send Lasse back, to keep you company. You show him spoons, okay?' Heckram bartered hastily as he pulled Tillu toward the door. But the boy only turned away from them.

'Kerlew will be safe?' Heckram asked as the flap fell.

'I think so,' Tillu replied, glancing back uneasily. She hoped he would do nothing foolish while she was gone. Whenever he was displeased, he acted it out in strange ways. Well, there was no time for fretting now. She found herself staring at a reindeer tied to a boat. The animal reared up on its hind legs and lashed out at them as they approached.

Heckram seemed to find nothing strange in this. With a swiftness born of practice, he reached, grabbed the reindeer's jaw, and brought it down. 'Get in!' he shouted to Tillu, gesturing at the boat. She stepped up beside it to stare hesitantly down into it. There was a nest of furs inside, and the long trailing leather strips that ran up to the reindeer's neck. Yes, it was a boat, made of planks of wood bent and pegged together. 'Get in!' Heckram roared again, and she clambered in.

She was scarcely settled before he seized the reindeer's harness and they started off at a run up the trail. Tillu's head was snapped back by the suddenness and she gripped the sides of the sliding boat. Pulkor, Heckram had called it. Trees, snow, and darkness slid past her at a frightening speed, all the more unnerving for the smoothness of the movement. The hind legs of the reindeer flashed very close before her, flinging up bits of snow that stung when they struck her. There was the creak and rush of the pulkor, the crunching footsteps of man and reindeer on the trail, and the black night pressing down. Tillu shivered deeper into the nest of furs.

FOURTEEN

Tillu had thought she was immune to screaming. She had heard so many kinds: the screaming of a woman in her first childbirth, cries swiftly forgotten when the babe was put in her arms; the screaming of a child, more frightened than hurt, when Tillu had to pry his grip loose from his mother to treat a badly cut lip; the startled scream of a brave man, the sound bursting from him when the broken ends of a bone grated together. Yet they were nothing compared to the constant mewling that flowed from Elsa's torn mouth with every breath she expelled. Heckram's panted words had not prepared Tillu for this.

She shivered with apprehension and chill as Heckram thrust her before him into the sod hut. His faith in her was pathetically apparent as he pulled her toward the injured woman. His face was red and white from his run, his chest still heaving with exertion. There was hope in his dark eyes. She dreaded it. 'The healer is here; all will be well now,' it seemed to say. She hoped he was right.

The two older women in the room parted and moved

aside, surrendering Elsa to her. Their faces were expectant and waiting. Tillu tried to appear calm as she knelt down by Elsa. Her medicine bag slipped from her grip to the floor beside her. Heckram stepped forward to set the chest of extra supplies beside her. He staggered as he stood upright again. Tillu felt the eyes of the women drilling into her like the spiral seeds of summer. With an effort she forced her attention to Elsa.

It was difficult to recognize the fit and capable woman who had come to trade with her. Elsa was a huddled wreck. Tillu wondered what merciless instinct kept her conscious. Whatever had savaged her had been thorough. Tillu touched Elsa with her eyes only, cataloging those injuries she could help, and the order in which to work. There was little she could do for the broken jaw and torn cheek other than to place them into their former positions and hope the body could heal itself. Whether she would ever again speak normally, Tillu could not tell. From the way one arm lay, it was dislocated at the shoulder. The hand on the other arm was a puzzle; it looked both sliced and broken. Later, when the broken pieces of Elsa's knife were found by the spring, Tillu would realize that these injuries had been caused by her desperate struggle to keep her weapon, to no avail.

Her torn clothing might hide other injuries, but these were the wounds that most frightened the others. Spilled blood and broken bones were a fearsome thing to look on. But healers learned to fear most the secret hurts, the ones that damaged the hidden places of the body and defied healing. Places where the eyes could not see, or the fingers touch. Tillu would wait to be sure before she told them of her own fear. She had not seen it all that often. Once, it had been a child who had tumbled down a hillside and struck his head on a rock. Another time it was a man who had received a glancing blow from a rival's club. Tillu did not like to remember them. They had been long in dying. First there was the slight bulging of the eyes, such as she thought she detected in Elsa. Later the pressure within the skull would build, distorting the face with swelling. No healer could cure it, though she had tried, with cold compresses and bleeding and warm poultices on the wound. It was a killing thing, mysteriously caused by a blow to the head. An unseen, unhealable injury.

Heckram sank slowly down beside her, kneeling on the hides right at Tillu's elbow. His body blocked her light, his quick panting breath distracted and unnerved her. As she reached a hand toward Elsa, he gasped, anticipating his woman's pain.

Tillu turned to him and gripped him by the shoulder. 'Heckram. You're in my way.' She spoke kindly but firmly. He didn't hear her. She turned to the women, glad to distract them. 'Take him away. Soup. Sleep. Or he'll be sick.' Her eyes caught on an old man in the corner who rocked himself wordlessly, helplessly, his eyes vacant. 'That one, too. Take away from here, out of my way. Big help to me.'

The alacrity with which the men were seized and urged from the tent was an indication of how helpless the two women had felt, and how badly they needed to help. As soon as the flap fell behind them, Tillu turned back to Elsa. She must work swiftly now, to get the worst of her pain-causing done while they were not here to witness it. 'Elsa? Elsa?' she asked, but there was no sign the woman knew she was there. There was only the sound that welled from her agony. Tillu debated whether to give her a soporific before she began. Reluctantly, she decided against it. The semiconscious woman would have been more likely to choke than to swallow.

Her jaw was broken in more than one place. Tillu's deft fingers manipulated the swelling flesh, trying to align the hidden fragments of bone. She eased the jaw back into an approximation of where it belonged and smoothed the ragged edges of torn flesh together. Someone had had the sense to leave water warming by the fire, and snow water melting by the door. Tillu chose the warm water for this. She wiped the wound carefully, ignoring the sounds of the woman she worked on. A careful binding held flesh and jaw in place. There. She looked better now, but a glance at her eyes told Tillu it would make no difference. Elsa was going to die.

As she worked over her hand, she wondered why she did it. What good to bind the poor crumpled fingers, to spread soothing unguent on the torn flesh, to bandage from sight the bloody and broken places? The new pain of having her broken fingers straightened changed the cadence and pitch of Elsa's moaning. As Tillu carefully drew one finger straight, Elsa gave a sudden gasp. Her heels drummed against the hides she rested on. Then she was still, at last unconscious.

Tillu seized her opportunity. Elsa would not feel the pain now. She would do the rougher healing. She snapped the wrenched shoulder back into its socket. She looked for and found a better knife than her own and used it ruthlessly to cut through the leather and wool and bright woven bindings of Elsa's garments. Tillu laid her tunic open, to reveal the blackening bruises down the left side of her rib cage. Her fingers probed delicately, and she decided no ribs were broken. A small frown creased her brow. She wondered briefly why the woman had been beaten so, and who had done it. She did not appear to have been raped; merely mauled and left to die. Perhaps she had broken some tribal rule.

Tillu shook her head at her own curiosity. These were not questions for a healer to ask. She had seen women of other tribes beaten this badly, sometimes by a rapist, sometimes by a lover or father. Kerlew's strange prediction that Elsa would not return with bear grease rose in her mind. Had Heckram done this? It might be so. She had seen men just as repentant and guilty as he seemed to be. It was possible. And none of her worry. Over the years, she had learned to ask no questions. The answers never made the healing any easier. She covered the poor battered body gently. Her fingers touched Elsa's skull, gently probing through the thick, black hair. She found the spot, as she had known she would, and felt her stomach turn over as she touched it. No blood flowed from it. All the damage was within.

Turning her back on Elsa, Tillu drew closer to the fire. She felt chilled and weary, more than the long ride through the cold night and her interrupted sleep could explain. It was this 'healing.' A healing that was more a preparation for burial. There had not been many of this kind in Tillu's life, but each one dragged at her, making her question her skills. This Elsa would die. Any of her other injuries, she might have survived. But Tillu could no longer ignore the signs. Still she did not call for Heckram and the others yet. Elsa had been strong. Her dying would take days and nights. Their vigil would be long enough. Let them rest now.

She unrolled a piece of scraped, bleached hide. On it she arranged packages and bundles of herbs, tossing spoiled bits into the fire as she selected others and put them in two small piles. Her fingers and nose knew each dry leaf, each curl of bark, as she sorted. Here was strong-scented yarrow that could start a woman's flow of blood or treat a wound, and the long leaves of deer tongue for an emetic. Here was the curling bark from the bear-berry shrub, good for urinary disorders, and the long dandelion root for a tonic or a mild laxative. Some herbs she had known from her lessons when a child, others she had learned from the folk she moved among. Their names might vary from people to people, but not their properties. Tillu chose carefully. Into the first pile went those for cleansing bleeding wounds and ones for easing the pains of cuts and gouges. Into the second pile went those that eased pain and encouraged sleep.

She turned next to the wooden box Heckram had brought along. Opening it, she began to assemble her tools. Her mortar and pestle were the ball and socket from a reindeer calf's joint. Tillu scooped up the first pile of herbs and began to grind them together. The fine powder was mixed with lukewarm water. She soaked a fresh bandage in it, and wrapped it dripping over the bound fingers. She wiped blood from Elsa's face, noted that her torn cheek no longer bled. She tried to ignore the bulging of her closed eyes.

The second mixture she hesitated over. Elsa's wounds were severe. She knew she must increase the strength of the mixture for it to have any effect. But Elsa was already weakened. Too much would . . . perhaps be merciful. Tillu pushed that thought aside. True healers refused such decisions. Her profession was to repair the body and cure the illness. Let others decide when someone was beyond her help. Her vocation demanded that she always believe her patients would survive. Her hand hovered over the neatly arranged piles of herbs. After a long hesitation, she picked up two night berries and added them to the small pile before her. Death's Seeds, Benu's folk had called these, and another folk had named them Bitter Sleep. She wanted a mixture that would heavily sedate and separate Elsa from her pain, but still allow her to bid her family farewell. If ever she opened those eyes again.

Tillu crushed the berries and herbs together into a coarse mixture, added it to water, and set the vessel to heat by the fire. It might never be needed, but if Elsa awoke to pain, Tillu did not want her to have to wait for relief.

She placed her palms on the earth and pushed herself upright. The walls of the hut swung slowly before her for an instant; she had stood up too rapidly for one so weary. She rubbed at her gritty eyes as she stumbled over to sit beside Elsa. She tucked covers gently against her. 'Rest now,' she told Elsa. 'Rest.' With a sigh, Tillu leaned back against a cool sod wall.

A sound turned her head. One of the women was coming back into the hut. Something about her face . . . A memory twisted elusively through her mind, and then Tillu realized she was seeing Elsa's features subtly reflected in this older face. A relative. Behind her came a handful of men that Tillu didn't recognize. Last came the other woman who had been in the hut when Tillu first arrived, followed by Heckram. Tillu sighed to herself. He should be resting. He looked weary and bed-raggled, and angered at something. She hadn't noticed before the tracings of gray in his black-bronze hair. It reminded her of a wolf's pelt. There were lines in his face that had deepened this night, and she wondered suddenly how she could have thought he was a young man. He was older than she was.

The people filed in silently, their very silence a continu-ation of whatever argument had created the tension stretched among them. It was plain the other men had not seen Elsa's injuries before. Their faces reflected various emotions, and cloaked others. One was the headman of the village. Tillu did not need to be told of his importance. His rumpled black

230

hair attested that he had been roused and dressed hurriedly, but he had not neglected to deck himself with a necklace of amber beads. His clothing was richer than that of the others, the furs softer and more lush, the colors of the woven strips brighter and wider. The skinny whelp beside him must be his son. Tillu disliked him instantly. His face mirrored none of his father's concern for Elsa. There was only the avarice of one fascinated by blood and pain. He licked his narrowed lips and peered at the girl. Muscles twitched around his eyes as he stared.

The third was a barrel-chested bear of a man. Had Tillu not seen him, she would have supposed Heckram an anomaly to the herdfolk. But this man, too, showed the marks of mixed blood. He stood half a head taller than Heckram, and his hair was brown bleached by the sun with streaks of gold. He had started life with a good face, Tillu judged, but along the way had spoiled it. There was a heavy cast to his features and his eyes didn't seem to open completely. A waiting, hiding man. His clothing was plain, but well made. Its reserved color and simpler braid suggested wealth more than the gaudy decorations the headman's son wore. Moreover, this man bore himself as the son should have, but did not. As he gazed on Elsa, he expelled a deep sigh like a hiss, and crossed his heavy arms across his thick chest. He was the first one to break the silence.

'If she had accepted my offers,' he said sternly, 'I would not have let her go out to the spring alone at night, to take her chances with beasts. Why is it some men claim what they cannot care for? You've only yourself to blame for this, Heckram. I understand why you did not report it to Capiam until now. No man of any pride would want to admit a thing like –'

'Joboam.' The headman's voice stopped him. The woman seizing Heckram's arm aborted his swing at the man rebuked as Joboam. Tillu made herself smaller, crouching by her patient as she scowled at this drama. This sort of tension never did an injured person any good. If there was any more disturbance . . .

Heckram shook the woman off and stepped clear of her. Tillu wondered if he were aware of the way he put his body between Joboam and the woman on the floor. 'It was no beast,' he growled. 'A man did this. And I went for the healer first, because I knew this is exactly what you would do. Stand over her and make useless remarks, seeking to fix the blame on someone rather than finding out who did it.'

'It could have been a demon,' Capiam's son breathed. His eyes glowed at the prospect. No one paid him the least attention. Tension sang between Joboam and Heckram. They could have been alone in the hut.

The woman who had clutched at Heckram's arm spoke abruptly, changing the direction of everyone's stare. 'Capiam. Are you the herdlord or not? Do you lead this sitor? Then there is someone among us who has done this thing. If you lead us, then it is you, not my son, who must answer for letting one such as that live among us.'

The very softness of her voice made the accusation sharper. The herdlord's son gasped. The jaw of the other woman sagged open an instant. Then she snapped it shut and her gaze hardened.

'She's right,' she said, her voice cracking. 'She's right! Never has there been a time when a woman was afraid to go to the spring alone! Never has a woman been savaged like this, on the very edges of our camp! What are we coming to, when there is among us one who can do this? Where are you leading us, Capiam?'

Her voice went shriller with every word, and suddenly she was gasping. She clutched at herself and sank slowly down on the floor, her face caving in as her tears found her.

'Who are you to speak to the headman like that, old woman!' Joboam demanded in a voice laced with fury.

Heckram spun on him, the cords in his neck leaping out like plucked bowstrings. The headman's son scrambled backward in his hurry to be out of the way, stumbling against Tillu's pot of pain potion and nearly upsetting it. Heckram took a step forward and suddenly found the little healer woman thrusting herself in front of him.

'Quiet! Quiet!' Tillu hissed furiously. In a moment more, they would be fighting, and she would have more heads to bind and hands to set. Not tonight, she promised herself. 'Out! Men out!' she added firmly as they showed no signs of obeying. 'Elsa needs quiet. Elsa needs rest. Other men, out! Healer say, Heckram stay here, help take care of Elsa,' she added shrewdly, thinking to occupy one of the combatants. 'You. Headman.' Capiam might not have recognized her word, but he recognized the finger that jabbed at him. 'Take men away, not let them fight here. Talk in morning, not now. Not now! Out. Quiet!' she hissed again when the headman's son opened his mouth.

For a long instant they held their positions. Then Capiam clapped his son on the shoulder and propelled him from the hut. 'Joboam?' He made the burly man's name a question and a warning. Joboam clenched a fist and let Heckram see the small movement of it. Then he backed from the hut, his eyes on Heckram as he departed. Heckram stared after him like a snarling dog.

Tillu gave in to the rubberiness in her knees and knelt beside the keening mother. She put her arms around her and rocked with her, letting her take the comfort of weeping, and feeling a small relief herself in the rhythmic movements. One day she would trust too much to her status as a healer. She had gambled that she could order a headman from a tent and not be beaten for it. She had been right, but now she trembled at what might have been the consequences had she been wrong.

The other woman came to take her place, her tears and soft cries mingling with her friend's. Tillu eased away from them. Healers had no time to grieve. Instead, she moved to her herb chest and took from it chamomile and sleep's ease, bilin root and willow bark scrapings. She put fresh cold water on the hearth to heat while she mixed and measured her herbs. When the water boiled, she took it from the fire, added the herbs, and set it aside to steep. These were the herbs for sleep, and to ease the headaches of weeping. All would need them this night.

She turned from her work to find that Heckram, too, had obeyed the orders of the healer. He sat flat on the floor by Elsa, her unresponsive hand resting in his. He was looking earnestly into a face that looked less and less like Elsa. With a sinking heart Tillu wondered how long it would take her to die. For now she could have no doubt of the pressure building inside the skull like the festering inside a closed wound. She did not understand this injury. It could not be lanced like an infection or a boil, could not be eased down with a poultice like the swelling of a twisted joint. Nothing to do but watch her die.

The tea had steeped to a honey darkness. She chose a dipper at random from those hanging from the rafters, looked about, and found the carved wooden cups. The women had wept themselves to silence. They leaned against one another and watched her passively as she brought them tea. 'You should rest,' she told them, and each nodded, believing she spoke to the other. She left them holding one another and took a third cup to Heckram. She offered it to him, but he did not notice it. When she touched it against his empty hand, he started as if she had stabbed him. Slowly he put Elsa's hand down, tucking it gently beneath the covers. Then he took the cup Tillu still held.

For a long moment he just held the cup as he continued to look at Elsa. Finally he shifted his gaze to Tillu, and she regretted telling him to help with Elsa. She saw now the effort it had taken for him to hold that lax hand.

'She's dying.' She read the words from the shape of his lips, the sound barely breathed out. He was not questioning her, was not asking for a lie to ease himself. He was telling her what he knew, passing on information to the healer. She bowed her head in assent. The next words he spoke made no sense to her. 'I didn't love her enough,' he confessed. Then he lifted the cup and drained it, scalding as it was.

Tillu waited to receive the empty cup back from him. He gave it to her, then stretched out slowly on the floor hides. His reaching hand touched, not Elsa, but the edge of the hide that covered her. She heard his stiff swallowing and turned to leave him alone. The women were talking still, in soft, thick whispers. They no longer wept or ranted. The passion of their grief was spent for now. Soon they would sleep.

As Tillu would now. A little distance from the fire, she made a place for herself, baring the floor's covering of birch twigs as she took one of the hides to cover herself. She stared into the fire and then closed her eyes, letting her mind glide just under the edge of sleep as she kept her ears alert for the slightest stirring from Elsa.

The fire had burned low. The softening shadows in the hut, the gentle sound of breathing, calmed the night. Heckram lay silent, listening and staring. The healer's brew had not put him to sleep. Part of him wondered if there was any left in the pot, if a second cup would let his mind sink into emptiness. But the other part of him was too occupied to think of rising and looking for a cup of soothing tea.

He was trying to remember the first time he had touched Elsa as a man touches a woman. He couldn't. It had been during a time that no longer seemed to fit into the general context of his life. He had awakened to his manhood later than most boys, and been prey to that awakening for a shorter time. He tried to remember the Heckram of those days, a male with burning blood like a leaping, snorting sarva in its first rut. Like a sarva, he had bounded from one willing female to the next, sharing but a moment with each, taking his pleasure with eyes closed, his own heart loud in his ears. It was a time he regretted.

No member of the herdfolk condemned him. Did not all, men and women, pass through the first heat of knowledge, to emerge as adults? The older folk turned their eyes aside from the excesses of youth, trusting to time that these things would pass, or deepen into permanent relationships. Heckram had been so steady and sober a youth, and was now so settled and responsible a man. Yet those two lives were divided by that wild season. He had fought like a sarva, too, finding insults in the most innocent of teasing, and battling all, youths his own age, and those years older. He had not

won all his fights, nor bedded every woman he courted. But
though he couldn't seem to remember his losses in either
kind of struggle, his victories were equally blurry.

Elsa had been one he had won, but he could not remember
much of the conquest. Like him, she had been flushed with
the first touch of fertility, but she had been younger, so much
younger. He tried to remember something, a word in the
dusk, a touch, the shape of a bared young breast. Nothing.
She had been but one of the many for him. It made it so
much worse to know that of her many, he had been the one.

It took a few seasons to cool his blood, but when his
passage was complete, he saw himself in a cold hard light.
It did not matter to him that no one else faulted him for his
conduct. He found his own peculiar shame in knowing that
the heat of his body had never touched his heart. Elsa, so
simple and trusting, had found ways to let him know that
she would come to his call. She had been willing to wait for
him to feel ready for commitment, never doubting that in
time he would want her. Now he wished he had found the
courage to turn her aside, to find some gentle way of telling
her to find a better man. She might have had children by
now, be a wife and a mother. So much she had missed waiting
for him.

He waited for tears to come, but his eyes were dry, the
lids abrasive when he closed them. He sighed, then stiffened
at an answering sigh from Elsa. In an instant he was on his
knees beside her, whispering 'Elsa? Elsa?'

She answered with a trailing moan that rode on her breath.
It was followed immediately by another. He took her lax
hand. The fingers twitched lightly against his rough palm.
He closed his hand over them, hoping she could feel he was
there.

A rustle of garments, and the healer was beside them. Her hair straggled about her face and her eyes were old as she bent closely over Elsa to peer at her. As she straightened, she looked into his face. Slowly she shook her head at him. 'Don't torment yourself,' she whispered softly. 'Don't hope.'

'She hurts,' he replied.

Tillu said nothing, but returned to the fire. Taking a ladle from her own chest, one stained dark at the dipper end, she scooped a measure from the pot she had kept simmering by the fire. She signed for him to ease her up to drink. Elsa's bandaged head was stiff against his shoulder as he supported her. Tillu held the dipper to her swollen lips, but gave her no more than would moisten them. He frowned at her stinginess.

'Night berry,' she explained in a whisper. 'Too much kills. Little bit, sleep deep.'

He eased Elsa back to the floor, but continued to sit by her, gently holding her hand. For long moments her breath moaned in and out. Then her sounds became softer and finally were stilled.

'She sleeps,' Tillu told him. 'Heckram sleep now, too?'

'No,' he told her, but lay down once again beside Elsa. He longed to tuck her into the curve of his body and hold her close. He wanted to feel he was protecting her, holding death at bay with the warmth of his own life. But he knew that the pressure of his body against hers could only cause her pain. He contented himself with taking her hand. He stroked her small fingers, pressed them once to his lips. He closed his eyes to the night. This time he kept her hand in his, followed her down into the darkness of deep sleep.

Morning came, a chill gray beast that nosed Heckram from the comforts of sleep. He kept his eyes closed, resisting consciousness. But his body complained it was chilled, stiff from the cold, from being still all night. He grumbled softly and started to shift to a more comfortable position, only to become aware of a cold hand in his. The events of the night before swept him remorselessly into wakefulness. Heckram jerked his body up, kneeling straight, to stare at Elsa in silence.

She was dead. He had felt her death chill in his hand and known it in his sleep. He had dreamed her dead, watched her walking away through the snow to Saivo. Her bow had been on her shoulder, her embroidered game bag swinging at her hip. Her stride had been easy, carrying her across the crusted tops of drifts. She had pulled her red cap off to the early spring sunshine, and her unbound hair had gleamed brighter than the snow drifts. So beautiful. He had watched her go, smiling after her. He had not called her back.

This morning did not find her so beautiful. He turned from that chiseled face, not wanting to remember these new colors flushed across it. Carefully, he pulled the covers up to hide it from the light seeping in the smoke hole. As he did so, something rolled from where it had rested on top of her bedding. It thudded softly on the floor hides, rolled in an arc to rest against his knee. He stared down at it. There was a grimness to its plain, ungraceful handle and black stained bowl.

His eyes traveled to the hearth, and the near dead embers on the flat stones. The small pot that had held the potion sprawled on its side. His mind whirled slowly as he refused conclusions. He would not check to see how much was left in the pot, would not try to remember if Tillu had put the dipper back in the pot the night before. Had she been asking him something, when she said too much of it would kill? Had she thought she read an unspoken answer in his face? He had a sudden vision of Bruk foundered in the snow, his own calming hand preceding the seeking knife. He moaned softly.

Picking the ladle up by its handle, he carried it back to the pot. He dropped it beside the hearth and it clattered once against the stones. No one else stirred. Ristin and Missa slept side by side, huddled together in sorrow. Elsa had been the last living child of Kuoljok and Missa. With her had gone their grandchildren. They ended today, the unraveled ends of a long line. He thought of poor old Kuoljok, soon to awake in Heckram's hut, alone and puzzled. He had seemed so confused last night. 'What happened?' he had asked over and over again, long after Heckram had wearied of telling him he didn't know. The simple question had stung worse than Joboam's foolish accusation.

And the healer? He turned slowly to find her asleep in a shadowed corner of the tent. Inexplicably, Kerlew was curled beside her, smiling in his sleep.

FIFTEEN

Clumps of soft wet snow were dropping from the trees with dull plops. It was an erratic, stealthy sound, as if some great creature were stalking through the woods. It was not the only sign of the change. The papery bark of the birch trees was suffused with a pink glow, while the tips of the reaching willows showed red against the snow. But the dropping snow load was the most apparent sign. The lightened branches sprang up as they shed their burdens, shaking the trees and triggering a new flurry of falls. Even the small dark spruce of the clearings had doffed their white caps to spring's entrance.

Earlier in the day a falling load had found Heckram's back and shoulders, and some had slipped inside his tunic collar, sliding icily down his chest. He was still chilled and wet. The daily thaws of early spring were miserable. The thin sunlight that softened the snow and tried to warm his back glinted up into his eyes from the sinking snow drifts, making him squint. The wet snow he waded through soaked into his boots and trousers, and clung to his legs to weight his every stride.

The change of seasons that used to lighten his heart now only wearied him. He stood on the side of the hill, looking down at the reindeer and frowning.

The reindeer struggled through the heavy wet drifts, sinking in the clinging stuff, surging through it in plunges when they were startled. They pawed through it for lichen, lowering their heads into the snow hollows and nibbling it from the frozen ground. And every night winter returned, to lock the soft snow into a thick icy crust that could chafe and cut the deer's legs as they tried to work through it. Worst of all, when the reindeer did paw through the upper crust, the savve layer, they found flen on the ground. The thick layer of ice on the ground beneath the snow locked away the tender white lichen known as reindeer moss. Stubbornly, the hungry animals pawed up the frozen chunks and ate it, becoming sluggish and sometimes ill from consuming too much ice. His own animals still looked all right, but those of Elsa's parents were beginning to look thin and pinched. He would have to act.

'Heckram!'

He turned, startled, and already irritated with whomever came to break his solitude. In the last few weeks he had had enough talk to last a lifetime. At first he had wanted only to sleep, to hide from thought in unconsciousness. Then he had roused from his lassitude to anger. Against the advice of his mother and Elsa's parents, he had gone to Capiam. He had boldly voiced his suspicions before Capiam and his elder advisers. And they had rebuked him. His stomach clenched as he remembered.

Capiam's eyes had shone like angry black gems. His chest had swelled with his wrath, but he had demanded calmly, 'On what basis do you accuse Joboam of this abhorrent act?'

Heckram winced as he remembered his faltering effort to put his uneasiness into words. As he told how Joboam had pushed himself upon Elsa, how Joboam moved among the huts by night, and that even since their joining, Elsa had complained that the man followed her when she hunted. Even to his own ears, it had sounded like the querulous complaints of an imaginative child. The elders had listened, exchanging glances as he spoke. And then Capiam had spoken the most scorching words of all. 'Cannot you let it go, Heckram? It is pain enough for Joboam that the woman he desired chose you instead. It is anguish enough for him that she has perished. I will not accuse him of this thing. I know that he was playing tablo with Rolke when first we heard of Elsa's misfortune. It is also known to all of us, Heckram, that you followed her out into the night. Yet, none spoke against you on so slight a basis. You would do well to follow our example. Set the petty jealousies of childhood aside. Mourn Elsa, as is fitting. But do not seek to set the blame for her death on a man who showed only concern and affection for her. Your father was a man I trusted, Heckram. I leaned upon his wisdom. I wish you had inherited it. Go now. Say no more about this. Whatever beast or demon killed Elsa has escaped us. There is no sense in dwelling upon it.'

So he had left the herdlord's hut and said no more. But it was soon obvious that all had heard of his accusation. Most thought it an act unworthy of a herdman.

But he could not let it go, nor could he lose himself in sleep anymore. His thoughts chased themselves through his brain, leaving him unable to eat or sleep. He had felt his mother and Missa watching him, been pestered by Lasse's repeated efforts to get him to go hunting. He thought occasionally of the healer and her son, but felt no desire to face the boy he had slighted for too long, let alone the woman who had practiced such a deadly healing upon Elsa. His thoughts had run and worried him like a pack of wolves encircling an old sarva. Then one day he had risen and gone out alone into the silence of the grazing herd. He had immersed himself so deeply in work that he could not think beyond the next moment. Except when some fool came to talk to him.

Lasse was toiling up the hill, sinking into the snow with every step. Heckram looked at him critically. The boy was thin, but his hair was glossy in the sun. He still tended to carry the long-healed arm closer to his chest. Fond as he was of Lasse, he wished the youth would go away. Lasse seldom spoke of Elsa to Heckram. But somehow his silences were worse than the consoling words of the others. So he called to Lasse before the boy could come closer and fix him with those sympathetic eyes.

'Keep the deer clear for me, Lasse. I'm going to bring a tree down.'

He fumbled at his belt for his hand axe. The handle was made from the natural curve of a reindeer antler, the head of ground and polished stone. 'Wait!' Lasse called, and Heckram saw that the boy was carrying a full-sized axe with him. He waved it at Heckram, and the man returned his smaller axe to his sheath.

'I thought you might want this,' Lasse panted as he drew close enough for words. 'And I wanted to tell you I saw the godde making for the higher hills. What do you think?'

'I haven't thought about the wild herd for days. I've no time to hunt anymore. I've my own animals to watch, and my mother's, and Kuoljok's and Missa's.' He didn't mention Elsa's. Their ownership had reverted to her parents, though Missa had tried to insist that Heckram, as her intended, should take them. The memory of the painful argument stung again.

'I didn't mean we should go hunting. I meant we should follow them, move our animals up to better pasturage until spring is stronger. The flen is so thick; you can't get a staff through it. I know, I've probed it.'

'That's why I want to bring a tree down for them. Keep them clear, would you?'

He took the axe from the boy with a silent nod of thanks and chose a tree that already had a pronounced lean. Moss and beard lichen festooned its branches. The first few blows brought the heavy wet snow crashing down. It spattered the snow around him and he danced back to avoid it. When he had loosened most of its load, he stepped in, set his feet, and swung in earnest. The axe bit into the wood, sending bits of bark and then white chips flying. Lasse floundered in the snow, trying valiantly to drive back the older animals who knew that the sound of the axe meant food. When the leaning tree began its groan, Heckram roared, 'Get clear!' As the youth rushed to one side, the hungry animals surged forward. With a sudden crack the tree fell, its outstretched branches slapping the muzzles and shoulders of the most eager reindeer. The animals staggered from the impact, but immediately plunged back. In an instant the tree was surrounded by reindeer stripping it of beard lichen.

While the deer were occupied, Heckram and Lasse cut two more trees in rapid succession, taking turns with the axe. Lasse's animals, hearing the falling giants, came from their place farther down the hillside to join in the easy feeding. The two herdmen sat down, panting, on the stump end of one of the fallen trees and watched their beasts feed.

'You're right. It's about time to move them,' Heckram said

as if their conversation had never been interrupted. 'The godde know where the feeding is best. A wise herdman sees that his animals follow them.'

'Good. Tonight?'

Heckram considered. Night was the best time to move in this weather. The colder temperatures froze the top of the snow in a hard crust that men and beasts could walk on. He and Lasse could move their animals up higher in the hills, where the thaws of spring had not yet ruined the grazing. Then, when spring reached that high, they would bring their animals down again, to begin their longer migratory trek from the forests across the flat tundra to the summer grounds.

'Tonight. Is your grandmother coming?'

Lasse looked aside, squinting across the bright, snowy hillside. 'No. Not this time.'

It was a bad sign, and Heckram knew it. When the older folk began thinking they were too old to move from the talvsit to the temporary camps in the higher hills for the early spring grazing, it was a sign they were wearying of life. 'I don't think my mother will come this year either. Nor Elsa's parents.'

Lasse considered this gravely. But all he said was: 'It will make a lot of animals for you to manage.'

Heckram snorted, trying to speak lightly. 'They say our fathers managed this many and more, and all belonging to themselves. We've a way to go before we regain all they had.'

'It's so important to you.'

Heckram gave Lasse a strange look. 'And isn't it to you? Besides, what else is there? Wouldn't it be nice to kill a fat, strong harke for meat this autumn, instead of having to harvest the sickliest one that might not winter through anyway? How would it be to have fresh, thick hides on the floor of the kator this winter, instead of making do with the old worn ones? Wouldn't you like to load pulkors and harkar with your excess meat and hides, and go south to trade? To have tools of bronze instead of stone and bone, and shirts of warm wool instead of patched leather?'

'Do we live so poorly, then?' Lasse asked softly.

Heckram was startled into silence for an instant. 'No. But it's not so rich, either.'

Lasse stared off across the snow while he spoke, and Heckram wondered if he spoke to him or to himself. 'Yet, there's poor and poor. There's Joboam, with twice the animals that you own, the richest furs, the sleekest vaja, the best of everything. Yet, with all his wealth, Elsa wouldn't have him. And there's you, with enough to go around, if you are thrifty and careful. But Elsa was willing to wait for you to be ready. I think you two would have been wealthier than Joboam or the herdlord himself. Heckram, do you ever wish you hadn't waited?'

Heckram looked at Lasse, seeing him anew. His color was high, and his grandmother had put new braiding on his old hat. He wasn't sitting like a boy waiting for Heckram's reply. His posture said that he was a man now, and they were men discussing the ways of herd life. Idly he wondered who the girl was, and how well Lasse would herd the impulses of his heart. But when he spoke aloud, he said coldly, 'No. I've never regretted my waiting.' Only hers. But he did not add the last aloud, and Lasse would never suspect it.

If Lasse heard, he gave no sign of it. Instead, he abruptly announced, 'Capiam is thinking of asking Tillu to come with us to the summer grounds.'

Heckram stiffened slightly. 'What for?'

'What for?' Lasse echoed incredulously. 'As healer, of course.

How long has it been since we've had one? The old women do their best, but all they know is what they have from their mothers. They aren't really healers. And Tillu is good, even if she couldn't save Elsa. Look how well my arm healed.'

After she shot you, Heckram thought to himself. And you'll never know just how effective her 'cure' for Elsa was, my friend.

'Lanya took her son over to see Tillu,' Lasse was gossiping on. 'For that rash he's always had. Tillu asked a lot of questions and then told the boy, "no more reindeer milk or cheese." The rash is nearly gone now. And she made a rub for my grandmother's shoulder that takes the stiffness out, even in the cold weather.'

'I expect she'll come with us, then,' Heckram observed. He hadn't spoken to her since Elsa's death. His lack of feeling puzzled him. Either he should be grateful to her for ending Elsa's suffering, or hate her for ending Elsa's life. This peculiar emptiness he felt was inappropriate. It was too close to what he had felt at the thought of marrying Elsa. Did he think the healer was as inevitable? Idly he took out his belt knife to cut a slender whip from a nearby sapling. He began to whittle at it, half listening to Lasse.

'If Capiam asks her, I bet she'll come. There's some talk against the idea. Joboam can't stand her half-wit son. He says the boy has wolf eyes. Some of the others feel the same. Kerlew didn't seem all that strange to me, but the other –'

'Kerlew is not a half-wit,' Heckram said firmly, and this time it was the strength of his emotion that surprised him. His knife bit deeply into the bark.

'Well, that's true, I suppose. I mean, he doesn't go about drooling or anything like that. But when Missa tried to send him for water that morning, he acted like he couldn't understand what she wanted. Finally she gave him the bucket and pointed at the spring. When he got to the spring, he turned the bucket upside down and sat on it. Didn't go any farther, just sat and stared at the water, with that spooky look in his eyes. Then he knelt down and touched the blood-stained snow . . .' Lasse's voice suddenly faltered. He cleared his throat, obviously shortening his story. 'Two of Kelr's little boys tried to talk to him, but he didn't answer. So they pelted him with snow, just to stir him, you know how boys are. And Kerlew, twice their age, ran back to Tillu, howling. And wouldn't go back, for the bucket or the water. You can't say that isn't strange.'

'The strangest part is that Kelr would let his sons so treat a stranger.' A chunk of bark flew.

'It was just a boys' prank!' objected Lasse. He bent to pick frozen clumps of snow from his damp leggings.

'Perhaps to Kelr's boys it was. But what was it to Kerlew? And you can't judge a boy's worth from a minor thing like that. Look how he came alone to the talvsit that night. I still can't believe he followed the pulkor trail all the way from his tent to our camp that night. Alone, in the dark.'

'But that's another thing,' Lasse objected stubbornly. 'Why didn't he stay in his tent, as he was told?'

'I'd promised I'd send you to keep him company. And, in the rush of things, I forgot to even ask you.'

'That's not a very good reason to walk all that way in the cold and dark.'

'Perhaps not for one of us. But Kerlew strikes me as a very single-minded young man.'

'Single-minded, you say. Simple-minded, say the others. Well, it's no difference to me. Tolerating Kerlew is a small price to pay for having a healer with us again.'

249

Heckram was silent for long moments. Then he gave a harsh bark of laughter that made Lasse jump. He looked at the crooked arrow shaft he had just fashioned and flung it away into the snow. In a tired voice he asked, 'I wonder if anyone has ever asked what price Kerlew will pay for us to have Tillu as our healer?'

'What price?'

Tillu turned slowly from her fire. She had just finished pouring steaming water into a small wooden trough. 'What you want to give.'

Joboam thought it was a question. He sat bare-chested on her pallet, cradling his left forearm in his lap. A poultice of cooked and pounded inner bark from a spruce tree covered the angry suppuration on the back of his forearm. The cut was no longer than a man's finger. But the swelling it had caused had puffed and stiffened his elbow, and made his fingers into fat sausages on a thick hand. Despite his pain, he bartered. 'Two wolf hides, without the tails. Or a sausage and two cheeses?'

'Whatever you choose. How long, this hurt?'

Joboam glanced down at the injury and wrinkled his brow, as if looking at it increased the discomfort. He took his time to answer. 'Long time. Long, long time ago. I was carving, and cut myself. Not bad. It didn't bleed that much. It heals for a while. Then swells, and oozes. I take my knife, open it, wash it. It starts to heal. Then, again, it swells up, bigger, worse. Again, I cut it. I think it is healing. Then, one morning, sore again, swelling. This time is the worst it's been.'

Joboam spoke slowly in simple words, matching Tillu's speech. She didn't bother to tell him she understood their language now. Specific words she might not know, but she was comfortable with the flow of the words and their strange inflection. And she could speak it more fluently than she did. She found it easier to speak very simply and briefly. Maybe to keep from having to talk about anything besides healing. Maybe to keep a distance.

'Lucky man. Lucky you're still alive, not poisoned. Bad kind of hurt. Maybe something in there. If something is in there, we have to find it, get it out. Going to hurt a lot to find it. But going to kill you if we don't.' As she spoke, she opened a tiny leather sack and spilled from it a small pile of salt. Biting her lower lip, she reluctantly added more to the heap of gleaming crystals. The salt was precious, not only as seasoning, but for its drawing properties when used in poultices and soaks. From the look of Joboam's arm, it was going to take most of her supply to heal him. She wondered idly why those with the most were the stingiest when it came to offering payment.

'Stop staring, boy!' Joboam growled suddenly.

Tillu glanced up. Joboam had arrived very early. She had been preparing food for the boy and herself, but had set that aside at the sight of Joboam's arm. Kerlew was waiting on the hides by the fire. He watched her like a hungry dog as she took out her healing supplies. Kerlew didn't answer Joboam, but hung his head. His hands toyed listlessly with his precious spoons. Tillu spoke softly.

'Kerlew. Go outside. You can gather firewood for me.'

'But I'm hungry!'

'Then take cheese and sausage with you and eat that.'

'I want hot food.'

'Out, boy!' Joboam growled. Kerlew's eyes flickered sideways. Other than that, he gave no sign of hearing the man. He sucked his lower lip in tightly as he looked at Tillu.

251

Tillu set her jaw. She forced herself to speak calmly. 'Go for the firewood, then. Have cheese and sausage now, and pile up some wood. Then I will cook some of the reindeer that Lanya brought us. Go, now. Then I can work faster. Go on!'

She didn't look at Joboam as she urged her son from the tent. There had always been men like Joboam, would always be men like Joboam. Men who felt they could take charge whenever there wasn't another man around. Men who could not meet Kerlew's peculiar stare, who were offended by his slow speech and odd mannerisms. Men she couldn't trust not to strike the boy if he came too near or looked at them too long. Men who feared him, as they feared the touch of disease or madness.

As she dissolved the salt in the steaming water and set out clean white moss, she reminded herself that Joboam was in pain. And probably tired from traveling here, and uneasy in a strange place. She had to be patient and remember that she was a healer. A healer. After a moment, she sighed and let the tension ease out of her shoulders. She would be able to treat him as she did everyone else. And then he would go.

'Hot water. Slowly, slowly,' she cautioned him as she set the trough before him. It was just large enough for him to submerge the festering arm. She removed the poultice from the wound and motioned toward the water. She watched his face, saw him wince as his elbow touched the hot water. He set his jaw and narrowed his eyes, but slowly his arm entered the water. Sweat sprang out on his chest and forehead, but he made no sound of pain. She found herself turning away, unwilling to admire the control he exerted over himself.

'Why didn't you come sooner?' She picked through the moss, discarding bits of sticks and dirt into the fire.

252

'I thought it would heal by itself.' His voice was slightly strained. 'How long must I leave my arm in the water?'

'Water let wound open. Wound drain, then we clean out pus, then we reach inside, dig and probe, look for thing inside it.'

'Oh.'

His reply was soft and Tillu looked over her shoulder to see lines of stress embedded in his face. She started to speak, then bit her own tongue, ashamed. Her description had made him squirm as she had known it would. She was a healer, and she must not be petty. Breaking his control and making him cry out would not gain his respect for Kerlew or herself. It would only make her lose her respect for herself.

She moved to his side, eased her hands into the hot water, and gently touched the surface of the wound. It opened almost immediately, releasing its foulness into the water, and Joboam gasped at the release of pressure in his arm. 'Steady. Sit still. Be still,' she said softly, keeping her eyes on the arm. He smelled of sweat and fear and maleness.

She worked deftly, using her moistened bits of white moss to clear the pus from the wound. Tillu motioned Joboam to lift his arm from the water. The wound gaped wide and angry in his flesh. 'Something in there,' she decided. 'Have to find it, get it out.' Rising, she took the fouled water outside to dump it.

Kerlew was standing beside the tent, looking bored. 'I'm cold,' he began whiningly.

'No, you're not.' Tillu's voice brooked no argument. 'This is the warmest it's been for days. If you're cold, work. That will warm you. Bring down more wood.'

'Is it nearly done?'

She took pity on him. 'Nearly. I'm working as fast as

253

I can. If I can heal him well, we will have wolf hides to sew with. New leggings for Kerlew, hmm?'

'No one needs new leggings in spring,' the boy pointed out, but looked pleased anyway.

'More firewood,' she reminded him, as Joboam's voice boomed from the tent.

'Healer! Healer, what is keeping you?'

Tillu didn't bother to answer as she pushed her way back into the tent. She wiped the trough clean with moss and set it to one side. Measuring more salt, she poured it into the trough and set water to heat again. She came then to kneel beside Joboam and peer closely at the injury. She could guess where the problem was. There were signs of the flesh trying to close over an object, only to break open again when Joboam used his arm. Whatever it was, it had gone in deep. Yet it probably hadn't been much of an injury at the time. Just a short, deep cut.

'Going to hurt. Cut open, get it out. I make a medicine first, help with pain.'

Joboam hesitated, then nodded. Wise. She stood up, measuring his size and weight, and then turned to her herbs. This was going to take a strong brew. She knelt by her fire, measuring out and crushing the herbs. She set raspberry root and willow leaves and bark to soak. Bound on a wound, they controlled bleeding. She hoped she would not need them.

'Where is your man?' he demanded suddenly to her back. She didn't even turn. 'Gone.'

'What happened? Is he dead, or did he just leave you?'

'Gone.' She repeated it flatly, and went on with her work.

Joboam gave a knowing snort. 'The boy, eh? Well, it would be a hard thing to live with. But don't you have other people?'

Tillu finally turned to face him. 'Gone.' Her eyes were flat, her lips thinned to a line. Joboam didn't falter.

'All alone, hmm? Must be hard. Would you like to join with the herdfolk? Go with us?' There was a strange note in his voice, a voice like a trader holding up prime merchandise.

'Go?' Tillu was doubly puzzled. She had seen the talvsit as a permanent village, but now this man spoke of 'going' as if they were a wandering, hunting people. Go? With a wrench she realized how accustomed she had become to the idea of living alone, but within reach of a village. She had thought she had a place as a healer, and yet the privacy she needed for Kerlew to be safe. She had thought . . .

'Yes, go.' Joboam hadn't sensed her confusion. 'Capiam say, you might go with us to the summer grounds, be our healer. Better life for you. You have food and hides and help to move your tent, even if no one needs healing. Maybe even give you some reindeer. Maybe. What do you think of that?'

It was too many new ideas, too fast. She was trying to juggle the idea of so many settled people suddenly rising up and going somewhere else with the idea of giving reindeer. Since the night she had ridden in Heckram's pulkor, she had accepted that these people used reindeer as domestic animals. But to be, possibly, the owner of one herself was too strange. Like owning a tree or a spring. And she was not happy to give up her image of planted fields and a settled life again.

'Herdfolk go soon?'

'Yes. Not very long from now. We'll go to the tundra. We'll leave the talvsit behind. If you don't go with us, you'd be alone all summer. Completely alone.'

There was a subtle taunt to his words. A veiled threat of

some kind? Why? For what? 'Not alone,' she corrected him calmly. 'Kerlew with me.'

Joboam gave a snort of deprecation. Tillu almost regretted the sense-dulling mixture that was now simmering on her fire. She should have dug it out of his arm as he sat. She quelled her temper and turned back to stir the mixture. She could not say exactly why she found this man so irritating. The sooner he was healed and bandaged, the sooner he would leave.

She poked at the sodden mass in the bottom of the small pot. It would do. Carefully she added warm water, stirred, and ladled off a scoop of the dark liquid that formed. She advanced on Joboam. His nose wrinkled at the odor.

'Bitter,' she told him, trying not to sound satisfied. 'Drink all. Make you sleepy, not hurt so much.'

Joboam took the ladle carefully and stared down at the dark brew. 'Maybe I don't need it,' he suggested.

Tillu shrugged. 'I cut, you hurt. You decide. But must not jerk arm while I cut. Maybe Kerlew hold arm down for me.'

Glaring at her over the rim of the ladle, he drank. A shudder ran through him and he swallowed with an effort.

'Water?' he asked.

'No. Make you sick, vomit. No water. Lie down. Wait.'

He didn't like it. She didn't care. But she still helped him lie back on her pallet. He swallowed noisily and looked up at her with wary eyes. She stood over him, waiting for the medicine to take effect. She watched the steady rise and fall of his wide chest. She had been surprised when he took his tunic off. He was more hairy than the men of Benu's tribe had been. Dark hair formed a triangle on his chest and tapered down the line of his belly. The ridged belly muscles showed clearly, tight with worry. He was cleaner, too. She wondered if all the men of the herdfolk were so. Heckram's stubble-cheeked face came into her mind. What did his chest look like?

With a snort of contempt for herself, she turned aside. If Joboam was going to sweat and worry and fight the medicine, it was going to take longer to work. In the meantime, she would cook something for Kerlew and take it to him. She was no eager girl to spend her time staring at a man's chest and smirking. She was a woman with a son to tend and a healing to do. As Joboam's breathing became more steady, she cut a generous slab of meat from the chunk suspended from the tent support. It was not that she had so much to spare; it was the recent warm temperatures. The meat was dripping and would soon spoil unless it was eaten or turned into jerky. That was one thing she regretted about the coming spring. Meat would not stay nicely frozen as it did all winter. There was more work to preserving a kill, and more pests that tried to ruin it.

Skewering the chunk, she put it across the spit supports to roast over the low flames. Drops of blood fell from it to sizzle on the fire below. The rich smell made her remember that she had not eaten yet, either. But she could wait. She had mastered the control of her appetites. She turned the meat, searing it on all sides, and then left it to cook through while she made a quick check of Joboam.

He lay on his back, his injured forearm cradled on his chest. His eyes were only half open. He was not asleep; he was in that dreaming state before sleep, where wakefulness has lost its importance. Taking his arm at the wrist and elbow, she eased it off his chest and out from his body. She arranged it, palm down, atop a clean piece of scraped hide. Joboam dreamed on, staring at the peak of the tent poles.

Tillu laid out clean moss, a damp pack of the herbs that would control bleeding, and finally her knife. She wished it was sharper. She should have told Joboam that she would heal him for a sharp knife. Maybe when he awoke, he would agree to such a trade. Kerlew always carried the knife that Heckram had given him. And he was still adamant that she must not touch nor use it. But the hilt of Joboam's own knife showed above his belt. Why not? He didn't move as she eased it free and examined it.

She had not expected the bone haft to clasp a bronze blade. She stared at it, entranced. The metal was cold and sharper than any blade of bone. Decision tightened her grip on it. She would use it. She set it down beside her own and leaned once more over Joboam. She touched his cheek. He didn't stir. She pinched it, lightly, and then harder. He grumbled, his eyes still not turning to her. After a few moments, he turned his head aside, pulling his face from her hand. He was ready.

'Mother?'

Tillu turned. 'There's meat on the spit on the fire. Don't burn yourself. Take it outside and eat it.'

'Good!' Kerlew bounced in. His nose and cheeks were red from being outside, but his hood had been pushed back, so he was not all that cold. He knelt by the fire, took one end of the spit in each hand, and bore his prize away. He was already trying his mouth against it before he even reached the door, exclaiming as it burnt his lips, but not ceasing in his efforts to eat. Tillu said nothing. He'd learn. She added a few dry sticks of wood to the fire for better light, then took out a stone lamp. She had little fat for it, but it would not have to burn long. She knelt carefully by Joboam. She was just lifting one knee to set it firmly on the back of his wrist when she heard the voices outside.

'Give it back!' Kerlew, outraged, angry, already close to tears.

'In a moment. Did you tell her I was here?' A superior, taunting tone.

'Tell her yourself. I'm hungry. Give it back or I'll kill you!' Kerlew, already pushed to making wild threats. Tillu sighed.

'And you such a mighty warrior. I tremble. I think I shall eat it while you go inside and tell her I am here. Stop that!'

She had risen at the first sound, but the struggle had already begun before she was out of the tent. An older boy held the skewered meat out of Kerlew's reach. His other hand gripped Kerlew by the hair on top of his head and held him at arm's length as he struggled and swung and yelped. At the edge of the clearing, a reindeer still harnessed to a pulkor stared at the struggle with round, brown eyes.

'Let him go!'

Neither heard her. Tillu stepped resolutely in, to grip the older boy's wrist. Her competent fingers squeezed down on the tender spot between hand and wrist bone. 'Let him go!' she repeated, and the stranger quickly did. She found herself eye to eye with a youth she suddenly recognized as Capiam's son. She still remembered that look, both sullen and avid. His tunic and hat were gaudy with bright braid and beads. The amount of it went beyond decoration to braggery. He met her stare boldly.

'So here you are, healer. I asked the boy to tell you I was waiting.'

She wasn't going to be sidetracked. 'Give him the meat back. Now.'

He refused to be cowed. 'I didn't want it. I was just keeping it from him until he did as I told him. Here, boy, take it and stop your sniveling.' He flipped the skewer at

259

Kerlew as he spoke. He did not intend that the boy should catch it, and Kerlew didn't. The meat sizzled as it hit the snow and sank from sight. Kerlew howled as if he had been kicked and ran to dig after it like a little dog.

The older youth smiled snidely at the sight. He twitched his wrist free of Tillu's grip and straightened his tunic. 'I am Rolke,' he announced grandly. 'And I bring you a message from my father, Capiam, herdlord of the herdfolk.'

He found he was speaking to Tillu's back. Kerlew had already retrieved his meat from the snow and was brushing the icy particles from it, sobbing as he did so. She stepped to his side and bent to speak to him. She would not humiliate him further by hugging him in front of this stranger, though she longed to. She knew from past experience that Kerlew would only pull quickly away. She was the one who wanted comfort. He only wanted his meat back, as it had been, hot and dripping. 'Take it inside,' she told him softly. 'And put it over the fire again. In a minute or two, it will be just as hot as it was. Do it!' she warned him, stepping in front of the glare he was giving Rolke, 'I will see to him.'

As Kerlew vanished into the tent, she turned to Rolke. She drew herself up to her full height. It was not enough to allow her to look down on him. She doubted that he would have been impressed anyway. There was very little respect for anything in this young man. But she would teach him some.

'Do you want the message from the herdlord, or don't you?' Rolke demanded.

'I want nothing from you.' Tillu set her jaw, hoping she wasn't turning aside a plea for healing. But surely one sending such a message wouldn't choose so rude a messenger.

Rolke was speechless. Tillu turned and lifted her tent flap.

He hiccuped as he caught his breath, and then seemed even angrier because of it. 'Then I shall not give it. I shall tell my father that you and your brat turned me away! You are not fit to join our people anyway. But my father will be angry that you have not heard my words. Very angry. You will be sorry if he sends Joboam to deal with you.'

'Will he send someone who is already here?' Tillu asked in an innocently curious voice. She turned away from the youth's reddening face. Over her shoulder, she observed, 'If the herdlord wishes to send me a message, it must come by a courteous messenger.' She entered her tent. She stood just inside, letting her eyes adjust to the dimness after the brightness of the snow. In a moment she heard Rolke berating his poor animal. She pitied any beast that belonged to such a master. Somehow she did not think the boy would improve with age.

Kerlew crouched by the fire like a small beaten animal. His hands were curled at the ends of his wrists as he held them before his chest. He stared at his meat as the higher flames licked against it, blackening the bottom of it.

Tillu sighed lightly, but said nothing. Any other boy his age would have known better. She stepped forward, to take the rewarmed meat from the fire and hand it back to him. He took it, gripping it like a squirrel, and looked up at her with pleading eyes.

'All right,' she said softly. 'You can eat it here. But be silent, and don't get in my way. Don't come asking me questions in the middle of this healing. Do you understand?'

He nodded silently, already trying to nibble at the meat. Another question occurred to her. 'Why didn't you come and tell me there was someone to see me, when Rolke first got here?'

261

Kerlew's forehead wrinkled with concentration. 'I did. But you gave me the meat and told me to go outside, so I did.'

'Must one thing chase another out of your head? Next time, give the message first. Anytime you have a message for me, give the message first. From now on.'

'I didn't know,' he complained as he went back to his meat. 'You never told me that before. It wasn't my fault.'

She gave him a warning look and went back to Joboam. As she knelt beside him and put his wrist back in position, his lashes fluttered. He rolled his head toward her, to ask in a thick voice, 'It's done?'

'Nearly,' she lied. The interruption had occurred at the worst possible time. He was already rousing from the medicine and she dared not give him any more. She moved the oil lamp into position, poking at the wick for a taller flame. She placed one of her knees on his wrist and the other on the inside of his elbow. She let most of her weight rest on her buttocks atop her heels, but was ready to rock forward and pin the arm still if he struggled. She took up his knife and set the blade tip into the wound at the deepest point. Something had dug in there and stayed. She probed with the tip, lightly at first, but when she encountered nothing, she pressed it gently down. Joboam groaned, but did not twitch. Deeper. The blade touched something hard that moved. As it did so, Joboam gave a deep grunt and lifted his head. Tillu rocked her weight forward to pin his arm down. 'Steady,' she told him. 'Lie still.' Again she put the tip of the knife against the object. Joboam's fist clenched suddenly and he took a shuddering breath. She slid her thumb down the knife blade. Bright blood was welling up in the wound; she could not see what she reached for, but went after it by touch. Her thumbnail found it and she clenched it down, pinning it against the blade. She pulled at it. It was stubborn, half grown into the flesh. Joboam was panting now and she smelled pain in his sweat. Quickly. She gripped hard and tugged.

Joboam gave a wordless cry as it came free. Blood gushed up to fill the wound. Tillu dropped the knife and object onto the skins and pinched the wound closed with a blood-slippery hand. 'It's out now. It's out!' she assured him. She rocked her full weight onto his arm as he writhed. 'The worst is done.' In a reflex action, Joboam had gripped his injured arm, clutching it above the elbow as if to pull it out from under her. 'That's it, now, hold it tight. Grip as tight as you can,' she encouraged him.

She freed his arm, to grab the herb poultice she had laid out. Joboam lay half on his side now, gripping his arm and staring at the welling blood. She arranged the poultice on his arm, pressed it gently against his flesh. His breath hissed out, but he held steady. The flow of blood was slowing. He was strong and in good health. He would heal well, she thought. 'Keep it tight,' she encouraged him as she wrapped the arm. Her fingers were slick with his blood and the bandages were stained before she had them in place. But she wrapped it firmly, the wound held closed. 'This time it will heal and stay healed,' she reassured him. She rose to rinse her hands off. She glanced at the salt in the trough, glad she had not needed to soak the arm a second time. She knelt beside him again.

'Better now?'

'I don't know.' His eyes were shiny, his breathing shallow and fast. 'I feel dizzy. Weak.' His voice trailed off. Tillu eased him back flat on her pallet. She set the injured arm on top of his chest and covered him warmly.

'Rest, then,' she told him needlessly. His eyes were already closing. She pulled another skin over him and snugged it down around him. There had been more pain for him than she had planned. Sometimes pain could disable a man more than the injury itself. Only rest healed that.

She rubbed her face, feeling suddenly tired. And hungry. But the habits of tidiness were strong. She wiped the knife and set it aside. Herbs and salt were stowed away neatly, the dish lamp extinguished and set away. It was when she was taking up the piece of skin that his arm had rested on that the small object fell to the dirt floor. Stooping, she took it up and turned it curiously in her hand. This was what she had taken from his arm. She wiped it on the piece of skin and stared at it curiously. 'I know that I know what this is,' she murmured to herself. 'I just can't remember what it is.' It was shaped bone. A line had been etched into it and stained black, perhaps as a decoration. Something Joboam had been working on that had shattered?

She set it down by the knife and with a sigh rose to her feet. Now she could eat.

Kerlew: The Night

He awoke. As he often did, after a period of not sleeping. He did not need to open his eyes. They were already open, had been open since he lay down on his skins. He had been staring at the peak of the tent, at the smoke hole and the few stars beyond it.

Now he had come back to awareness of himself and his surroundings. A shiver ran over him, and he wondered what had drawn him back. He flared his nostrils, taking in the smells of the tent. There. Joboam. He bared his teeth in the dark.

He turned softly on his skins, but the birch twigs still cracked beneath his bedding. It did not matter. The big man slept deeply. Kerlew smiled thinly, remembering the man's pain when Tillu had healed his arm. He had been tight and silent, even when the blood flowed red. It was only later, when he had become feverish, that he had cursed and roared. His head had tossed about, and his undecipherable words had been full of fury. Kerlew had giggled to hear him, and Tillu had gotten angry and told him to go to bed. So he had, but he had still enjoyed Joboam's pain. He had giggled until Tillu had threatened to beat him. Then he had felt angry with her, so he had gone away with the smoke. And now he was back. And Joboam was still here.

By day, Kerlew feared the big man with the cruel hands. Joboam's eyes were hard and mean, angry that Kerlew existed. He was one of the ones who looked and struck. Kerlew knew and kept clear of his hands. But, in the clear darkness of a shamanic night, Kerlew had only hatred for Joboam. No fear at all. He slipped silently from his bedding.

This was a power time. Carp had spoken with relish of the times when the night opened itself to shamans and the spirit world merged with the day one. Kerlew had never known one until now. Now he could not doubt it. The night surrounded him and intensified him. He felt engorged with its darkness, immune to the daylight world. Cold did not touch his skin and his body knew no hungers. Another shiver ran over him, erecting every hair on his body. Something called him this night. What?

For a long moment, he stood listening. Then he turned back to his bedding, knelt, and gently pushed aside the birch twigs that cushioned his skins from the cold earth. From the hollow he had scratched there, he took his shaman's pouch. Carefully he lifted the pouch and set his ear against the side. He listened. Knife. Knife was calling him.

Reverently he untied his pouch, reached in with blind fingers. Knife touched them. He drew it out slowly and returned the bag and other talismans to the hollow. Then he stood again. 'Knife?' he breathed questioningly. He held it in two hands, pointed it toward the dying embers of the fire. He held it a long time, until he felt it grow heavy in his hands. Knife was ready. Slowly he drew the sheath off.

266

The pale bone blade gleamed even in the dying firelight. It would lead him. It would not be the first time he had followed it. But the first time, he had stumbled frightened and cold in the blackness of the woods, with Owl-spirit peering from every shadow and branch. Then he had wept and pleaded with Knife, and Knife had heard. Knife had led him to the herdfolk's village, to the very hut where his mother slept.

Only one had been awake in that place. In the dimness of the hut, he had stood over her. She who had shaped Knife was there, breathing her pain out in a soundless sigh. She did not rant and roar as Joboam did. Her pain was silent, sealed into her. Heckram held her hand. He shivered, remembering. Her eyes had been closed and she had been still, but the pain vibrated out from her, like ripples in a still pond. Her pain washed over Heckram and put lines in his face. The Knife in his hand had shivered with her pain. He had known she wanted to rest.

He knew the black ladle of the sleeping potion. He had used the back of the knife to hold her lips open while he trickled the sleeping tea in. A last word had bubbled up through the tea, broken against the back of Knife's blade. Some secret or word had been passed between she who made Knife and Knife. Knife had trembled with it, and then he had felt the ebbing of all her pain.

And now Knife had awakened him. There would be a reason, and Knife would lead him to it. He held the tool at arm's length in front of him. His arms ached with holding it still, but finally he felt the tug of the blade. It drew him forward and down. He followed it.

The blade did not hesitate or wait for Kerlew's stumbling feet. It pulled him through the fire, so that Kerlew felt the brief lick of unbearable heat against his bare legs, the bite of a small coal on his callused heel. He barked his shins against his mother's chest of herbs, clattered over it and on. Despite the noise, no one stirred. He alone felt the power of his night and moved through it.

Two more steps and he stood over Joboam. Knife halted and hovered, dragging on Kerlew's arms.

The man was heavy in his sleep, bigger in his laxness. He lay on his back. One arm was flung wide, hanging over the side of the pallet, the back of his wrist resting on the ground. Sleep held him like a thick fog around him. Kerlew smelled it, a fog of blood stench and sweat and the odor of his morning's food that he breathed out of his sagging mouth. His hair clung in damp locks to his forehead and cheeks. In his fevered sleep, he had pushed aside the hides meant to warm him. His chest was wide and gleaming, his bandaged arm cradled protectively against it.

The darkness swirled sweetly around Kerlew as he stood over the man. Knife's hilt was rough and sweaty in his hands. The blade turned slightly in his grip, catching and cradling the wan light that filtered in from the smoke hole. Light ran down the blade in wavering forms that shifted and changed, reminding him of a dark stain on clean snow. Knife soaked up the light and the dark, taking power into itself. It smiled.

Then it plunged down swiftly, dragging him to his knees with the force of its descent. It passed narrowly between Joboam's chest and outflung arm, to sink haft-deep in the earth of the tent's floor.

Kerlew dragged himself up from his bruised knees. No one stirred. His heart thundered inside the cage of his ribs, leaping in its struggle to be free. He rubbed his sweaty hands across his face and looked down at the floor. The hilt of

Knife stuck up from the cold dirt, but a portion of the blade lay beside it. Knife was broken.

He sat down flat in astonishment. He scooted himself closer, stared woefully at the fragment of blade that lay atop the earth by Knife's upright hilt. Wolves of despair devoured his heart. Slowly he picked up the fragment of bone and stared at it. Even in the dim starlight and rusty glow of the dying coals, there was no mistaking it. Half of a swirl and one flying hoof were on the shattered blade. He lifted the piece, held it sorrowfully against his cheek. It was cold. Cold and broken and angry with him. As angry as Carp and the Blood Stone. In his eagerness, he had failed again. Tears flooded his eyes.

With a trembling hand he took hold of the hilt and drew Knife from the earth. It dangled between his forefinger and thumb as he stared at it. It was whole.

He brought it close to his deep-set eyes and studied it. Whole. Not a splinter out of it, not a nick. One reindeer still galloped, the other grazed with her calf at her side. The swirls still spun like stars. His slow gaze traveled from Knife to the fragment of bone. Gradually his two hands brought them together. For long silent moments he studied them side by side. Here was the hoof of the galloping reindeer; here was the hoof alone. Here were the swirls spinning on the blade; here was one swirl and part of another. Here was . . .

He stopped. His mind leaped the gap, and the knowledge swelled in him. This knife from the knife-making woman. This piece of a knife from Joboam's arm. Kerlew smiled. Shifting his weight carefully, he knelt by Joboam, leaned over the sleeping man. He held the fragment of blade before the closed eyes and grinned down. A prickling chill ran over his body as he felt the power that coursed though the broken blade.

Yes, it was cold and angry. But not with Kerlew. No. It was angry with Joboam. And in its anger, the fragment of blade offered much power to Kerlew. Much power.

He curled his fist around his own Knife, held it close to his chest as he knelt over Joboam. He leaned very close, studying Joboam's closed eyes to be sure he really slept. The man's breath was hot and rank against his face. Slowly Kerlew lifted the knife chip. He touched it softly to Joboam's forehead, then to each of his closed eyelids. He carefully traced the outline of Joboam's sagging mouth with the tip of the broken piece. The man twitched, closed his lips.

Kerlew held up Knife and the fragment side by side. He turned them slowly, letting them catch the light and then grow black as old blood in the shadows. He leaned very close over the man, his eyes wide and fixed on Joboam's for any sign of wakefulness as Knife and the fragment wove a slow pattern over his bare chest. He could feel the power the fragment was drawing out of the man. He felt almost dizzy in the great clarity of the night and of the forces that whispered through it.

He gave voice to them. 'Joboam.' Softly he called him by name, the word no more than a shaping of his exhalation. No one could come to such a call, except for a spirit. His spirit would hear Kerlew's words. 'Joboam. It has soaked in your blood, Joboam. You cannot deny it. It knows the inside of your flesh. It has tasted your life, and longs to taste your death. Feel the knife that failed, Joboam.' He drew the fragment lightly down the man's bare chest. 'The knife hated to fail, Joboam. It wished to be true. So it has called out to its brother Knife. And its brother Knife has called to me. And I have made it a promise, to give it what it wants.'

He leaned closer over the sleeping man. Ridges divided

Joboam's brows and his breath was becoming uneven. Joboam's spirit was uneasy. Kerlew fixed his wide eyes on Joboam's closed ones, breathed his breath into his face as he said softly, 'You know what the Knife wants, Joboam.'

The big man's eyes flickered open wide.

SIXTEEN

'Wolf! Wolf!'

The hoarse cry rang in Tillu's ears and jerked her from sleep. It was inside the tent. She heard the rustle of flung hides and the sound of quick movement, panting breath. Tillu rolled from her pallet onto her knees and came to her feet with a short jabbing spear in her hands. She gripped the close-quarters weapon, glaring with sleep-blurred eyes around the darkened interior of the tent. Nothing stirred. Her eyes probed the shadowed corners. All was still and quiet. Her heart slowed its hammering. Kerlew was a hunched bundle under his sleeping furs. She saw him twitch them in closer and guessed he was awake. Awake and hiding from wolves. She sighed as she stepped to the tent door and peered out into the darkness. Nothing at all. Just the cold and the empty darkness under the trees beneath the starry skies of early morning. She turned to Joboam. He was propped up on one elbow. His wide eyes shone black.

'What did you see?' she demanded.

'I . . . yellow eyes. Staring at me.' His breathing was

coming in ragged gasps. Tillu set down the spear and stepped to the firewood stacked neatly by the door. She tossed a few sticks onto the dying coals of the fire and then crossed the tent to kneel by Joboam. She touched the side of his neck and then his bandaged arm with quick, cool fingers. His face was still heavy with sleep and the pain of her healing.

'Your fever's broken. That's all. Sometimes when one goes from fever sleep to dreaming, the dreams are bright and hard. There's nothing here. Go back to sleep.'

'I . . .' Joboam seemed both dazed and exhausted. He looked about her tent in bewilderment. 'What am I doing here?'

Tillu hunkered down on her heels beside him. The earth was cold under her bare feet. 'You came to have me heal your arm, remember? I gave you a tea to relax you, and dug a bone splinter out of your arm, and bandaged it. Your arm bled again, you were sleepy from the tea, and draining the swelling of your arm gave you a fever. That sometimes happens. We healers say the body burns itself clean. So I let the fever burn, but not too high. And now you are better. Remember? You woke twice and I gave you water. Remember?' She spoke soothingly, as if to a frightened child. After a moment Joboam relaxed.

'Yes. Yes, I remember now. Drink and rest, you told me. But the wolf . . . I felt his hot breath in my face. His eyes were yellow and he laughed at me . . .'

'A dream. Only a dream.' Tillu pushed the sweat-soaked hair from his forehead, checked once more for fever. The man smelled sour with fear. 'You've sweated out the poisons. That's good. Sleep now, and by morning you'll be ready to go home.'

'Yes. I'll sleep.' His words started to drag, and then

suddenly he was up on one elbow again, deep creases furrowed between his brows. 'A bone fragment? From my arm?'

'Not your own bone. A piece of worked bone or horn.'

'Where is it? Let me see it. I want it.'

'It's here, it's right here, just a moment,' Tillu soothed him. Shadows in the tent were deep. She was tired and sleepy and growing impatient with his dream fears and compulsions. Her fingers trailed along the earth floor, finding first his knife, then a piece of bark, then some bits of the moss she had used to clean his wound. She groped some more, her toes going numb against the cold earth. 'I'll find it in the morning,' she promised, wondering why he was so anxious. She offered him the knife, hilt first. 'I borrowed your knife to open your arm. My own is old and dull, and a sharp blade is best for such work.'

He took it from her wordlessly, stared at it in puzzlement, and then let it fall from his fingers back onto the dirt floor. He rolled onto his back and stared into the shadowed point of the ceiling. 'Wolf. It was Wolf, and he showed me two knives. One was whole, and one was . . . broken. He showed them to me, and then he laughed. He said . . . he laughed. That was all.'

'A dream. Just a fever dream.' She wished he would go back to sleep. She was getting cold, crouched here in just her long shirt. She was taken by surprise when his good arm shot out suddenly and his hand gripped her upper arm hard.

'Tell no one,' he ordered her fiercely. 'If you tell anyone you healed me, I'll kill you.'

'Easy.' She pulled at his digging fingers, wincing as his grip only tightened. 'You're dreaming still. Let go, you're hurting me. Let go!'

'Tell no one!' he repeated insistently. His eyes blazed.

'I won't tell anyone. Why would anyone be interested? Let go.'

'Good. Don't tell.' He stared at her. His grip loosened but he did not free her. Instead he pulled her close, until she was leaning over the pallet. His eyes darted to the shadows behind her, then came back and moved slowly down her body. 'I didn't mean to hurt you. I'm sorry.'

'Let go of me.'

'Don't be angry. I was . . . it was just the dream. I didn't mean to hurt you.' His voice was low, soft.

'I know that and I'm not angry. Just let me go.'

'Why?' His eyes still burned, but with a different fire. He winced slightly as he moved his other hand up to touch her face. 'I saw you looking at me. Before you healed my arm.' She pulled back from the caress, baring her teeth.

'Let go of me, or I'll hurt you.' She spoke quietly.

'You? You're no bigger than a child!' He smiled indulgently. His free hand touched her breast through the thin leather of her shirt, pinching her nipple. Then he gasped as her hand fell on his injured arm and tightened on the bandage.

'I'm not pretending. Let go of me, or I'll give you pain.'

His grip dropped from her arm and she sprang back instantly. 'You leave my tent tomorrow morning.' She bit the words off. She could feel Kerlew watching, listening. 'As soon as it's light. Do not come back.'

Joboam eased himself back onto the pallet. He stared at her with round eyes. 'Like a little wolverine. I didn't mean to hurt you, Tillu. And you shouldn't try to hurt me. Come here.' He smiled crookedly, only encouraged by her rebuff.

She stared at him. He had actually believed she wanted him. Still believed it, still believed her reluctance was a game.

Had she wanted him? She turned her back on him and went silently back to her pallet. She could not hide from his eyes; they followed her as she lay down and covered herself again. Her heart beat a little faster and she felt more vulnerable lying down. He was a big man, and strong. She let her arm slip down beside her pallet, to find the short spear. She closed her eyes, but listened for movement. She would not sleep again this night. She opened her eyes slightly, peered through her lashes at the fire as it devoured the sticks and fell into coals again. Beneath her lashes she glanced at Joboam. His face was turned toward her, watching her. Smiling.

She pulled her eyes away. Had she wanted him? No. A man, yes, her body hungered for a man. She was a woman, she had her needs. Desire swelled and ebbed inside her with the cycle of the moon. Some nights her thoughts were filled with images of men, and her thighs tingled and her nipples grew hard with longing. But not this man. It had been a long time for her, but it would never be so long as to make her want a man like him. Even if he had not been so arrogant and rude, she would have turned him away. He was too large, too daunting. He would make her feel helpless and childish. Again she felt the suffocating weight of a man's body atop her, pinning her to the earth, smelled the smoke of a burning village.

Her desires vanished. She shook her head, banishing the old memories. Never again. She wanted nothing of men larger than herself, nothing of dominant, crushing men.

There had been Raduni, of Benu's folk. He had been a small, quick man, his smile almost bigger than his face. When she had first joined Benu's folk, he had smiled at her often. She had admired his litheness. She had marveled at his quickness as he lay on his belly and scooped shining

276

trout from the stream. And offered a share to her, unasked. She had hoped he would approach her. But too soon he had become aware of Kerlew. Strange Kerlew. His strangeness had been enough to make Raduni hesitate and then turn aside from her. Her son tainted her. She wondered what made men behave so. Raduni was not the first. Did men believe all her children must turn out as Kerlew had? Did she believe so herself? She wasn't sure. She only knew the outcome. She had been left with the attentions of Carp, another man she did not want.

She shifted in her bedding, sighing. Rolke's offer came to her mind. She wondered if the offer would be extended again. And if it was? Did she want to travel with these herdfolk? She did not think so. Kerlew was not ready for such a life. Nor was she. Why would she wish to give up her independent life for a place within the herdfolk? With men such as Joboam, so ready to assume control of her household? With men like Heckram, so quick to assume the decision of life and death?

Something very like betrayal squeezed her heart. She had thought better of the man. Her mind roved back to that night, to chew again at the puzzle bone. She had warned Heckram that too much of the medicine would kill. Why had he given it to Elsa? Because he could not watch her suffer, because he cared for her? Or had it been colder than that? Was that the fate of women among the herdfolk when they became disfigured or useless?

Neither piece fit. She had seen Heckram when Lasse was injured. He had not tried to hide the sympathy and concern he felt. She had sensed his friendship with the youth. And with Elsa? With Elsa, it had been just the same. A deep friendship, a loyalty. Not a relationship of the kind that presumed power over life and death. Yet the same friendship was what made her sure that the killing had not been a casual disposal of a useless chattel.

Only recently had Tillu come to understand the strange status of women among the herdfolk. In no other tribe had she encountered women who not only possessed their own property, but retained their private ownership even after marriage. The meat Leyna had paid her with had been meat from Leyna's own animal. The women made their trades independently of their men, hunted alongside their men, or alone. Her weaving and sewing had the same value as his carving and building. In a society where a man could not assume possession of his wife's handiwork, a woman of the herdfolk knew her own worth. For the first time in her life, Tillu had encountered women who took pride in their independence. She envied them.

But always the speculation took her back to Heckram and Elsa. It could have been no one but him. The women in the tent did not know what the brew was, would not have given it to Elsa without asking. And there had been the way he turned aside from her that next morning. His eyes had been empty when he looked at her, his face held straight. Guilt. Useless to tell herself it did not matter, that Elsa would have died anyway. Sometimes she tried to convince herself that Elsa had simply died, that she had let go instead of lingering in pain. She wanted to believe that, but couldn't. Even more, she wanted to understand why he had done it, why he felt guilty about doing it. Then perhaps she would know why she thought less of Heckram since then. Perhaps she would even understand why it saddened her that he could no longer meet her eyes.

What did it matter? She sighed to herself. A glance at Joboam showed that sleep had claimed him again. Good.

Tomorrow he would be gone and, soon after that, all the herdfolk. Gone from her life, leaving her to her independence. Alone again. She remembered her terror of being alone when she had first left Benu's folk. But she had overcome it. A small pride swelled inside her. She could take care of herself and her son. Could hunt for them, sew for them. Could even repulse the advances of someone like Joboam. And Kerlew was doing so well lately . . . In some ways, she qualified it to herself. He carved now and even tried to hunt, though as of yet he had had no success on his own. He remembered things now, to gather the wood, to watch the fire. And he remembered them on his own. It was good he had not become attached to Heckram, it was good that he was doing things on his own. She felt they were nearing a day when Kerlew would make his own decisions, would see himself as a person independent of her. She waited, watching him silently, conscious of the small changes in him. She smiled to herself and realized she had no regrets. Let the herdfolk go.

Morning found her none the better for her sleepless night. Her eyes were reddened and itchy as she steeped the inner bark of alder, brewing a reddish tea from it. It was a useful tonic for anyone trying to recover from illness. Or after a sleepless night, she told herself as she poured a cup.

She drank it standing, staring around the tent. It was not the poor place it had been in midwinter. Everywhere she looked were the signs of her trade with the herdfolk. Their mark on her life could not be denied. She cut up the last of Leyna's meat and dropped it into the very battered bronze kettle that Bror and Ibba had given her for worming his best harke and mixing a herbal wash to discourage lice. She stirred the simmering meat with a ladle of knurled birch with bright colors carved into the handle. These things were hers, even if the herdfolk left her. She did not need to go with them, for summer was near, the time of plenty. She did not need to go with them.

She woke Kerlew and he ate. As was usual when they were alone, they spoke very little. Few words were needed. It was only after he had eaten that she had to speak to him. He had finished his bowl of stew and sat crouched on his heels, running his finger around the greasy inside of the bowl and licking it. This Tillu could have ignored. But Kerlew had chosen to perch at the end of the pallet where Joboam still slept. He stared at the sleeping man as he licked his fingers. When he noticed Tillu watching him, he snickered his brittle little laugh.

She stared at him solemnly, refusing to be baited. He giggled again.

'Leave him alone,' she told him coldly.

'Wolf!' he sputtered and trailed off in helpless laughter. Joboam's eyes flickered. Kerlew leaned forward, heedless of how the man might react. 'Did Wolf really visit you in the night?' he asked delightedly. His hazel eyes sparkled.

'Kerlew!' Tillu exclaimed angrily, even as Joboam growled, 'Keep that brat away from me!'

'Outside, son,' Tillu directed calmly. 'Firewood.'

'I got it yesterday,' Kerlew complained.

'Then get more. We can always use it.'

'Not if we go with the herdfolk. Comes the herdlord now, to ask you to be healer.'

'Outside!' Tillu repeated sternly. 'Take the bowls and clean them with moss and snow. Now!'

He turned from Joboam, who clutched the sleeping skins about himself as if Kerlew were vermin that might be warded off. Laconically the boy gathered Tillu's bowl and lifted the door flap. As he lifted the flap, the gray light of morning filtered in. Distant shouting reached their ears, the words indistinct.

'Capiam,' breathed Joboam. His eyes narrowed with suspicion or fear as he stared after the boy. An instant later, he had flung back the bedskins and was struggling to rise. 'I will leave,' he told Tillu tersely as he kicked clear of the skins and groped after his boots. 'And you will not tell I have been here. Understand?'

She didn't understand why he wouldn't want Capiam to know he had been in her tent. It was pointless, anyway. 'Capiam knows you are here. Yesterday, his son came. He knows you are here.'

Joboam dropped the boot he had been pulling on. 'Rolke? Rolke was here yesterday? What did you tell him?'

'I tell him, Capiam cannot send to me one who is already here.'

'And that was all? You didn't say you were healing my arm?'

Tillu cast her mind back to the day before, tried to recall her exact words. 'No. I just say he could not send someone who was already with me.'

Joboam sat toying with his boot. Unreadable emotions flickered over his face as he sorted ideas. Tillu heard now the crunch and squeak of the snow as it gave under hoof and sledge. To her surprise, Joboam eased back on the pallet. He dragged the furs across himself and stretched out. 'Go out!' He gestured at her authoritatively. 'Go out and meet him. Say nothing of me, unless he asks. Then say I am here. Go out! Hurry!'

'This is my tent!' Tillu spoke through clenched teeth.

'Hurry!' Joboam urged her.

She went slowly, smoothing her hair back from her face. She gave him a final glance as she went out. He was staring after her, his face set in a grin born of both tension and satisfaction. She couldn't understand him and didn't want to.

Two sledges had pulled up in front of her tent. Rolke was there, as sullen-faced as ever, with his father standing behind him. Capiam's face was stern. He stood straight and solemn, his black eyes fixed on the healer. Short and stocky he was, as were most of the herdfolk, but his bearing and dress conspired to give an impression of height. His garments were both opulent and severe. His cap was of knotted black wool, his coat and leggings of black wolf. The hem of his coat had been trimmed with the black-tipped tails of weasels. The braid that decorated his cuffs was a stark pattern of black on white. His coat was cinched tightly around his waist by a thick leather belt held with a large bronze clasp. A leather thong about his neck supported another massy piece of bronzework. If he had intended to impress Tillu, he had succeeded.

She tried not to imagine how she must appear, in her tunic and leggings of worn leather. She stood straight and returned his gaze, trying to ignore her son's foolishness. Kerlew crouched behind a tree much too slender to hide him, peering around it at them, but not giving any greeting. Tillu pressed her lips together, took a breath, and advanced to meet them. She did not smile as she spoke, but kept her voice even and her face calm.

'Capiam. Rolke. I am honored that you visit me.'

Capiam said nothing. Nor did Rolke, until Capiam nudged him violently from behind. The boy's eyes glittered angrily when he spoke, but his words were courteous.

'I wish you good morning, Healer Tillu. I come bearing a message from my father, Herdlord Capiam of the Herdfolk. May I speak it to you?' She could nearly hear his teeth grate as he closed his jaws on the last word.

'Certainly,' she replied serenely. 'I am always glad to receive a message courteously delivered.'

He flinched at her words, and she knew she had hit the mark. Capiam had come to be sure that his message was politely delivered.

'The Herdlord Capiam' – Rolke glanced aside to find Kerlew grinning at him from behind the non-shelter of the tree. He caught his breath in frustration, and jerked his eyes back to Tillu – 'The Herdlord Capiam invites you to join our people on our spring migration. Long have our folk been without a trained healer. Last year both humans and reindeer suffered injuries that a healer could have eased. A child ate tainted meat and died. A herder's broken leg healed badly, so now she must limp. Herdlord Capiam is a man who cares for his folk. He would not see them crippled and scarred for lack of a trained healer to tend them. So I am sent to offer you these things, if you will come with us.' He took a deep breath and began his listing. 'Hides for a new tent, and the use of a harke to carry your belongings. Meat as you need it, and woven cloth for clothing for you and your son. The herdlord will see that you do not hunger or lack any necessity. And so I ask you: Will you go with our folk, to be our healer?'

Tillu stood silently, a decision still eluding her. But Kerlew leaped out from behind his tree, crying, 'Yes, oh, yes, Tillu, say yes! I am sick of eating rabbit, and tired of always staying in one place. Let's go with them!'

Rolke's face flared with hatred as Kerlew capered wildly

283

in the snow before them. Distaste showed an instant in Capiam's eyes; then he regained his stoic bearing. If she went with them, their feelings for Kerlew wouldn't change. They would only deepen. Kerlew would be like an annoying scab to Rolke, a thing to be picked at and irritated endlessly. She should stay here, by herself with the boy, and teach him and protect him.

But the healer in her spoke through her jangling need to protect her son. Her belly had tightened when he had mentioned the child dead of tainted meat, the herder who now must limp. For so many people to be without a healer was not right. Her skills gave her a duty. As she had so many times before, she could always leave them if things became too uncomfortable. Her resolve of the night before melted.

'I need to think,' she said softly, her voice carrying clearly through Kerlew's babbling. 'At least for a while.'

Rolke nodded curtly and hung his head to hide a venomous glare at Kerlew. He was not pleased with his success as a messenger. For a moment the herdlord's eyes met hers, assessing her. His face was serious, as if he knew of her private doubts. He gave a slow nod of acceptance. Then his eyes darted suddenly past her, to widen in surprise. Tillu turned in consternation to see what was behind her.

'Joboam? You are here?' Capiam asked in disbelief.

'As you see.' The big man emerged from her tent, standing to stretch in the daylight. His hair was still tousled from sleeping and he had not bothered to put on his outer tunic. Tillu was baffled. Had not he just ordered her not to speak of him? And now he wandered out in plain sight of them, as if to flaunt his presence.

'But what are you doing here?' Rolke demanded, curiosity making him forget what courtesy he knew.

284

'I –' Joboam began and then hesitated long.

'Rolke!' his father reprimanded him, and the boy's eyes flew wide with sudden understanding. He swung his stare to Tillu, and a slow, offensive smile spread across his adolescent face. He leered at her knowingly.

'I came to speak to the healer and to add my . . . persuasion that she should come with us.' Joboam's voice was oily with self-satisfaction. Capiam looked uncomfortable, Rolke avid. Tillu wondered what message she was missing. Even Kerlew stopped his hopping about and stared from one adult to the next, his mouth agape. Tillu knew their language well enough now, but what had passed among the men was a non-verbal implication that eluded and annoyed her. A moment longer Joboam stood in her door. Then he ducked back within her tent. Capiam shuffled his feet awkwardly.

'Healer, we are hopeful you will come with us. I promise you that you shall lack for nothing, though I am sure that Joboam will make sure that you have all –'

'I think I shall drive back with you, Capiam, if you will wait a moment. My harke and pulkor are behind the tent. It will take but a moment to harness up.'

Joboam buckled his heavy belt over his tunic as he spoke. He gave Capiam a bright smile of good fellowship, then stepped close to Tillu. He smiled down at her, and she looked up into his teeth. When he spoke, it was in a soft, fond voice that still carried clearly. 'Tillu. I am sorry to leave so abruptly, but there are things I must attend to, especially since you have decided to be one of us. But you know I'll be back soon. What shall I bring you?'

His syrupy voice and the masterful way he loomed over her were impossible to mistake. She couldn't understand what his game was about, but she could play it, too. She smiled up at him, all teeth and thinned lips. 'I have not decided yet,' she said clearly, 'but you may bring me a bronze knife. As healer for the herdfolk, I would need one. If you come back to see me, bring a bronze knife for me. A thin blade is best, but I can manage with a wide one.'

She saw the quick flash of anger in his eyes as she named the exorbitant fee for not betraying his game. He masked it quickly. She felt a small quiver of worry as she realized how important his deception of Capiam must be to him. 'A knife, then,' he agreed smoothly. He was not so foolish as to try and touch her in farewell. But the way his eyes wandered over her face was touch enough to inspire unease in Tillu. He turned from her abruptly, and the snow crunched under his boots as he went around her tent to where his tethered harke waited.

The silence was back, hanging between them like a curtain. Kerlew had completely lost interest in the proceedings. He had hooked his hands over a low branch of a nearby birch, and he dangled by his arms, feet on the ground still, but knees bent so that the tree swayed with his weight as he bounced. Rolke was staring at him, his upper lip drawn up in distaste. Kerlew spoke suddenly. 'Joboam had a vision of Wolf in the night. He yelled out, "Wolf!" and Tillu jumped from the bed to grab her stabbing spear!'

'Kerlew!' Tillu rebuked him, not so much for the gossip as for the way he told it, his amber eyes probing Capiam for a response to the story. For an instant, it might have been Carp hanging in the tree, working his magic on Benu's folk with his sly intimations and cryptic insinuations. But if the story meant anything to Capiam, he covered it well. He gave the boy the sickly smile adults often gave her son when they did not know how else to respond to his strange behavior.

'He does well to fear Wolf,' Kerlew added, ignoring Tillu's glare. 'For one of Wolf's own will pull him down one day. Joboam may fancy himself a Bear, but that is not what looks out of his eyes at me. I am to be a shaman; did you know that?'

Before anyone could respond to this latest comment, the squeak of Joboam's pulkor was heard and he drove his harke from behind the tent. He seemed oblivious of the changed mood that greeted him. He pulled his animal to a halt and, smiling, glanced from one face to the next. 'Well. Shall we be going, then?'

'When will the herdfolk be leaving?' Tillu asked suddenly.

Capiam answered her. 'Some of the folk are still in the higher country with their animals. When spring is a bit stronger and the ice has left the moss, they will come down from the hills, and we will go.'

'West?' Tillu guessed, thinking of more hills and forest.

Capiam looked surprised. 'North. From the hills out onto the wide tundra, and across it to the Cataclysm. To follow the wild herd, and to meet with the other herdfolk for the summer.' He turned a bemused smile on Joboam. 'She has much to learn of our ways,' he commented affably.

'I shall not mind teaching her,' Joboam assured him. Tillu seethed at his proprietary air, but said nothing. She'd let him keep his game intact, until she had her bronze knife. Then they would come to an agreement on her terms. The thought brought a real smile to her face as she bid them farewell. She marked how Joboam brought his pulkor abreast of Capiam's, to converse with him while Rolke trailed behind them. She sighed softly when they were out of sight. If it were only the healing she had to deal with! But if she went with them, it would be the day-to-day life among the herdfolk that would be hardest for her. And for Kerlew. She glanced about, but didn't see the boy.

'Kerlew!' she called, hoping desperately he hadn't followed the men and reindeer. There was no answer. 'Kerlew!' she called again sharply and pushed her way into the tent. He bounced up quickly, guiltily, from his pallet, furtively stuffing something inside his shirt. She knew of the shaman's pouch he had made by taking one of her herb bags and marking it with charcoal and blood. She had even seen it once, when he had thought she was asleep and had come to the fire to examine his treasures. She never spoke of it; she didn't want to encourage him. She knew it held his red stone and other oddments. What other bits he added to it were no concern to her. His behavior was.

'Whatever made you speak out that way?' she demanded angrily. Snatching up a cup, she dipped up some of the tea she had set to steep earlier.

'Whatever made you keep silent?' he returned, his eyes gone flinty.

The tea was cold and bitter in Tillu's mouth as she met his stare.

SEVENTEEN

'It's the last flurry of winter,' Lasse observed.

Heckram assented silently. There was a peace to the thickly falling curtain of white flakes that he was reluctant to disturb. All day he had sensed the snow coming. The thick clouds had been snagged on the near crest of the mountain like a swatch of gray woolen stuff. All day the softening snow had been slogging underfoot, sinking undetectably, glistening on the trodden paths but white and blue-shadowed under the trees. The reindeer had grazed easily, nuzzling the soft wet snow from tender moss, or reaching their shaggy necks to nibble the suddenly tender tips of the birches and willows. Even the sunset had not brought the cold back. The snow that fell now was wet, sticking to the branches of the trees but doomed to melt before noon tomorrow.

Heckram and Lasse sat back to back in a crude shelter of branches leaned against a tumble of jutting gray boulders and shist, memorial of some glacier's ancient passage. The tangle of branches kept out most of the snow, but not the diffused light of the overcast moon or the soft placidity of the snowy night.

For the first time in many days, Heckram felt at peace with himself. Here at the winter pasturage there were no reminders of pain and failure. But for Lasse's company, it was like any other early spring he had passed in the mountains. They hadn't bothered to bring a skin tent with them, but only sleeping hides sewn into a sack. The bunched hides were beneath him now, atop a cushioning pad of pine boughs. The night was too mild and Heckram too comfortable for him to think of crawling into his bed and sleeping. He would doze back to back with Lasse, occasionally stirring to look out on the gray and brown backs of the forty-odd animals scattered across the slope below them.

A soft, almost warm wind crept through the trees, now parting the snow flurries, now swirling the falling flakes more thickly than ever. The steady fall of the white stuff was almost as restful as sleeping. Heckram was not sure he was awake when he heard Lasse's whispered 'What's that?'

Heckram cleared his throat quietly. 'What's what?' he murmured softly. He squinted his eyes, tried to focus his gaze through the falling snow. He could see nothing. Confiming his own lesser senses were the peaceful attitudes of the animals below. They were not milling in agitation or muttering to one another in their coughing grunts. Whatever had disturbed Lasse had not bothered them at all.

'There. Hear that?' Lasse whispered.

'Just the wind,' Heckram muttered irritably. The wind had many notes on a night such as this. It soughed through bare branches, overbalanced snow loads on heavy ones to make soft plopping sounds, and set smaller limbs and twigs to creaking and clattering softly against one another. Lasse should know those sounds as well as Heckram did himself.

He tried to go back to sleep, but found himself annoyingly

alert, listening for whatever peculiar note had roused Lasse. The wind blew harder, the snow swirled and for one moment seemed to coalesce into a crouching wolf by a pale-trunked birch, but the next swirl of wind dispersed it and revealed the cheat of an old lightning-blasted stump. Heckram sighed, letting the tension ease out of his back. Was he a child to be spooked by shadows and shapes in the night?

Lasse's back was still tight against his. 'See anything?' Heckram asked, his deep voice soft in the night.

'I almost did. I mean, I thought I did. Like the biggest wolverine ever made, but white, every bit of it. Just the snow playing tricks on me.'

'Moonlight through clouds on new snow will do that,' Heckram acceded. Silence followed his words, falling and drifting as deep as the snow. His eyelids began to sag again.

'What will you do when we go back?' Lasse asked suddenly.

Heckram opened his eyes, frowned into the night. 'Do? What do we always do in spring? I'll put my winter gear up on the rack, load my summer gear onto a harke or two, and follow the herd. What will you do?'

'The same, I suppose.' Lasse sighed. Heckram felt it more than heard it. 'I'll spend the first day or so listening to my grandmother recount every little incident that occurred while we were gone. And the next few days trying to account for every moment that I was up here, while she imagines a dozen things wrong with every reindeer I've tended.'

Heckram nodded. 'There's a lot of silences up here. But all the talk when I get home somehow seems lonelier than this.'

Lasse paused, considering the sense of his words. Then: 'Won't it be strange for you, to go back to your own hut in the talvsit? You'll be going back to silences.'

'Yes.' Heckram bit the word off short. 'But it will only be for a night or so, and then we'll be off for the tundra.'

'But you'll be taking your own tent this time, won't you? The one Elsa and your mother made?'

'I suppose.' After avoiding these thoughts for days, the questions stung like fresh scratches. He realized suddenly that his guilt cut more sharply than his grief now. And knew in the same moment that while his grief might fade with time, the guilt he felt would not. It would not be any easier to meet Missa's eyes when he returned. Kuoljok's were even worse, for the death of his daughter had turned the old man's mind. When he looked at Heckram, he did not seem to see him at all. When he spoke to him, he looked through or beyond him. Neither one had ever spoken a word of blame; they didn't need to. Joboam's accusation that night had been enough. He remembered, sometimes, that Missa had spoken out against Joboam's words. When he did, he took comfort from it, but could find no ease from his own self-accusations.

Lasse had fallen silent, but hadn't relaxed his vigil. The sleep that had come so easily moments before now eluded Heckram. His temples began to ache as his thoughts raced around and around like reindeer in a sorting pen. Around and around and around, pounding like rolling thunder, but finding no escape. Who had killed Elsa, and why? Joboam, he wanted it to be Joboam; he wanted a reason to challenge the man and unleash his fury and guilt on him.

But what if it were not Joboam? Sometimes in the night, it seemed impossible that Joboam could have hurt Elsa. Had he not been courting her just a few months ago? No herdman would kill a woman he wanted. He might try to lure her away from the man she had joined, with gifts and sweet words. There was nothing dishonorable in that. But why would any man destroy a woman he desired? For Joboam to have killed Elsa made no sense. Maybe Heckram only suspected him because he had always hated Joboam, and longed for a reason to act on that hate. The other herdfolk, true to their tradition, had set the death aside in their minds. Elsa had died; no one had seen, so no one could say what had killed her. They did not feel pressed, as Heckram did, to find something or someone to blame, to make someone pay for Elsa's death. Such was not their way. It should not have been Heckram's way. Yet he hungered for vengeance as a wolf hungers for meat in the dead of winter. The aching need for revenge set him apart, made him a stranger among his own folk and put lines upon Ristin's brow. Yet he could not turn his thoughts away from the unfairness of that death. Someone must pay.

But if not Joboam, then who? There was no answer to that. Had Elsa made an enemy he knew nothing about? Had it been a single marauder, one of those wild men old women spoke of, on late evenings around the open fires during the migration times? They were supposed to come by darkness, to carry off young women for mates. He had always thought them scaretales, nothing but a woman's device to keep her daughters from straying too far from the fire on warm spring nights.

His temples were thrumming. He reached up to touch his own face, felt the deep thought wrinkles between his brows, but could not remember how to smooth them out. Around and around and around. A demon, perhaps, as Rolke had suggested on that horrible night. Heckram did not know if he believed in demons anymore. Yet if ever he had seen a demon's work, it was what had been done to Elsa.

He closed his eyes against the swirling snow. The peace

had fled from it. Now it danced before him, a demon that wrought itself over and over into images of Elsa. Again and again he saw her shattered hand lift in that terrible greeting. Slowly he drew his knees up to his chest, curved his neck down to rest his forehead on his knees. His body felt hard and hollow, like a sucked out marrow bone, a thing thrown aside.

Lasse spoke softly, without moving. 'I'm sorry. I didn't mean to remind you again.'

'It's all right,' Heckram lied. His voice came out hoarse and thick. Sometimes he regretted letting Lasse come to know him so well. To grieve was bad enough. To know that the friend who sat back to back with him knew the depth of his pain did not ease it. It subtly intensified it.

Back to back they stiffened simultaneously, speaking no word as they listened to the soft drumming that suddenly filled the night. Had it just begun, or had it only now increased in volume so they were aware of it? Its rhythm was one piece with the night. The sound was sourceless, eternal, soft and yet undeniable. 'Heckram,' Lasse began softly.

'Shh,' the older man cautioned him. Neither one moved. The drumming went on, in infinite variations that yet formed an elaborate pattern. Heckram could imagine the fingers on the drumhead, tapping, brushing, rapping, moving from the edge of the tight-stretched hide into the center and then back again. An old image from a time he had thought forgotten came suddenly.

It had been a night in fall, on the trek back from the summer grazing grounds. He had been small, still looking up to his mother, and his legs had ached from walking all day. The smell of death was in the unseasonably warm air. Behind them, on the tundra, like scattered berries from a leaking basket, were the bodies of the reindeer that had fallen to the plague. Their bellies were bloated and their legs stuck up stiffly at obscene angles from their bodies. Flies buzzed audibly in the twilight.

Around a large fire the herdfolk had gathered, circling in rows around Nadunin the Najd. The najd's hair was streaked with white and hung long and wild past his face. He knelt on the hide of a white reindeer, so close to the fire that sweat streamed down his seamed and wrinkled body. He was clad in a loincloth of twisted yellow leather and his skin was a sallow brown like old bones moldering by a stream bank. His flesh was tight over his bones; Heckram had watched his ribs move with his breath. His kobdas was before him, and its strange voice filled the night. He tapped it with his hammerlike drumstick, making it cry out, now loudly, now softly. Gods were painted on the drumhead in red alder-bark juice, and also the Trollskott, the emblem used to inflict harm on the herds of an enemy.

The herdfolk ringed him; men, women, and children, gathered to see if respite might be gained through magic. Not far from this night's resting place was an ancient seite. They passed it every year on their annual migration. The great gray stone streaked with black reared up from the earth, jutting out of the tundra, visible for miles in any direction. Over the years streaks of color and bits of fluttering cloth had been added to it by passing peoples, enhancing its mystical appearance. No one gave a name to it. It was a seite, a place of power, a stone idol erected by the mother earth herself, beyond the worship or appeasement of men. Earlier today they had watched Nadunin as he took an antler cut from a plague-killed reindeer and rubbed it over the surface of the seite. Eight times he had circled the seite,

295

dragging the clacking antler against its rough surface, making one circuit for each season of the year. At the end of the final circuit, he had broken a tip from one antler prong and buried the rest in the gravelly clay at the foot of the seite. The tiny bit of antler prong he had taken back to the the camp. All day Nadunin had sat before his fire, making his sorcery, singing his magic into the prong in a monotonous joik. With his knife he had worked into its brown surface special symbols of his trade. No one had disturbed the old najd or asked him what came next. His was the magic; they could but witness it.

When he had begun to gather dung and dried moss and bits of sticks for a fire that evening, all the herdfolk had wordlessly joined in his task. Soon the heap was mounded taller than a man, and they had watched him start the fire in the old way, with his own firebow. His bow was a rib, and the string on it was sinew. Heckram had heard older boys say that his firebow had been made from the body of the old najd before him. He had never doubted it. When the smoke had wafted, then billowed, from his bow's work, the herdfolk had gathered closer. The najd sat very close to the fire. He set the bit of antler, a charmed pointer of their fate now, atop the head of the red-figured drum and began to tap upon the skin with his little drum hammer.

With each tap of his hammer, the tiny charm skipped across the drum's surface, touching first the heel of this god, then the cheek of that one. Only the herdfolk's najd could know the meaning of its passage, and they watched, breathless, as the striking of his little bone hammer vibrated the surface. It skated, it danced, it jounced, and the sweat poured from the najd's skin. His eyes were far, far, and his lips moved soundlessly as he drummed. Closer and ever closer to the

Trollskott the charm skipped. Finally it settled on the red and black figure and clung there. Louder became the drumming, the little hammer striking the drumskin incessantly, but the hopping, jumping charm would not be budged from its chosen spot.

The words of Nadunin's chant began to be heard, breathless at first, then taking strength and filling the night. The essence of the sacred herbs he had ingested while making the charm could be smelled in the sweat that streamed down his ribs and the hollow track of his spine. His words were not in the language the herdfolk spoke to one another in their daily doings, but the tone was clear. He importuned, he pleaded, he begged, but still the charm clung stubbornly to the Trollskott. Then, with a dullness more deafening than the sharp thumpings that had preceded it, the drumhead split. The gap in the stretched leather opened as suddenly as a good knife opens the belly of a rabbit, racing from the hammer's head to cross the drum and open a mouth in the Trollskott. The Trollskott swallowed the fate of the herdfolk. Drum and najd were suddenly silent.

Heckram couldn't remember what had happened next. He thought he had been bundled away by his mother, carried off hurriedly to their tent and tucked into his blankets, closed off from the terrible omen of the split kobdas. The herdfolk had been swallowed in their own curse. So he had heard whispered the next day. At the next deep lake they passed, the najd had slit the throat of a fine, fat vaja. He had opened her belly and filled the hollow within with stones, and caused the body to be sunk deep in the lake. The offering should have helped. But three days later the najd himself was discovered crouched by his arran inside his tent, staring into the dead ashes on the stones. The murky smoke of sacred herbs had been thick inside the skin tent. Ranged before him were the bits of bone, feather, and stone from his shaman's pouch. No one else could read what his castings had told him on his last journey into the spirit world. The najd was dead.

'Maybe one of the other herders brought a drum. Maybe they're trying to signal us,' Lasse suggested softly.

Heckram gave a doubting snort. 'No one else followed us up this canyon. The others stayed in the lower hills, closer to the stream. And no one would drum to call us. They'd whistle.'

'I know,' Lasse admitted and fell silent again. Heckram could feel the tension in the back that pressed against his. He didn't blame the boy. His own muscles were stretched tight, ready to knot in their tension. The drum thudded on and on in its unhurried rhythm, the sound carrying hollowly through the night and the blowing wet snow. Steadily it tapped on, but its very regularity seemed to mean it was building to something, to some ominous change. Every tap of the thrumming drumhead drew his muscles a notch tighter. He strained his eyes into the darkness until points of light danced before him. He still saw nothing. Most eerie of all, the reindeer dozed placidly.

The snow fell more thickly, swirling into the rough shelter to cling to his eyelashes. They melted on his lashes and shattered his vision with prismatic distortions. He could see nothing clearly, but the things he could almost see were not of the daylight world. The hair prickled up on the back of his neck, the flesh on his body crawled, as the remnants of ancient hackles rose in hostility and fear. He dared not speak to Lasse, but took comfort from the solid warmth pressed against his back.

The hide of the world had been peeled back and he looked on its mysterious inner workings. Lights and shapes and shadows surrounded the little camp and peered at him. That brief flurry of silent snow that stirred the branches of a small birch might have been a white owl, but for the way it disintegrated into snowflakes after peering at him. From the corner of one eye he spotted the white brush of a snow fox, only to have it dematerialize into a fall of snow from a branch.

The drum thudded on monotonously, and Heckram's heart matched its beat. His head jerked as his eyes twitched from one vision to the next, each creature disappearing just as he almost recognized it. He heard sharp panting breath behind him, thought it was Lasse's, and in that instant missed the warm press against his back.

'Lasse!' he cried, springing to his feet so that he stood up through the dry branches that had formed their shelter. A stub on a dead branch raked down his cheek, tearing the flesh, and he felt the warm blood run. He gasped with the pain and clapped his hand to it as he stared wildly about. He could see no sign of the boy. Enraged with fear, he ripped the crude shelter open, flinging and kicking the branches aside. He watched as the falling snow began to coat their sleeping skins and gear bags. Lasse was gone, and he was alone with the muffling snow and the deafening drumming that now rose one notch in rhythm and pitch. It drove him to a frenzy, and he roared wordlessly at the night, at the cloaking snow and the unseen drummer.

He sprang clear of the collapsed shelter, feeling its poles and branches tumble as he leaped away. He scanned the snow about the camp for tracks of the fleeing boy, but the falling snow had already masked them. 'Lasse!' he roared, pushing the sound from this throat with all his strength. But the covering snow bore the sound to the ground and buried it while the steady drum throbs marched over his cry. There was no reply.

'Lasse!' he cried again, and his voice broke on the word. He thought he spotted a shadowy movement by the blasted stump, and he walked toward it. Nothing. But there, again, in the blackness under that pine something shifted. A dozen steps took him close enough to see that the shadows were empty. 'Lasse?' he called again, more softly. Whatever it was slunk deeper into the shadows.

Fear such as he had never known assailed him. He knew it was luring him on, deeper into the woods, and yet he knew he would follow it because there was no safety in returning to the tumbled shelter. His bow was back there, buried under scattered boughs and drifting snow, as was his great knife, and had he been hunting any beast of flesh he would have returned for them. But the drum had transformed the night. He no longer moved in a world ordered by logic, in which the hunter armed himself and went after his prey. The reality of the forest had shifted, and he knew he moved in the spirit world, where man was seldom the hunter. He walked forward blindly, following whatever summoned him, entering a tunnel of swirling snow. The drumming followed.

The night was a small place, bounded by falling snow and tree trunks. He followed something he never saw, but felt as a darker place that moved ahead of him, blocking the swirling snow and lighter trunks of the birches from his vision. Occasionally he glimpsed other things on the periphery, pale shapes that altered for an instant the pattern of the constantly swirling snow. He refused to let them distract him. He no longer called for Lasse, for he knew it was not Lasse he followed. Wherever Lasse was, he could not help him, nor could Lasse aid Heckram. On these journeys, a man was alone.

He came at last to a clearing. He could not see its boundaries, but as he stepped away from the last trees, he saw no more trunks, no more swoop of needled branches to block his vision. There was only the eternally swirling white around him and, far above, the muffled silver of a full moon behind the clouds. He stumbled forward, his feet and legs heavy with the clinging damp snow. He was not cold, but panting with effort, and sweat ran salty and stinging into his eyes and the cut on his face. He scooped a handful of cold snow, held it against the wound. The white flakes increased suddenly, rushing into his face, blinding him with their light. He closed his eyes, then flung up an arm before his face to ward off their cold touch.

When he let his arm fall again, the snow and the drum had ceased. Around him the night was black and silver. The round moon dangled heavy in a black and starry sky over an endless clearing of smooth white snow. There was no boundary to the plain on which he stood; it was vast as the tundra. Briefly, he wondered about the trees he had passed; then, as he took in the scene more completely, he did not dare to look back for them, forgot them completely.

In the center of his vision, dominating the endless plain before him, was the seite. He recognized it and knew it, though he had never seen it as he saw it now, coated thick with the snows of winter. Gray and black it reared up before him, its rough irregular surface almost suggesting a living creature, but never baring enough detail to make it clear which one. White snow clung lacily to the uneven planes of its face. Red as blood were the symbols someone had painted on it. He knew them from the drumhead of the kobdas before

301

it had split, recognized their awesome significance. He took a step forward, and his keen nose knew then that they were painted in blood, fresh warm blood that scented the clean cold night with its strength.

The Wolf atop the seite sat up. So huge he was, Heckram did not understand how he had not seen him before. So huge he was that no wolf could he be, but only Wolf. A light wind ruffled his coat, and the silver tips of his guard hairs sparkled in the moonlight. Mighty thewed shoulders rippled beneath his lush hide. His small ears were pricked sharp, swiveled toward the man. His nose was black, and his nostrils flared thrice as he took in Heckram's scent. Wolf was silent and still, staring at Heckram with eyes that were now red, now green, now yellow. Heckram returned his gaze, silent and still as Wolf himself.

Wolf stood suddenly, looming over Heckram. Slowly he stretched, his chest dipping down behind his outstretched forelegs in a movement that could have been a greeting. He rose from his stretch, then leaped, higher and farther than any mortal wolf could, to land with silent lightness before Heckram. Heckram did not move. The rules of the day world did not apply here. One did not flee or challenge Wolf. Eye to eye he stood with the enormous creature. Hot, rank breath puffed against his face. The yellow eyes measured him as Heckram stood firm in their glare. Slowly, a great gray paw lifted from the ground. Wolf held it before Heckram's face, let him study the black claws on the wide-spread foot. He did not flinch. The great paw touched his face. He felt the roughness of the toe pads, the strength and weight of the huge beast behind it, the drag of the dull nails down his cheek. Then Wolf turned from him, leaped once more to sit atop the seite. He looked down on Heckram.

Something ran on his face, dripped from his chin. Slowly he drew his hand free of his mitten and lifted it to his cheek. The wound stung as he placed his hand against it. Then he lifted his hand free, saw the blackness of his blood on his palm and fingers. Silently he stepped forward, to press his bloody hand against the seite's cold surface. He felt the seite press back against his flesh, felt it suck the warm blood from his hand and take it deep within itself. When at last he drew his hand back from the stony surface, the handprint that remained was not red, but white as snow. He looked up at Wolf, smiling, and Wolf looked down at him and parted his jaws, showing his red tongue and white teeth as he laughed joyously. It was done. The bargain was sealed.

The snow fell again, suddenly and solidly, in a sheet that coated Heckram's face and filled his mouth and nose, making him sputter for air. He heard the drum muttering again. The wind pushed against him, and he staggered blindly through the snowstorm. He opened his eyes a crack, and the wind drove icy flakes into them. He reached to wipe the snow from his face and felt the brush of branches as they dragged against his sleeve. He clawed the snow from his eyes frantically and stood for a long moment in disorientation. The black night was silent around him, the snowfall long over. But where was he? A huge whitened stump loomed up immediately before him. This was what had snagged at his sleeve. Then from behind him he caught the familiar click and shift of the herd's movements by night. He turned.

Their animals were spread out on the slope below him. The stump behind him was the same one that had tricked him earlier. The crude shelter he and Lasse had built was but a dozen steps away from him. It was as they had built it, and within it he could make out the shape of Lasse burrowed into

303

his sleeping skins. He staggered toward it, confused and strangely grateful.

A lump rose in his throat. Lasse was safe, and he himself was returned alive from that other place. How had the world seemed such a bitter place earlier this night, when it was the only place where one might know the sweetness of life? The heart-thumping euphoria of survival washed over him.

He was within arm's reach of the shelter before he noticed the man who sat by the door. He was perfectly still, his hooded head bowed over his bent knees. His attire of white fox skin had merged him with the drifted snow he crouched in. Heckram stopped still. His dream was too recent and the man too motionless. What might look out at him from that hood?

'Who are you?' he demanded in a low voice. He swallowed the quaver at the end of his words.

The man turned his face up. The clouded eyes fixed unerringly on Heckram's, chilling him to his soul and beyond. The old man smiled, and the gaps between his teeth were black and bottomless in the moonlight. 'Carp I am,' he said in a soft voice. 'An old man whose long journey is nearly at an end. You would be one of the herdfolk of Capiam's tribe?'

Heckram nodded briefly, reassured by the man's mention of the herdlord, but still not liking the circumstances. 'I am.'

'And your name is . . .' the old man pressed.

'Heckram,' he conceded. 'My companion is Lasse.'

'Heckram,' the old man repeated in a voice well pleased. 'Ah, Heckram. You wouldn't have a bit of meat about your camp for an old man to gnaw on, would you? Or anything at all? I have come far seeking your folk, and am both weary and hungry.'

'I'll see what I can find,' Heckram muttered. He felt naked as he stooped to crawl past the old man into the shelter.

Something about the seamed old face and murky eyes made him feel vulnerable to the darker side of the night. He didn't want ever to be alone with that old man. He took care to nudge Lasse awake in passing. Inside his gear bag he found strips of jerky and a rind of frozen cheese. Lasse grunted complainingly as Heckram carefully crawled back over him to the old man.

'I was asleep, you gut-bag,' Lasse muttered grumpily.

'We've got a guest,' Heckram informed him.

'I know. He arrived right after you decided to go off into the woods. But he would hardly speak a word to me; said he was waiting for you, and I should get some sleep. If he doesn't mind if I sleep, why should you? And what took you so long, anyway? Too much cheese?'

Heckram let the conversation die. It was something he might sort out with Lasse later, in private, or perhaps not at all. While he was very curious to know what Lasse had experienced that night, he was not at all eager to share his moments with Wolf with anyone. They had become, inexplicably, precious and private. Terror could be a form of intimacy. He considered for an instant, as he handed the food to the old man, that Lasse might be guarding a similar treasure.

Carp took the food, sniffed it curiously in a way that put Heckram in mind of Kerlew, and then began gnawing damply at one end of a piece of jerky.

After several moments of watching his guest chew, he ventured a question. 'You say you are looking for Capiam's herdfolk. Why? You don't look like a trader.'

Carp bit off the partially masticated piece and swallowed it. 'I'm not. I'm a shaman. I'm seeking for Kerlew, my apprentice. Capiam's herdfolk will lead me to him.' He thrust the end of the jerky into his mouth again and spoke around it as he chewed. 'Tillu, his mother, is a healer. When you go to have her mend that gouge down your face, you can take me along.'

Heckram put cautious fingertips to his stinging cheek. It wasn't that deep a gash. 'It won't need healing. It'll close up on its own.'

'Do you think so?' asked the old man. 'I don't.' He cackled short and sudden, then grinned at Heckram around the jerky in his mouth. 'I wouldn't be surprised if it was infected. Wolf claws can leave a nasty scar. The sooner we go to the healer and her son, the better.'

EIGHTEEN

The cavalcade of reindeer crunched their slow way down the hillside. Their toe bones clicked as their wide cloven hooves spread their weight out on the frozen crust of the snow. Their heads bobbed, their white tails flicked in an endless pattern too complex to be deciphered. Somewhere, at the head of the line, Jakke guided the herd's lead animal down through the dark pine fells. They returned to their talvsit now, traveling by night under white stars in a black sky. Usually he was sensitive to the stark beauty of these nights, but tonight Heckram felt irritable, and deadened to such things.

Jakke was an experienced herder, and he set an easy pace that would still have them back at the talvsit by morning. The vajor were heavy with their calves now, their sides bulging out like misshapen packsaddles. They minced awkwardly down the trail, their swollen bellies swaying gently from side to side as they felt for the best footing. Heckram guarded them jealously, seeing the doubling of the herd in their bulging sides.

He had another reason to travel slowly. While Lasse skied

ahead of him through the darkness, alongside their animals, Heckram came at the rear of the herd, leading a harke with Carp perched atop it. The old man had attached himself to Heckram; Heckram did not enjoy the role. Heckram made enough sense of his strangely accented words to know that a shaman was a najd, a wizard, one who crossed ceaselessly between the day world and that other world of which no man spoke lightly. Heckram knew enough of that world to know that Carp was not a man it would be wise to offend. Yet he did not want to know more of the man or be drawn into his confidences. Just being physically close to Carp made Heckram nervous. It was hard to ignore his endless bragging stories and impossible to avoid his nagging questions. But while Heckram patiently led the harke with Carp clinging and swaying on its packsaddle, he made no effort to befriend the old man or to ask any questions of him. He deliberately kept his eyes fixed on the rump of the animal in front of him, ignoring the shaman at his side. It didn't discourage the najd.

Carp nattered on, unashamed of riding a harke like a child while Heckram plodded beside him in the dark. His words rattled off Heckram's bent shoulders like flung pebbles. '. . . and in that hunt, three men were able to bring down the bear that had been raiding our food stores. Enu fell to the bear, but that was as the spirits decreed and not a thing to mourn. Enu had offended Bear in the first place, by letting his woman eat of the heart of the first he-bear killed that season, or none of that bad luck would have found us. Then, after we had skinned the bear and taken the meat, I put the skull in the hollow of a burned birch stump, and within its jaws I placed the bear's heart and Enu's heart, joined together by a pine stake thrust through both of them. Thus was Bear satisfied, and we lost no more meat caches that year. And four moons later, Enu's woman birthed a man-child, and on his skull and on the back of his shoulders was coarse black hair, just like Bear's. Such a hunter as that boy grew to be! What furies could take him! Sometimes in the heat of a hunt, he would fling his weapon down and leap at the beast, his teeth flashing whiter than a wolf's. He would grab the deer by its antlers and force its nose to the earth, and then . . .'

Heckram plodded on, letting the old man's voice blend with the clicking of the reindeer's hooves and the crunch of snow under them. By morning they would reach the talvsit, he told himself. And then . . . Images of a sod hut, its hearth cold, of old Kuoljok's empty eyes, of Ristin's careful smile. The unfinished traveling chest crouched in his hut like a reproached dog. In the gray light of dawn, he'd have to face it.

Each thought dragged at him, pulling his spirit down deeper into a cold, numb place. He pushed his mind on. After a few days of rest, the real spring migration would begin. All the herdfolk, all the animals, moving from the foothills and forest out onto the open tundra. Sweet spring grasses springing up as soon as the snow bared the ground, the vajor dropping their gangly calves, the gentle wind smelling of tundra flowers as it wandered in and out of the scattered tents. The wide places under the unsetting sun.

It was no good. None of it would be any good, until this thing with Elsa was finished. It was like a task that would give him no peace until it was accomplished. The rest of his life would have to be put off until it was solved. He would take no joy in spring, would not find satisfaction in the new calves, would not relish the fresh greens, until he had made some sense of Elsa's death. Like a terrible debt he must pay.

He scratched at the cut down his face, distracting himself. It was healing well, despite Carp's prediction.

'. . . but that is the value of a shaman. We are the go-betweens, who stitch the worlds together like sinews joining hides into garments. People without a shaman are people alone and half blind. Their lives can make no sense, for they are only living half of it. Things happen to them, and they cannot understand why, or what they can do about it. Some lose their spirit guides, and sicken and die without knowing why. Children are born and grow and go blindly through their lives, sometimes offending the very spirits that would shelter and guide them. Their days are long and sad and filled with misfortune. Life becomes a burden to them, and they are vulnerable to any who wish to work harm upon them.'

Heckram found himself nodding to the najd's words. Long, sad days, filled with misfortune.

'Don't you want to ask what I can do for such a one?' Carp's words hung black in the night. Heckram turned to him slowly.

The old man's pale eyes showed almost white in the night, gripping him with their strangeness. He stared into them, unable to reply. Carp answered his own question.

'Such a one can be put on a pathway, and ushered into a journey back to his spirit beast. The journey is dangerous and only the strong return. No one can go with a man on that journey; he must undertake it alone. Along the way, he may meet spirits. If he has wisdom, when he meets his spirit guide he will know him, and he will know how to bind his spirit guide to himself. Then, when the man returns from his journey, his spirit guide comes back with him. If he is very wise, he listens to his spirit beast and accepts his aid. Wisest

310

of all is the one who seeks the guidance of a shaman to find what his spirit beast desires, and what he must do to restore balance to his life.'

Heckram realized with a start that he was standing still, his feet numb in the snow as he stared into Carp's clouded eyes. He no longer heard the click and crunch of the moving herd. He was alone in the blackness of night with the peculiar old man crouched on the back of the harke like some predator ready to sink its claws. A wind slipped past them and wandered off through the trees. An unworldly silence followed it, quenching all familiar night sounds. No branch sighed in the wind, no twigs rustled to a lemming's passage. The stillness was complete.

'Look!' The shaman's shrill whisper cracked the silence. 'Look who follows!'

Heckram turned wide eyes back the way they had come. There was nothing there, only the trail wending off into darkness. He held his breath, listening, as his eyes scanned for any shift of shadow. There was none.

'Nothing follows us, old man,' he rumbled softly.

'Not us!' hissed Carp, a note of laughter in his whisper. 'Not us. You!'

Unwillingly Heckram looked back once more. He stiffened. His grip tightened on the harke's lead rope. Something large and shaggy slipped across the trail behind them and merged with the trees on the other side. He did not breathe as he eased the reindeer into movement. The harke's eyes shone round and black, his nostrils flaring as he snorted out his fear. When Heckram tried to breathe, the air jammed in his throat and he wheezed. He stumbled off the hard crust of the trail and plunged knee-deep into softer snow. Frantically he dragged himself up and tried to increase his pace. On the harke's back, Carp rocked back and forth in silent paroxysms of laughter. Heckram longed to strike him and knew he did not dare. Only a fool offended a najd. His movement made the panicky animal stagger. It jerked against the halter and tried to rear despite the shaman's weight on its back. Heckram dragged it on, taking long swift strides.

A part of him knew what followed. Another part of him refused the possibility of such a thing. Glancing back did no good. The treacherous moonlight showed a flash of fang, a glint of silver guard hairs, a gleam of lambent eyes, but never betrayed the follower entire.

Sweat broke out over his whole body, trickling down his back and ribs. 'Grip to the pack frame,' he croaked to Carp. 'Hold tight so that if we have to run, you won't be thrown.'

'There's no outrunning him!' Carp cackled, spraying spittle. The old man rocked in the packsaddle.

'Maybe not,' Heckram muttered. 'But we'll try. I'm not going to try to stand and face that.'

'Run, then!' cackled the old man. 'I'm sure he won't mind! The faster you run, the sooner we'll get there.'

Heckram burst suddenly into motion. The reindeer beside him sprang forward gladly, stretching and straining to put distance between itself and that which followed. The najd clung to the lurching packsaddle. Heckram gave the harke the best part of the trail, so that at every fifth or ninth step he plunged through the snow crust and had to wallow up again. Twice he dared to look back, and each time found his pursuer no farther behind. The whisk of grayish shape, the flash of glowing eye, haunted him.

He lifted his eyes to glance down the trail before him, hoping to see the other reindeer and herders. Wolves did not attack groups of men and animals. In numbers there would be safety. His feet pounded on. Any moment he expected to see the gray shape slip past him, to head the reindeer off and turn them back into the pack that certainly followed. He ran until the reindeer was staggering and a lancing pain stabbed up through his ribs. Sweat stung his eyes, the najd stoically bounced on the packsaddle, the reindeer made a bad step, and, as the snow gave way beneath its hooves, it went to its knees.

Heckram turned, pulling his knife, to face their pursuer. He caught a glimpse of something blending suddenly into the gray shadows and trunks of the surrounding forest. It should have been pressing its advantage, rushing forward to harry the exhausted man and animal. Nothing. The blowing reindeer shuddered its way back onto the path and stood with its head drooping. Terror had wearied it as much as exertion; the old shaman was no heavier than its normal workload. The harke had run as only wolves make a reindeer run.

'It was real!' Heckram turned defiant eyes to the old man.

Carp no longer smiled. 'Real. That's what I've been telling you. But you did not seem to be listening.' He leaned so close that Heckram saw the tiny bubbles in the spittle on his lips. 'You insult him,' the old man whispered harshly. 'Was not the bargain made last night, and sealed with blood? Trust him. Give over your vengeance to him, and let your own mind be emptied, ready for what he will ask of you.' Slowly Carp straightened on the reindeer. 'Let us go now.' Despite the jostling ride, Carp sat calmly. His fogged eyes looked deep into Heckram's eyes, but barred all entry to themselves. Heckram turned aside from him, shaking his head wearily, baffled and somehow angry with him.

He looked back again. Nothing. Just white snow. He

realized abruptly that dawn was well begun. Looking about himself again, he recognized the trees and the lay of the hills. The village was not far now.

As if to prove him correct, he heard a glad call from down the trail and turned to find Ristin hastening toward them. Welcoming words spilled from her.

'I was worried when you did not come in with the rest. Lasse said you were right behind them, but did not know why you were coming so slowly. He offered to look for you, but he was nearly asleep on his feet, so I told him not to bother.' Her words were nearly apologetic, but her eyes roamed over her son in obvious relief. Heckram's glance was equally piercing. Was the dawn light that harsh, or had she aged in the days he had been gone? There was strain in the lines about her eyes and mouth, but also relief and gladness as she looked on him. Then, as she noticed the man with him, she became more formal.

'You must be Carp, of whom Lasse spoke. Welcome to the talvsit of Capiam's herdfolk.' She glanced quickly at Heckram. 'When Lasse said you were bringing a guest, I took it upon myself to kindle a fire on your hearth and prepare food for you both.'

'It will never be said that Capiam's herdfolk were inhospitable to a stranger,' Heckram said to Carp, but he wondered for whom she had really kindled the fire. Had she known how much he had dreaded coming home to a hut with a cold arran and the musty smell of emptiness throughout?

He smiled his thanks at his mother, and she met his eyes with warmth and sympathy. Then she frowned. 'What have you done to your cheek?' she asked, reaching to touch his face.

'Scratched it on a branch. It looks much worse than it is.' He pulled away from her touch.

'Let's hope so. Still, I think you should see the healer as soon as you can.'

Heckram frowned. 'Can't you make me a poultice for it, Ristin? We used to manage without a healer.'

Ristin moved her head, studying the slash. 'Yes, we managed well enough, if you don't count the people scarred and dead that didn't have to be. If that gash were on your arm, I might try to treat it myself. But not that close to your eye. It's for a trained healer, and as soon as possible. Eat first, and get a bit of sleep, but then go to her. An infection like that is nothing to trifle with.'

Heckram reached to pat at his face. It was swollen stiff, and throbbing pain echoed through it. He glanced with narrowed eyes at Carp, but the old man said nothing.

He made no move to dismount from the harke either. With a sigh, Heckram tugged at the weary beast's halter. They started down the path to the talvsit. His mother gossiped as they went. Heckram listened numbly, letting the words slide by him, responding to her questions by rote as his tired brain chewed at other mysteries. He thanked her for unloading his gear and putting it in his hut. Yes, he knew they'd have to break a few more harke to pack this year; no, he hadn't decided which ones yet. No, he hadn't had any problems with the reindeer on the grazing grounds; yes, it might very well be an early spring. He nodded as he heard that two of Bror's vajor had already calved. It was early, but calves born now would keep up with the herd better on the migration. He was rather hoping his own vajor would calve soon. It never hurt a calf to have a few days to find its legs before having to follow the herd.

Then Ristin was saying that Capiam had decided they would leave ten days from now. Everyone was in the usual spring uproar, putting winter equipment up on the racks, taking down summer gear, mending the worn or making new harness.

Heckram nodded to her endless commentary as they walked through the talvsit. He noted with detached humor that many folk were turning to stare at his companion. Carp's outlandish garments marked him a foreigner, and Heckram noted how quickly the eyes of the villagers turned aside and down when they met his gray-filmed gaze. Carp was enjoying his grand entrance. He sat up straight on the harke and nodded down on the herdfolk they passed. His mouth hung slightly agape with pleasure. Heckram was torn between being annoyed at Carp and enjoying the stir he caused. Pirtsi watched them with gaping mouth; then the youth whirled and ran up the path. Well, the herdlord would soon know there was a stranger in the village, staying at Heckram's hut. He wondered if he would send Joboam to investigate, or come himself. The old herdlord would have come himself to welcome any stranger, no matter how humble, and to ask news of the far places. That had been in better times, though. Heckram was willing to wager that Capiam would send Joboam.

'Heckram?'

He paused at the questioning note in Ristin's voice, and, as he halted, he realized that he had unthinkingly been making for her hut. His own was off to the left, past Stina's. His tragedy, forgotten for a moment, weighed on his heart again.

'Let me take the harke for you,' Ristin said. 'You must be tired. I'll peg him out near good feed. You take care of your guest and settle down for some rest. I'll come by later this afternoon.'

Heckram felt the sudden weight of Carp's hand on his

shoulder. The old man leaned on him as he clambered heavily down. He smiled at Ristin, dismissing her with a benign wave. 'Don't come back this afternoon,' he instructed her grandly. 'Heckram will be taking me to the healer Tillu.'

Ristin's back stiffened at Carp's condescending tone. Heckram didn't blame her. But she turned graciously, seeming to remember that the old man was a stranger to their talvsit. She would tolerate his foreign rudeness and attribute it to ignorance. She looked straight into Heckram's eyes as she spoke her next words. 'The meat on your rack is thawing. Best use it up soon, perhaps to pay Tillu. Though she may have no need of meat.' She paused for half a breath, touched her son's hand. 'Joboam may be at Tillu's. He has been finding out for Capiam what the healer will need for the journey. So, if you do go that way . . .' She let the sentence dangle, but her meaning was clear. Avoid trouble. She tugged at the weary harke's bridle.

Heckram felt his mind whirl and questions filled him. 'Joboam is bringing the healer on the migration with us?' he muttered bewilderedly, but Ristin was out of earshot. Carp grinned his gap-toothed smile and tugged at Heckram's sleeve.

'First, eat. Carp is very hungry. Then, sleep, and then we will go find Tillu the healer. Yes, and Kerlew, my apprentice. You are surprised that Tillu is going with the herdfolk? Before the day is over, others will be much more surprised than that. Much, much more surprised!' Carp laughed sprayingly and dragged him toward his own hut.

The hot throbbing of his face woke him. Dim afternoon light seeped in through the smoke hole of the hut. Carp snored noisily on the hides Ristin had placed by the hearth. She had prepared all for them. Soup had been simmering in a pot near the hearth stones, dry firewood piled neatly by the door, the sleeping hides aired and spread smooth. He wondered briefly how it would have been to have come home with Elsa. For a moment he imagined how he might have unloaded the harke as she gathered dry wood and rekindled the fire on their hearth. He stared at the unfinished chest in the corner and then pulled his eyes away from it. Why couldn't he just say to himself, 'That's done,' and let it go? Let it all go and get on with his own life. He tried to roll over and find sleep again, but the press of his swollen cheek against the skins was a throbbing agony. He touched the pulsing swelling with careful fingertips. Last night, he had thought he was healing well. Today, this ugly festering demanded attention.

He glared at the smug old najd and then started as Carp's eyelids slid up and his snoring stopped in midrasp. The shaman sat up smoothly, regarding Heckram with his blank stare. He didn't yawn or stretch or scratch himself. He simply sat up and announced, 'And now we go to see Tillu the healer. Bad infection, yes? Face hurts a lot, right?' He grinned at Heckram amiably. 'Tillu's a healer. She cannot tell a man with an infected face to go away.' Carp laughed jovially, as if at a marvelous prank. Heckram did not join in.

The path to Tillu's hut seemed longer than he remembered it, and better trodden. To either side of them, the afternoon sun was melting the soft snow that lay in the open places between the trees. In the shadows snow lingered, more icy than soft now, and the path itself was a packed ridge of ice that meandered under the trees. He tugged at the collar of his tunic, loosening it to let more of his body heat escape. He wished he were alone. Give his revenge to Wolf? He needed to mull over that idea. He needed to know what Wolf would ask in return.

He had expected Carp to complain when they set out on foot, but the old man scuttled willingly along. Heckram had never seen legs so bowed or an old man so spry. But then, he had ridden down from the mountains on the back of a harke, and he hadn't made a wild dash with a wolf at his heels in the dawn. Heckram sighed away the memory of the encounter, pushing it down with all the other things he didn't want to consider. Vainly he tried to just keep on living his life, ignoring all the events that tried to jar him into action. He wanted, if he wanted anything, to just keep on being himself; to hunt the wild herd for more animals to add to his stock, to sit of an evening and plait a lasso or fletch an arrow, or carve a spoon. Kerlew and his spoons. How was he doing with his carving? he wondered. Then he shook his head at himself, marveling how once more he had dragged himself back to thinking of his problems. Could he just give them over to Wolf?

He took a deep breath of the air. Spring smells. Moss awakening to life after its frozen dormancy all winter. Sap was moving in the trees, their buds just starting to swell, yet the bite of their odor scented the air. And why was Kerlew one of his problems? he suddenly asked himself. Forget it.

'Top of this rise and we'll see Tillu's tent.' He spoke over his shoulder to Carp. He had taken the lead, ostensibly to show the way, but mostly to prevent conversation. He'd be glad to be rid of the old shaman. Then he felt a twinge of guilt at leaving his problem at Tillu's door. Ridiculous. Carp was not a problem to Tillu, he was her son's mentor. And the old man had hinted that he was more than that to her. He glanced back at the crook-legged old man with his foggy eyes. He frowned to himself. Well, it wasn't any of his business, anyway.

He paused at the top of the hill to let Carp catch up with him. Wordlessly he pointed through the trees to the just visible tent. Heckram spotted a harke, then two grazing to one side of the tent. Probably hobbled there. He recognized one as Joboam's and felt a tightening in his gut. He remembered Ristin's warning and set his jaw carefully. No trouble. No problems. Take the old man to Tillu, get his face tended, and then go home and sleep. And sleep.

He had been so deep in his own thoughts, and the sight that greeted him as he stepped into the clearing was so unexpected, that he stood staring.

Kerlew, rolled into a ball, lay on the melting snow and exposed earth before Joboam. His long narrow hands were clasped over his head, his eyes squeezed shut, and his mouth quavered as the long ululating wail of a very small and frightened child escaped them. Even as Heckram stood frozen by consternation, Joboam, unaware of them, stooped to grip Kerlew's tunic and drag the boy up. He lifted him high, his dangling feet clear of the earth, his leather shirt tightening about his throat and stifling his cries. 'When I tell you to do something,' Joboam said in a deadly, pleasant voice, 'you will do it. Swiftly.' The great muscles in his upper arm bunched, and then Kerlew was flying through the air. He landed, rolling, and curled into a ball. He made no sound, only gasping for the air knocked out of him. Joboam advanced on him, and suddenly Heckram knew that what he had witnessed was a repetition of what had gone before and was about to happen again. A rush of angry strength flooded him.

'Joboam!' he hissed as the big man reached again for Kerlew.

Joboam's attention twitched up from the boy to Heckram

moving in on him. Joboam set his weight and crouched like a snarling wolverine, and the same unholy anticipation lit his face.

'Heckram!' wailed Kerlew with the first breath he drew. With the resilience of children and madmen, he scrabbled to his feet and raced to intercept Heckram, flinging himself at him. Kerlew gripped him around the waist, dragging at him, panting into his shirt, wordless with fear. Caught between strides, Heckram all but fell over the boy. He lurched to a halt and put his hands on Kerlew's shoulders. He tried to loosen the boy's grip, but he clung like lichen on a rock. Beneath his touch the boy was shaking still; Heckram glared wordlessly at Joboam, no words strong enough for the promises he wished to make the man.

For a moment Joboam was likewise wordless, expecting Heckram to cast the boy aside and come after him. When he knew that Kerlew's clinch had stopped him, Joboam bared a mocking grin. 'Two of a kind,' he sneered. Then, as he studied Heckram's frozen face, he added, 'The cut's an improvement. Wish I had done it myself. If you want Tillu, she's busy now. You'll have to come back later.'

'I can tell she isn't here,' Heckram growled so low that the words were barely intelligible. 'You'd never dare to treat the boy that way if she were.'

Joboam's smile never wavered. 'No? Things have changed while you've been gone. The little healer has come to appreciate me. I'll be seeing that she travels comfortably when she joins us for the spring migration. And I think that the boy will have learned some manners by then.'

Kerlew made a fearful noise and buried his face deeper in Heckram's shirt. He tried to untangle himself and step around the boy, but Kerlew only gripped tighter.

'You are wrong, big man. I am the one who will be giving the boy his lessons from now on. Come, Kerlew. Look up. Have you no greeting for me?'

For a long moment Kerlew didn't move. Then his face lifted from Heckram's shirt front and he peeked warily at the source of the voice. 'Carp!' he cried out, relief and joy in his voice. Abandoning Heckram, he flung himself toward the twisted old najd. 'Every day I have sung the calling song. Every day!' the boy rebuked him gladly.

'And every day I have heard you, but some days not as loud as others. It was a long way for me to come. And some trails an old man travels by ways longer than a boy's, and somewhat slower. But here I am. I have come.' His old hands patted the boy, smoothing the tousled hair, lightly touching his shoulders and arms as if to reassure himself that the boy was real. Kerlew wriggled under his touch like a pleased puppy. Heckram watched them, trying to decipher the emotion spilling through him. Hadn't he believed Carp when he said Kerlew was his apprentice? Hadn't he known Kerlew would be glad to see him? Then what was this he felt; surely not jealousy? His hands hung empty.

Joboam stared at the old man whom Kerlew greeted so strangely. There was appraisal on his face and bafflement. The scrawny little man spoke so boldly, but had nothing visible to back up his authority. He did not keep a wary eye toward Joboam; he dismissed him altogether. It made no sense. No one treated him so. No one dared to ignore him. As if reading his thoughts, Carp suddenly lifted his eyes from Kerlew and fixed Joboam with an ice-white stare. Joboam expelled air from his lungs as if he had been struck. He could not meet that stare. But when he looked away from Carp, he found Heckram, his arms now free, staring at him. He was not smiling, or glaring. His face was impassively cold as he stepped toward Joboam.

'Carp!'

The word that cut across the clearing was more a cry of disbelief than a greeting. All eyes turned to Tillu. She stood at the edge of the clearing, an armload of white moss held to her chest. Her face was as white as the moss, and she rocked where she stood. Yet the old najd looked up with a grin to her cry, while Kerlew danced about him, fairly shouting, 'He's come, mother, he's come, just as I knew he would! Didn't I tell you he'd come to us! And this time he will teach me all of it, all the magic, all the songs!'

Heckram had halted at Tillu's cry. Now both men looked from her to the najd. Silently she came across the slushy clearing. Bits of the moss she had gathered dripped from her arms; she paid no heed to it. Her face was white and strained. As if she looked upon a ghost, Heckram thought, and felt a night chill creep up his back. From what he knew of the old man, he very well could be from the spirit world. The najd gripped Kerlew by the shoulders, turned him to face his mother, and held the boy in front of him, like a shield or a hostage. There was defiance in the cold smile he turned on Tillu over the innocent boy's head. The contrast between Kerlew's ecstatic grin and the najd's sneer grated on Heckram and raised a strange guilt in him. What had he guided to Tillu's tent?

'You did not forget me so soon, did you Tillu? Surely you knew I would be coming for my apprentice?' Carp asked sweetly.

'Your apprentice?' This from Joboam. 'You've come to take him away?' There was appraisal in his voice, and Heckram didn't like it. Why was Joboam so interested in Kerlew?

'He is mine, yes. Mine to train. But not to take away. No. A shaman must have a people to guide. I have chosen the herdfolk for Kerlew.'

'Shaman?' Joboam tried the strange word on his tongue.

'Najd.' Heckram filled it in softly and enjoyed the look of sudden wariness that spread over Joboam's face.

But in another instant, Joboam was hardening his face and asserting an authority that was not his. 'And what does Capiam say to this?'

'Nothing, yet, for no one has told him. But I expect the headman will be most welcoming. I have never yet met a headman who was inhospitable to me.'

There it was again, that arrogant assumption of authority and power. This najd, with his manner so like Joboam's, already made Joboam's jaws ache. Heckram could tell, and he took a furtive delight in it.

'Kerlew,' Tillu said brokenly.

The boy reached up to pat one of the wrinkled hands on his shoulders. He seemed impervious to her distress as he asked, 'May I take Carp into the tent and give him tea and some of the salt fish that Ibba brought us? I am sure he is both hungry and weary.' His speech had a new fluidity to it, his face a new confidence. As if his encounter with Joboam had never occurred.

'No, no,' the najd cut in. 'Heckram has fed me well and I have rested. I would rather walk with you, Kerlew, and speak privately of things that are not for women's ears. Besides, your mother has a healing to do. Heckram has an infected cut on his face. Let her practice her craft while we discuss ours.'

Carp put his arm around her son, smiled at her as he turned the boy and walked him away, showing her how easily he took her child away from her. Kerlew did not look back, and Heckram felt an echo of the abandonment that sliced Tillu's soul. She aged before his eyes, the lines at the corners of her mouth and eyes going deeper. She shut her eyes, shook her head slowly.

Joboam snorted. 'Don't be a fool, woman. Let him have the boy. I see no problem with that. But he may be surprised when he announces to Capiam that he will be our najd.'

Tillu waved a hand at Joboam, in an angry gesture of dismissal, heedless of the moss it spilled.

'So now you tell Tillu what to do with her son, as well as advise the herdlord about najds,' Heckram observed. 'I wonder if she knows how you "discipline" Kerlew when she is absent?'

Joboam turned to him. Color rose in his face, but his words were calm. 'I wonder what would happen if I hit you on that slash? Looks as if your whole face would break open.'

'I wonder if you have the courage to try?' Heckram met his gaze. 'Here I am, Joboam. There's nothing hampering you.'

'Shut up, the both of you!' Tillu whirled on them suddenly, anger flaring. 'Do you think I have nothing better to do than mend your stupid heads after you've broken them? Make me extra work, Joboam, and Capiam will hear of it. Yes, and of other things, too.' Her dark eyes snapped from Heckram to Joboam. Joboam's eyes narrowed at her threat. 'Now. Joboam, you may tell the herdlord what I have told you several times already. That I am not decided to go. You may even tell him that your daily visits here have reminded me of all the reasons that I have for avoiding people. And Heckram. If you want me to clean up that gash, then go to the tent. But if you stand here and fight, I shall do no healing for either of you. And I shall tell Capiam you interfered with my gathering of supplies.'

She turned, clutching the moss to her chest as if it were a child. She walked to her tent without looking back. Heckram saw her shudder once, as if she held back a sob or a cough. He turned to look at Joboam through narrowed eyes.

Joboam snorted. 'Let her stamp and shake her head now. She'll learn the harness soon enough.' The look he sent after her was proprietary. Heckram's anger went one notch tighter.

'Aren't you still wondering about my face?' he asked softly.

Joboam turned aside from him. 'You'll keep,' he said casually. 'News won't. Since you haven't informed the Herdlord Capiam of the troubles you have dragged home, I will. A najd. Even a simpleton knows the problems that can create. And you had to bring him here. Still, if he takes the healer's son with him when he goes, that may solve a problem. For me.' Joboam's voice had become speculative. He began to walk back toward the talvsit.

'Joboam!' Heckram called. The man stopped.

'Stay away from Kerlew. Not because he's the najd's apprentice. Because I say so. And one more thing. If you won't fight me now, be ready to later. A time will come.'

'That it will,' Joboam agreed. He started to walk away, but Heckram's voice stopped him again. 'Be sure to give Capiam all the healer's message. I'll be stopping by his tent this evening to be sure it was delivered correctly.'

Before Joboam could walk away from him, Heckram turned and walked toward Tillu's hut.

NINETEEN

It was dark and stuffy inside the tent after the bright coolness of the spring afternoon. The earth floor had softened with the warmer weather. It gave beneath Heckram's heavier tread. Moisture, unlocked from frost, damped the furnishings of the tent, giving them a musty smell. Tillu should take everything outside into the early sun to air. The herdfolk always aired their possessions before packing for the migration. Heckram wondered if Tillu were really coming with them, but couldn't muster the courage to ask. He stood awkwardly inside the door flap, feeling an intruder. Tillu hadn't spoken, hadn't even acknowledged him with a nod. She crouched, stirring herbs into a pot of water beside her hearth. Something in her physical attitude was familiar; her back bowed like a shield, chin tucked into her chest as if she awaited the next blow. Recognition hit him. She, too, tried to go on with her life as she struggled with an insolvable problem.

He looked around, trying to think of some neutral comment. Her poverty had given way to meager comfort.

There were more hides on the pallets, and dried meat and fish hung from the tent supports beside utensils of wood and bone. Her dealings with the herdfolk were prospering. The thought recalled the last time he had seen her. The day after Elsa died. They had had little to say to one another amid the hubbub of grief. And just as little now. The things he shared with this woman were not the things that drew folk together. He wished suddenly he hadn't come. She was ignoring him, crouching with her back to him, stirring something in a pot. He wondered if he could simply back out of the tent and return to his own hut.

As if she had heard his thoughts, Tillu spoke. 'Leave the tent flap up. The light is better that way.' She glanced over her shoulder at him, irritable. 'Sit down on the pallet. You're too tall for me to work on that slash if you stand.'

Without a word, he looped the door string around its support. A narrow triangle of light spilled into the tent and across one pallet. He went to it and sat, silent. Not talking seemed easier.

She lifted the steaming pot and set it on the floor by his feet. As silent as he, she took a handful of white moss from a basket near the fireside. Her capable fingers picked through it quickly, discarding bits of twigs, a pellet of rabbit dung, the skeleton of a leaf. He watched her. The rising steam from the pot had a pleasant fragrance, like the forest in true spring, when the rising warmth from the leaf mould smelled of generations of pine and alder. He relaxed, until Tillu knelt suddenly before him. It put her face on the same level as his. She dunked the moss into the water and let it soak as she studied his face.

It was an uncomfortable arrangement for Heckram. He had no place to put his eyes and he didn't know what to do with his hands. He folded his arms across his chest, then, feeling foolish, let them fall to his sides. Her face was close to his as she examined the cut. Her mouth was impassive, and when he did look into her eyes, she didn't notice. The injury had all her attention. He started slightly when she took his chin in a firm, cool grip and turned his face toward the light. Her fingertips rasped lightly against his chin. She kept her hand there, holding him steady, as she moved her head to study the injury. He stared at her frankly, noting the fineness of her hair, the way it pulled free of its binding and strayed around her cheeks. Her nose was narrow and more prominent than was thought attractive among the herdfolk. Much like his own. Her cheeks were not broad and flat, but were molded back over high cheekbones. Her dark eyes were sharp and bright as they peered at him. Like a vixen, turning her head and cocking her ears as she watched and waited at a vole's burrow.

'What happened?' she demanded suddenly.

It took him a moment to reply. 'I scratched my face on a tree branch.'

'Oh?' She turned his chin again. 'It looks like an animal scratch. Not as bad as a bear swipe, not as big, but similar.'

'I stood up inside a branch shelter that Lasse and I had built, and scratched my face on a snag.'

She didn't agree with him. 'Then it shouldn't have become infected like this. But even a mild swipe from a predator usually becomes infected. Like this.'

'It was a branch,' Heckram repeated irritably.

'Mmm. It's close to the eye. You should have come sooner. Now it's going to hurt.' With no more warning than that, she scooped a handful of moss from the warmed water and held it firmly against his face. The heat accented the pulsing pain of the wound. He set his teeth and held himself still. Sweat sprang out all over him.

'I can hold it there,' he offered after a moment.

'I've got it,' she replied. 'It will take a little while. It has to open. Sit still.'

It was unnerving to sit so close to a woman, face to face, being touched by her. There was the hot pain of the wet moss and its pressure against the swollen slash. But the smell of her hair and skin was another pressure against him, as warm as the poultice, and stirring. Her touch on his face, the brush of her warm breath, the points of her breasts so close to him, and the serious eyes that stared at him but didn't meet his gaze were all combining to disturb him.

His face flushed suddenly and he looked away from her. His sudden arousal surprised and shamed him. He expected better control of himself. He hoped she wasn't aware of it. A drop of sweat tracked a line down his face.

Why, she wondered idly, would a man lie about being clawed by an animal? Most hunters bragged of their struggles with beasts, as if being maimed were a feat to be proud of. She saw the pinch lines around his mouth go deeper and white. 'I know it's uncomfortable,' she said quietly. 'But in a few moments we'll ease the pressure.'

She lifted the spongy moss away to inspect the swollen gash, then dipped it again into the warm water. 'Here. Hold it against your face while I make a poultice to draw out the infection. It may not be as bad as it first looked.' He put his hand against the moss as she lifted hers away. Their fingers brushed in passing.

She stepped clear of him, glad to put a cooling distance between them. I should be thinking of Kerlew, she told herself sternly. I should be worrying about what nonsense Carp is telling Kerlew, and how to get rid of that horrid old man. Instead, she had been lost in Heckram. She had meant to examine the gash. But when she had touched his chin to turn his face, she had become aware of the rasp of his unshaven skin. With a sudden ache, she had remembered the brush of her father's whiskers against her cheek when he hugged her. He had been a big man, strong, like this Heckram. When he carried her on his shoulder, she had been safe. If he had been home the day the raiders came . . . but he hadn't, and she had never felt safe since then. She swallowed against a rising lump in her throat and half angrily pulled her thoughts away from those lost days. She should be concentrating on her work. On Heckram.

Like an intruder breeching a broken wall, he had made her aware of the man behind the injury. There was his smell again, as she remembered it, the smell of live reindeer and behind it the subtler musk of his own maleness. She had felt his eyes trying to meet hers and resisted them. Bad enough that she could not bring herself to take her hand from his face. His body warmth had crossed the small space between them, touching her and making her blood quicken. She quenched her rising warmth firmly. It had nothing to do with the man, she told herself. It was only that she was at that time of her days when her body ached for a man's touch, warmed and quickened at the thought of one. Another hand of days and her blood time would come, and this foolishness be forgotten. Was she a girl to be ruled by such urges?

Going to her herb box, she began to sort through it. The sorrel leaves were shriveled brown, nearly too dry to use. Put them in anyway, it couldn't hurt. Yarrow. Willow leaves. Goldenrod root? Well, it worked on burns and scalds. She added a little. She'd be glad of the fresh green herbs of spring. These old gatherings had nearly lost their potency. She began to pound them together on a slab of wood. She could mix them with lichen, cook it with a little water into a soggy paste, and –

'You're angry at me, aren't you?'

Tillu turned in surprise to his question. 'What?'

'You're angry at me. For helping the najd to find you and Kerlew. And for threatening Joboam.'

For a long moment she did not reply. Then she gave a great sigh. She rocked back on her heels, her pestle forgotten in the hand she raised to prop her chin. 'I'm not angry,' she decided. 'You couldn't have known that he wasn't what I would choose for Kerlew. And even if you had . . . it wouldn't have mattered. I believe that he still would have found us. Sooner or later.'

'And Joboam?' he pressed. She wondered why it was important to him.

'Joboam is a . . . problem,' she admitted grudgingly. 'But it is a problem I have had before. There are always men who like to control things. Men who believe they should rule anyone weaker than they. I wasn't protecting him when I interfered between you. What I said was true. A healer sees so many injuries that could not be avoided. We get weary of treating the ones deliberately caused. And soon he will be gone. Soon you will all be gone.'

She heard the dilemma in his voice as he pushed on. 'Why do you let him . . . treat Kerlew like that?'

'Let him?' She let her bitterness bloom in her voice. 'What am I to do? He doesn't strike the boy when I am here. And I try always to be here when Joboam is. But sometimes he comes when the boy is here alone, and then . . . but I have told Kerlew not to be alone with him. To come and find me as soon as Joboam arrives, not give him a chance to be angry.'

'And Kerlew forgets.' The understanding in his voice surprised her.

'And Kerlew forgets,' she agreed. 'It is hard to explain to someone who doesn't know him. The thoughts of this moment drive from his mind the instructions of a moment ago. It is not as if he were stupid. He is always thinking, but of something else. He has his own ideas of what is important and what is not. Two days ago I saw a bruise on his arm, and asked him about it. Three days ago, Joboam grabbed him there. Why didn't he tell me? Because he forgot, because that was the day he found the patch of frozen berries and dug them up and ate them, and I asked him what the red on his mouth was, so he told me about the berries instead. And, to him, that makes sense!'

She heard her own voice shaking. She turned abruptly to Heckram. He was sitting quietly, the dripping moss still cupped against his face. His eyes were brown, she realized suddenly, not black. And there was no pity in them. What she saw in them startled her. It didn't seem possible that he was sharing the pain she felt for her boy. 'The sleeve of your tunic is soaking wet,' she said with a calmness she didn't feel. 'Take it off and hang it by the fire. You'll want it dry to go home in.'

She became aware again of the pestle in her hand and used it with a vigor the dry herbs didn't require. She heard him ease out of his shirt. She mashed the herbs with some lichen in the bottom of a small pot, added water, and put the poultice to heat. She turned to find him naked from the waist up, wringing water out of the sleeve of his woolen undershirt. There was a tracing of hair on his chest, starting just below his throat, widening slightly on his breast, and stretching in a line past his navel.

'The men of my grandfathers' blood,' he said, a husky embarrassment in his voice, 'are hairy, like this. On the face and chest.' She had been caught staring.

She lifted her eyes, tried to meet his gaze nonchalantly. 'It is so with my people, also,' she admitted.

'The women also?' he asked incredulously.

She laughed aloud, caught the look in his eyes, and wanted to stop, but couldn't. He was blushing, embarrassed by his ignorance. She caught her breath, found a solemn expression, but lost it again. Perhaps it didn't matter. He was starting a smile now, rueful and shy, but a smile.

'That was stupid, wasn't it?' he admitted, chuckling.

'Not really.' She got her face under control. 'You have probably always been with your own people. How are you to know the ways of other folk?'

'I haven't always been among the herdfolk,' he defended. 'When I was very small, I once made a trading journey with my father. It was when he was wealthy, before the plague. I saw the village of the traders, like, like . . .' He groped for words. 'Like two great square huts, made into many little huts.'

'Rooms,' she suggested.

He paused, shrugged his shoulders, and gave a tentative nod. 'Two of them, with many families living there, each family with a "room." And the wide path between the two great huts. The men had beards that billowed over their chests. And the women had hair like different shades of wood. Some of the children were my cousins, but we could not talk well together. Still, we played.'

'Was it far from here?' Tillu found herself asking.

Heckram frowned to himself. 'It didn't seem so at the time. But I was small, riding in my father's pulkor, so the distance meant little to me. Still, it couldn't be that far. Some years the traders come from that village to trade. Not as often as they used to, but then, we used to have more to trade. Now it is more common for the herdfolk to go to their village. The year my father took me, it was an unusual thing. All the folk in the village were surprised to see us and marveled over our harke and pulkor. Do I have to put this back on my face?'

He had caught her dreaming, her thoughts riding on his tale. She looked at the handful of moss he held out.

'Wet it again and put it back. It will soften that gash.'

He made a sound between a sigh and a growl and sat down again. She heard him slosh the moss in the pot. She bent to study her own pot of lichen and herbs. She poked at it with the pestle, decided it had softened enough, and removed it from the heat. The white lichen was very useful as a binder. It could be used to thicken a stew, or to make a poultice, or even to be cooked into a sort of bread. She touched a finger to it, flinched, and set it aside to cool a bit. She felt both reluctance and anticipation as she walked over to Heckram.

He took the moss away from his face as she knelt before him. A few strands of the white moss clung to the edges of the slash. She picked them off carefully with her fingernails, then touched the injury. The soaking had taken down most of the swelling. It was red and warm about the edges, with a yellowish crust down the middle. The herbal soak had softened the scab so it would slough away easily. 'This doesn't look near as bad as it did.' She picked cautiously at the edge of it and felt him wince. 'We'll try the poultice now.'

'What do you say to him, afterward?'

'Who after what?' she asked absently, poking at the mass in the pot. It was a little too runny.

'Joboam. After he's been rough on Kerlew.'

'Very little. It does no good. He denied it the first time I accused him, and the next time he said he had been wrestling playfully with the boy and the boy misunderstood. I've told him to keep his hands off my son. Then he said something about Capiam making him responsible for us, so he must make the boy understand your rules before we go with you. Then I said if it involved beating the rules into Kerlew, I'd as soon not go. After that, he left Kerlew alone. Until today.'

'Have you ever spoken to Capiam about it?' Heckram asked.

Tillu shook her head silently. She brought the poultice pot over beside him, took up a handful of white moss, and mixed it into it. The result was a warm fibrous mass that would cling together when she smoothed it onto his face.

'Do you want me to speak to Capiam about it?' Heckram offered softly.

'Would he listen to you?'

Heckram hesitated fractionally. 'The herdlord is supposed to listen to all of his folk. But Capiam has not been herdlord long. Nor did he have the benefit of a father's long experience. Relf, who was herdlord when I was a boy, died about five years after the plague, leaving no children. Capiam's father had been one of his most trusted men, and he assumed the leadership. Some were not happy about it. Several spoke up in favor of Eike, who was Joboam's father and another of Relf's men. But Eike's father was not of the herdfolk, but was a trader, like my grandfather. A friend of his, in fact. So many said the herdfolk needed a leader with the blood of herdfolk strong in him. So, Capiam's father was chosen, despite his great age. He died three years ago, and Capiam became herdlord.'

'Was Eike bitter?' Tillu asked thoughtfully.

'No. Eike was a good man, big in both size and heart. He supported Capiam's father right up until his own death. But I know what you are thinking. Yes, Joboam resented it. We were only boys at the time, but I remember it still. When no grown folk were around, he often said that the leadership should go to a man strong enough to lead. Then, if any disagreed, he would wrestle them and hold them down until they were shamed. And say that good men take pride in a strong leader. Meaning Eike; he was large, like Joboam.'

'And you,' Tillu added.

Heckram bobbed a nod of agreement. 'Same blood. But we were seen differently. Joboam was strong, and his family had plenty, even in the worst times. No matter how angry the other children got with him, it was easy to forgive him, because in his tent there were cheeses and suet puddings for his friends.'

'And what about you?' she pressed curiously, even though she sensed he remembered pain.

He smiled ruefully. 'I was a bit of the fool. Then, and some still think now. Clumsy, always too big for my clothes. And Joboam disliked me.' Heckram gave a deprecating laugh. 'He could wrestle me down, but I was never smart enough to admit he had won. I'd always keep struggling until he had to let me up or until one of the adults came to end it. So I was never welcome in his tent with the other children. Most of the other children avoided me, for Joboam was unfriendly to any who befriended me.' He shook his head suddenly.

337

'It wasn't a good time. I was glad to grow up, glad when the wrestling and struggling stopped.'

'So glad that you nearly started it up again today,' Tillu observed wryly. 'But I think I understand now. Enough to know that your speaking to Capiam would not make any difference. I will have to think, and decide. It may be that the only way to spare Kerlew from him will be for us to go our own way. Lie back on the pallet while I put this on, or it will drip off your chin. It's not as thick as it could be. Close your eye, too.'

He eased back on her pallet, feeling the soft prickle of the furs beneath his bare back. Her smell was on the furs, rising to make him aware of her closeness. She knelt beside the pallet, scooped some of the poultice up on her fingertips, and then leaned over him to pat it softly onto his face. She was very close, her face intent. The poultice was runny. Some of it trickled down by his ear, tickling unbearably. She scooped it back with a finger. Her hands were warm, her breath sweet. Her small face was so solemn. He could reach up and pull her down on top of himself. She probably weighed nothing at all. He gave his head a slight shake to rid it of the impulse, and Tillu exclaimed in annoyance. 'Be still!' she chided and steadied his face with her free hand. It made it worse. The throbbing of his face under the poultice wasn't painful enough to distract him from the sudden throbbing in his loins. He tried talking.

'It would be a sorry thing for the herdfolk if you did not go with us. Long have we needed a healer –'

A glob of the poultice slipped into his mouth, flooding it with bitterness. He made a move to sit up, but Tillu held him down, exclaiming with annoyance, 'Be still, or it will go all over!'

He reached to claw the glob from his mouth with his fingers and more slid in. He nearly choked on it. Her free hand was on his forehead now, trying to hold him flat while her other hand was laden with more poultice. He managed to turn his head slightly under her grip and scoop the offending gunk out of his mouth. That left him with a handful of it and no place to put it. Embarrassed, he glanced up at Tillu who chose that moment to burst out laughing.

The transformation was remarkable. The years dropped from her face, her cheeks dimpled in, and her eyes shone. Kerlew's resemblance to her became obvious when her white, even teeth flashed in her smile. Without her habitual small frown, she seemed young, almost girlish. Her laughter was good, low pitched and earthy. Their eyes met, and he found himself grinning in response as the poultice slid down the side of his face.

'It's too runny,' she apologized. Still smiling, she shook the poultice from her fingers back into the pot. Her hand had not left his face. 'Here,' she said and took the gloppy poultice from his hand and flicked it into the fire. She reached over him toward a worn square of hide on the other side of the pallet, could not quite reach it, leaned further, slipped, and was suddenly sprawled across him. Under her, his chest shook with laughter. Her cheeks burned. She snatched up the square of hide, wiped her fingers and handed it to him as she rocked back onto her heels. He took it from her, still grinning, and wiped his fingers clean. He could feel the poultice dripping down the side of his face and neck.

His eyes sought hers, but suddenly she was not smiling. Her lips were pursed, her face grim as she took the patch of old leather from him and wiped the side of his face. 'We'll have to start all over,' she said gruffly. The smile faded from his face as he looked up at her. There was such constraint on her face, such control. Over what? The failure of the poultice?

'Anyone can make a mistake.' He hesitated. She paused, the square of leather wet with poultice hovering over his face, but didn't meet his eyes. He didn't pause to think. Reaching up, he took the leather from her, wiped his own face clean. She didn't move. He dropped the scrap to the floor, touched her hand. 'What's wrong?' he asked.

The gentleness in his voice broke her. Her eyes met his, frank with hunger. She saw his eyes widen as his own warmth kindled. His hand moved very slowly to cup the back of her neck and pull her face down to his. He moved his face against hers, taking in first the smell of her skin, then the taste. His mouth was warm and tentative. She was transfixed by the sensation. There was no resistance in her body as he reached out a strong arm to pull her closer. She stopped thinking and moved her mouth against his. Time stopped. Warnings and cautions hammered frantically in her mind. She blocked them. This, now, this man, this touching, she took for herself, she stole from the world as a gift to herself. Atop him, she could forget the differences in their size. His strength was no threat to her.

She lost herself in him. The skin of his chest was warm under her fingers, stretched firm over muscle. She lifted her mouth from his, brushed her lips over his flat male nipples, watched the black hair spring back from her touch. She let her fingers trail down the center line of his chest, over his belly to his navel, then heard Heckram's sudden gasp as she set her hand flat below his navel. It broke her trance and she lifted her eyes to the face of this stranger in her bed.

She could not name what was in his eyes – a stillness, a wonder almost. He was breathing rapidly, shallowly. But he did not move. There had been other men for her since those raiders had first carried her away. She had taught herself that not every mating was pain. But always, with every man, there came a time when he asserted mastery, a time when he gripped and took her, a time when his own needs were all he responded to. It was a time she always steeled herself against, that moment when gentleness was routed by force. She pulled back slightly, testing him. But he did not drag her back. He only touched her face with tantalizing fingers that trailed down her cheek and throat.

Voices. A murmur she could not decipher, and then Kerlew's voice lifted high in question. She stiffened against Heckram and then pushed firmly away from him. For an instant the circle of his embrace resisted her. Then as he became aware of the voices, he made a sound between a sigh and a groan and released her. She lifted herself clear of his body, feeling the cool air blow in between them. 'Tillu?' he questioned softly, but she did not look at him. She tugged her tunic down straight, righted the pot of poultice that had tipped and nearly spilled. She pushed her hair back, felt the stickiness of the poultice that had smeared from Heckram's face to hers. She rubbed her sleeve cuff down her face, felt unreasonable tears sting her eyes. A sudden shakiness beset her knees and the pit of her stomach. Taking a long deep breath, she forced steadiness onto herself. She glanced at him, to find him leaning up on one elbow, looking at her anxiously. She turned away.

'Tillu?' he repeated, but the crunch and squeak of boots over damp snow was right outside the tent now. She shook her head wordlessly without looking at him. Heckram fell back onto the pallet with a sigh. She knew how he felt.

'Heckram?' The old man's querying voice cracked as he called. 'Is the face better?' He ducked into the tent, squinting his eyes as he came from the brightness to the dimness.

Heckram was silent, looking to Tillu for an answer. Kerlew bustled into the tent and up to Heckram. 'It doesn't look so bad to me!' he exclaimed.

'It wasn't as bad as it looked at first. It was mostly swelling,' Tillu filled in.

Heckram was staring at Kerlew. Even with sharp anticipation fading into aching disappointment, he was not blind to the change in the boy. The difference was like that between fall and spring. Kerlew's narrow shoulders were no longer bowed in on his chest. There was confidence and self-importance in his face as he met Heckram's gaze squarely. But there was also an unworldly translucence to his gaze. As if Heckram were not as substantial as whatever it was that Kerlew saw behind him. His face was evasive, dreaming. A chill rose in Heckram, as if he had seen the boy sucked down and swept away by a river. The contacts he had made with the boy were gone, the ties unbound. The certainty that he would never reach Kerlew again rose in him. The boy he had begun to know was gone. Gone, in one afternoon. Carp was smiling also, a smile with cutting edges for Tillu. A smile of triumph and vengeance. Tillu withered in that gaze, shrinking in on herself. Heckram sat up slowly.

'Get your shirt on,' Carp directed him calmly. 'Time for us to go.'

'Go?' Kerlew asked in sudden bewilderment, and in that instant Heckram glimpsed the vulnerable boy he had known. 'Go away, Carp? Why? Where?'

Carp laughed his cracked old man's laugh. 'Not far, Kerlew, don't worry. I am staying with Heckram. He has a fine warm hut, with much food and many soft skins. I am very comfortable there. And I must see the Herdlord Capiam, to tell him I will be shaman of the herdfolk now. But I will be back tomorrow, to teach you. And soon we will all be traveling together.'

'No.' The firmness of the word was spoiled by the sharp note that broke Tillu's voice. 'No,' she repeated, gaining control. 'You may go with the herd, perhaps. But not Kerlew, and not I.'

'Oh?' the najd asked coldly. 'And is that so, Kerlew?'

The boy turned his face to Tillu, and in that moment all in the tent knew she had lost. His small jaw was set. His eyes were distant as he spoke. 'I go, Tillu. I am a man now, and the decision is mine. For a few days more, I stay here with you. But when the herdfolk follow the herd, I will follow Carp.' The words were Carp's, spoken carefully. But the decision in his voice was all Kerlew's. Tillu stared at him.

Here, before her, was what she had dreamed about. Her boy, standing as a man, making his own decision. Speaking with confidence, standing straight before her. And here, beside her, watching her face with sympathetic eyes, was a man such as she had imagined. A man to make part of her life, part of her own life, separate from Kerlew's.

Bitterness filled her mouth. 'No,' she said again softly. But it was an internal denying, a forbidding of tomorrow to come. The new day had already dawned in her son's eyes.

Something long fastened within her let go. Weariness was a part of it, the sense that she could no longer battle to keep Kerlew safe from the world he had chosen. But there was also a certainty that if she fought Carp for the boy, she would destroy him. The self-confidence that set his shoulders was too new and shining a thing to crush with bitter words.

Better that he walked straight without her and failed than that he huddled forever in her shadow, safe but without substance.

'You are going,' she said, looking deep into her son's eyes. Kerlew nodded. 'And so am I,' she said aloud, and the surprise was loud in her voice.

There was too much to read in Tillu's eyes. Heckram pulled his eyes from her face. Rising awkwardly from the low pallet, he found his woolen shirt and pulled it on, holding it away from his face. Next he dragged on his skin tunic, its heaviness suddenly unwelcome in the soft spring air. As he cautiously poked his head out the collar, he found Tillu standing in front of him, looking up at him. Reaching up, she took him firmly by the chin and turned his face to the light again. Her brow furrowed slightly as she studied the gash.

'It looks better. It may heal itself now. But' – she paused, a ghost of a smile in her eyes – 'you should come back tomorrow and let me check it.'

He nodded slowly, but she turned aside hastily, leaving him to wonder if he had understood what she hadn't said. 'Come on, come on,' Carp was urging irritably. 'The walk back is long and already I am hungry. And I have yet to see Capiam today. I have important things to tell him.'

'As have I,' agreed Heckram, and followed him out into the early spring evening.

Kerlew: The Seeing

It had taken long for Tillu to fall asleep. Kerlew had had to lie awake and still, distracted by her shiftings, her sighs and mutterings. But now she lay still on her pallet, her arm flung across her eyes as if to blot out the sight of what must be. Foolish woman. Still she thought she could change it. Still, she did not understand that Kerlew had been born to the magic, and the magic to him. One and the same they were, intertwined. She had sought to separate him from the magic, but that was like separating the warp from the woof of the herdwomen's weaving. What was left was not cloth at all. Nor was Kerlew to be Kerlew without the magic. Someday, she would see.

Now that she lay silent and did not distract him, he rose from his bed. He slipped clear of his body and slowly climbed the thin spiral of smoke that drifted up from the banked fire. Up he climbed again, always going up when he should be going down. But he had a feeling someone was waiting above to speak to him.

Outside the worn tent, the wind was rising, swirling snow

within its belly, reminding the herdfolk and forest that spring's grip on the land was still a feeble one. Kerlew felt the chilling of night air, saw the snow reclaiming the forest for its own. Briefly he frowned; this was not good for the herdfolk, for his new people. Then he looked farther and felt Carp's hand in the sighing of the wind and the drifting of the white flakes. There was a reason, then, behind this late storm, and all would be well. Carp was shaman of the herdfolk now, their najd. He cupped their fates in his wizened old hands; his clouded eyes would guide them now. Satisfied, Kerlew let go of his worry and climbed higher.

He broke free of the storm suddenly, standing with his bare feet atop the wind and churning clouds. Blackness arched above him; there were not stars or moon, but only the light of his own eyes to see by, yet it was enough. He sat down cross-legged atop the clouds to await the one that must come.

As if from afar, he heard Tillu rise and put more wood on the fire. A part of his mind wondered that she had not asked him to rouse and do it. Another part of him asserted that he was too far away now, too far beyond her, to ever do any task for her again. The pallet and hides beneath his body were more distant to him now than the sky over his head.

She knew he was gone, and it grieved her. She was a narrow, earth-bound person, unable to see the true shapes of the world or how she fitted into them. He pitied her. He could see her grief, like a fine stain running through the thread of her life, bleeding darkness into the color. Tillu, he realized, was but a thread, as was Heckram, yes, and even Carp.

'I am the hands of the weaver,' Kerlew thought to himself, and suddenly the image was real. Here were the lines of their lives, of Heckram and Tillu and Carp, of Lasse and Elsa and Joboam, coming into his fingers like the strands of fiber

and root that the herdwomen wove. He it was who plaited
them together, who made a pattern of their days. They passed
through his fingers and were changed by his touch. He it
was who could shape their days to come. He wove them,
making power for Carp, and for Elsa, revenge. The thin
strands, red and brown, that were Heckram and Tillu were
limp in his hands. Idly he twisted them together, marking
the contrast of the colors. It pleased his eyes and he left them
so. He took up the cold rough cord that was Joboam. It was
white against his fingers, biting his skin, scratching as if to
escape his will. He twisted it around his fingers, longing
to snap it off short. But it was a stout and ugly thread,
twisted like badly cured hide. It ruined the pattern of the
other threads. It could never be made to blend.

'Little shaman, what do you weave?'

Kerlew looked up from his weaving. Wolf's eyes were on
him, yellow against the bright blackness of the world. Kerlew
was careful to keep the smile from his lips. He did not answer
Wolf with words, but only stretched forth the rough twine
of Joboam. Wolf frowned, his lips drooping red all about
his white teeth.

'Who has given you that which is mine?' he demanded in
a low growl.

'I have taken that which I would shape,' Kerlew replied.

'And that, too, is mine. It is for Wolf to take what he
would. Not some shaman's brat.'

'But I have it,' Kerlew challenged and held up the thread.

Wolf stared at it, and Kerlew let himself grin. Come closer,
spirit beast, he murmured to himself. Come within the touch
of my hand.

Wolf's yellow eyes narrowed. 'Do you remember, little
shaman, what I told you the last time we met?'

Kerlew nodded slowly. '"If you would be Wolf's brother, learn to follow the herd." I go, and soon, with the herdfolk, to follow the herd. I will be as you are. Wolf. Following the herd and taking what I want.'

Wolf rose suddenly. His breath was hot and smelled of meat. Kerlew's words had been too bold. But he did not flinch from that hot breath or look away from the shining yellow eyes. Wolf held his tail higher, then shut his jaws with a snap. 'Follow the herds, then. And hold what is Wolf's.' He turned and trotted away. He glanced back at Kerlew over the long fur of his shoulder and grinned. 'But not too tightly, little shaman. For you are not yet Wolf's brother, and may never be. That which you hold will be demanded of you one day. See that you give it then, for I have made a bargain about it.'

Kerlew looked down at the rough strand in his hand. 'I have a Knife,' he said to the night. 'I could cut this off short, at any time I please.' Then he thought of Wolf, leaping from star to star, setting the night sky a-thunder with the clattering of panicky hooves.

'I will wait for you to claim what is yours,' he promised. 'But then I will claim you. I will be Wolf's brother.'